MITIGATING
CIRCUMSTANCES

MITIGATING
CIRCUMSTANCES

．

Nancy Taylor Rosenberg

ORION

Copyright © Nancy Taylor Rosenberg 1993

First published in the United States under the title *Mitigating Circumstances*
by Nancy Taylor Rosenberg. Published by arrangement with Dutton,
an imprint of New American Library, a division of Penguin Books USA Inc.

First published in Great Britain in 1993 by
Orion
An imprint of Orion Books Ltd
Orion House, 5 Upper St Martin's Lane, London WC2H 9EA

A CIP catalogue record for this book is available
from the British Library

ISBN 1 85797 042 X (Csd)
1 85797 084 5 (Tpb)

Printed in England by Clays Ltd, St Ives plc

CHAPTER 1 ■

Inside the windowless courtroom, a man awaited sentencing for murder. There were no reporters and no spectators. His victim had been a rival gang member. The female prosecutor's voice echoed in the empty courtroom as she made her closing argument.

"Your Honor, the people feel the maximum sentence in this case is both appropriate and justified. The defendant has a lengthy criminal history, a prior offense for assault with a deadly weapon, and by his own words he's demonstrated his callous disregard for human life." As she started shuffling papers on the counsel table, the air conditioner emitted a loud noise and died. "I read from the probation report: 'After you stabbed him once, you then proceeded to stab him three more times?' The defendant's reply: 'He took a licking and kept on ticking.'" She paused. "Your Honor, this was a human life, not a Timex watch."

At the defense table, the defendant snickered, cupping his hands over his mouth like a child. The public defender shot him a look of utter disgust, and he sat up in the seat, solemn and alert. The judge glared at the man, peering over the top of his glasses. The prosecutor opened her mouth to continue, then stopped and removed her jacket. In minutes she would be dripping wet.

"It's the people's position that the defendant be sentenced to the California Department of Corrections for the term of twelve years to life; that the enhancement for the use of the weapon, as well as the prior offense, be served consecutively for a total term of nineteen years to life. There are no mitigating circumstances in this case." She dropped into her chair. The air was heavy and still; perspiration trickled between her breasts. Her mind began drifting to other cases.

"Young man," the judge said after the imposition of sentence, "if the law allowed it, I would sentence you to prison for the remainder of your life. You're a blight on the face of the earth."

With that, the gavel came down, the prisoner was remanded, and the hearing over. Even with the maximum sentence, he would be eligible for parole in less than ten years. She grabbed the heavy case file and headed for the exit, the public defender right behind her.

"So, we're not going to have to contend with you in the courtroom much longer," he said, referring to her recent promotion. "Gosh, that's a shame, Lily."

They hit the double doors and he followed her down the hall. "That little snicker probably cost your client five additional years in the slammer. He could have served the five for the prior concurrently," she snapped. "You need to keep your animals under control."

"Right, Forrester, right."

She was buzzed through the security doors, leaving the public defender standing there shaking his head.

Even after eight years as an assistant district attorney, she still let the vermin she prosecuted get to her, touch that exposed wire leading to her nervous system. Sparks were flying all around her, inside her. Reaching her office, she took the file and threw it with every ounce of strength she had against the glass window, watching as the contents spilled out and tumbled to various resting places all over the new commercial-grade carpet. The same names, the same faces, kept reappearing. The system was spitting them back out like rotten pieces of meat viler than when first digested. She thought of the guillotine, wondering if it had really been barbaric. They certainly didn't reoffend.

Seeing the open cardboard box by her desk, she started packing her remaining personal effects. Tomorrow she took charge as chief of the Sex Crimes Division, one more step toward a black-robed seat on the bench. What she wanted was to look down at the courtroom, her domain, where no one could even approach her without permission. She wanted the rulings and decisions to be hers. She wanted the power, but more than anything, she wanted the control. At least she wanted something she could possibly obtain. She was married to a man who wanted nothing, aspired to nothing, accomplished nothing. John didn't even want his own wife anymore, not as a man. But this was something that had started not long after her daughter's birth. It wasn't anything new. They'd slept in the same bed without sex for years.

She looked around the office, the scattered file, the boxes. Glancing at her watch, she realized that she was late to the agency cocktail party celebrating the promotions of her and others, the shuffle in assignments that occurred every six months.

On her hands and knees, she reached under the desk and pulled out two items: an autopsy photo and a birthday card. The photo was replaced in the file, but the card she carried to her desk and opened it, standing it upright. It was one of those musical cards that played "Happy Birthday." Yesterday had been her thirty-sixth birthday. No one had remembered but her mother. Her husband had not remembered; none of her so-called friends had remembered. Maybe if her mother had not sent her the card, Lily herself could have forgotten.

She stood and listened to the musical serenade while red, white, and yellow sequential lights flashed on the front of the card. The notes got weaker and weaker and flatter and flatter before she realized that the minuscule battery was wearing out. It sounded like a birthday anthem for a mouse. With one abrupt move of her fist, she smashed the card flat and put it out of its misery, asking herself what kind of sentence she would give for mercy killing a birthday card: four minutes, out in two.

Tossing the last certificate in the box for the short ride down the hall, she also tossed the card in the trash can, where it emitted one pathetic dying squeak. She grabbed her briefcase and left the office.

When she stepped outside the building, a large man approached her. "Forrester," he said. "The jury just came in with a verdict of second-degree murder on the Owen homicide. I was just coming up to shoot the breeze with one of your investigators. You know, brag a little."

The man was an Oxnard detective, one of the few good ones. The case was one he'd worked on for years. She wanted to stay and talk, but she was late already. "Congratulations, Cunningham. Chalk one up for our side, huh?" She liked this man. He was what the job was all about: people who really gave a shit what happened, who were willing to give it their all. "We need it. Let me tell you, the way it looks right now, the other side's winning the war."

Jaywalking across the busy street, she looked toward the corner and wondered how many times she'd walked all the way down to cross at the crosswalk and then had to walk all the way back to the bar. She wasn't exactly concerned with a ticket. If people could go out there and kill and maim, sit around for a few years, and do it again, she should be able to walk anywhere she damn well pleased. She was an underpaid servant of the people, there had to be some fringe benefits. A car screeched to a stop in front of her, and the driver flipped her the finger. Smiling sweetly, she made a point of walking even slower.

The Elephant Bar was filled to capacity with suits, both the male and female versions. Since the completion of the massive new government center complex, the legal community had claimed the bar as their own. The atmosphere was straight out of *Casablanca*, circa 1992, with whitewashed walls, ceiling fans, and a black piano player who played when no one could hear and everyone was too preoccupied to listen. But deals were cut here daily, plea bargains and under-the-table transactions, the days of a person's life dealt out like so many playing cards. Attorneys would brag that they had settled a case in Division 69; everyone knew that meant over drinks at the Elephant Bar.

Clinton Silverstein and Marshall Duffy, both A.D.A.'s, were at a table near the front door. It was one of those high tables with no stools, the kind used by establishments like the Elephant Bar to cram more bodies into a small space. Silverstein was running his fingers around the glass rim of his gin and tonic while Duffy poured beer from a pitcher. Duffy was black and handsome, dressed in a stylishly tailored pin-striped suit and a crisp white shirt and tie. He towered over the short, stocky Silverstein.

"You're a righteous nut case, you know," he said to Clinton, "even if I do call you a friend."

"I'm a nut case. Right. Well, at least I don't wear tinted contacts. Do you know how weird those make you look?" Clinton stepped back from the table, loosening his tie, smiling at the other man.

Duffy tipped his glass and let the beer slide down his throat before speaking. "My baby blues. My wife loves them. All the women love them. So what's the big deal with this transfer? I thought you put in for it."

"Before, I put in before. When Fowler still had the unit. I'm sick of the Misdemeanor Division. Shit, if I have to handle one more drunk driving, I'll throw it all in."

"So you don't. You got the transfer. What's the big deal about the lady? She can't be all that bad. Nice little ass. Reminds me of my wife." Duffy stepped back and almost toppled a plastic palm tree.

"I don't care what she looks like. I just know she's one tense lady. What she needs is a good tranquilizer, a good fuck, or both. That's what I think. She's going to run that unit with an iron fist. Mark my words." Clinton ran his hands through his permed hair, making it stand on end like the boxing promoter Don King.

"Sounds like the pot calling the kettle black, my man." Duffy's eyes turned toward the door. "Take a big slug of that drink, Clinty. Calm yourself down. Your new boss just arrived."

"Lily," a man's voice called to her. "Over here."

The bar was dark and smoky, and her eyes were still adjusting to the outside light; she followed the voice. "Hello, Marshall. Looks like the party started without me."

She was anxious, scanning the room. From the looks of it, the entire agency and half the private attorneys in the area were here. She seldom attended these parties. There weren't enough hours in the day as it was, and socializing wasn't her strong suit.

"Hey, we're all waiting for you. You're one of the guests of honor tonight. What're you drinking?"

She started to order her standard glass of white wine, then changed her mind. "I guess a margarita, with salt." As Duffy started to flag the waitress, she added impulsively: "And order me a shooter of tequila on the side." Might as well do it right, she thought. This is what the men did when they had a bad day, came over here and got smashed. It appeared to work for them. Maybe it would work for her. Today had been a rough one, and the new job assignment was weighing heavily on her mind.

"Whoa, there. I'm impressed. Clinton and I were just talk-

ing about you. He's been telling me how excited he is about
working with you."

"Guess he's not too excited. He just walked away." She
laughed, but it really wasn't funny. Attorneys like Silverstein
represented another problem Lily had to contend with, a new
problem brought on by the promotion. Now she had to su-
pervise other attorneys, some with far more experience and
much larger egos. It wasn't going to be easy. She could use a
good stiff drink.

Duffy turned his head to the side, surprised. Clinton was
standing a few tables over talking to Richard Fowler, Lily's
predecessor.

Lily tried to look into Duffy's translucent blue eyes, but
her gaze was drawn to Fowler. "You transferred into Homicide, took my slot, right?" Her eyes burned into Fowler's back,
willing him to turn around. Instead of bending down and placing her briefcase and purse on the floor, she dropped them
with a loud thud. The noise was lost in the bar, and Fowler
still didn't turn. Her face felt flushed. "Where's the waitress?"
she asked Duffy, thinking she'd change her order to a glass of
wine. She didn't want Fowler to see her tossing down shot
glasses of tequila like a truck driver, but it was too late. Duffy
had already given the girl the order.

"Guess you can call me a victim of the Big Butler Shuffle,"
Duffy said, placing his elbows on the table.

His words drifted past her and once again her thoughts
turned to Fowler. For the past two weeks he'd been working
with her, coaching her to make the shift in supervisors as
smooth as possible. He was tall, maybe six-five, with the lean,
hard body of a runner or a swimmer. His hair and eyes weren't
just dark, they were actually black, a sharp contrast against
his fair skin. He moved his long body and long legs without
sound wherever he went, fluid and relaxed like a large cat
ready to pounce on unsuspecting prey. He moved the way Lily
wanted to move. And he moved Lily.

He saw her and headed in her direction. The waitress approached with the drinks, and he lifted the margarita off the tray, looking at Lily. She nodded. Then he saw the shot glass and again looked at her. "Yours?" he asked.

"No . . . yes . . . I . . ." She blushed. She was stammering like a fool. Fowler did that to her. "It's been one of those days. Thought I'd try to drown it."

Setting both glasses on the table, he slid in close to her, in front of Duffy. A cloud of his cologne drifted to her nostrils, a hint of lime. For the past two weeks she'd been inhaling it, even found it lingering on her clothes like cigarette smoke when she was forced to work closely with a smoker.

"Shooters, huh?" he said with a slight smile, lifting only one corner of his mouth. "Was it really that bad a week?"

"No, you've been great. I mentioned the sentencing I had today, didn't I? You know, the sweetheart who thinks human life is comparable to a Timex watch."

"You mean, 'takes a licking'? Well, it's kinda cute, isn't it? The guy might become a stand-up comic when he gets out."

"That's the problem. The fact that you can kill a person and be out on the streets to do it again in a few years. It makes me sick. It's just something you don't get used to, no matter how many times you see it." She saw the waitress and bent down to get her purse, turning her back and digging for her money. "Let me buy you a drink."

"The waitress is gone. Next round if you insist."

He was so close now that their hips were touching. Lily downed the shooter of tequila in one swallow and chased it with the margarita, licking the salt off her lips. The closer he stood to her, the more flustered she became. She was talking like a rookie D.A., like she'd never prosecuted a homicide case before.

"Do you remember the last party we were both at? I do," he said. "You were wearing this white backless dress and your hair was down, all the way down your back. You looked gorgeous."

"The last party was a barbecue at Dennis O'Connor's, and

that was over five years ago. If my memory serves me right, you were wearing jeans and a blue sweater.''

Their eyes met and he refused to look away, searching there, prying where he didn't belong. The tequila was still burning her throat and she felt uncomfortable. She took her cold glass and pressed it against her cheek. "Have to make a phone call. Watch my briefcase, okay?'' She turned to head for the back of the bar, then said over her shoulder with a smile, "Anu, Richard, I've never in my life owned a white backless dress.''

There were a lot of things Lily had never done—things far more significant than wearing a backless sundress to a party. One of them was to have an affair. Although her husband had accused her of cheating behind his back for years, Lily had remained faithful despite the accusations and the complete disappearance of sex in their marriage.

Elbowing her way through the people, she spotted District Attorney Paul Butler on his way to the door. He was a short, serious man in his mid-fifties who seldom mingled with those who worked beneath him. She was surprised to see him.

"Paul," she said, "I didn't see you earlier or I would've come over. I guess your secretary informed you of our conference tomorrow on the Lopez–McDonald matter.'' The tequila had hit Lily hard on an empty stomach. She willed herself to appear sober, carefully articulating her words.

"Oh, yes," he said with a blank look in his eyes. "Refresh me.''

"Double homicide, teenagers, lovers . . . the boy was beaten and bludgeoned, the girl raped and mutilated. Five suspects in custody, all Hispanic—possibly gang related.'' It was front-page and sensational, both kids honor students, college bound. "You asked for the conference yourself, Paul. The case was assigned to me prior to the promotion, and I've already done the work-up. Do you recall?'' She tried to sound nonchalant, not wanting to emphasize the fact that he was uninformed on such an important case.

Butler looked down and coughed. "The budget is due this week and the mayor is all over me. Also, the employee relocations. We'll discuss it tomorrow."

As he moved to pass her, she reached out and took his hand, something she never would have done without the alcohol. "I just want to tell you how I appreciate the promotion. I know you had others to consider."

Even in the dim light of the bar, she could see his face turning beet red in embarrassment. She was holding his hand far too close, a bad habit resulting from vanity, refusing to wear her glasses outside the office. She looked down on the top of his head and saw how thin his hair was, something she'd never noticed before. He stepped back as if he knew.

"Certainly, certainly," he said. "Well, I guess we'll discuss this Lopez–McDonald case tomorrow."

As he started to pass, he was pushed into her, against her chest, her breasts. The terrified look in his eyes almost caused her to laugh out loud. Did he actually think she was flirting with him? How ludicrous. If she was going to flirt with anyone, it sure wouldn't be Butler. She leaned against the brass rail of the bar and watched him scurry away on his short little legs, musing on a world where a genuine expression of gratitude was so rare that it raised suspicion. Maybe Butler wasn't even aware he'd promoted her. He didn't remember the Lopez–McDonald matter. Perhaps his assistant just picked her name out of a hat?

No, she rationalized, impossible. He had called Richard into his office on a rampage and demoted him, offering Lily his position only a few hours later. Richard was still a supervisor, but over the Municipal Court Division, a clear step down. The story went that Fowler had became enraged over a lenient sentence on a particularly vicious sex crime and had stormed into Judge Raymond Fisher's chambers without announcement, all the way into his private bathroom, where he had found the forty-year-old judge snorting lines of cocaine off the bathroom counter. This was one of the reasons Lily wanted a position on the bench. Like oil in water, some of the slimiest had risen to the top and floated there, untouchable, their shifting shadow spreading and darkening all the lives beneath them. Judge Fisher got caught snorting cocaine; Fowler got demoted. That sounded like a fair and impartial judgment.

In the back of the bar, Lily spotted the phone outside the ladies' room. She thought it was the ladies' room, the name said Bwanagals or something weird. She'd been here many times but never drinking tequila. With the alcohol flooding her bloodstream, the floor moved and swayed like a ship at sea. Searching for the little stick figure of a woman with a skirt and finding none, she decided what the hell, barging through the door. She almost ran over Carol Abrams.

"Lily," the petite blonde said, "congratulations on the promotion. That was really quite a coup."

She patted Lily on both shoulders with dainty hands and bright pink manicured nails; the movement caused her blunt-cut, shiny hair to swing forward, and Lily watched, mesmerized, as it fell back to the exact position, every hair perfectly aligned. Pushing an unruly strand of hair off her forehead, Lily spotted the chipped paint on her own fingernails and quickly dropped her hands to her sides.

"I won't say I didn't want that promotion. No, I won't deny it. But I'm glad that at least it was you, a woman, and not some idiot that will sit in the office all day and make paper airplanes. You know what I mean?"

Lily went into the stall and shut the door, carefully pulling the latch. Carol Abrams might follow her inside or open the door to continue the discussion while Lily sat there with her panty hose stuck around her thighs. Brilliant and never tiring, Abrams was an asset to any department. In court, she simply wore them down: judge, jury, defense attorneys, every last one of them.

"I don't know how you feel about Fowler, but I don't mind saying I'm glad to see him go. I mean, he clearly knows the law, but recently he has lost all semblance of self-contr'

Everyone knows you don't go after a judge like a madman. My God. I think he's suffering from burnout. You know what I mean?" She stopped and took an audible breath, preparing to continue.

"Carol, why don't we talk tomorrow?" Lily said. Just as she flushed the toilet, she realized she didn't want to leave until Abrams had left and wished she hadn't flushed. She had an urge to tell her off to her face: open the door and tell her that Fowler knew more than she would ever learn in her hyperactive life, but . . .

She opened the stall and the woman was gone. Thank God for small favors.

Seeing her bedraggled face in the mirror, she ripped the bobby pins out of the loose knot and brushed her bright red hair. She reapplied her lipstick, tried to resmudge her eyeshadow, and headed for the phone to call her thirteen-year-old daughter.

"Shana, it's me."

"Hold on, Mom, let me put Charlotte on hold."

Lily thought it was insane for a child her age to have a private line as well as call waiting, but her father . . .

"What do you want?"

Lily opened her eyes wide and stepped back from the phone a few steps. Shana was getting more sarcastic every day. Lily remembered what it was like to go through puberty, and she was trying her best to let it slide, thinking it was just an adolescent phase. "Are you doing your homework or just talking on the phone, sweetie? Where's your dad?"

"Charlotte's helping me on the phone, and Dad's asleep on the sofa."

Lily pictured him there as always: the dishes piled in the sink, the television blasting, stretched out on the sofa snoring. This was one of the reasons she had begun staying late at the office. With John sleeping in front of the television and Shana in her room on the phone every night with the door closed, there wasn't really a compelling urge to go home. "Tell him

I'm tied up in a meeting and will be home in a few hours."

"*Mom*. Charlotte is going to be cut off. Tell him yourself."

"I love you," Lily whispered. The line was dead. She saw Shana's adorable face in her mind and tried to match it to her tone of voice and actions. Her own child, her precious little girl, was becoming rude and obnoxious. She'd just hung up on her. Only a few years ago, Shana would sit on the floor in front of Lily for hours, enthralled at every single word that came out of her mother's mouth, her face bright and beaming. Now she was hanging up on her. If Lily had spoken that way to her father, she would've been slapped to the floor. But John said those days were over; children had a right to talk back. And Shana adored her father.

Lily started searching for another quarter to call John and then decided against it, closing her purse. She'd say something to him about Shana talking on the phone and not studying; she couldn't stop herself. She could only be what she had already become. John would hang up and then march to Shana's room and tell her that her mother said she had to get off the phone, but it was okay; he wouldn't tell if she didn't. He might even add that her mother said she had to clean her room or she was grounded. That would go over great. If that didn't make Shana despise her, he could also remind her that her mother once said she'd have to become a waitress because she'd never study hard enough to get into college. One of those off-the-wall comments that a parent makes to prove a point to the other parent, it was not something to repeat to a child. But John repeated it and said a lot of other things that were outright lies.

He should have been an attorney, Lily thought as she walked back into the noisy bar, straightening her skirt and smoothing down her jacket. He should have been a defense attorney. No, maybe a divorce lawyer.

Back at the table, she saw a fresh margarita, a new shooter, and Richard Fowler. She slid the shot glass away and took a sip of the margarita, letting her hair fall seductively over o corner of her eye while she took in Fowler from his shoes to the top of his head. She was looking at a determined man, she thought, a man of conviction, a warrior, not the type of man who needed to fight with a child as his shield; nor a man who could be happy with a mediocre government job where his hours had been cut to only thirty a week and his wife carried the weight of the family while he puttered around in the kitchen. He wasn't a wimp like John.

Silverstein's New York twang rang out from the adjoining table, where he was throwing popcorn into his mouth and trying to talk at the same time, complaining about some case; four out of five kernels ending up on his clothes or the floor. Duffy had apparently gone home.

"Your hair looks great," Richard said. "I had no idea it was still so long. You never wear it down to the office." He reached out and touched a strand, twirling it between his fingers.

"Not too professional. I don't know why I don't cut it. Guess I'm trying to hold onto my youth or something." She inhaled deeply. She was breathless. He was so close.

Fowler's fingers disappeared from her hair. Lily wanted to reach for his hand and put it back, feel the electricity again, feel his fingers on her face, her skin, but the moment was shattered. From across the room, they both saw Lawrence Bodenham, a private-practice defense attorney. He honed in on Lily and headed their direction. The new rage with those in private practice was to wear their hair long, almost shoulder-length, and Bodenham's curled at the bottom. Reaching the table, he put his hand out to shake hers.

"You're Lily Forrester, right?" he said. "Lawrence Bodenham."

"Right," Lily said, really feeling the tequila now, wishing the man would leave and she could think of something brilliant and seductive to say to Fowler, particularly now that she'd had a few drinks and was feeling the false courage of alcohol. She made no move to shake his hand, and he withdrew it.

"I'm representing Daniel Duthoy on that 288 matter, and I've been having some real problems with Carol Abrams regarding discovery."

The case was only vaguely familiar to Lily. Richard evidently knew it well and turned to face the attorney with a look of contempt. Two-eighty-eight was a sodomy and the victim had been a ten-year-old boy, the defendant a pillar of the community—a Big Brother. "Remember me?" Richard snapped. "If you have any problems, Bodenham, just tell it to the judge. Or why don't you call up Butler at home on your car phone from your Porsche? He just adores you guys who pull down two hundred G's a year defending these good folk who like to butt-fuck little boys."

Bodenham stepped back a safe distance before responding. "I hear you're back assigning drunk driving and petty thefts to new A.D.A.'s who don't know their ass from a hole in the ground. Good career move, Fowler. You're really on the way up." As soon as the words had left his mouth, the attorney disappeared into the crowd.

Richard pushed back from the table, slapping it with both hands. His eyes were red-rimmed and he reeked of bourbon. "That about makes an evening for me. See you around." He turned to leave.

Lily caught his coattail, stopping him. "You've had too much to drink, Rich. Let me drive you." She was standing with her purse and briefcase, ready.

For the first time that evening, he smiled broadly, flashing perfect white teeth. "Come on, then. If you want to save me, now is the time. But if you think I'm going to let a drunk like you drive me, you're crazy. Come on. You never bought me that drink, so now you can buy me a cup of coffee."

CHAPTER 2.

He was waiting.

His hands and face were pressed against the thick, tinted glass windows of the shiny new jail. Intrigued by the circles his warm breath made, he was entertaining himself by making a pattern of them. It was dark and the little red car stood alone directly under his window. Every morning and evening, he watched her long legs appear from the door of the car, her skirt hiked up. Depending on where she parked, the angle of the car, he thought he could see up her skirt, see the fabric of her underwear. He imagined that she was naked under her clothes and what he had seen was her pubic hair. It would have to be red, he thought. Red pubic hair.

He was angry at her now. She didn't always come out at the same time, but never this late. She was fucking someone, he was certain. He had given her the eye, making her his woman, and she was fucking someone right now, right this very minute. He saw those long legs wrapped around another man's neck, saw her reaching for him with lust-filled eyes. He wanted to take his fist and beat the lust right off her face, see some pain instead. She looked like a schoolteacher or a probation officer, but she was nothing but a whore. They were all whores.

He kept his body against the glass but craned his neck around toward the common room, where other prisoners were sitting at the stainless steel picnic tables and laughing at some sitcom or cop show on the television. Laughing like a bunch of hyenas in a cage. They loved cop shows. When one of the television cops got shot or hurt, they all applauded and whistled. But that would stop soon—the laughter. In a few hours they would be locked down for the endless night and the laughter would stop; the other sounds would begin. They would talk to each other in the dark, their voices echoing off the bars from one cell to the other. And they would listen. In the blackness was another world.

Sometimes he heard men crying like babies. It made him sick. They would talk about their wives, their children, even their mothers. They would talk about God and the Bible, about redemption and forgiveness. And the other sounds. The groans and moans of sweaty, smelly, disgusting sex. They tried to stop it, the keepers, but they never would.

Men were men, he thought. And men needed sex. But he would never stoop that low—become an animal like the others, allow them to steal his manhood, his machismo. Not him. No matter what they did to him, or how many years they locked him up. He was a Latin lover, a ladies' man. Women always said he was handsome. They all wanted him. All he had to do was choose the one he wanted.

He pushed the lower half of his body against the window, looking down on the parking lot. He imagined himself on the floorboard of her car, waiting for her, and felt himself hard and erect against the glass. Then he saw her face, heard her scream, and the aching between his legs intensified. He rotated his hips against the window, his mouth falling open. His heavy breath smoked a circle and spread to ragged edges, reminding him of bloodstains. He jerked his body away from the glass, stood completely still, let anger fill him. He was no pussy boy who jerked off in a cage.

They'd put him in a cell with a black. Not only a black, but a stupid black, an older black. He had friends inside, home-boys from the streets. But they'd put him in a cell with a fucking black and now he had to watch him, keep his eyes open even in the dark of the night.

Laughter, hoots, and whistles rang out from the common room. This was the best part of the day. But he couldn't leave the window, not until he saw her. She had taken this time away from him, this redheaded whore.

"You'll pay, bitch. You'll pay," he uttered against the glass. "And you'll fucking beg. You'll beg."

This morning when she'd come to work, he'd been at the window, waiting. Something about her troubled him, triggered a blinding rage to see her beneath him, her mouth open in a scream of terror. He'd seen her somewhere before. Not from the window, but close. He remembered that she had freckles, little alien dots across her nose and cheeks, something he could never have seen from the window. But he knew they were there. He could see them in his mind. Most Hispanic women didn't have freckles. He'd never had a woman with freckles.

"First time for everything, man," he said, chuckling. "First time for everything."

"What youse laughing 'bout, boy?" a large black man said, shuffling into the cell. "Youse always standing at dat window and laughing likes a crazy man. They gonna cart you off, they sees you. You listen to Willie, boy. Willie knows. They done get plenty pissed they sees you."

He spun around and spat at the black man, "Fuck you. They'll drag your black ass off, but they ain't touching me. I got friends, you know, family. I got connections. I'll be out of this place when you're on a bus to the joint."

"Maybe so," the black man said, heading to the bunk, his head down. "Maybe so."

He pressed on. The black man was big, but he was old. "You're a fucking loser, man. You got your ass busted for shooting some dumb kids for trying to steal your car. If that'd been me, I'd never got caught. I've gotten away with things make you look like a pussy. You hear?"

The black man had rolled over on the bunk, facing the wall.

"You look at me when I talk to you, boy. You know who I am?"

The black man remained motionless on the bed. The Latino moved closer, sure of himself now, excited at his power. In the bunk the black man looked small, defenseless.

Leaning into the bunk, he hissed, "I've done things make your frizzy hair stand on end. Man, I've done things make shooting a couple of kids nothing. Richard Ramirez. You know him? The Nightstalker." He started poking himself in the chest. "Friend of mine. That's what. Fucking friend of mine, man. Fucking brother. Front page in the paper too, man. On every front page in the country."

The black man slowly rolled over and fixed him with his huge round eyes. "Boy, youse not right in your head. Get 'way from me now. Let old Willie alone. I ain't starting nuthin'. Let old Will alone."

"You ever fucked a white woman, Willie? You ever put your black dick in a white woman's pussy? How 'bout a redhead? You ever fucked a redhead with freckles and skin as white as a fucking baby? Soft, too, Willie. They soft, man. Their skin's like velvet, like one of them paintings."

The black man ducked to keep from hitting his head on the upper bunk and stood to his full height, at least six-six or more. He put his hands in front of him to shove the other man back, but it wasn't necessary. The Latino was backing away, his face ashen.

"I knows whats youse done, boy. I's heard whats youse done. And if'n I was you, I'd be quiet 'bout it. Willie's been to the big house, boy. They don't like boys like you. Boys do the things you done."

He was cowering in the corner, pressed against the back wall, only inches from the filthy open toilet. Just the mention of prison filled him with terror. He was small, his body unconditioned and wasted from drugs and alcohol, his power sucked from the helplessness of his victims. In jail he could survive, but not in prison. He knew what would happen to him there.

He took the few steps to the window and stared out again. "This is your fault, you bitch," he whispered. "This is all your fault."

CHAPTER 3 ■

They were sitting in a booth at Denny's, two blocks from the Elephant Bar, sipping black coffee and eating cheeseburgers. They were laughing and getting sober.

Lily picked her burger apart and with a fork poked the meat, displaying the bloody insides. "This is raw."

"Send it back," he said. "They'll kill it for sure this time."

"Think I'll just pass." With one hand she shoved the plate away and moved the coffee cup in front of her. "So tell me exactly what happened with Judge Fisher."

"I found the little bastard snorting cocaine. Not much more to tell than that."

"But how did he have the gall to call Butler and complain? Wasn't he the least bit concerned?"

"Hell, no. He just told Butler that I was a madman and barged into his chambers and that he didn't want to see my face anywhere near Superior Court again." He dabbed his mouth with a napkin. His black eyes were now alert and mischievous. "I did happen to go up and down the hall and tell a few people that Fisher was having a little party and that they better hurry if they wanted to do a few lines of the best Colombian coke around."

"What's wrong with you?" Lily said, laughing at the scenario. "Do you have a death wish or something? I thought you and Butler were on great terms, that he thought you could do no wrong. Why didn't he back you up?"

"Oh, Butler's a good man. He believed me. Just took the easy way out, the path of least resistance. His theory is that when the dirt flies, we all get buried in it. I actually think he felt bad about the whole thing. When all is said and done, he'll probably give me homicide. Maybe in six months."

Lily brushed her hair off her face. The waitress came with the check, and she grabbed it and threw a twenty on the table. "I don't know how I'm going to handle this new job, Rich. Isn't it hard to become involved in the cases and then have to rely on someone else to actually try them?"

"That's what supervision is all about. If you can't trust people or feel you have to track every single proceeding in that unit, you'll lose your mind. Don't nag and don't be a baby-sitter, Lily, or you'll fall into that age-old stereotype of the woman manager."

Lily stared into space, digesting his advice.

"Ready," he said, sliding out of the booth and then looking down at her twenty. "By the way, you have to pay at the cash register."

Outside in the cool air, he stood close to her. "I'll walk you to your car. Where did you park?"

In her mind she saw herself already walking through the door of her ranch house. The first thing she saw every day was the backyard. "I parked at the center," she said, looking straight in front of her. John had decided to redo the sprinkler system himself about six months before and had dug up the entire yard. He had then planted one side in with sod, leaving the other side dirt after he couldn't figure out how to get the sprinklers working.

"My car's at the bar. I'll drive you," Richard said. "You shouldn't be walking around alone at night."

On weekends John would sit in a lawn chair and sun himself on the grass side as if the dirt side didn't exist. No matter how many times she told him how it irritated her and how ridiculous it looked, he made no attempt to correct it. She looked at Richard and replied: "Thanks." She didn't want to go home. She didn't want to be the primary decision maker, the disciplinarian, the strong one in the family. She wanted to laugh and feel pleasure, feel attractive and physically desirable. She wanted to believe that a birthday was a cause for celebration.

They walked in silence. She'd have to settle for the moment. Soon it would be gone. She'd be at home in her bed with John. After all these years of abstinence and John's accusations that she was fooling around on the side, for the first time she wished it were true. And it could only be the man walking beside her, the same man she called forth in her fantasies. But he was married and there was no reason to believe he was even attracted to her. If John was no longer interested in her sexually, why would another man want her? She was no longer desirable. She might as well accept it. She'd accepted everything else about her life. She was thirty-six. Just a few more years and she'd be forty.

He unlocked the passenger side of his white BMW and tossed what looked like his gym clothes into the backseat. In the driver's seat, he put the key in the ignition and then dropped his hands in his lap and turned to her. He reached across and kissed her fully on the mouth, his hands buried in her thick hair. His face scratched her sensitive skin with day-old stubble. "Come home with me," he whispered. "Please, I need you. I want you."

"But . . ." Lily said, thinking of his wife and teenage son, the fact that she should go home; the fact that she might want it now and regret it later. His lips were there again and his tongue probed in her mouth; his hands on her back pressed her to him.

23

She was flooded with warmth, pushing herself closer into his body, her flesh alive with nerve endings. Everything washed away: the job, John, Shana, her birthday, her childhood, her caution.

"Please," he said. He lifted her chin, forcing her to look into his eyes. "No one is there if that's what you're thinking. And no one is coming home tonight." He took her hand and placed it on the crotch of his pants, on his erection. She let it stay there as he kissed her again.

She was a normal woman with normal desires. Richard wasn't going to use her as a receptacle, as John would say. He was the repairman, the doctor, the magician. He was going to plug her back into the wall outlet again and turn on the lights. She wasn't broken. She had just been put on the shelf.

"Drive," she said, "and fast. Drive fast."

They were standing in his living room, looking out over the city at night; he was nude, she was wrapped in a large bath sheet. The house was in the foothills, contemporary, with high ceilings and an open, airy feeling. Her jacket, her shoes, her bra and hose were scattered across the living room floor. They'd never made it to the bedroom.

Once in the house, she had stripped her clothes almost ahead of him, and they had stood there facing each other in the darkness, a foot away, both their arms at their sides.

"I always knew your body would look like this," he said.

"What does it look like?" she said.

"Lush. It looks like mounds of strawberry yogurt. I want to taste it."

They made love on the sofa, their feet sticking off one end, arms and legs everywhere. It was the only piece of furniture in the room. With his long, sinewy arms he held her upper body down and buried his head between her legs. He lingered there even when she protested and sighed and cried out. "No. No. No."

She finally could take it no longer and dragged him up by

his hair and forced him to switch places with her, and with her hair spread over the hard muscles of his stomach, she took him in her mouth, hungry for the taste and smell of him, the feel of him. "Oh, God," he cried, "God."

She crawled on top of him and straddled him, riding him like a horse, pushed up on her arms, tossing her hair, leaning down to kiss him and then throwing her head back again. This was her fantasy. She was living her dream. She actually imagined she was on a great white horse, galloping over huge hurdles and streams, heading for the white light of pleasure. Finding it, she collapsed on his chest, sweating, satiated. He rolled her off onto the floor and turned her around and took her from behind, holding her buttocks in his hands and slamming against her until he exploded and fell on top of her. She fell onto the carpet, his heavy body on her back, his warm, heavy breath in her ear. "Jesus," he said, "did I hurt you?"

"Not hardly," she said. "Did I hurt you?"

He lifted her wet hair and kissed the back of her neck tenderly. "I don't think you can call that pain."

Suddenly embarrassed, she broke free, sat up with her knees drawn and her arms wrapped around them. Already feelings of guilt were fluttering in the pit of her stomach, but a quick look at Richard made them disappear. She'd finally met John's accusations and suspicions. And it had been easy, too easy. And it had been good enough to want much more. Her body was screaming at her, begging her, demanding more. Perhaps she could actually feed this desire, this need. She could go on wanting Richard until he ignored her and disappointed her and no longer cared if she walked alone at night. This is what it must feel like when two people meet each other on an even level, she thought, share similar points of view. She let her eyes drift down with mock coyness, a smile playing at the corners of her lips; her behavior had been shocking, wanton, thrilling. People felt this good all the time, at every second in every day, somewhere in the world. Getting a divorce was not a crime punishable by death. She could feel this way again.

They showered together in the master bathroom. Passing the bed, she saw it was unmade and the room was strewn with clothes and newspapers and glasses sitting on tables without coasters. In the shower, they rubbed soap all over each other's bodies. He dumped half a bottle of shampoo on her head, and it dripped down into her eyes. "Get me a towel," she screamed, actually laughing, listening to the delightful sound bounce off the walls, amazed that it had been manufactured inside her. "You've blinded me." She took the little soap, greatly used, and made him turn around and rubbed it between the two muscular white cheeks of his ass, like she'd done to her daughter when she was young. He jumped and told her to stop, but she knew he loved it. Outside the shower, he wanted to comb her pubic hair with his comb so some of the hairs would be there in the morning. She couldn't believe it, but she let him. It tickled. He commented on the fact that she was a real redhead, causing her to take one of his nipples and twist it hard, "Because you doubted me," and because she just wanted to, had always wanted to do something like that. Afterward, he gave her the only clean towel and he walked naked, dripping water onto the carpet, to the living room, where they now stood and talked.

He moved behind her and put his arms around her. "Do you want something to drink? I don't have any tequila, but I can find something else."

Her head ached at the mere mention of tequila. "No, thanks. I have to go, you know, and soon." She had already decided that his wife no longer lived there. She wanted it to be true so badly that she couldn't ask. "I hate to do this to you, but you realize you're going to have to drive me to my car."

"I don't mind, Lily," he said, his voice reflecting the beginning of a letdown. "But do we have to end it so fast? Can't we just stay here a minute and relish it?" He turned her to face him and held her face in both hands. "This was much more than just an office fuck and you know it."

She sighed deeply, letting the air leave her lungs as if she were exhaling a cigarette. "I know."

Lily picked her clothes off the floor and put them back on piece by piece. She turned away from him when she hooked her bra in the front and turned it around, shaking her breasts into the cups. She put on her blouse first and then her panties. They were plain white comfortable cotton panties, and she was ashamed that they were not French cut lace.

He was still looking out at the city as he spoke. "My wife left me for someone else. A month ago. It was a month ago today. She told me she was in love with someone else, and while I was at work, she came with a moving van and moved half the furniture out."

"I'm sorry, Richard. Did you love her?"

"Sure, I loved her. I lived with her for seventeen years. I don't even know where she is now. She's here in the city somewhere, but she doesn't want me to know where. Our son is with her."

"Do you know the man?" Lily asked, curious about the whole thing, wondering how she could want him so badly and someone who had lived with him for seventeen years no longer wanted him at all.

"It's not a man. Lily, my wife left me for a woman."

"Your son?"

"He doesn't know and I would never tell him. He just thinks the woman is her roommate." His face was bathed in shadows. He was facing Lily now, but he quickly turned back to the window. "I mean, I don't believe he knows."

"You might be surprised, Rich. Kids know a lot more than we think. He might know and have already accepted it. He is living with his mother, right?"

"He's a strange kid, off in his own world." He glanced at Lily over his shoulder and saw that she was dressed and waiting. "Greg used to be an honor student and now he's a surfer. Instead of studying, the kid surfs. He'll be lucky to get into a junior college. I always dreamed he'd be an attorney, that maybe we'd someday have our own private practice. Dreams. Things don't always work the way you plan them."

Lily came up and stood beside him. He draped an arm over her shoulder. "I'm curious, Richard. Forgive me. But did your wife explain any of this to you—you know, tell you how long this had been going on? Surely you knew something?"

"Believe it or not, I didn't know shit. I never knew a thing until she left. Oh, now she tells me she's been seeing this woman for three years, but all that time I would have never known."

She saw his need to talk but knew she had to go. "Can we talk in the car? I wish I could stay and we could talk more, but I am married. It's not a good marriage,"—she paused— "obviously, or I wouldn't be here with you. It may end soon, for all I know, but I don't want it to end badly. Can you understand that?"

"Just give me a second. I'll get dressed."

At the government center complex, she leaned against the car and he kissed her. "Why do you park here? Don't you know they can see you from the jail?"

"Well," she said, nuzzling him and softly biting his ear. "One day I might be able to park underground where the judges park. What do you think?"

"I think there's a good possibility if that's what you really want. Did you know I recommended you for my replacement?"

She didn't and was pleased. "Thanks, and that was even before tonight." She smiled, unlocking the door to her red Honda. She started the ignition and waved and then stuck her head out the window. "To be continued, huh?"

"Right," he said, "to be continued."

CHAPTER 4 ▪

A loud clap of thunder woke her from a deep sleep, and the child jerked her body upright in her bed, feeling the warm, soggy sheets and her flannel gown beneath her. She had wet her bed but was relieved that it was still warm and not cold yet; it was so warm that it was almost comforting. Eyes glued to the window, she saw the lightning illuminate the large cedar tree. She began counting: "One one-thousand, two one-thousand, three one-thousand, four one-thousand." Crack. She put her hands to her ears and held her breath, trying to keep the fear from making her cry out. Silence. She let out her breath in one long whoosh and fell back onto the bed, covering her head with the blankets. She had to get up soon and get the towel and place it over the mattress; she had to change her gown or the wetness would become like ice and she would start shivering. Inching the covers down slowly, the light was again there and the shape outside the window now moved. She screamed, unable to stop herself. She was in the mountains, at the ranch, and there were bears who wanted in from the rain, hungry bears.

She ran barefoot, oblivious now to the wetness, to her grandparents' bedroom down the long, dark hall, looking over her shoulder for the bear, jumping up in the air as she ran so it could not grab her feet. She leaped into the big bed. Safe. "Granny, Granny," she cried, big sloppy tears running down her face. She remembered: Granny had gone to the neighboring town and would not return until the morning; she had gone to buy presents for her birthday tomorrow. Only the big barrel tummy of her grandfather swelled beneath the sheets. He moaned and turned over onto his side, a big arm reaching out to her, still asleep. "Granddaddy," she said, poking his stomach with a finger, not really afraid anymore and liking the funny feeling she got when her finger touched the soft flesh, went in and came out, like a pillow. "Granddaddy," she whispered now. He was breathing funny, rattling and wheezing; the air filled with a sour odor coming from his mouth. She was shivering. She climbed under the thick blankets and felt the dry sheets, shoving the wet part of her gown away from her body. In seconds she was asleep.

A long time later, while she was dreaming of her birthday party, of the presents and ribbons and cake, she awoke to feel pain somewhere near her bottom, bad pain, the worst pain she had ever felt. The bed was shaking under his weight and she was facedown on the mattress, unable to move, unable to scream, gasping for air; her arms stretched out horizontally, frantically clawing and grabbing. Before everything went black, she heard him call her grandmother's name: "Lillian."

"Lily," John said, shaking her, hands on her shoulders. "Wake up." She was sleeping facedown on the pillow, not sleeping really, but drifting in and out of that early morning state of semiconsciousness when dreams, memories, and reality are all intermingled. "You just clawed my arm and your gown is soaking wet. You're going to be late for work."

John knew she was having the nightmare. He was all too familiar with the signs: the sweating, clawing, screaming out in her sleep. She would never tell him or anyone else the whole truth, but he knew that her grandfather had sexually abused her. She raised her head and looked at him as he walked out the door. If he just thought about it, he'd realize that he'd forgotten her birthday. The nightmares always got worse around her birthday.

Not long after they were married, she'd told him and all it did was support his beliefs about most men and sex. John said he didn't crave sex like the majority of men. To him it was an act of great beauty and purpose—procreation. During the early years of their marriage, he had rocked her in his arms when she awoke in the middle of the night, sometimes even wetting the bed as she'd done as a child. When she couldn't go back to sleep, he would go into the kitchen and bring her back a cup of hot chocolate or a grilled cheese sandwich. Then he would gently stroke her and hold her until she fell asleep again. He loved her then, and his love and understanding, his lack of sexual desire, all allowed her to heal and recover from the past. He wanted her to go to law school, had encouraged her, but when she finally graduated, their relationship changed dramatically. Like a cripple who finally walks, she waited for the applause, the tears of joy. They never came. This was when she learned about John. When she had been scared and afraid, John was devoted, loving, supportive. When she broke through the wall of fear and became a confident professional, with a career, a future, a mind of her own, John's love disappeared. He didn't want to walk next to her, evidently. He wanted only to carry her.

By the time she put her feet on the floor, she heard the garage door and knew John had left for work. He had been asleep when she came home the night before, snoring loudly. She'd taken off her clothes in the closet and slipped into the bed, turning him on his side to stop the snoring. Lying right next to him, she'd thought of Richard, wanted John to disappear and Richard to take his place. Everyone thought John was wonderful, a great father, a perfect husband. He'd been the ideal husband for the broken child she had been. But she wanted more. She didn't want to be that person anymore. Time was running out, the clock was ticking. If she stayed until Shana went to college, she would be forty-one, too old. Sorry, missed the boat, they would say.

Naked, about to step into the steaming shower, she reached for a towel and observed her reflection in the mirror. Turning sideways, she viewed her profile, placing one hand under a breast and lifting it, then letting it fall. Gravity was pulling her down, her face, her breasts, her behind. John was pulling her down, an albatross around her neck.

Her head was throbbing, her stomach growling with hunger, but she felt great. Today she had a reason to go to work, and it wasn't just another hearing, another case. Richard Fowler was there, at the office, in the same building, right down the hall.

She started searching her closet for something special to wear. She would wear her favorite outfit, the one that made her waist and hips look so thin and that everyone always complimented her on. It had just come back from the cleaners the previous week. Perfect.

After ten minutes of going through everything wrapped in plastic, she found only the skirt. The top was gone.

She stomped into Shana's room, flinging the door open in anger. "Where's the top to my black-and-white outfit with the buttons up the side?"

Shana, who had been sound asleep, rolled over and stared at her mother with puffy, unfocused eyes. "What time is it? I don't have it." She rolled back over and promptly went back to sleep.

Lily went to Shana's closet, piled three feet high with clothes, and started digging through them all on her hands and knees. Seeing three or four items that were hers, she tossed them aside, leaving the rest in the middle of the floor. "I know you have my top. I want to wear that outfit today. You have no right to take my things without my permission, particularly my expensive things—my work clothes."

"Chill out, Mom!" Shana screamed at her shrilly. "I loaned it to Charlotte. You'll get it back."

"You're grounded. Do you hear me? Grounded," Lily yelled, hating herself for yelling, but it wasn't an isolated incident. Shana took her clothes almost every day, and on many occasions Lily never saw them again. Every other morning she had to go through Shana's closet before she could even get dressed to go to work, generally finding her things tossed in a heap, wrinkled and stained. John just shrugged his shoulders and told Lily it was typical, a teenage thing, suggesting they get a lock for their door. He couldn't fathom that a child might respect another person's property.

As she walked out the door, she heard Shana mumble the word "bitch" under her breath and pull the covers over her head.

Outside the room, Lily leaned against the wall, her eyes moist with tears. What had gone wrong between them? They'd always been so close. She remembered all the Sunday afternoons they'd gone roller skating together in the California sunshine, their hair blowing in the wind, Shana skating as near Lily as possible, so close that she sometimes knocked her down. Until just a few months before, Shana used to come into the bedroom every night while John was still watching television and tell Lily all about her day, jabbering on and on about who said what and who did what at school, asking Lily's advice on everything from homework to boys. Was it all just puberty? Raging hormones? Had Lily's own childhood been so twisted, so painful, that she couldn't remember what it was like to be thirteen?

She wiped her eyes and headed for the kitchen. She popped a slice of wheat bread in the toaster and poured herself a cup of coffee. She was overreacting to everything. It was all her. Shana was just becoming a teenager. Even the situation with the clothes was her fault. She'd always told Shana she could borrow her clothes, had an open-door policy on everything. But back then Shana had respected her. She never took things without asking and absolutely never took her work clothes. She never glared at her and called her names. She never hung up on her. And every day the child seemed to get closer to her father, pushing Lily further and further away.

It was nothing more than the Oedipal phase of puberty, Lily knew. Shana was daddy's little darling and now her mother was her rival. It all made perfect sense. She even wanted to wear her clothes in order to compete for her father's love like a woman, not a child.

She carried the coffee to the Honda in a styrofoam cup. Then she left it there, sitting on the hood of the car, and returned to the house.

In her bathrobe, Shana had just stepped out of the shower and was headed back to her room. She saw Lily and stopped, a look that said "what now?" on her face.

"I'm sorry I screamed at you."

Shana did not respond. She stared.

"All I ask is that you don't take my clothes without asking me, and that you don't loan my expensive things to your friends. Every parent wants their child to respect them." Lily moved a few steps closer, extended her hand, and touched the girl's shoulder. She smiled. Shana didn't smile back.

"Look, if you get your homework done early, maybe we can go to a movie tomorrow night. Just the two of us, like we used to."

"I can't. I'm grounded, remember?"

"Okay, let's start over. We'll pretend this morning never happened. What do you say? Tomorrow night."

"Too much homework."

Shana had always been an outstanding student, but lately her grades had dropped. According to her, even that was Lily's fault. It was because she had pushed her into accelerated classes. "I know your classes are hard. We discussed that before you took them. I just want you to have everything in life. That's why I want you to take school seriously, work at your highest level. You can do it, Shana. You're a smart girl. I don't want you to marry someone just to get married. If you have a career, you'll be your own person. Do you understand what I'm saying?" Lily glanced at her watch. She was going to be late for work.

"Yeah," Shana answered, "you're saying you married Dad just to get married."

"No, Shana. When I married your dad I was not the person I am today, but I didn't marry him just to do it. I married him because I needed him. When I was a young girl, in a way I stopped living. I didn't know what it meant to be happy. I let something hard and ugly grow inside me. I didn't take control of my life."

"I'm going to be late for school, Mom," Shana said and started walking to her bedroom. With her back to Lily, she said: "Don't worry. I'm not going to be a waitress." Then she closed the door in her mother's face.

So much for child psychology, Lily thought, hurrying down the hall to the garage. She was never going to live down the waitress comment. She might have said it, but she owed John for repeating it.

By the time Lily got to the complex, the parking lot was almost full. After circling a few times and seeing the time on the clock on the dash, Lily headed for the rows directly under the jail, knowing she would find a spot. Looking up at the smoked glass windows, no one could tell it was a jail facility —that is, unless you looked up at the roof, where searchlights were positioned. Other than that, it looked exactly like the rest of the modern complex. Prisoners were moved through an underground tunnel to the courts and back again, never seeing the light of day; law enforcement personnel saved hours traveling from one location to the other, as did the prosecutors and public defenders. During the planning stages many had protested, arguing against housing the prisoners in the same complex. County officials ignored the concerns, pointing out that it was a presentence facility, not a prison. Once a prisoner was convicted, he was transported to the Department of Corrections. Only the lightweight offenders served time here for things like petty theft, parole violations, drunk driving.

Except for the fact that they were all housed inside, all breathing the same recycled, stuffy air (windows didn't open anywhere in the complex) and all the offices were now glass-partitioned cubicles which everyone despised, you could say the new center was functioning as designed. Lily hated it. If they had not moved from the old facility, she would now be walking into a prestigious office, complete with real wood paneling and bookcases and a wooden door that shut out the relentless office noise. There would be fresh air drifting in from open windows with ledges where pigeons roosted. But this was progress and it was here to stay, she thought with a sense of loss, getting out and walking across the parking lot in the crisp morning air.

The meeting with Butler went as she had expected: once she had briefly described the atrocities of the Lopez–McDonald case, he was both shocked and outraged. Sitting in his large corner office, with real leather studded chairs, a desk large enough to play a game of pool on, and the built-in bookcases Lily lusted after, she looked straight into his small dark unblinking eyes and told him the problems she could foresee with the case.

"The eyewitness was a schoolteacher and she saw, quote: 'Several Hispanic youths running from the area by the bleachers,' the area where she made the grisly discovery of the two bodies. She didn't see five of them, Paul, and she's uncertain if she saw even three of them. She did tentatively identify three of the suspects from a photo lineup. We need to coach her into saying that she saw three or more and eliminate the word *several* from her testimony. The police stopped the defendants on an expired registration one block and five minutes from the time the crime was reported. There were five of them in the car, but two insist they were picked up at the corner by the driver only seconds before the stop. Unfortunately, there were no witnesses to this, and it's our guess that they were all involved. No confessions and no incriminating statements. Paul, these boys are tough." She stopped, sighing deeply before continuing.

"Semen extracted from what was left of the murdered girl's vagina reflects more than three different blood types. We have powder burns and blood stains from the victim on two of the defendants' clothing, and what I would call a pretty good case." Lily paused, waiting for Butler to ask questions, then interjected, "But not a case without pitfalls."

Butler leaned back in his chair and gritted his teeth. "The problem lies in convicting all five and not confusing the jury by the eyewitness testimony," he stated. "Defense is going to use this to the max, trying to make the jury think at least two of these boys are innocent and confusing them about who did what. The optimum situation is to get one of them to roll over for a deal and put the whole thing together air-tight."

Exactly what Lily was thinking. "But how far will we go to get what we want? Will we go second-degree, accessory to murder, all the way down to manslaughter?" Lily was still holding the file in her lap, and now opened it and removed the crime-scene photos. Pictures said more than words, and she wanted Butler to have these nightmare images in his mind as he mulled over possible deals. "The problem is not getting someone to talk—any of these animals would sell his own mother down the river to save himself. The problem is knowing which one did the least in this massacre." She offered the photo and Butler accepted it. "This is a close-up of the tree limb that was shoved into Carmen Lopez's vagina, piercing her abdominal wall."

Butler was visibly shaken and his lower lip trembled slightly. There were leaves on the end of the branch, covered with blood. "God," he said.

"And this is a close-up of her breasts—what was left of

them after they played target practice on them with a small-caliber handgun." She handed another photo to Butler.

"No deals as of right now," he said flatly. "I want two investigators from our office on this full-time. Question everyone who ever said so much as good morning to these boys and bring me the reports. We'll pray that forensics comes up with enough to make it stick on all five. Anyone who merely watched this happen and didn't stop it deserves life, and of course we hope to get the death penalty. If any case merits it, this one does."

The meeting was over. They decided that Carol Abrams would handle it due to the sexual nature of the crimes and Marshall Duffy would assist her from homicide.

When Lily returned to her office, the phone was ringing and she bent over the front of her desk to answer it, dumping the file on top of the existing clutter. It was Richard. "Meet me in interrogation room three in five minutes. I have to see you."

Her heart raced and her breath quickened. "I want to see you, too, but I don't have a minute to spare." She paused and then realized that she would never make it through the day without seeing him. "I'll be there."

She carried several files for appearances and walked into the interrogation room, closing the door and taking a seat at the small table, tapping her feet while she was waiting. There was a phone for attorneys to dictate notes on the on-line system to the word-processing pool. Lily had finally settled on a lavender silk dress that clung to every curve, dangling silver earrings, and a big silver clasp tieing her long red hair at the nape of her neck, letting it hang down her back. She knew she looked feminine and attractive. Several people had complimented her already. Richard opened the door, then shut it and locked it behind him. He kissed her, smearing her lipstick, and placed both hands on her breasts beneath the thin silk fabric.

"I've been thinking about you all night. I want you so bad. I can't get your face out of my mind." He slid his hand up her skirt, along the silk of her panty hose, stopping at her crotch.

"Stop it, Richard," she said. "I don't think it's my face you've been thinking about." She smiled, trying to remain detached while her body was responding to his every touch. The same reckless abandon she had felt the night before was taking over as he pulled down her panty hose and placed his hand inside, touching her lightly, making her wet, making her ache. His mouth was on her neck, her head thrown back, her hair touching the top of the table. Her blouse was open and his other hand inside. He unzipped his pants and entered her, spread out on the table; it moved beneath them. She was afraid to speak, fearful someone would hear them, unable to stop him.

He picked up the phone and handed it to her; his face was twisted with passion, his voice deep, his eyes half closed. "Pretend you're dictating something."

She could hear the phones ringing outside and hear footsteps passing the door. "*State of California* v. *Daniel Duthoy* . . . case No. H23456." The dial tone rang in her ear as her body moved with his. "Additional pleading should read: The defendant occupied a position of trust while committing the crime." Richard was moaning now. "Don't stop," he said. She continued: "By his role as a Big Brother to the victim, he was therefore in a position to gain his trust in order to perpetrate the crime and used this position for this purpose." She bit her lower lip to keep from crying out and let herself fall back onto the table, trying to make as little noise as possible. There was a recording now on the phone. "If you'd like to make a call, please hang up and call again." It was over.

They repaired their clothing and Lily wiped her lipstick off his mouth and cheek with her finger, leaving only a pinkish blush. "I love you," Richard blurted out. "I know you don't believe it . . . I wouldn't either. You're the woman I've been looking for all my life. You're strong, smart, passionate . . . you're radiant."

Lily put her finger across his mouth. "Hush," she said, "or

I'm going to be unemployed and humiliated beyond belief. Besides, I'm up to my asshole in work.'' His words of affection she discarded; all men loved you the few minutes after they left your body. He looked crushed. She continued in a tender, soft tone. "I know something big is happening here. I don't know exactly what. I know I want it to keep happening. Not like this, not in the office, but . . . my life and my emotions are going a million different directions right now. Can you understand that?" She was pleading with him with her eyes, her fingers playing with the edge of his jacket lapel, still sitting on the table and thinking how irresistible he looked this minute with his dark hair falling onto his forehead. "I need time," she said, "and I can't afford to be reckless." She didn't want to bring up her marriage—to tell him that she wanted out, that she wanted more than an affair. She wanted the whole ball of wax.

"There's never time, Lily," he said. He crushed a piece of paper into her hand with two numbers on it: his home and car phone. He left first, and after a few minutes she also left, looking up and down the hall, relieved that no one had seen them.

She returned to her office and started plowing through the cases, infused with energy. Not an inch of veneer showed on top of the desk; it was littered with papers, files, open law books. The credenza in back of her was stacked with files. Her head propped up on one arm, her tortoiseshell glasses down on the center of her nose, she was fully engrossed in the case in front of her when the phone rang. She pushed the hands-free button but continued to read. Clinton Silverstein appeared in the doorway, holding a file in one hand and slapping it against the other, his mouth tense, his brow furrowed. She caught him out of the corner of her eye and waved him into the room.

"Which case? Oh, Robinson. It's assigned. We pled the prior and the enhancement for the weapon. Peterson should have it in the morning." She tapped off the speaker and directed Clinton to one of the green chairs in front of her desk with a diagonal glance of her eyes.

"This case you just assigned me is a fucking joke." He waited for her to respond, but all he heard was metal crackling on plastic as she sat back in her chair and it moved on the heavy mat beneath it. "The victim weighs over two hundred pounds—probably from the waist down, from the butt shots —has a record of prostitution, and even admits she was working at the time of the offense. What I'd call it is 'failure to pay.' She decided to cry rape when the trick didn't pay."

"It's a kidnapping and attempted rape," Lily snapped.

"But *no deals?* You can't be serious. Your victim is not credible. Have you seen the mug shots of this defendant? Hell, he's a good-looking guy. He even smiled for the camera; he knows he's going to walk even if you don't." Clinton dropped his stocky body in the chair.

Lily removed her glasses and tossed them; they appeared to fall in slow motion, landing on the paper-padded desk without a sound. "Do you think a woman can't be raped if she weighs two hundred pounds?"

"It's the entire case. The victim's a hooker. All the witnesses are hookers. She admits she negotiated a price for sex. All he did was punch her in the face a few times. So what's the big kidnapping all about: the fact that he shoved her head down and drove her to a city dump and then tossed her out of the van? What the hell do you expect when you're in that line of business? Did she think the guy was going to get front-row seats at the opera?" Clinton shook his head. "I'd say we offer him a plea on misdemeanor battery and he'll plead out at arraignment; as part of the agreement, we'll ask for ninety days in jail and three years supervised probation. Then we'll have a conviction on record. Taking it to trial means we may end up with nothing but egg on our faces." Clinton sat back in his chair, smug in his analysis.

Lily's eyes were cold steel. She leaned forward. "What makes this case so weak in your eyes makes it even stronger in mine: the fact that this young man could easily find sex partners but he picked this woman—this disgusting woman, in your eyes—to vent his rage." She stopped and swallowed air, aloft now on her beliefs. "You know what? I think he was going to kill her, and it just wasn't as easy as he thought it was going to be."

Clinton ran his fingers through his permed hair. It stood on end. "But what is the whole point if he walks? I still don't agree with you."

"The point is that we give it our best shot and treat this case with as much outrage as we would if the victim had been a Sunday school teacher . . . that we don't demean her or demean ourselves. That's the point. Prepare the case for pre-lim, Clinton."

He stood to leave. "It's also moving the calendar, Lily—trying cases it makes sense to try and disposing of the others. I know Butler is against plea bargains on sex offenses, but he can't mean all of them. We'll do all the preparation and the victim won't even show. Mark my words."

She called him back from the door. Her voice was almost seductive, chilling in its purposeful modulation. "This is your next case. Perhaps you'll be more willing to champion her cause."

He walked to a position near her desk. There was only one photo in her outstretched hand.

Lily's voice was a commentator's monotone. "You're look-ing at Stacy Jenkins, age eight years, nine months. Stacy at-tended school for about six months during the first grade and was never allowed to return. Her stepfather is an accountant with a salary of about $65,000 annually; her mother a registered nurse."

"Is she dead?" Clinton said.

Lily saw his hands shaking and just looked at him without answering.

"I mean, her eyes are open, but was the picture taken posthumously? Is this a homicide?"

Lily had thought the same thing when she first saw the picture. The child's eyes were void of the essence of human life, her brown hair was stringy and limp. All over her body were round, angry red circles, and on her chest were jagged, fresh scars.

"No, she is not dead," Lily said flatly and continued. "Stacy's stepfather began forcing her to commit sex acts about the time he removed her from school. Each time she cried, he burned her with his cigarette. One time she defecated. He pried off her nipples with a pair of pliers. Mother went along with everything, it seems, and used her nursing skills to treat her wounds."

"How did this come to light?" he asked. "My own daughter will be nine next month." His mouth was open, jaw limp, his voice elevated. "This is my first case involving a child."

Lily's head was down, engrossed in another case. She spoke without looking up. "Mom brought her into E.R. one night with a raging infection on the verge of death. Apparently, even she had her limits. We're charging her as a codefendant on all counts." Lily now looked up, her eyes dull and tired. "Our biggest hurdle is to stack the counts as high as they will go, but of course, we have to document each one as a separate crime and a lot will depend on Stacy. You'll be interviewing her with a social worker next week." She stopped and looked hard at Clinton. "By the way, either cut your hair or get some conditioner. You'll scare the child to death with that hair."

As soon as Clinton wandered out of her office, Lily hit the number one button on the auto dial and called home. She massaged the throbbing in her temples as the rapid tones came out over the speakers. Trying to ease the tension in her neck, she rolled her head around. She looked at the case file in front of her and saw Stacy Jenkins's face, then her own face superimposed over the child's.

"John, it's me. I don't think I'm going to get out of here before eight. I'm buried. Tell Shana for me." She could hear pans rattling in the background; John was making dinner. He got home every day at four-thirty. Some days he didn't work at all.

"I'm coaching Shana's softball game tonight. You promised her you'd come, you know."

Lily's chest was burning, and she reached behind her and unsnapped her bra through the fabric of her dress. Had she really promised she would come tonight, or was she losing her mind? John sometimes manufactured statements like these to increase her guilt, tighten the screws.

"Don't worry, she never expects you to show anyway." His deep voice throbbed with venom. "We know your work is more important. For the past two years that's all you seem to be concerned about—your work."

"I'll see you at the ballpark." She wanted to scream at him, tell him that she'd buried herself in her work to escape the emptiness of her life, her marriage—that she felt like an outsider in her own home, with her own child. But it was no use. She started to hit the off button, but stopped. "And, John, even though you and Shana have a short memory, I've only missed one game."

She disconnected and placed her head in her hands for a few brief seconds. Thumbing through the stacks of files on the credenza, she counted seven that had to be reviewed and assigned by four o'clock the following day. She was working on three simultaneously and even now realized that valuable time was slipping through her fingers. Looking at Shana's dazzling smile in the photo on her desk, she observed Carol Abrams in the doorway. How long had she been there?

"I need to talk to you about Lopez–McDonald, but it can wait." She spoke slowly and looked at the floor, moving her feet around. "I didn't mean to barge in, but your door was open."

So she had heard the conversation with John. Lily mustered up a feeble smile. "How about nine o'clock sharp? We'll both be fresh."

"I have an appearance at nine; make it ten and you're on."

She paused, an awkward silence, her eyes still searching Lily's face. "You know, we should have lunch someday, if time ever permits. I have two kids, ten and fourteen. It's tough sometimes, really tough. You know what I mean?"

Lily compared herself to Carol, so pert and perfect at the end of the day. Every blond hair was in place and her suit was hardly wrinkled, her lipstick a bright, moist pink. Hard to believe it was so tough for Carol when she looked so good. Lily ran her tongue over her cracked, dry mouth. "Maybe they made a mistake, Carol. You should have this job instead of me."

Carol smiled and shook her head. "Nope. You can keep it. By the way, I personally think you're going to be the best damn chief this department ever had. How about that?" She winked and bounded out of the office.

A few hours later when Lily left, a heavy briefcase weighed down each arm. The sun was setting and it was getting chilly; she felt it through the thin silk of her dress. Jogging at a stiff pace to her red Honda in the parking lot, she pulled one arm up to look at her watch and realized she would have to speed to get to the ballpark—the game had already started. She dropped both the cases on the ground and started digging blindly in her purse, willing her fingers to touch the cold metal of her keys. She dumped the entire contents of her purse on the hood of the Honda, and the keys hit metal with a ting, rolling to the asphalt along with a lipstick and a phone bill she had failed to mail. The breeze picked up the envelope and she had to chase it across the parking lot.

Finally in the driver's seat, she saw the garbage from her purse still on the hood on the car. She started to just drive off and let it fall, knowing most of it should have been discarded long ago. Then she thought better and the same reasons she had collected it caused her to get out. With the palm of her hand, she shoved all the business cards, receipts, and old validated parking tickets back into her open purse, except for a small piece of paper, the one Richard had crushed into her hand earlier that day with his phone numbers. Her fingers ran across the paper, smoothing the wrinkles, touching something he had touched. She folded the paper like a note passed in high school and put it into her checkbook. Something had started in her life, and soon she would never be the same. She knew it, could feel it. Something was vibrating all around her, like the white noise they used at the office to disguise the relentless office clamor. When she got back in the car, she turned the heater on high. It might have been sixty-five degrees, but Lily was freezing.

CHAPTER 5.

He was laughing, excited, watching her run around in the parking lot, fumbling for her keys. He slapped his hands in glee against the window and left his fingerprints there. He never left fingerprints, never touched things when he was in places where he didn't belong, and he had been in many such places. "I'm here," he yelled at the window. "Look up."

"You fucking crazy man," Willie said. "Who you yelling at, boy? Why you always standing at da window?" Willie was reading a thin paperback called *Charly*, and he rolled over on his bunk. Every time they came with the little cart, the big black man took another book.

He turned and looked at the man, his face frozen, his eyes glazed, the excitement gone. "'Cause I'm leaving this shithole. That's my woman out there. Comes to see me every day, man."

Willie put his size-thirteen black shoes on the linoleum floor, leaned forward, arms on his thighs. "Dat ain't your woman. I've seen what you lookin at, boy. She call da cops on you even open you mouth ta her. Don' you hyeah me when I speak?"

"You're nuthin' but a fuck-ass killer, man. Your black ass'll be in the joint and I'll be out fucking. They gonna let me out. They never gonna let you out."

The big man stood and took heavy steps toward the window, toward his cell mate, backing him into the corner. Then he turned and unzipped his pants, urinating in the open commode. "You be back, boy, ev'n dey let you out. Don' make me come crost dis floor." Then he turned and looked at him, his eyes large white beacons.

Just then the doors to all the cells in the quad opened with an electronic whine and metallic clang. Willie stepped out into the common room. The Latino remained in the corner, afraid to move. He heard dinner trays rattling on the stainless steel tables, smelled the food, but he didn't go out. Crawling onto his top bunk, he turned his face to the wall and thought of her. This was her fault. The more he thought about her, the more anger filled him, the less afraid he was of Willie. This morning he'd watched her and remembered something, another time and place that he'd seen her. For a second he thought that she might be a judge, someone who had sentenced him in the past. There were a lot of lady judges now. They were the worst, absolutely the worst. All the inmates felt the same. Having a woman judge punish you was like having your fucking mother punish you. And they all hated men. Everyone knew that. No woman would want to dress up in a long black robe and be around criminals all day who was normal. Women were basically whores. They let their tits hang out and wore their dresses so any man could see between their legs, and then they screamed when men looked at them and wanted to fuck them like the whole thing was one big surprise. Woman were stupid, cock-teasing whores.

Latin men knew how to train their women. They didn't let a lousy woman push them around, tell them what to do. Latin men were the bosses. They did what they damn well pleased and if the lady didn't like it, they'd just find a new lady.

He couldn't get her face out of his mind.

She could be an attorney, he thought. Maybe one of the court-appointed lawyers he'd had in the past. But he'd never had a woman lawyer. He'd never let a woman fuck up his case and land his ass in prison. Then he remembered who she was.

She was a district attorney.

It wasn't his case, but he'd been in the courtroom at the time, waiting for his case to come up. He'd been fascinated by her freckles and her legs. She had long legs, good legs—legs he could imagine pinned beneath him. They'd be shaved and slick as glass. They'd slide against his skin.

He leaped from the bunk and headed for the glass window, wanting to see her car again, wanting to remember her. Sometimes she came to her car at lunchtime. She hated Hispanics. In the courtroom the day he had seen her, the defendant had been Hispanic, a rival gang member, someone he knew from the streets of Oxnard. She had called the man an animal, told the court that gangs were like a black plague taking over the city. What did she know about anything? In his neighborhood the cops didn't protect a person. Gangs were the only way to survive. She probably lived in some fancy house, in some fancy neighborhood. She probably pulled her little red car into her own garage, never having to come out and find the windows smashed in and the radio gone. Once they had even stolen the seats from his car. He'd come out to go to work one morning and his car had been sitting there at the curb like an empty tin can, everything of value completely gone, the car gutted and stripped. What did she know?

He was going to fuck her and make her beg. He was going to teach her about fear. Then she'd know.

After he fucked her, he'd find the brother on the street that she had prosecuted, and he'd walk right up to him and tell him, "I fucked her, man. I fucked the redheaded whore who sent you to jail that time." He laughed. "You owe me, man," he'd say. "I fucked her for you, man."

She would beg him, plead with him. His chest swelled in anticipation. Willie was nothing to be afraid of, he decided, confident again. He went outside and got his dinner, banging the tray against the metal table.

"What is this fucking shit, man?" he said to the man sitting next to him.

"Dog shit. See, they keep a big black dog—like a Doberman or something—downstairs in the kitchen just to shit us dinner. Saves the taxpayers a lot of bread."

"Yeah," he said, pushing the food around on his plate. He could almost smell the dog shit. The other inmate had long, stringy hair past his shoulders and tattoos covering almost every inch of his exposed flesh. He looked like a biker. On one muscular bicep he sported a Harley-Davidson tattoo. The Latino sniffed and realized it was the man he was smelling and not the food. He picked up his fork and started shoving the substance on his plate into his mouth. "You stink, man. Smells like that dog been shitting on you."

The man stood and tried to topple the table, grabbing it under the lip with two tattooed hands. He looked like a fool. It was bolted to the floor. Instead he tossed his metal dinner plate in the air like a Frisbee and threw his head back laughing. Then he growled and suddenly reached down and grabbed the other man's shirt near the collar. With one hand he lifted him off the bench and held him several feet off the ground.

"Put me the fuck down, you stinking piece of dog shit," he yelled, his stomach rolling over and over in fear and humiliation, his bowels rumbling, ready to explode. The other men were laughing and crowding around, obscuring the commotion from the television monitors.

"Look what we got here," the biker said, holding his shirt now with both hands, moving him from side to side, causing his legs to swing in the air. "Looks like we got us an Oxnard cockroach. What we need is a little sombrero. This fucker's so small, we could use one of those little hats they put in them drinks and put it right on his greasy little beaner head."

They were all laughing now, hooting and hollering, slapping their sides. A small older man with neatly trimmed hair reached out suddenly and squeezed his balls, a sly expression on his face. He tried to kick the man's face but missed and kicked out at air. Sweat was popping out of his pores, soaking his shirt, dripping onto the tile floor. Just then a shrill tone went off, the man instantly released him, and he fell. He started to get up, pushing himself off the floor with his hands, when a black shoe came from the sea of legs and rushed toward his chest, connecting and knocking him on his back, taking his breath away.

The loudspeaker blasted: "All inmates return to their cells. I repeat, all inmates return to their cells at once."

Suddenly he was alone in the middle of the floor, on his back, dazed. He saw Willie walking toward him. The big black man bent over and offered his hand. "Get the fuck away from me, man," he said, his voice weak and cracking. The guard was standing outside the quad, staring at him through the bars.

"You hurt?" the guard asked.

He didn't answer. This was all her fault. He got up and headed to his cell. His chest throbbed where the man had kicked him, and the disgusting man who had grabbed his balls was smirking at him, winking at him from his cell. The biker walked up behind the small man and draped an arm over his thin shoulders. Together they smiled at him. The biker's teeth were yellow and cracked. The little man was the biker's woman. Willie had told him that the two men had known each other for years from San Quentin and had set up housekeeping on the outside when they were released, living like man and wife. The little man had robbed a bank to get back inside after the big man had violated his parole. How they got in the same cell, he didn't know. They must have paid someone, one of the jailers. Because he couldn't pay, he'd ended up in a cell with a black instead of a homeboy. He didn't steal—most of the time—it wasn't his style. Stealing was dishonest. He hated thieves. They were the real scum—the lowest of the low. Anyone could steal.

The biker probably stunk because he had AIDS, he

thought. People with AIDS always smelled. It was because they were always shitting and sometimes there was no toilet paper in the cells. In here, everyone knew everything, even when you took a crap.

He held his head up and threw his shoulders back, spitting as he walked by their cell. "I'm gonna fucking slice you, man," he said under his breath. "One day I'm gonna slice you both like ripe tomatoes. I'm gonna carve your assholes out and feed them to my cat, man."

The two men laughed. Soon all the men in the quad were laughing and banging their cups against the bars. They were laughing at him. He was an object of ridicule now. The harassment would be relentless. Unless he killed someone and risked going to the slammer for life, he'd have to endure it until he was released.

And he would be released. It was just a matter of time.

She'd been the reason he'd been late to dinner, he thought, tasting the bitterness on his tongue like he'd been eating with a rusty fork. If he hadn't been late, this would've never happened, he would have never mouthed off to the biker. The other inmates didn't know him. They didn't know what he was capable of, what he'd done, what he could do.

But she would know. Soon, he thought, walking into his cell. She'd know soon enough. He stood there, his body rigid with rage, staring out over the common room, seeing nothing, waiting for the electronic doors to clang shut. He'd teach her humiliation. He'd teach her to cry. In his mind he saw tears as red as blood running down her cheeks, washing over the freckles, staining her face a bright pink. The image he saw reminded him of a statue of the Virgin Mary—one of those miracles they talked about all the time where tears mysteriously fell from the statue and people came from all over the world, thinking they would be cured from some disease. He chuckled, his shoulders moving up and down. A miracle. She'd pray for a fucking miracle, he thought, feeling better now. When he finished with her, people could come and look at her and take pictures of her. Maybe they'd put her picture on the front page of the newspaper. Then people would know him, fear him, give him the respect he deserved. Then they'd all know what he could do.

After lockdown, in the dark, he heard Willie talking from the bunk below. "I seen your back, boy. When you takes off'n your shirt, I sees it. You been whupped. An' you cries. In da night, you cries."

He pressed his hands over his ears. Lies . . . it was nothing but lies. It wasn't him crying, it was them.

"Don' you be 'fraid now. I ain't gonna hurt ya, you hyeah me? Sees, I was grown in Alabama an' my daddy was whupped. I ain't nev'r gonna hurt a man been whupped. Dat man been hurt enuf."

He tasted his own salty, silent tears, his fingers closing on the crucifix around his neck, his mind erasing the words Willie had just spoken. He closed his eyes and dreamed he was swimming in a sea of frothy violet blood. It burned his eyes. He tried to reach the surface and then found that the blood had changed into millions of long tentacles. Around his neck, thick strands strangled him, choking him until his eyes popped out of his head and immediately disappeared in the mass of tentacles. Around his legs and feet he felt the rope-like cords cut into his flesh.

He was drowning in a living, swirling mass of red hair.

CHAPTER 6 ·

Lily's heels sank into the soft dirt as she walked to a position behind the plate at the community center playing field and laced her fingers into the wire fence. Shana was pitching and she made eye contact as her right arm moved back for the pitch. The other parents in the bleachers wore down-filled jackets and sipped steaming coffee from styrofoam cups. Lily wrapped her arms around herself in an attempt to stay warm.

Her daughter was charismatic. That was the only way to describe the type of popularity that she had been blessed with since the first grade. A ball of energy, beauty, and quick wit, she had been the most adorable little girl Lily had ever seen. And she had been Lily's life. Up until the last few years, no matter what was going on in her career, Lily saw her entire universe spinning around Shana. Her daughter had been the one who convinced Lily that there was goodness in the world, real goodness. She had taught Lily how to smile, laugh, cry tears of joy. And she was slipping away, growing up, changing into a woman. She didn't need Lily anymore. She had her father to meet her every need. Whereas Lily had always been

John's baby, his little girl in many ways, Shana was now all he cared about.

The problems with Shana were more than just the Oedipal phase of puberty. John was turning her own daughter against her for reasons Lily just couldn't understand. Was it because she had told him she wanted to become a judge? John had always dreamed of her entering private practice, where she would "make a ton of money" and he could retire and spend his time managing their investments. A position on the bench might be prestigious, but the salary was only a notch above what she presently earned. John didn't understand. He told Lily she was a fool, insisting that she wanted the judgeship for the power alone, simply to feed her ego.

Shana had been only a few months old when Lily decided to enter law school. It was a major decision. Lily was working as an admitting clerk at a local hospital and John at a personnel agency. His salary varied from month to month, and the only way they could afford to get by was for Lily to continue working. John encouraged her to go, talking constantly about all the money she would make and how they'd never have to pinch pennies again. "You go to law school," he had said, "and I'll open my own personnel agency. We'll have it made." Lily worked the graveyard shift and attended classes during the day. She left her daughter with the sitter only during the hours she was in class. The remainder of the day and evening, Lily carried her around with her, constantly chattering to the baby just as if she were an adult.

To this day, Lily could remember the exact second Shana had started to talk. It wasn't so remarkable, she only said "da da" like all babies say. Then she started chattering away like a magpie; all the words Lily had said to her seemed to pop back out like magic. The more the child talked, the more Lily talked to her. She knew all kinds of legal words. People would ask her what her name was and she would smile and say, "plaintiff." Thinking she had said "plain tough," they would roar with laughter. Shana would clap and giggle and say it again.

Lily never once spanked the child. She read every book she could get her hands on relating to parenting and used them all. "We don't bite children," she would say to her, "but we can bite an apple."

Although Lily slept only a few hours a day, napping when Shana napped and nodding off at work in the early morning hours, she was happy. She had no time to worry about her relationship with her husband. Her grueling schedule left little time for him. He didn't appear to notice. She accepted a position with the district attorney's office about the time Shana went to school. Every morning Lily would make her lunch and walk her to school before work. Her classmates loved her. She knew how to share, loved to make children and adults laugh, and was a regular Pippi Longstockings with her carrot-colored hair and freckles.

In a way, those first words, "plain tough," also applied to little Shana. She feared nothing. Lily wanted it that way, wanted her to be able to protect herself against anyone and anything. Just as she taught Shana how to share and be kind to others, she tried to teach her to be strong, brave, and mature. "When I'm not here," she would tell her, "or your daddy's not here, if anything bad ever happens, then you must pretend you are a grown-up and do exactly what a grown-up would do and believe you can do it, because you can." Shana would always blink her eyes and smile when Lily made her speech. She looked for occasions when she could prove herself to her mother, knowing it would make Lily smile with approval. With Lily's encouragement she climbed trees, played ball, would stomp on a spider rather than scream, and once punched a neighbor's dog in the nose when it growled at her. Then she ran all the way to the house and leaped into Lily's arms, bursting with pride. To John and Lily, she was the golden child, the magic child.

As the years went by and the magic persisted, Shana learned to see it and use it for the power it afforded her. Seeking to bask in her light, her fans would do her homework, give her money, let her wear their new clothes before even they had worn them. Shana had started to change a few years before. John's influence grew stronger. Shana began snapping at her parents at home and developed quite a temper. Lily refused to tolerate it, but John undermined her and allowed Shana to order him around like a child. The fissure between them as parents widened.

Lily tried to talk to her, to use the old psychology tricks, but nothing worked. Finally she had sat down with her and discussed her behavior at home.

"You just don't understand," Shana told her. "All day long I have to smile and be nice to everyone. Sometimes when I get home I can't control it any longer."

She had to defend her turf as the most popular girl in school. Other girls would get envious and make up stories about her. Like a politician constantly seeking reelection, she would have to seal her position, take polls, make certain her constituents would vote for her. On one occasion a girl punched her in the face after school. Shana punched her back and got expelled. Lily told her to give it up, but she couldn't. It was a hard thing to give up, this being on top. Like Lily, Shana was tenacious and driven to control the world around her.

Just the past month Shana had come home in a particularly nasty mood and Lily had broached the subject again. "Most people have a few good friends in their life that they enjoy. Why do you have to persist in having ten or fifteen? Why is it so important that everyone like you?"

"You don't understand," Shana said. "It's not like that at all. They need me."

Lily shook her head, incredulous. "That's absurd. They don't need you. What are you saying?"

Then she had thought about it. "Are you saying that someone has to be a leader? That if that person isn't you, it will be someone else?"

"Yeah, that's it," Shana said. "See, Mom, I don't smoke or listen to death rock or go all the way with boys. I get good grades—pretty good, anyway—and I give people advice, listen to their problems. Girls get into fights with other girls and I get them to make up."

So that's the story, Lily had thought. Sounded like her reasons for being a district attorney and wanting to be a judge. Since she had defeated the demons of her childhood, she had held the reins in her own two hands and had taught her daughter to do the same.

The short brunette at bat swung and connected; the parents in the stands screamed as she raced the short distance to first base. The next batter hit the ball as well, but was tagged at first base. The game was over and Shana's team had won.

The girls moved to the dugout, the majority getting as close to Shana as possible. Post-game activity had changed since the year before. Instead of going for the cookies and sodas the team provided, a number of girls were taking out brushes and lipsticks from their purses.

John infiltrated the group of girls, putting both hands around Shana's waist and lifting her into the air. "I'm so proud of you," he said. They both saw Lily a few feet away and smiled. They weren't smiling at her. Lily knew they were flaunting their closeness, showing her that this was their private moment, one they didn't care to share. Placing Shana back on the ground, John stared straight at Lily and draped his arm over Shana's shoulders, walking with her the short distance to the dugout, pulling her close, glancing back again to see if Lily was still watching, the other girls crowding around John now as well as Shana. Lily winced, locking her fingers on the wire fence. They both looked away.

A few minutes later, John headed in her direction, stooping to pick up a few bats on the way. The baseball cap made thick crevices appear in his forehead. At forty-seven, he was eleven years older than his wife. Even though his hair was thinning to the point where more scalp showed than hair, he was still an attractive man, with a robust laugh and a bright smile, displaying rows of even white teeth in his tan and masculine face. His expression was not pleasant, though, nor was it the adoring look reserved for his daughter.

"Made it, huh?" he said flatly, tipping his baseball cap back on his head. "Pried yourself away to catch the last five minutes of the game. You sure you're not missing something at the office? I mean, you don't want your family to get in the way of your big ambitions to be judge, now, do you?"

"Stop it," she said, looking around to see if anyone was in earshot. "I'll take Shana home in my car." She turned and plodded through the dirt in the direction of the dugout.

Shana's face was flushed with excitement. She stood almost a head above most of the other girls. Her long red hair had more gold tones in it than Lily's, and she wore it in a ponytail pulled through the back of her baseball cap. Her wide-set eyes were such a deep shade of sapphire that they almost matched the navy blue lettering on her uniform. High, pronounced cheekbones gave her face an ethereal, elegant quality far beyond her years. With the right makeup, clothes, and photographer, the right push-up bra, Lily thought, Shana's face could be on the cover of next month's *Cosmopolitan* magazine.

One girl followed as she broke away and headed for the car. "Call me in thirty minutes," Shana said. Once they were home, the phone in her room would ring for the next hour, each girl calling at a preselected time.

"Oh, this is my mom. Mom, this is Sally."

Sally stood there with her mouth gaping. "You look so much alike. I can't believe it."

Shana got into the car and slammed the door, her eyes cutting to her mother with resentment. Lily felt her heart sink. Shana had always been so proud that they looked alike. She used to tell Lily how all her friends thought her mother was so pretty. Lily remembered how she'd gaze up at her and ask her if she'd be that tall when she grew up. The past week, Shana had screamed at her that she was a giraffe, the tallest girl in school, and ended the tirade by saying it was Lily's fault.

She tried to start a conversation. "That was a great job of

pitching out there. Sorry I didn't get to see more of the game. I rushed, but the traffic . . ." Shana stared straight ahead, refusing to answer. Lily swallowed. It was going to be one of those days. "How was school?"

"Fine."

"Do you have much homework?"

"Done."

"Want to go roller skating with me Sunday?"

"I practice softball everyday and have gym class. I don't need the outside activities."

"How about the mall? Do you want to go to the mall?"

"I thought I was grounded." She shot Lily another look full of animosity. "Can Charlotte and Sally go?"

"No, I want to spend time with you alone. I don't want to spend time with Charlotte and Sally. Besides, where is my top you loaned Charlotte without my permission?"

"Don't worry, you'll get your precious top back. I just forgot. Will you *chill out, Mom?*" With this last statement her voice went high and shrill. Then something came to mind and she turned to her mother with a sweet smile and a sugar-coated voice. "I need a new outfit. There's a dance in the gym next week and we're all going."

Here we go, Lily thought, feeling the burning in her chest again. In desperation she had found herself recently doing something she despised. She'd started buying her things in the past year or so just to get that one little smile. As a parent, she felt she was on a seesaw. One minute she tried to uphold her long-standing rules and restrictions. The next minute everything fell away, and she broke all her own rules. To compete with John she had to play a new game, his game. His game was to give Shana anything she wanted. "I just bought you all those things two weeks ago, Shana. Can't you wear one of those to the dance?"

"*Mom* . . . I've already worn them to school. I don't want to wear them to the dance."

"We'll see," she said, stalling, pacifying.

Shana stared out the passenger window.

"So, what else is going on? Any gossip?"

"I started my period today."

Lily was excited and it showed. Shana rolled her eyes around in disbelief at her excitement. This was something strictly feminine, something they could share. Now, Lily thought, they could go home and lock themselves in the bedroom and talk about this, the way they'd used to talk about everything. "I knew you'd start any day now. Didn't I tell you that I started at your age? That's why you've been so snappy and emotional. I was, too. It's normal. You're a real woman now. Do you have cramps? How do you feel? We'll stop at the drugstore. What are you wearing now?" Lily knew she was rattling on and on, but she didn't care. This could be a new beginning for them.

"Dad already got me some pads today."

Lily's knuckles turned white on the steering wheel. She took her foot off the gas, and the car came to an abrupt standstill in the suburban traffic. Cars honked and then passed. She turned to face her daughter. "You could have called me at work and told me. Why didn't you? Why are you shutting me out of your life?" She had to hear the words; like a masochist, she sought the pain.

"Dad said you were too busy and not to bother you."

The words "Dad already got me some pads today" were ringing in her ears; now they were joined by "Dad said you were too busy." In the act of not sharing that one historically female moment, the rite of passage, and the fact that she could go to her father without embarrassment, her daughter had destroyed her. They drove home in silence.

John arrived home shortly after Lily and Shana. Located in what once had been the farming community of Camarillo, twenty minutes from Ventura, the house was a spacious twenty-year-old ranch with paned windows. John went and made a bowl of ice cream for himself and Shana, and carried her dish to her in her room; she was on the phone with the door shut. He walked in, handed the bowl to her, and started to walk out. Shana reached up without looking and tugged lightly on his shirt, still talking to the girl on the phone, until he leaned down near her face. She kissed him on the mouth and immediately returned to the conversation. He smiled and left, returning to the family room to eat his ice cream in front of the television. Lily was standing in the hall. She stepped back for John to pass, glaring at him. Then she went to take a shower. They did this after every game, and John had never once asked Lily if she wanted a bowl of ice cream.

She stood in the bathroom fully clothed and stared in the mirror. She was an unwanted intruder—an outcast in her own home. Without her salary they couldn't even afford this house. Without all the late nights and the hard work and the stress that had put years on her face. John just wanted to punch a time clock, collect his check, coach softball, watch television, and wait for the day he won the lottery. When they did talk, which was rare, John wanted to talk about spaceships and aliens and life after death, issues that delineated the world he lived in from the stark reality of Lily's world.

She walked into the den and looked at him on the sofa. "Can we turn the television off? I want to talk."

He jumped up. "I just remembered. Shana has the cramps, poor baby, and I told her I would bring her some Tylenol." He headed to the kitchen cabinet.

Lily grabbed the two pills out of his hand and snapped, "I'll take her the Tylenol. Afterward, I'll meet you in the backyard. I want to talk." In the backyard, Shana would be unable to hear. At least on one issue they agreed: not arguing in front of their daughter.

She opened Shana's door. She was still on the phone, sitting on the floor in the corner, so much junk on her bed that there was nowhere else to sit. "Please get off the phone now and go to bed. You'll never get up in the morning."

The phone was left on its side as Shana strode over to her mother. "I'll get off in just a minute."

"I brought you a few Tylenol for the cramps."

"Did you bring me any water?"

"The bathroom is just two feet away, Shana. Look. See, it's still there."

"*Dad, bring me a glass of water on your way,*" she yelled.

"On my way, darling," he answered and was there in a second, entering the room as Lily backed out.

Lily stood with her back against the hall wall and listened to the two of them talk, discussing the game—John praising and bragging on her pitching. She could tell that Shana was standing on tiptoes and hugging him around the neck as she did every night, kissing him tenderly on the cheek. He walked out the door and saw his wife standing there, her hands crossed over her chest. He waited for her to pass and followed her into the backyard.

John took a seat in the lounger; Lily sat in a nylon chair across from him. It was dark and the only light was from the neighboring house. The only noise was their television heard through an open window. The amber end of his cigarette reminded her of the fireflies she used to chase as a child, sometimes capturing one in a jar.

"Where did you go last night?" he said.

"I had a late meeting. I told Shana to tell you, but I guess you never woke up." Lily was thankful for the darkness, so he couldn't see her face. She had always been a poor liar. He had once told her that whenever she lied, her nostrils flared.

"I saw you," he said, his voice a mixture of anger and sadness.

Lily rubbed her arms in the damp night air, his words playing in her mind. She laughed nervously. What was he talking about? Surely, he didn't mean what she thought he meant. "Oh, really," she said, "and what exactly did you see?"

He was silent. Then he repeated himself. "I saw you."

"Look, John, don't play games with me. What are you talking about?"

"I want you to move out." He stood and the voice now was all bitterness, all conviction, the voice of a man who was no longer playing a game. "Did you hear me? I want you out of this house by tomorrow."

He was standing over Lily, and she looked up in the dark. Her eyes followed the glowing end of his cigarette, the dark outline of his arm in motion as he flicked it toward the dirt side of the yard. She waited for it to explode like a firecracker, counting the seconds, holding her breath. She thought of spontaneous combustion, her body erupting in flames, burning from the inside out.

His arm was flying toward her, a night bird, a bat, the sound of his shirt wings flapping, the slap across her face the dreaded collision. "Move in with your boyfriend—the guy you were making out with last night in the parking lot."

Lily caught his arm in an iron grip. In front of her she saw an enormous stack of white dishes crashing to the ground and the pieces flying in the air. "You want me to move out?" she screamed. "You disgusting piece of shit. You think I want to spend the rest of my life with you, working my ass off while you lounge around in front of the television and turn my own daughter against me?"

He yanked his arm away. "I never turned Shana against you. You're just too busy with your cases and your career to pay attention to your own child." He was spitting the words out between clenched teeth, his chest heaving.

"What do you suggest? That I quit my job? That we go on welfare or something so we can both be here every minute in case Shana needs a glass of water? You've spoiled her rotten. She was a beautiful child and now she's a disrespectful, demanding brat." She stopped, regretting her last statement. "Now you're probably going to run in there and tell her what I said. Don't you realize that you hurt her, too, when you do this, repeat things I say to you in private? Go ahead. Tell her. I don't give a shit anymore."

She stepped back into the nylon chair and almost tripped. With one hand she seized the chair and threw it onto the dirt side of the yard. "Look at the yard, John. You don't even see that one side is dirt. It doesn't bother you at all. You only see what you want to see."

"You're a slut, a whore. You let that man use you like a whore."

Her voice lowered to a controlled level. "Like a receptacle, John? Is that what you want to say? That I let him use me like a receptacle?" He didn't answer. "Maybe if you were a man and treated me like a woman, a wife, then I wouldn't have needed another man." She stepped closer, inches from his face. "You know, John, people have sex, married people, and for more reasons than just making babies." Her voice rose again and she screamed at him. "They have it because it feels good and because it's normal."

He was shaking, moving back away from her, retreating. "You're sick, Lily. You're not fit to be a mother." He turned and started walking toward the back door.

"I want a husband, John. I don't want a wife."

He slammed the door and left her there in the yard. The neighbor's dog was barking and howling at the commotion. Lily picked up a stick off the ground and tossed it over the fence, hearing the little dog squeal and run.

Her breath was coming slower now. The tempest was over. She felt a lightness in her body, a floating sensation. She was finally going to be free. The only problem was Shana.

Walking down the hall, she saw the light under her daughter's door—it was only ten o'clock. When she cracked the door, Shana was cramming papers from the bed back into a spiral notebook. "Can I come in for a few minutes?"

It took the younger woman only a moment to see the expression on her mother's face and she said, "Sure. Have you and Dad been fighting? I thought I heard yelling out there."

"Yes." Lily turned her head, hoping Shana wouldn't see the red handprint on her face. "Can we turn out the light and get in bed the way we used to when you were little?"

"Yeah, sure." Shana flicked off the light and climbed onto the side nearest the wall. "What's going on?"

"Your dad and I are going to get a divorce," Lily said, sniffing in the darkness and feeling the wet tears run down her face. She had felt so good in the yard; it was what she wanted, but now she was terrified. "Things have been bad for a long time. You knew that."

"Will we be poor now? Sally's parents got divorced and she says they're poor."

"I guarantee you won't be poor, Shana, even if I have to work an extra job. I love you; I'll always provide for you, and I'll always be there for you."

Shana sat up in the bed in the dark, her voice thin and cracking. "Where will we live if you and Dad get divorced? We won't be a family anymore."

Lily sat up, too, and reached for her, but the girl pulled away. "We'll always be a family, Shana. I'll always be your mother and Dad will always be your dad. We both love you very much."

"I can't believe this is happening to me. I can't believe you're doing this to me." She started crying. "Today. You're doing this today."

The fact that she had started her period for the first time that day surfaced in Lily's mind. She fell back onto the small bed. Shana would remember this day the rest of her life. "Please, Shana. Try to understand. I know it's hard. I just can't live with your father anymore. I wanted to wait until you were out of high school, but—"

She cut her off. "Then why don't you?"

"Because I can't take it anymore. Because I'm too old to wait that long. If we do it now, we both have a chance to find something else in our life."

Shana leaned back next to Lily, still sniffing. "You mean another man? Find another man?"

"Possibly. Or your dad might find another woman who will make him happy."

Shana was silent, thinking. Lily continued, "One of us has to move out. Too many bad things were said tonight. Dad wants me to move out. I have a right to stay here, Shana, and things might be different if it was just the two of us. You know, sometimes when I go to my room or stay late at the office, it's because I don't want to be around Dad. I mean, you stay in your room all the time and he sleeps on the couch. Try to see my side just once."

"I want to stay here with Dad."

Lily felt her heart sink. She'd known it would be this way. She got up and turned on the light, sat on the bed, looked into Shana's eyes. With her hand she brushed a tear off her cheek. "Why? What is it I've done? What haven't I done? Tell me."

Shana reached for a tissue off the nightstand, blowing her nose. "Dad loves me more than you do."

Resentment rose in Lily's throat. She snapped, "That isn't true. No matter what you think, that simply isn't true. You know what it is? It's because he gives in to you more, waits on you more, never demands anything from you. Isn't it?"

Shana's blue eyes roamed around the room before returning to her mother. "Maybe."

What could Lily say? The child had answered honestly. She stood and was leaving the room when Shana spoke up. "You can sleep with me, Mom. Turn out the light."

Back in the bed, Shana moved close and put her head on Lily's shoulder. "I do love you. I just want to live with Dad. You know?"

"I know," Lily said. "I know."

CHAPTER 7 ▪

Clinton had called from Division 42 and told Lily that he wanted to speak with her before she left for the day; she had agreed to wait but was anxious. John was dropping Shana off at the house she had rented in thirty minutes, and Lily had been working toward this evening all week. They had been separated for eight days, and today was the first time Shana would see the house.

She had the entire evening planned. After she cooked Shana's favorite meal, fried chicken and mashed potatoes, they would curl up together on the sofa and watch television. All the furniture had been purchased at a local antique shop, and although most of the pieces were actually inexpensive reproductions, the outcome was charming and warm. The greatest portion of the money and effort had been applied to Shana's room, and Lily had rearranged the furniture three times until it was perfect. It contained a high four-poster bed with a canopy, an antique wardrobe, a pedestal nightstand, and the bed sported a brand-new quilted pink and lavender floral-print comforter with matching curtains that Lily had hung herself.

She had framed a lot of small snapshots of her and Shana and even her father, and placed them in tiny silver and jeweled frames on the nightstand and dresser. The drawers were full of new casual clothes, underwear, nightgowns, and multicolored socks so that Shana would not have to pack a suitcase every time she spent the night with Lily.

The house had been a godsend. It had belonged to an elderly woman who had passed away, and the family wanted to rent it to someone reliable until the estate was probated. It was in an older, quiet neighborhood a few blocks from the office, and the deceased owner had been an ardent gardener. Almost every square inch of yard was planted in rose bushes and blooming flowers.

Clinton came blasting into the office, out of breath, his hair standing on end. He slammed his briefcase on the top of her desk. "Just so we don't have a problem with this, I wanted to tell you face to face. I asked for dismissal on the Hernandez matter. They're probably releasing him right now."

Lily was relieved. She was sure Clinton had asked to see her about a new development in the Stacy Jenkins case. He had interviewed the child a few days before and had gone bonkers. Learning that she was in foster care, he wanted to take her home to live with his family. Lily had put a stop to that immediately and gave him a long lecture about becoming overly involved.

"Hey, earth calling Lily," he said, seeing that her mind was far away. "You know, the prostitute case—the one you were so hot about. I thought you were going to ream me out for dismissing."

"So, the victim didn't show again, huh? What was this, the third time you had continued?"

"Exactly. I would have kept the damn thing rolling, but no one even knows where she is, and without a victim . . ." He paused, waiting for a reaction.

"It's fine, Clinton. At least you tried. I had a feeling it would end up like this. Give me the file and I'll add a few notes regarding the dismissal just in case he surfaces in the system again." She was already standing and took the file from his outstretched hands and loaded it into her briefcase, containing six or seven cases she planned to work on after Shana went to bed. She hurried to the door.

"See you tomorrow, boss. Hey, what did you do to your arm? That's a pretty nasty bruise there. You mud wrestling on the side or something?"

She was beginning to like Clinton. "Oh, that," she said, smiling, lifting her arm to inspect the bruise. "I was moving furniture in my daughter's bedroom."

Clinton headed off in the opposite direction, and Lily made her way to the elevators. She decided to cross the floor on the side near Richard's office, hoping to catch a glimpse of him. He had called almost every day, and on each occasion she had found an excuse to cut the conversation short. How could she tell him that her own daughter had elected to live with her father? Everyone knew that the children stayed with the mother unless there was a serious problem. If Shana had been a boy, the situation would have been easier to explain. But now that she was settled and Shana was right this minute on the way to her house, she felt she could finally see him.

He was on the phone, in the midst of a heated conversation. Seeing Lily, he waved her in and then put the call on the speaker and walked over, kicking the door shut. "I don't care if the guy is Jesus Christ, Madison," he shouted. "He's going to do jail time. Three times and you're out, baby. That's the way we play the game in this county." Looking Lily in the eye, he reached over and hit the off button.

"How's it going?" she asked, standing in front of his desk.

"Misdemeanors. Do you have any idea how many cases we process in this unit? Sit," he said, "I don't bite."

"I can't," Lily said softly. "I only have a minute."

"You haven't had a minute all week. I'm beginning to think this whole thing between us never happened." He leaned back in his chair and then flopped forward. His eyes softened.

"Come home with me tonight. I can't get you out of my mind."

Lily's eyes darted to the window and then back. "I can't. My husband and I split up. I've just been so overwhelmed by the whole thing. Between this and the new job, I . . ."

"I guess I'm supposed to say I'm sorry that your marriage is over, but I'm not. When can I see you?"

Her body felt hot and flushed. She wiped sweaty hands on her skirt. "Soon. I've thought about you too. Believe me . . ."

Before she knew it, he was around the desk and pulling on her hand. There was a certain spot in the offices that was blocked from view, the small space between the desk and the credenza. Once she was there, he embraced her, pressing his lips against her neck. "Stop," she said. "I really have to go. My daughter is waiting. Please . . ."

He released her and leaned back against the credenza as she left. At the door she turned and looked at him. "I'll call. Maybe tomorrow."

The front door had an overhang, and she didn't see Shana waiting there until she was halfway up the little path to the door. The smell of roses drifted through the crisp evening air. Lily smiled and rushed to her, wrapping her arms around her. "How long have you been waiting?"

"A long time. I was afraid you weren't coming."

"I'm sorry, honey. I had to wait for one of my attorneys, and then I had to stop off at the store. Hey, I have a surprise for you. I hope you like it."

Once inside, she took the girl by the hand, dropping both Shana's overnight bag and her own briefcase by the front door and leading her down the hall. "This is your room now. What do you think?"

Shana tossed her long red hair and strolled confidently into the room. She was wearing a matching pants outfit that Lily had bought her only a few weeks before, pink, the top trimmed in lace. She was tall and lean, a gorgeous young woman growing

in beauty with each day. Surveying the room with her back to
Lily, she ran her hand over the top of the comforter and picked
up one of the small framed pictures, the one of the two of
them together last year at Christmas. She turned and smiled,
a broad, spontaneous smile, not phony or forced.

"I love it, Mom. It's great."

Lily felt a wave of pleasure surge through her body; light
was shining in through the lovely curtains, and she felt the
darkness of the past eight days disappearing. "Look in the
dresser drawers."

"Oh, Mom . . . wow . . . these are great." She was really
excited now as she pulled all the new clothes out of the drawers
and placed them all on the bed so she could examine them.
"This is adorable. I love it. Oh, look at these . . ." She held
up a pair of bikini panties that Lily had purchased at the lingerie
store in the mall. All the price tags were still dangling from
the items; knowing her daughter valued things by their costs,
she had left them on. Lily somehow wanted to make up to the
child for the pain she had suffered, would suffer during the
divorce. She also wanted her to see this house as her home
and associate it with pleasant things. Then, she hoped, Shana
would spend more time with her. The clothes and room were
a start. A small start, for sure, but a start. Her instincts were
confirmed as she watched Shana read the numbers on the tags
with a look of contentment. With clothes all over the bed and
spilling onto the floor, the room now looked like her daughter's
old room, but a prettier, fresher, more feminine version.
Shana's furniture at home was older and scratched, the surfaces
marked with water stains and nail polish she had spilled.

Shana leaped off the bed with joy and hugged her mother.
Lily buried her face in her hair and smelled the fresh scent of
herbal essence shampoo. "Thanks, Mom. I love it all: the
room, the clothes, the pictures . . ." She pulled away and
stopped, surveying the room again. "I do need a stereo,
though."

"Open the door to the wardrobe," Lily said, having anticipated this need as well. "Now, I have to start frying that chicken. I'm starving."

Lily didn't want to take time to change clothes, so she merely tossed her jacket onto her bed as she headed for the kitchen. "Dinner in forty-five minutes."

Soon the oil was crackling hot in the skillet; Lily was rolling chicken in flour and seasoning, having donned one of the new print aprons she had purchased. The table was set, the sliding glass door brought a breeze in through the garden, and in the background the stereo was pounding out rock music. All was right with the world. She placed the chicken in the hot oil and began peeling the potatoes.

"What'd you think?" Shana said, modeling one of the new outfits, twirling around on the white tile floor, her long copper hair swirling around her.

"It fits perfect and you look at least fourteen in it."

"Is my butt too big? Does it make me look fat?"

Lily started laughing, wiping her hands on the apron and leaning back against the counter. Shana was mimicking one of her own frequent statements. "You look reed-thin and fabulous. Hey, don't start on that fat thing. You'll never get fat anyway, it not in your genes."

"What jeans? Did you buy me a pair of jeans too?"

"No, silly. What I'm talking about is genetics; you'll probably study it in biology next year. It relates to inheriting things from your parents. Like, I've never really had a weight problem, nor has anyone else in the family. You'll be just fine."

Shana moved close to her mother and looked up at her face earnestly. "Will I be as smart as you someday, then?"

Lily saw the admiration in her eyes. This was her daughter of old. She felt relaxed and happy, basking in her eyes. "Of course you'll be as smart as me. In fact, you'll be much smarter. You already are right now."

"I'm not as smart as you think, Mom. Sometimes I don't feel smart at all. I struggle so hard with my school work, and most of my friends don't try at all and get straight A's. You were always smart. That's what Dad told me. He said you even made him feel stupid."

"Well, maybe it's your popularity that interferes with your work. If you lived with me, I would limit your phone calls, make you discipline yourself and develop better study skills."

"Discipline myself? That's stupid," she snapped. "Like I'm really not disciplined. What does that mean? What do you think I am anyway, a juvenile delinquent?" Then she looked down at her tennis shoes. When she looked back up, a pronounced sadness was reflected in her vibrant blue eyes. "Dad needs me. I can't leave him. Why did you leave him?"

"Maybe I need you too, Shana. Have you ever thought of that?" Lily went to the stove and turned the heat down. She regretted that last statement. The child was stuck in between. They couldn't keep pulling on her. "Okay," she spoke up quickly, "you have a right to know what happened. I just don't know if I can explain it to you. Dad and I are very different in the way we look at life, in the things we want from life. I worked very hard to get through law school, to make something of myself, and I work very hard today, every day. I'm pretty good at what I do, Shana. And not only that, it's an important job." Lily stopped and wiped her hands on the apron.

"And Dad doesn't have an important job. Is that it?"

"Not exactly. I don't care if he has an important job, but he certainly should have a full-time job. And he should appreciate my efforts." She turned and looked at Shana. "And he was wrong in trying to cause friction between us . . . using the time he had with you, forcing me to be the bad guy all the time, the one who had to punish you, telling you I said negative things about you."

"Dad says you changed."

Lily sighed deeply, leaning back against the kitchen counter. "Maybe I did. Maybe I did." She smiled. "Enough of that for tonight. Go change and we'll eat."

After dinner, the dishes piled in the sink, they sat side by side on the sofa, looking through Lily's old photo albums, most from the days when she was a photographic model earning her way through college.

"You're so pretty here," Shana said, holding one of the photos up to her face and examining it. "Everyone thinks we look alike. Why can't I model?"

"You can someday, but right now you're too young. You know how I feel about you being around a lot of strange men. And besides, you need to concentrate on your school work, decide what you want to be. Modeling is just something you do for extra money." Lily stared out over the room, lost in the past. It was during these days that she had first met John, when she had been so young and afraid. Her grandfather's sexual abuse had been a secret wound, something so dark and filthy that she had never told a soul.

Finally, Shana tired of sitting and stood and stretched her lanky frame. While they had been chatting, she had been playing with her hair, braiding it. With no fastener it fell loose, and with a burst of energy she began jumping around and flinging her arms in the air. She was at that age when the child and the woman coexisted in the same body. One moment she was all little girl, unaware of her actions or her body, and the next she was all woman, with pouty little poses and gestures copied from movie stars, like the hair tossing and the way she shook her slender hips from side to side as she walked.

"I wanna call Dad now," she said. Lily's mouth fell open with disappointment. Then she turned and flashed that golden smile, lighting up the room. "The room is nice, Mom. I mean, it's not like being at home, but it's nice. Can I have a television?"

"No," Lily yelled back, but she smiled. "You're a case, Shana. A genuine case."

CHAPTER **8** ∎

He was out.
In his property he had twenty dollars, and he went to Stop
'n' Go across from the jail and bought a six-pack of beer and
two hot dogs for seventy-nine cents. When he got in line to
pay, he saw her.

Even from the back he knew it was her. He had watched
her enough from the window. Up close, she looked different
—even from what he remembered from that earlier day in
court. That day she'd looked sterner, taller. She was a good-
looking chick, but she was older than he thought. There was
one stocky old man standing in line between them. He stepped
aside in order to see her better. Luck is a lady, he thought,
smiling to himself and dropping his head as she paid for a
bottle of Wesson oil and actually brushed up against him on
the way out. He caught a whiff of her smell: clean . . . sweet.
He couldn't believe it. First they had released him and now
he had found her only a few minutes after walking out of the
jail. This was a sign, he thought, a fucking sign if he'd ever
seen one—right up there in league with the statue of the Ma-

donna crying. They should put him on the front page of the newspaper instead of that Nightstalker asshole. He was a fucking winner today.

He watched her go through the glass doors, headed right to that same little red car he'd watched from the windows of the jail. "Shit," he said out loud, just as the man in front of him was paying for a pack of smokes. He slammed his beer and dogs down on the counter and ripped out his twenty, his eyes darting back and forth to the parking lot. Change in hand, he turned, thinking she would be gone by now. But no, he chuckled, she was digging in that dumb-shit purse for her keys, just as she had in the parking lot. Stupid bitch, he thought. Stupid hot-shot D.A. whore.

Once she was inside the car, he bolted through the doors, jumped in his car, and followed her. Did she look in her rearview mirror? Not once. Fucking women. Sometimes he thought they deserved everything they got just because they were so fucking stupid. And this lady thought she was smart, putting people in prisons, locking them away like animals in the zoo. He could outsmart her with both hands tied behind his back.

He stayed several car lengths behind her as she drove through the rush-hour traffic. He'd have never thought his luck would be this good. She was fucking pulling into a driveway and parking her car, getting out and walking to the front door. Once she got near the doorway, he couldn't see her. Should steal her car too, he thought—probably left the keys right in the ignition. Might have a husband in there. Might have a fucking gun or something. Might be just the lady.

Parked a block from her house, he ate the rubbery hot dogs and slugged down two or three cans of the beer. Loaf—they served this thing they called loaf all the time in the jail. Tried to call the shit meat loaf, but everyone knew there was no meat in it. Willie had told him that they served it because they couldn't hurt each other with it. Sure couldn't kill someone with a fucking loaf, but a chicken bone, that might work.

As soon as he thought of Willie, the scene at the jail with

the biker and his little playmate returned to his mind. The biker's cocksucker lady had touched his balls. He rolled down the window and spat. It made him want to puke. And the tattooed motherfucker had called him an Oxnard cockroach. This bitch had caused that, he thought, staring at the front of the house. Never would have happened except for her. He felt the anger rise inside of him. Willie had said other things. Willie had seen his back. "Fuck . . . fuck . . . fuck," he screamed. He grabbed the empty beer cans and started throwing them at the windshield of the car. One popped back and hit him in the face. His stomach was twisting. Snakes—it felt like snakes in there—a pit of snakes crawling in circles in his stomach.

Switches—that was what she used to beat him with—big, skinny sticks torn from the tree out back. First it was the closet, the dark, stinking closet. He sat in there for hours and cried and cried, beating the door until his hands were bloody and raw. But when she opened the door, it was worse because she had the switches. Over the commode . . . she made him bend over the fucking open, reeking john with his shirt off. And she whipped him and whipped him, screaming that she wouldn't stop until he quit crying. But she was a liar. Even when he quit crying, she never stopped. She didn't stop until blood dripped from his back onto the filthy, cracked linoleum. Then she made him mop it up, scrub and scrub until it was all gone.

He could still smell the awful stuff she put on her hair. The stuff to make it red—whore's red. It smelled so awful that his eyes would burn. He had loved her long black hair that hung all the way to her hips—before the switches and the beatings. He used to brush it and braid it for her, feel it sliding through his fingers like silk. He'd stand behind her on a stool and gather it gently in his hands like a horse's tail. Then he'd close his knees on it and hold it there while he picked up each strand to braid.

After she made her hair red, she started staying out all night and sleeping all day. She stopped making them food. Sometimes she'd walk in the door with a sack and they thought it was food, but it wasn't. It was a bottle of booze. She'd throw a few dollar bills on the table and leave every night. He'd walk alone to the store and try to buy enough for them all to eat, but he never had enough money. He had to steal.

He turned on the car radio. Like dessert, he'd saved the best for last—the best was under the seat, waiting. His hand reached under there but couldn't find it. Starting to panic, he reached farther and then he felt it: the hunting knife. Just the feel of the cold metal made his dick get hard, and he rubbed it back and forth with his hand, thinking what he was going to do to the fucking whore in the house. Adrenaline surged through his body and he laughed. He could wait until dark— he was used to waiting.

He'd wait until he thought it was safe, and then he would get out and walk her house, try to figure who was inside. Then he'd come back and sleep awhile until it was right. He always knew when it was right. Tonight it was going to be right.

CHAPTER 9 ∎

She glanced at the bedside clock. It was almost eleven o'clock. Lily started to retrieve her briefcase from the living room to go over a few cases, but she couldn't muster up the energy and instead removed her clothing and climbed under the covers, thinking that tonight sleep might come. Almost euphoric knowing her daughter was asleep in the new four-poster bed across the hall and the evening had gone so well, she turned off the light. It then dawned on her that she had not checked the doors in the little house, a chore John had always handled.

With her terrycloth robe wrapped loosely around her, she padded barefoot in the dark, deciding to check the kitchen door first. It was a quiet neighborhood: no cars, no barking dogs, just blissful stillness.

Entering the kitchen, she saw the drapes billowing in the slight breeze, being sucked through the open sliding glass door. She chastised herself for not locking it but felt the area was so safe, it probably wasn't even necessary. As she pushed the drapes aside and started pulling the door in the track, a funny feeling came over her, a sense of something amiss. Holding her breath in order to hear better, she heard a squeak, like the sound a basketball player's sneakers make on the court.

It all happened at once: the noise behind her, her heart beating so fast it hurt, her robe pushed up from the floor over her face and head with lightning speed. As she struggled to scream and free herself, her feet slid out from under her but she did not fall. She was being carried in a suffocating embrace. What must be an arm was placed directly over her mouth. Trying to sink her teeth into the arm, she bit a mouthful of terrycloth instead. She was nude from the waist down and felt the cold night air against her lower body. Her bladder emptied, splashing against the tile floor.

She tried to move her arms, but they were trapped across her chest inside the robe. Kicking out furiously, her foot connected with what must be a kitchen chair, and it screeched across the floor, landing with a loud thud against the wall.

The backs of her calves and her feet were burning, and she knew she was being dragged down the hall—toward where her daughter slept. Shana, she thought. Oh God, no, Shana. The only sound she emitted was a muffled, inhuman groan of sheer agony coming from her stomach through her vocal cords to her nasal passages. Her mouth would not move. Her feet struck something. The wall? No longer kicking—no longer struggling, she was praying: ". . . as I walk through the Valley of Death . . ." She couldn't remember the words. Flashes of the past were meshed with the present. Not Shana, not her child—she had to protect her child.

"Mom." She heard her voice, first questioning and childlike and then the terror of her sickening high-pitched scream reverberated in Lily's head. She heard something heavy crash into the wall, body against body, the sound heard on a football field when the players collided. He had her. He had her daughter. He had them both.

In another moment they were on the bed in Lily's bedroom. When he removed his arm, the robe fell away and she could see him in the light from the bathroom. Shana was next to her and he was over them both. Light reflected off the steel of the knife he held only inches from Lily's throat. His other hand was on Shana's neck. Lily grabbed his arm, and with the abnormal strength of terror she almost succeeded in twisting his arm backward, turning the knife toward him, seeing in her mind the blade entering his body where his heart beat. But he was too strong and with eyes wild with excitement, darting back and forth, his tongue protruding from his mouth, he forced the blade sideways into her open mouth, the sharp edges nicking the tender edges of her lips. She bit down on the blade with her teeth, her tongue touching something crusty and vile. His face was only inches away, his breath rancid with beer. "Taste it," he said, a look of pleasure on his face. "It's her blood. Lick it with your tongue. Lick a whore's blood, a cheating fucking whore's blood."

Removing the knife from Lily's mouth and placing it back at her throat, he moved his hand from Shana's neck and shoved her gown up, exposing her budding breasts and her new bikini panties. Shana desperately tried to push the gown down to cover herself, turning pleading eyes to Lily. "No," she cried. "Stop him, Mommy. Please make him stop." He thrust his fingers around her neck. She choked and gurgling sounds came from her throat, a trickle of saliva ran from the corner of her mouth. Her eyes were glazed.

"Be calm, Shana. Don't fight. Do what he says. Everything is going to be okay. Please, baby, listen to me." Lily's voice was forced control. "Let her go. I'll give you the best fuck you ever had. I'll do anything."

"That's it, Momma. You tell her. Tell her how fucking good it is. Tell her you want it." His guttural words were uttered through clenched teeth. He had one knee between Shana's legs, forcing them open, and the other knee between Lily's, touching her genitals. "Unzip me," he ordered Shana.

Shana's terrified eyes again made contact with her mother's. "Do it, Shana," she said, watching while her child's thin, trembling arm reached for his crotch, unable to grasp the small end of the zipper. He raised his body up somewhat, but the crusty knife remained near Lily's throat.

"Do it for her, Momma," he said, shifting the knife to his other hand and positioning the point on Shana's navel. "Teach her how to take care of a man."

Lily had to distract him, somehow get him away from Shana. She had to find a way to get the knife. Quickly unzipping him and removing his penis, she placed it in her mouth, the ragged edges of the zipper scraping her face. She smelled urine and putrid body odor, but he was becoming erect and moaning, throwing his head back, moving the knife away from Shana's body. He grabbed a handful of her hair and jerked her head back. He fell on top of Lily, looking straight into her eyes and relishing the fear he saw reflected there. Something struck her chest, then her chin. It was a gold cross with a crucified Christ dangling from his neck.

Suddenly he thrust himself up. "No, I want her, Momma. I don't wanna whore, a fucking old redheaded whore." Once again he expertly tossed the knife from one hand to the other and placed it again at Lily's throat. "Watch, Momma, watch or I'll gut her."

With one vicious yank Shana's underpants were torn off and tossed aside. Her body bounced up on the bed and then fell under the weight of him. He forced himself inside her and Shana screamed in pain. Lily had never felt so powerless in her life, except once before, all those years past. There was no God. She knew it now. No reason to pray. She wished that he would just cut her throat and end it all.

"Oh, Mommy. Oh, Mommy," Shana gasped.

Lily found her hand beside her and squeezed it tightly. It was cold and clammy. "Hold on, baby. Close your eyes and make believe you are far away. Hold on."

A loud siren wailed in the street somewhere. He jumped and sprang from the bed. "The neighbors heard and called the police," Lily said, hearing the sound growing nearer and nearer. "They're going to shoot you, kill you." He was directly under the light emanating from the bathroom, his red sweatshirt and face completely outlined and visible as he frantically tried to snap his jeans. Lily sat up in the bed and screamed, in raw panic and fury, "If they don't shoot you, I'll kill you myself." The siren was blaring now, only a few blocks away. In seconds he was gone.

She held her daughter tightly in her arms, stroking her hair, softly whispering in her ear. "It's over, baby, he's gone. No one is going to hurt you ever again. It's over." The shrill of the siren was becoming distant, fading from earshot. No one had called the police. Their agony had gone unnoticed.

Time stood still as she rocked her daughter in her arms and listened to her pitiful, wracking sobs. A million things were racing through her mind. Two or three times she tried to wrench herself away and call the police. Shana was holding on so tightly, though, that she stopped. He was long gone anyway by now, lost in the night. Every sordid detail replayed itself in her mind. A hard ball of rage was forming in her stomach and spilling bile into her mouth.

"Shana, darling, I'm going to get up now, but I'll be right here. I'm going to get a washcloth for you from the bathroom, and then I'm going to call the police and your father." Lily inched away and pulled her robe back over her shoulders, tying the sash loosely around her waist. The rage was somehow calming her, moving her around like a machine with a great churning engine.

"No," Shana said forcefully in a voice Lily had never heard. "You can't tell Dad what he did to me." She reached out and grabbed the edge of Lily's robe as she tried to get up, causing it to fall open and expose her nakedness. She retied it again. "You can't tell anyone."

The face and voice were a child's, but the eyes were a woman's. She would never be a child again, never see the world as a safe place without fear. Lily placed a hand to her mouth, biting her knuckle, stifling a scream that welled up inside her.

In those eyes she saw herself. Back in bed with Shana, she held her and rocked her, comforting the child she had been. "We must call the police. We must call Daddy."

"No," she screamed again. "I think I'm going to be sick."

Shana ran to the bathroom. She threw up on the tile floor before she got to the commode. Lily dropped to the floor with her and wiped her face with cold towels. She went to the medicine cabinet and found the bottle of Valium a doctor had recently prescribed for her insomnia. Her hands were shaking as she poured two pills out, one for her and one for Shana. "Take this," she said, handing her the pill with a paper Dixie cup of water. "It will relax you."

Shana swallowed the pill, watched with round eyes as her mother tossed one into her own mouth. She let Lily help her back to the bed. Once again she held her in her arms.

"We are going to call Daddy and we are going to go home. Leave this house. I won't call the police, but we are going to tell Daddy. We have no choice, Shana."

Lily knew exactly what she would be subjecting her daughter to if she reported the crime. The police would stay for hours, forcing them to relive the nightmare, making every detail of it live forever in their minds. Then the hospital and the medical–legal exam. They would probe Shana's ravaged body and comb her pubic hairs looking for evidence. They would swab their mouths. If they apprehended him, months and months of testimony and court appearances would consume their lives. Shana would have to sit on the witness stand and repeat the sordid details of this night in lurid detail to a roomful of strangers. She would have to rehearse her testimony with the prosecuting attorney like lines in a play. In that room, breathing the same air, he would also sit. Then the ordeal would become known. Even some kid at school might learn of what had happened and spread it around.

The most despicable thought of all, a truth that Lily alone was far too aware of, was the fact that after all they had suffered, would suffer, while the nightmares were still the sweating, waking, screaming kind, before they could even begin to resume normal life, he would be free again. The term for aggravated rape was only eight years, out in four. He would even receive credit for time served during and prior to the trial so that by the time he was on the bus to prison, his countdown to freedom might amount to only three years. No, she thought, he could receive a consecutive sentence for the oral copulation, amounting to a few more years. It was not enough. It could never be enough. And she felt certain he had committed other vicious crimes. She recalled the taste of dried, old blood on the knife. Possibly even murder. This crime was a murder: the annihilation of innocence.

She also had to consider her career, her life's work, and the reality that although she could prosecute rape cases, she could never try them without bias as a superior court judge. A door was closing in her face. Thought by thought, she was getting further away from reporting this to the authorities.

His face kept reappearing before her, and somewhere in the far reaches of her mind, she knew she had seen him before. Her memory of the attack crowded out the past, and she was no longer able to distinguish reality from imagination. But that face . . .

Shana had calmed somewhat; the drug was taking effect. Moving slowly away, Lily called John on the bedside phone. He was in a deep sleep when she awoke him, his answer a muffled and annoyed "Hello" as if he was expecting a wrong number.

"John, you have to come over here now." She spoke softly and rapidly. "Something has happened."

"My God, what time is it? Is Shana sick?"

"We're both okay. Just come now. Don't ask any questions until you get here. Shana is right beside me." Her voice started to crack. She didn't know how much longer she could maintain her composure. "Please come. We need you."

She hung up and looked at the clock—only one o'clock. A mere two hours to destroy their lives and take away the happiness they were finally finding in each other. Her thoughts turned to John and what this would do to him. Shana was his life, his shining star, his protected and sheltered baby girl. When Shana was born, he had shoved Lily away and centered all his affection on the child: holding her, stroking her, kissing her when he no longer kissed his wife. Starting to tremble, Lily hugged herself. She had to be strong.

It seemed like only minutes passed before John arrived. Time had been standing still, hanging over them like a dark storm cloud, refusing to move, the unleashed downpour contained and waiting. He appeared in the door to the bedroom. "What in the hell is going on here? The front door is wide open." His tone was accusing, demanding, and it was vented at Lily.

Shana's muscles had began to relax in Lily's arms, and her breathing was shallow, her body too still. "Daddy," she said, hearing his voice, crying out to him. "Oh, Daddy." He ran to her side of the bed and Lily released her. As John engulfed her in his large arms, she pressed her body to his chest, sobbing. "Oh, Daddy."

He looked at Lily, his dark eyes full of fury, but in their depths, fear was rising. "What happened?" he shouted. "Tell me what happened here tonight."

"Shana, Daddy and I are going to go in the other room and talk," Lily said gently. "You'll hear us talking and know we are there. We'll only be a few feet away." She got up and motioned for John to follow.

The Valium had calmed her somewhat and she told John what had happened. It was an emotionless recitation of facts. If she allowed one tear to fall, the floodgates would open. They were sitting on the newly purchased sofa with the amber light from a Tiffany lamp creating an almost surreal atmosphere. The photo albums were still open on the floor. He leaned up close and with his fingers touched the small cuts at the side of her mouth, but it was not a gesture of concern or affection. It was more like reflex, confirmation of the reality of what she was saying. His eyes clearly said that she was responsible, no matter what reason predicated. She should have found the strength to stop him. That's the way he saw her, Lily thought. A tower of strength, invincible.

Then he sobbed, his masculine body wracked with pain, that unfamiliar and pitiful sound that signified a grown man crying like a child. He did not scream or yell or threaten revenge. He was quite simply heartbroken. His sorrow left no room for rage.

"Well, do you want to call the police? You're her father and I can't make this decision without you," she said. "It's not irreversible. We can always file a report later if we change our minds." As she spoke, her eyes darted to the kitchen, wondering about evidence, fingerprints on the door.

"No, I agree with you. It would only make it worse for her," he finally replied. Tears were still streaming down his face, and he wiped them away with the back of his hand. "Would they catch the bastard if we reported it?"

"How the hell do I know, John? No one knows. We don't have a vehicle description." She cursed herself for not running after him, for staying with Shana. "Maybe we're doing the wrong thing, for chrissake, by not reporting it. God, I just don't know." Her mind was so muddled, full of barely suppressed rage. Memories of the past and years of untold secrets were tainting her reason. Something inside her was diving, sinking, twisting. She had to stop it. She had to rewind the tape. Erase it. John's voice sounded distant. She stared at him and tried to focus.

"I want to take Shana home, take her away from this place." His voice was a choked whimper. "I don't know or care about anything else. I just want to take care of my child."

"I know," she shouted, and then lowered her voice so that Shana would not hear, "and she's our child, not yours. Don't you think I want to take care of her? I don't want her to suffer. I couldn't stop this. I tried, but I can stop it now. I gave her a sedative. Let's just bundle her up and take her home. I'll pack a bag and follow you."

He stood and then stopped dead in his tracks, staring at her. A look of utter horror shot from his ravaged eyes. He had not combed his hair over his bald spot, and a long strand dangled over by his temple. He looked so old, so haggard. "Could she get pregnant? My baby, my little baby."

She started to reply but found herself disgusted by his weakness; it was this that had caused her to lose respect for him over the years. As she had forced herself to overcome the past, to confront the violence of the world they lived in, he had lived in a fantasy world that didn't exist. Why couldn't he make the decisions that had to be made for once in their life? She couldn't stop herself from thinking of Richard, wishing he was there instead of John. For the first time she had reached for happiness, touched the soft edge of pleasure. Pleasure, she thought. That man had found pleasure in her terror, in Shana's terror. He had found pleasure in their degradation. Just as her grandfather had found pleasure in the forbidden recesses of her young body.

"He didn't ejaculate. The sirens scared him away. We can take her to the doctor tomorrow, and they'll give her antibiotics for possible disease and check her. There's a slim chance she could get pregnant from pre-emission sperm. We'll just have to pray."

"Will she ever get over this, Lily? Will our little girl ever be the same?"

"With you and I beside her and all the love and help we can give her, I know she will. I pray to God she will." As she said the stock comforting words she had said to dozens of victims, their worthlessness struck home. Shana was strong, had been strong. Lily had tried to make her strong, refusing to baby her and shelter her as John had. And if they didn't drag it on and on with the authorities, perhaps it would some-day become like a bad dream. Like her own bad dreams, and she had made it. The only alternative was to become a hopeless cripple, and no child of hers would fall into this abyss. She would not allow it.

After they wrapped Shana in the new comforter off her bed, John led her to the door. She turned and looked at Lily, and their eye contact locked and lingered. Lily had wanted to be her friend and confidante, to guide her without her father's intervention. Instead they had witnessed hell together, forming a bond, but one forged in terror.

"You go home and go to sleep. Daddy will sleep on the floor next to you." She embraced her. "I'll be there in the morning when you wake up."

"Will he come back, Mom?"

"No, Shana, he'll never come back. I'll move out of this house tomorrow. We'll never come here again. Soon we'll both forget this night ever happened." She knew this was a lie.

CHAPTER 10.

Once they had gone, Lily hurriedly started throwing things in a small duffel bag. The house was dead quiet again, that ominous stillness like before, and she was shaking. The memory of the attacker's face in the last few minutes before he had left kept flashing in her mind, and each time she dropped what she was doing and stood there, frozen in thought, trying to put her finger on what it was that she associated with his face. Suddenly the face appeared, but not as she remembered it. It appeared in a mug shot photo.

She ran to the living room, tripping and falling on the edge of her robe, soggy and reeking from Shana's vomit. From her position on the floor, she saw her briefcase and crawled the rest of the way on her hands and knees. Her fingers trembled as she dialed the combination lock. On the third try it clicked open. She threw all the files on the floor and frantically searched for the one she knew contained the photo. Papers went flying across the carpet.

Suddenly it was in her hands and she was looking at his face. He was the same man who had attempted to rape the prostitute. Clinton's case that he had dismissed today. The man was even wearing the same red sweatshirt. He had been arrested and photographed in it. Photographed with that smug smile. They must have released him about the time she left the building, giving him back his original clothes with the rest of his property. Someone either picked him up or dropped off his car. He must have followed her from the complex.

There was no doubt in her mind as she studied the hated image in her hands. No doubt at all. It was him.

Her breath was coming fast now, catching and rattling in her throat. Whatever effects the Valium had were gone. Adrenaline was pumping through her veins. She rapidly sorted through the pages of the file to the police report. There it was: his address. His home was listed as 254 So. 3rd St., Oxnard. His name was Bobby Hernandez and although Hispanic, he had listed his place of birth as Fresno, California. Lily tore the sheet with his address from the file and placed it in the pocket of her robe. She went into the bedroom and threw on a pair of Levi's and a sweater, transferring the address to the jeans. She dug into the back of the closet until she found her fur-lined winter hiking boots. John had insisted that she remove every single item that belonged to her from the house when she moved, as though he wanted to erase her from his life, everything except the furniture. That he wanted to keep. In the same box was a blue knit ski cap. She placed it on her head and stuffed her hair inside it.

She headed for the garage. Back in the corner, behind three or four boxes was her father's shotgun, a twelve-gauge Browning semi-automatic, the one he had used to hunt deer, one of the curious items her mother had given her after his death. She had given Lily his cast-iron barbecue, one Cross pen, and his shotgun. Nothing more.

In the stillness of the garage, as her hands touched the barrel of the gun, Lily felt his presence beside her and heard his voice. "Good shot, Lily girl. Good as any boy could make," he would say with his booming, gruff voice on the Saturday afternoon he had taken her to shoot tin cans lined up on a tree stump. He had wanted a son. She no longer dreamed of frilly dresses and bows for her hair. By the time her grandfather had died, when she was thirteen, Lily had wanted exactly the same thing as her father.

Spotting the small box containing the green slugs, she again heard his voice, right there next to her, clear and distinct. "These are called rifled slugs, Lily girl." She loaded them into the chamber and crammed several more into the tight pocket of her jeans. "These will make a hole big enough to throw a cat through. You can bet on that. You shoot something with this baby and it's gonna stop." She did not falter for a moment, his voice guiding her, pushing her on. "Once you get your sights on them and decide to shoot, shoot. You can't wait or you'll miss." He had taken her on a deer-hunting trip, proud of his daughter, wanting his hunting buddies with sons to see what a good marksman she had become. "It's meat, honey," he said, speaking to her in the car on the drive down. "Venison." Later, in the woods, she had the shot, the gentle, beautiful animal in her sights, but she had hesitated, teeth clenched, hands sweating, unable to pull the trigger. He was disappointed. She had let him down. She vowed she would never miss again.

As she left the garage, shotgun muzzle down in her arms, her footsteps echoed even when she had left the concrete flooring and was walking on carpet. She felt heavy, rooted to the ground with resolve, walking in another dimension, no longer alone in her body. The phone rang like a shrill bell, invasive, unwelcome, but a signal, a signal to begin. It was John.

"Shana's asleep. I'm worried about you. Are you coming over?"

"I'll be there in a few hours. Don't worry. I can't sleep now anyway. I want to calm down and take a bath. He's not coming back here tonight. Just worry about Shana." Do what you do best, she thought without contempt, accepting her role, and I'll do what has to be done.

She started to lock the front door and leave and then thought of something, returning to the kitchen. Rummaging through the drawers, her fingers seized a black Magic Marker, the one she had used to label the moving crates. She shoved it into her other pocket and left.

The moon was out, the night clear. A streetlight reflected half moons of light on the manicured green yards. She had only briefly seen the neighbors on either side the day she moved into the house. They were both elderly couples and she had heard their televisions blasting early on in the evening. The sounds that had earlier pierced the night had fallen on deaf ears. The block looked quiet and peaceful, as if nothing had ever happened, yet the stillness was audible now, a sound of its own.

She crouched at the rear of her car and began marking the license plate. The plate read FP0322. With the marker she altered it to read EB0822. It was a small change, but it was the best she could do. She threw the shotgun in the backseat, thought of covering it, and then decided that it didn't matter. The rage was an unseen inferno, burning all around her, blinding her, engulfing her, pushing her on. She kept seeing him over Shana, the knife at her navel, his body heaving on top of her precious child.

She drove toward Oxnard. The streets were quiet. She rolled the window down and let the night air blow in her face. As she passed the farming area of Oxnard, the smell of fertilizer reminded her of his rancid odor. She tasted his vile penis in her mouth—she spat out the window. The edges of her mouth stung from the razor-sharp nicks of the knife. The thought of where that knife had been and the dried matter she'd tasted made her force the thought from her mind to keep from vomiting.

Slowly she drove down the dark streets, passing from one streetlight to another, one stop sign, another traffic signal changing from red to green to yellow and back again. In her mind they were like runway lights, illuminating her descent into Hell. Cars sped past her now and then. Couples coming home from parties, dates, bars; lovers crawling out of beds and returning to other beds. At one red light she looked into the car next to her and for a brief minute visually connected with the driver, a middle-aged woman with tired, defeated eyes in a lined face. Lily thought she might be a late-shift waitress from an establishment like Denny's, going home to a little apartment somewhere. Maybe she feared someone would be waiting to jump out and attack her. "Be careful," Lily told her as their cars moved into the intersection. "You could be next."

She was trying to formulate a plan. It didn't take her long to find the house. The street was a major thoroughfare in Oxnard and she simply followed the numbers. The area was called Colonia. She knew it well, for it was infested with drug dealing and crime. His house was one in a row of tiny stucco houses. Across the street was a vacant lot. The yard was over-grown with weeds, dry and cracking from lack of water. On the front porch was an old refrigerator with a big heavy-link chain and padlock. They had probably been cited by the police, she thought with contempt, before purchasing the lock. In the driveway was a dusty black older-model Plymouth and a par-tially primered brown Ford pickup. In the attempted rape and kidnap, he had driven a van and there was no van. The screen on the front door hung haphazardly on its hinges. One window was boarded up with no glass. The other was open yet covered by curtains. The house was dark.

Like a burglar she cased the area, noting that the nearest streetlight was a block away on the corner. She had driven here with intent, her loaded shotgun in the backseat, but with no definite plan. She knew she couldn't enter his house and shoot him. That would be suicide. And she had no way of knowing for certain that he was actually inside. There was only one way: wait for him to come out. It could be broad daylight and dozens of people might be milling about on the street. Some of these houses had five or six families living together. She looked at the cars parked up and down the streets she prowled. Evidently, Hondas were not a common mode of transportation in Colonia.

Turning back toward the field she had passed earlier, she steered the car onto a dirt road, pressing down on the accelerator and flooring it. The car had been washed only a few days before. It was now absorbing the dust she was churning up with her tires. She parked by the road, with crops planted as far as she could see on either side. Taking the shotgun from the backseat, she pointed into the fields and fired it. The blast shattered the stillness of the night, and the butt of the gun smashed into her shoulder. Her father had been dead for ten years. She wanted to be certain her weapon of death would perform. Quickly throwing it in the backseat, she spun out and headed back onto the main road, making her way under the freeway and traveling into the safer, well-lit streets of Ventura.

She passed the government center complex and pulled into the parking lot. Lights were still burning inside the belly of the jail, but the windows were dark. Her eyes darted to those windows and she was instantly filled with visions of him watching her, watching as she fumbled with her keys as she always did, never having them ready in her hand, always reckless of her own safety, thinking she was impervious, invincible, spending so much time among criminals and crime that she had felt like someone watching it all from above, protected and safe. She thought of how her little red car had stood alone so many nights in the parking lot. A force more powerful than rage seeped into her mind: guilt. By her actions she had caused this to happen to her daughter. It had started with the night she had slept with Richard, a married woman out fucking around while her child and husband were home.

But no, John had not been home. He had been lurking in the shadows, spying on her, waiting to catch her at something he had repeatedly and wrongfully accused her of dozens of times through the years. There had been terrible rows. She had hated him for his distrust and even threatened to go out and cheat on him purposely because he didn't believe her no matter what she did or said. From the onset of their marriage, in whispered words from the soul, he had shown her again and again his fear that he would someday lose her. He had also said that she did not love him, had never loved him, had only sought refuge in their marriage. She had heard the words so many times over the years that she finally believed him.

Maybe he was right. She had shunned the social scene in college, the aggressive, egotistical young men who had asked her out. She had selected only the shy, bookish types to date and ended the relationships before they had a chance to develop. Their meeting had been chance, in a drugstore with a small lunch counter. He lied, overinflating his job and income at a personnel agency, courting her with flowers and cards. But it was his reverence for women and his nurturing nature that made her feel safe, protected. "Men will just use you as a receptacle," he had told her. "They think women are just for sex." He said he wanted to make love to her when she was his wife, the future mother of his unborn children, the "way it's supposed to be." In time, Lily initiated the sex between them, found her body seeking it. The more she wanted, the less he wanted her. It began after Shana was born and gradually got more pronounced, particularly the last year or so. Finally she had stopped wanting.

She circled the parking lot and then left, her hands firmly planted on the steering wheel, her back rigid. The darkness was slowly changing into the overcast gray of a southern California morning. She could hear birds in the trees as she passed the parkway leading to Oxnard. Here and there, the world was awakening.

She had to go to the bathroom but refused to stop. She willed the urge to disappear and it did. As she pulled up to a stoplight and glanced in the rearview mirror, she caught sight of her image. Her face was ashen. Her eyes bloodshot. She looked old and tired in the blue knit cap, pulled low on her forehead. As she realized that the stench of him still clung to her body and had now grotesquely blended with her own developing body odor, a wave of nausea assaulted her. She bit down on the inside of her mouth, tasting her own blood.

Slowly guiding the Honda onto his street, she saw a dark green van parked at the curb, its rear doors open. Her eyes turned at once to the shotgun in the backseat while her pulse raced and her stomach churned. Eyes back to the street, she saw no movement. A muted radio played from an open window, the words probably Spanish. She strained to pinpoint the sound. Pulling to the curb five or six houses away, hands locked and sweating on the cool steering wheel, she let go long enough to wipe them back and forth on her denim-clad thighs before she reached for the shotgun and transferred it to the front seat, the muzzle pointed at the floorboard.

When a dog barked somewhere, she jumped and took her foot off the brake. The car was still in drive, engine running; it jerked forward.

After staring so hard at the front of his house that her vision had blurred, she saw a distinct flash of red. She floored the Honda and covered the distance between the houses in seconds. Slamming both feet on the brake, she threw the gear shift into park without thinking and grabbed the shotgun. The sound of the barrel as it struck the top of her car was earsplitting in the morning silence. He was exiting the house, halfway down the curb, headed toward the van. He saw her and stopped abruptly, planting both his feet firmly on the ground. On his face was a look of shock and confusion.

Inside that second, reason flickered behind the eyes she lowered to the sight, coursed inside the finger on the trigger, a pinpoint of light before blindness. Her body moved back inches, but the light was gone, the sight a framed portrait of red fabric pulsating with the beat of his heart. Her nostrils burned with Old Spice after-shave. Sandpaper fingers dug into her vagina. The man in front of her was no longer the man who had raped her daughter, he was the old puppeteer, her grandfather.

She fired.

The impact knocked him off his feet. His hands and legs flew in the air. The green slug ejected onto the street. The explosion reverberated inside her head. A gaping hole appeared in the center of the red sweatshirt, spewing forth blood. She was drowning in a frothy sea of red blood: Shana's blood, virginal blood, sacrificial blood. Her throat constricted, mucus dripped from her nose, and once again the alien, detached finger squeezed the trigger. The slug hit near his shoulder, severing his arm.

Her knees buckled beneath her. The shotgun fell butt first to the ground. The muzzle came to rest under the soft flesh of her chin, stopping her. Moving her head, she vomited chunks of chicken onto the black asphalt, seeing pieces of flesh boiling. She pulled herself into the open door to the car, her arms locked around the shotgun. Everything was moving, shaking, bleeding, screaming. She saw objects flying through the air, trapping her inside the core of horror.

Move, she ordered her body, still frozen. Move. She grabbed the steering wheel, releasing the shotgun. Don't look. Drive. Her foot responded and the car surged forward. The intersection was there in a second. Turn. Breathe. Turn. Drive. She had not killed a human being. Turn. Drive. Turn. The sun was shining, but she saw only a dark tunnel in front of her. She knew she was in Hell and there was no way out. "Please, God," she prayed. "In the name of the Father, the Son, and the Holy Ghost." She screamed, "Show me the way out."

Her body was like ice, but she was dripping with sweat. The sign read Alameda Street. The sun was blazing, the streets teeming with activity. Seeing the stop sign, she braked, waiting while three school children crossed. She had been driving aimlessly for at least an hour. The shotgun, now on the floorboard, had rolled to a resting place against her feet. She kicked it back and continued.

It was as if she could see herself from a position outside her body. Somehow she no longer felt connected. The houses were larger and the yards well tended. She was no longer in Colonia.

In her mind she could visualize the crime scene: the police cars with their lights flashing, the ambulance and paramedics, the crowd of onlookers being shoved back by the police. If he had survived, he would have been transported to the nearest hospital, and the emergency-room staff would be trying to stop the bleeding, assess the damage. It had been so long he might even be in surgery, a dedicated physician trying to save his life. What she willed herself to see was his disgusting, inhuman body beneath a coarse dark blanket, lifeless.

Finding a major cross street, she made her way to the freeway and headed home. To Shana, she thought, she had to get to Shana. "He'll never hurt you again, baby. He'll never hurt anyone again," she whispered. As the words left her mouth, the voice she heard was not her own. It was her mother's voice, saying the words she'd yearned to hear as a child, telling her that her grandfather's perverted abuse of her body was over. Those words had never been spoken. Only his death had freed her.

She plucked the knit ski cap from her head and tossed it out the open window as she entered the on-ramp to Camarillo. She felt remarkably calm and controlled, both full and empty, horrified but at peace. The rage had been released, allowed to take its own shape and propelled toward its target, locked inside the green slug. The evil had returned to the person who had unleashed it.

Instead of turning left, in the direction of her house, she turned right. Her destination was an old church whose property included a steep slope planted heavily with avocado trees. She saw it every day on her way to work. The parking lot was deserted. Mature trees blocked anyone from seeing it from nearby streets. Exiting the Honda with the shotgun, she wiped it with the tail of her shirt and held it in the fabric until she released it to tumble down the embankment. As her eyes tracked it, she said, "I killed a mad dog today, Dad. You would have been proud."

Turning onto her street, her eyes scanned the gauges on the dash. The little needle on the gasoline gauge was not even a fraction above, it was locked on "*E*." A second later she saw the police car parked in front of the house.

CHAPTER 11 ∎

With the car sputtering on gas fumes alone as Lily approached her driveway, she knew she had no option but to enter the house and confront the police. She hit the garage-door opener and pulled the Honda alongside John's white Jeep Cherokee. As she let her head fall against the steering wheel, the engine still running, the garage door closed, her thoughts turned to asphyxiation. As her mind struggled toward lucidity, a capsized boat trying to right itself, she reached for the strength of rage and her earlier conviction, and knew it was gone. She was naked and exposed, fully aware of what she had done, face to face with the horror. Perhaps there was just enough gas left, lingering lethally in the tank, and some slim chance that whoever was inside could not hear the engine running before she turned blue and it was all over.

She quickly turned the key off. Killing herself would only inflict more agony on Shana.

How had they found her? Linked her to the crime in only a few short hours? There was no possibility of tracking the plate through the Department of Motor Vehicles, for she had altered it. Even if he had lived and recognized her in her blue knit cap? Maybe he had seen the Honda? That's it. He had followed her, of course. He might not know her name, but he knew where she lived. Here again, it didn't play. The house was a rental and would take more than a few hours to track, and she truly doubted that he—in what had to have been a dying statement—remembered the street and number.

Her life was over. She would be imprisoned and disbarred. There was no defense for the crime she had committed. No matter what he had done to her and Shana, she had not shot him in self-defense; she had tracked him down and assassinated him. She thought of defenses: diminished capacity, temporary insanity. Did she know her actions were wrong at the time? Was she cognizant of their wrongfulness? The answer was a clear and distinct yes.

Reaching for the car door handle took all the strength and courage Lily had. She almost fell to the garage floor when the door swung open, for her fingers were locked on the handle.

John opened the door to the garage just as she reached the first of the four steps leading to the house. "Where in God's name have you been? I was panicked. I kept calling the house. Then I dozed off until about six. You still weren't here, so I called the police." He paused, rubbing one hand across his brow. "I guess you saw the police car."

When he continued, it was in a tentative, uncertain voice. "I told them everything. They're talking to Shana in the den now."

Lily's hand flew instinctively to her neck; the noose she had been hanging from had been cut, but only for the moment. "What did you tell them? You mean, about the rape? You decided we should report it?"

"Yeah. And they said we should have reported it last night. They might have caught him in the area, somewhere near your house. With you being a D.A. and everything, they found it hard to understand why you didn't report it." There was more confidence in his voice now, his actions having the support of the police officers. He turned and entered the house, through the door leading to the kitchen. The den opened off the same area.

Lily stepped inside and took in the scene. There were two uniformed officers: a female sitting on the beige leather sofa next to Shana, the male standing back near the kitchen bar. Although she knew a lot of police officers, she had never seen these two. All eyes in the room turned toward her, yet she spoke as if she were carrying on a private conversation with John, her voice low.

"I'm sorry I worried you," she said, looking down at the floor and then back again to his face. "I was so upset. I got on the freeway to come home right after we talked and then realized I was halfway to L.A. I got off on some side street and got lost. By the time I found my way back to the freeway, I was stuck in rush-hour traffic."

Feeling the eyes on her, Lily threw her arms around John's neck in an awkward embrace, then stepped back. "I started to call, but I was afraid to get out of the car. It was a bad neighborhood. And I was afraid to wake you and Shana."

She acknowledged the officers' presence with a nod and hurried to Shana's side. She was pale, glassy-eyed, and dark circles were visible under her eyes. Only her head protruded from the blanket she was wrapped in. Choking noises rose from her throat as Lily put her arms around her and guided her head to her shoulder. Shana moved her body to get as close to her mother as possible, trying to wedge her head under Lily's arm as she had as a small child.

The female officer was blond, a bit stocky for her frame, but the uniform added bulk, and she wore her hair in a knot at the base of her neck. Her eyes were hazel and reflected concern and kindness, but her face was a practiced mask of authority. "I'm Officer Talkington, Mrs. Forrester, and this is Officer Travis."

The male had stepped back almost to the living room area and had his portable radio to his mouth, about to speak. He then apparently changed his mind and stepped back into the den. "Excuse me, but can I use your phone? We put out an attempt-to-locate on your vehicle and I need to cancel it." Trying to impress Lily with his professionalism, he added: "Any transmission regarding this incident is scrambled, so don't worry about your address or name or anything going out. That's why I have to use your phone. We can't scramble on the portable."

Her mind was racing, tracking at lightning speeds as she sat quietly and stroked Shana's hair. They would need access to the crime scene to collect evidence and take photos. Mentally starting at the front door, she recalled the file scattered there and felt the noose tighten again around her neck. Clinton knew she had taken the file, and whatever Oxnard detective assigned to investigate the murder might call Clinton, even ask for the file. She had to get it back, leave it as it had left Clinton's hands. That meant copying the torn page of the police report and replacing it. She had to eradicate anything that could link him to the crime, for that would leave her wide-open as a suspect. A suspect with motive and no alibi.

Prints. Before she could allow the police into the house, she must wash it down for prints. How long had he been in the house? What had he touched? Other than an eyewitness ID, fingerprints should be the only thread connecting her to his murder.

The female officer, Talkington, was speaking, but Lily had not been listening. A flash of green filled her mind with horror—the slug casing. The green slug ejected at the scene, placed in the chamber with her own hands. Surely, when the gun exploded, any prints would have been destroyed. But forensic science today . . . ?

". . . other than description, we were waiting to discuss the details of the actual crime when you were present, Mrs. Forrester," she spoke firmly, attempting to gain Lily's attention.

"I'm sorry," Lily said apologetically. "I didn't hear you. I . . . I haven't slept. John, can you get me a cup of coffee?"

She smelled the aroma of freshly brewed coffee and briefly wondered why John had not thought of offering her a cup.

"No, Mrs. Forrester, surely you are aware of the fact that you could destroy valuable evidence. Your husband gave us a sketchy outline of what occurred."

Lily responded, "I ate some chewing gum in the car, so there's no evidence in my mouth. I didn't think."

"Well, to repeat what I was saying, Shana here basically gave us a physical description of the assailant, and we, of course, have already put out a broadcast on that information. We'd like to get a full statement now. Then we'll take you and your daughter to Pleasant Valley Hospital for an exam."

"Certainly," Lily said.

Officer Travis stepped into the conversation. He was chewing gum and smacking it as he spoke. Tall and dark, he exuded arrogance and Lily found him offensive. He looked bored and eager to leave, probably fully intending to let his partner complete the mounds of paperwork while he had breakfast somewhere. "We need the keys to the house you were renting so we can order a crime-scene unit over there."

Lily sat up on the sofa, straightening her back, assuming a prosecutor's demeanor. "It makes more sense for me to be present. I could direct them to areas where I feel they may locate evidence. After my daughter and I complete the medical, I'll go to the house and call for a unit to meet me there." She turned with a degree of sarcasm in her voice. "You do agree with me, don't you, Officer Travis?"

"Sounds like a plan," he said, smacking loudly. Her attempts to deflate his enormous ego were like flies on the back of an elephant.

Travis was the type of police officer who didn't give a damn if Mother Teresa was raped. He would never make sergeant. He worked to kick ass legally. Looking at his black boots, Lily bet the toes were loaded with steel. Enough brutality cases had crossed her desk to spot those who teetered on the line, who without the badge would end up in jail.

"Officer Travis," she said now, "I would appreciate it if you left the room while my daughter and I give our statements."

He looked at her, not budging, as if to protest. This was probably the part he enjoyed. Then he turned and left, advising his partner that he'd wait in the cruiser.

Their statements took over an hour, as painful and embarrassing for Shana as she knew it was going to be. Talkington was good and Lily made a mental note to write a letter on her behalf to her commander. She took her time, didn't push Shana, and kept her voice soft and compassionate.

The officer stood, adjusting the heavy gun belt and nightstick. "So, that's all we'll need for now. Investigators will contact you for more details probably by tomorrow. If you think of anything else, here's my card."

"Thanks," Lily said and meant it.

"Are you ready now? We'll drive to the hospital."

"We'll drive ourselves," Lily answered.

"But, Mrs. Forrester, an officer has to be present during the exam for chain of evidence. This is all just procedure. Surely—"

"Right," Lily said impatiently, "but we don't have to ride over in a police car. We'll meet you there. My daughter has been through enough. I don't want the neighbors to know about this. We'll say that we were burglarized or something."

John had been busy in the kitchen the whole time, cleaning, embarrassed by the mess. It was as if he had been caught by unexpected company. He walked the officer to the door and closed it, returning to Lily.

"I'll go with you. Do you want to help Shana get dressed?"

She turned and said quietly to Shana, "Do you need me to help you get dressed?"

"No. I'll be fine. I want to take a bath, but the officer said I couldn't. How can she tell me not to take a bath?"

Lily wanted to cry. "Because there may be evidence on your body. You can't take a bath. We also need to take what you were wearing last night to the hospital. They'll want our clothes." Lily suddenly looked down at her feet, at the old hiking boots. "I couldn't find any tennis shoes last night, so I found these in an old box." She glared at John, wanting to draw his attention away from the boots, her appearance. "It was nice of you to insist that I took everything I owned. Thanks, John. Now I don't even have a change of clothes over here."

As soon as Shana shuffled down the hall, dragging the large blanket behind her, she turned to John. She wanted to slap him, scream at him in frustration, but the pitiful look on his face stopped her.

"You're angry at me, aren't you?" he said. "Because I called the police without asking after we said we weren't going to do it."

She sighed. "You did what you thought was right. What I'm sure is right. I'm not angry, John, I'm—I'm . . ." The lightheadedness she had felt caused her now to see flashing lights before her eyes. She was going to pass out. She started to fall; he grabbed her. "I'm okay," she said weakly, pulling away. "I was just dizzy for a moment. Why don't you take a shower while I make some phone calls? You look awful."

"Do you want me to make you something to eat? I can make you some toast or something. Maybe if you eat?"

She fixed him with ice-cold eyes, red-rimmed and void of makeup. "Take a shower, John. Let me do what I have to do."

Like a scolded puppy, he turned, shoulders slumped, walking off to the bedroom. The clock in the kitchen said nine forty-five as Lily snatched the phone and dialed the office. She started to ask for Butler's office, but instead asked the operator to ring Richard.

"Richard Fowler," he answered on the speaker phone.

"It's me, Lily Take me off the speaker."

When his voice no longer sounded like he was in a well, she spoke softly. "Tell Butler for me that I have an emergency and can't come in today. I'll call him later and be in tomorrow.

You'll need to review and assign some cases. They're on my desk, some on the credenza. Whatever can't wait."

"You got it. Are we on for tonight?"

"I can't talk now. I promise I'll explain everything later. Just cover me on this, please."

"Did you hear about Attenberg?"

Benjamin Attenberg was a superior court judge in his late sixties. He had once called Lily unconscionable in her interrogation of a witness, and they were not on the best of terms.

"Tell me about it tomorrow." She started to hang up.

He persisted. "He's dead—the old goat dropped dead yesterday of a heart attack. I got to the office real early this morning and ran into Butler. Then he called me into his office. In fact, I just got out. And Lily, Butler had just finished talking with the governor about an appointment to replace him."

Lily braced herself against the kitchen counter. She didn't reply.

"Are you listening?" His voice was low, secretive. "You are being considered, Lily. Believe it or not, Butler asked my opinion. They want to fill this slot with a woman, so it's between you and Carol Abrams. You may receive a call from the governor today even. If I were you, I would make it a point to come in no matter what's going on. Unless, of course, you're dying." He laughed.

"Or something . . ." she said out loud, not meaning to. Her mind was so jumbled now that she could no longer think. She blurted out the words. "Both my daughter and I were raped last night at knife point. We're on our way to the hospital now for the medical–legal."

"Jesus Christ. Why didn't you say something right away? Are either of you hurt? Where are you? I'll come—"

"Will they consider me now?" she said, her voice small and breaking as she spoke. Stretching the curly phone cord to the sink, she splashed water on her face.

"I'm so sorry about this, Lily. God, I am so sorry."

"Richard, will you answer me please? Will they still consider me for the appointment now that I'm a rape victim?"

"They'll consider you, of course, but you know as well as I do that it causes a problem. Hell, they might not rule you out. The presiding judge could shift all the sexual-related cases to other judges. There's no way you could sit unbiased on those matters." His voice dropped and softened. "It's you I'm concerned about, Lily. Can you talk? Tell me what happened?"

"You know I lost the appointment. Why don't you just say it? We have three or four attorneys sitting pro tem and two retired judges. They're not well versed enough with the complexities of the new laws regarding sex offenses to try them. What benefit can I be if I can't use my expertise to try these cases? They're flooding the calendar." She paused, sucking in air. "I lost it."

He was placating now. "Don't jump. Wait and see what happens. I think you should allow me to advise Butler, however, about your status. There'll be more phone calls involved and some conferring if they—"

"Go ahead and tell them about the rape," she said, defeated, "and tell them I'll decline if offered. No need to try to make it work. I don't want it that way." The blood. She could see the blood. The scene was surfacing; she had to stop it. "Let them appoint Abrams." Pert and perfect Carol, she thought. No blood on her white hands.

"When will I see you?" he said. "I'll come right now if you'll let me."

"No," she said. "You can't. I'm at the house with my husband. Just handle the cases. If you want to help me, do that. I'll call later."

Hanging up the phone, she tried to hold herself together. She rushed to the bedroom and was relieved to see the bathroom door still closed, the shower still running. The black Magic Marker was still on the license plate, and at close range, in broad daylight, it would be visible. Grabbing a bottle of nail-polish remover, she headed for the garage, picking up the roll of paper towels from the kitchen counter.

A minute later, Shana opened the door and was down all four steps to the garage level by the time Lily heard her. She was kneeling behind the Honda, and the towels were smeared with black Magic Marker. Shana approached her mother, sniffing, a puzzled look in her eyes.

"What are you doing?" she asked.

Lily's mind went blank. "Nothing. Are you ready? Is Dad ready?" She tossed the towels into the trash can in the corner of the garage.

"What's that smell? What are you doing?" Shana was antsy and persistent. She had on a pair of jeans and a pale blue blouse, and her eyes were darting around the garage as if she expected something to jump out at her.

"Let's go. Go get Dad. It won't take long, and then we'll come back and you can sleep. They'll give you something to help you rest." Lily followed her back into the house. She stopped in the kitchen and hugged Shana tightly.

"Do you want to talk about what happened last night? I mean, is there anything you want to ask me? How do you feel?"

"I dunno. I feel dirty and rotten and tired and scared. And I keep thinking he's going to come back here and find us and do it again."

Next door someone was mowing the lawn; the noise was invasive not because it was loud, but because it was normal and they were not normal. In school, kids were clanging locker doors and laughing. Right about now at the courthouse, they were having recess and attorneys were rushing to grab a donut and a cup of coffee.

"He's not coming back. Please believe me. I know about this type of person. He's afraid of being arrested. Right now he's probably a hundred miles from here. And, honey, he doesn't know where we live, not this house."

"In the movies, all the bad guys come back. Even when they think they've killed them, they get up." Shana placed her finger in her mouth and started biting on a nail. Her father walked in and started to embrace her, but she pulled away, her back stiff, her arms rigid at her side.

"I'll back the Jeep out of the garage," he said softly, visibly hurt by Shana's aloofness, unable to comprehend how she felt.

They drove in silence to the hospital. The female police officer was waiting in the lobby. She pulled Lily aside, explaining that unfortunately no female physician was on duty to perform the exam. She shrugged her shoulders and met Lily's eyes woman to woman, knowing, compassionate. "I'm sorry," she said, "but we can't wait any longer."

With the nurse present, Lily tried to prepare Shana for the exam, telling her more or less what had to be done. The child listened quietly, chin dropped, eyes up, staring without hearing, her body wracked by exhaustion. On the examining table, as the doctor attempted to perform the pelvic, she went wild with indignation, screaming and calling the doctor a "jerk nerd shit pighead" and kicking the top of his head. Her face turned bright red, a vein stood out in her neck, and she locked her jaw, transforming her soft face. Finally they gave her a shot and she calmed enough to complete the exam. To Lily, it was as if Shana was forced to endure another rape. Tears welled up in her eyes, and she had to leave the room. It wasn't difficult to understand why untold numbers of these crimes still weren't reported to the authorities.

They photographed them both. Shana had slight discolorations around her throat where his hands had been and other minor bruises on her buttocks. Drugged but awake, she had to roll over on the table, exposed, while Talkington photographed her. Lily leaned down by the table and placed her face next to her daughter's. With her fingers she wiped away the tears from under her eyes, and stroked her hair. "I love you," she said, her voice catching in her throat. "It's almost over."

Lily had nicks at the sides of her mouth, a grayish, darkening bruise on her right shoulder that only she knew was from the kick of the shotgun and not incurred during the rape. She had a substantial bruise on her wrists. She realized that if anything came to light, the photographs of her bruised shoulder would be used against her as evidence. There was nothing she could do. If they ever got that close to the truth, it would be over anyway. Just in case, she told them that she thought the injury happened when she was moving the furniture in Shana's room.

They treated the small cuts with antiseptic. They tested them both for sexually transmitted diseases and gave them both a shot of penicillin. On the issue of AIDS, they told Lily privately that they should be tested again in the future to be certain.

In the examining room, the doctor found a chain of blisters starting on one side of Lily's back and circling her upper torso. "How long have you had these?" he asked her. "Have you been having pains in your chest, around your ribs?"

Lily didn't know about the sores on her back, but the pains in her chest she had clearly felt. "I thought I was going to have a heart attack. Started a few weeks ago."

"You have herpes zoster. Shingles. It's very painful. I'm surprised you didn't visit your family physician before now." He removed the rubber gloves and tossed them in the trash can.

"I have herpes? How did I get herpes?" Lily asked, her voice high and shrill, her composure disintegrating.

He smiled. "You don't have genital herpes. First good news of the day, huh? This is a virus, usually caused from nerves, but it's in the same family."

"Great," Lily said. "Give me the medicine."

"I can give you some cream, but there's no cure. It will probably get worse before it gets better. You'll get even more blisters. But it will go away. It's not serious." He was young, younger than Lily. He touched her shoulder. "I'll give you some tranquilizers and, of course, something for your daughter. District attorney," he said. "Stressful job."

She didn't answer and he left. There were a lot more stressful things than being a D.A., like being raped . . . like killing someone. She sat on the table, her shoulders slumped, the hospital gown open in the back, her feet dangling off the edge like a small child's, her hair stringy and matted. She lifted an arm and sniffed her armpit. She felt filthy and disgusting, inhuman.

Then she got dressed. As she pulled on her jeans, she thought that any minute they would come in and tell her the blood work had shown she had cancer. Wasn't that what life was all about, a test of how much a person could endure? In the school of life, before this had happened, she had seen herself as passing. Maybe she wasn't in the top half of the class, maybe not the perfect mother. And others faced far worse adversity, achieved more, but she had persevered. She had used her average intelligence, with the force of hard work and drive; had endured through law school with a baby and husband. She had continued in an empty, unfulfilling marriage for the sake of her child, remaining faithful in the face of continued accusations. In her career, she was relentlessly dedicated and carried the full weight of her responsibilities. But she had failed to endure all. Turning her back on her beliefs, she had met violence with violence. Many of the men and women she had sent to prison had been abused and victimized. She was one of them now.

In the hall, she handed Talkington Shana's gown from the night before. "My robe's at the house," she said. "I'll give it to the crime-scene unit."

On the short ride home, Shana's lids were drooping and her head nodding, but she was still irate. "You didn't tell me they were gonna do that to me. Stick some metal thing inside of me with everyone watching, even that dog-face police officer. And they took pictures of me naked." She started screaming. "You made them do this. I hate you. I hate everyone. I hate the world."

John stared at the road and drove. He was speechless.

"It's okay to be angry, Shana," Lily said. "It might even

be good for you to be angry and let your feelings out. You can say anything you want to me."

She turned, leaning over the front seat, close to Shana in the back. "Here," she said, "pull my hair. Pull it as hard as you can. I can take it. Yank it. Go on, Shana."

Shana grabbed a handful of Lily's hair and jerked it hard, causing Lily's head to pull forward. She almost toppled over into the backseat. Lily didn't wince. Shana let go and fell back with a slap against the seat, fighting the drugs to stay awake. "Pretty funny, Mom," she said without smiling. "Did they do the same things to you?"

"Yes, just about, and I didn't like it any more than you did."

A slight smile barely moved the edges of Shana's pale mouth, but enough to be visible. "Want to pull my hair, Mom?" she said.

Lily responded, "No, thanks, little lady." She reached for her daughter's hand and smiled at her. "You might kick the hell out of me like you did that doctor."

Their hands laced together tightly and their eyes met. A ray of sunshine shot between their bodies. Lily saw the minute dust particles dancing and falling around their hands. She was still leaning over the seat awkwardly, and the motion of the car was pulling them apart, each one resisting, lingering. By moving her fingers, Shana rearranged their hands so they were palm to palm. She stretched her fingers until they were perfectly aligned with her mother's. She maintained the contact, pushing her palm slightly into Lily's, spreading her fingers and taking Lily's along. In this small gesture was a moment of beauty and utmost tenderness, that rare occasion when two human beings truly comprehend each other's pain and experience the purest form of emotion: compassion.

CHAPTER 12 .

Detective Sergeant Bruce Cunningham opened the door to his unmarked unit and tossed in a case file and his tape recorder. He caught a glimpse of his scuffed black shoes and gave thought to stopping by the barber shop for a shine. What he really needed was a new pair of shoes, but with three kids and a wife who no longer worked, a shine would have to do. Still attractive at forty-two, he was tall, tan, and masculine, but the suit that had once strained to contain his bulging biceps now hid an abundance of soft flesh. His bushy mustache was a darker shade of blond than his thick hair, and he had a bad habit of letting it grow until it almost covered his lip.

He glanced at his watch. It was almost five o'clock and he'd have to fight the rush-hour traffic all the way downtown to the morgue to look at today's stiff. The day shift had done a cursory workup at the scene and then dumped the entire case on his desk without so much as a word. This wasn't the way it worked in Omaha, where he'd been a cop for seventeen years before relocating to a position with the Oxnard P.D. five years ago. In Omaha, things were different. People were friendly and honest—basic hardworking midwestern folks. Cops were cops. They weren't thieves or killers or brutal, out-of-control animals. They were good guys. Nothing more, nothing less. Everyone in the department worked toward the same goals and assisted each other whenever they could. Here in Oxnard, he'd seen officers spend longer trying to kiss off a case to another officer than it would take to simply handle the fucking thing themselves. That was the kind of mentality he was surrounded by here in California. But it went much further than that. Being lazy and incompetent he could adjust to—he didn't like it, but he could accept it. What he'd seen in the past two months, though, was just more than he could stomach.

He stood there and stared out over the parking lot, flicking the stiff hairs of his mustache with one hand. Suddenly he slammed the car door shut and returned to the building. His anger built step by step as he made his way down the narrow hallway to the Internal Affairs Division. The two men sitting at their desks jumped and almost reached for their weapons when Cunningham came barreling through the door. "You incompetent motherfuckers," he yelled. "I gave you that case cold and you still botched it. These guys are as dirty as the Omaha stockyards."

Detective Stanley Haddock leaned back in his chair and laughed. Then the smile fell from his narrow face, and he flopped forward and fixed the big detective with a steely gaze. "Get out of our office, Cunningham. We have work to do."

"Work? You call how you handled that case work? Fucking disaster is what it was. Fucking national disaster. And the people of this city pay your salaries. If I were you guys, I wouldn't show my face in public after this fiasco."

The other detective came from behind his desk and took Cunningham's arm, physically pulling him out of the office into the hall as Cunningham kept glancing back at the other man over his shoulder. Whereas Haddock's face looked as though it had been carved out of stone, Rutherford's was as round as a beach ball. "Look," he said, his voice low and tense, "we did what we were told to do. Get the picture? These were veteran cops with years on the force. This came down from the top."

"Thieves and killers," Cunningham said, his face still flushed with anger, "not cops. Don't put me in the same category with them. It's bad enough I have to admit I work for the same department." He reached into his jacket for his cigarettes. After offering one to the other man, he stuck one in his mouth, but didn't light it, letting it dangle there as he spoke. "First, we got these animals in L.A. beating some guy to a bloody pulp on videotape for the whole world to see, and now we have our own guys blowing dope dealers away and pocketing the drug money."

"There's no proof. Your report was all speculation."

"Proof," he said, lighting his cigarette and inhaling the smoke, bracing himself against the wall. "The man had five bullet holes in him and the gun they say he pulled on them— well, forensics says the damn thing is so old, the firing pin fell out when they tried to test-fire it at the range. That gun was a plant and you know it."

The other man shook his head from side to side and dropped his eyes to the ground. "Let it go, Bruce."

"Look, Rutherford, this guy, this dealer, he owned three brand-spanking-new nine-millimeter Rugers. We have the sales receipts in the file. Why would a dealer carry an old rusted .38 to a twenty-grand crack buy when he owned an arsenal of the finest weapons? You answer that one, I'll let it go."

"The story's as classic as they get: Franks and Silver made the connection and the mark solicited the buy. He was supposed to show with the cash at the designated time and place. Instead he appeared with a gun and tried to take them out and steal the dope. Classic drug deal gone sour. Case closed."

Cunningham stared at the other man and then barked, "Answer my question."

"We aren't exactly concerned with designer guns here, are we? The next thing I'm going to be hearing from you is that

118

a gun makes some suspect's sports jacket pull, so he couldn't possibly have been carrying it and is therefore innocent as a babe in the woods. Give us a break, guy. Let it go. Just consider it one less crack dealer we have to worry about."

"Sure," Cunningham said, disgusted, then added, "Gosh, Rutherford, with a few sub-machine guns, we could go out there and clean up the whole city in a matter of hours. What a novel concept." He dropped his cigarette on the floor, grinding it into the linoleum with his heel. Then he pushed himself off the wall and adjusted his tie. "Keep up the good work. If I ever need any cash, I know how to get it." He turned and started lumbering down the hall.

"Hey, Bruce," the other man called to him, "I heard you finally got a conviction on the Owen homicide. Fine work you did there, guy."

He didn't look back but continued down the hall and out of the building. His anger subsided. The mere mention of the Owen case had a calming effect on him and made the fact that two of his fellow officers were no better than perps off the street a little easier to swallow. There were still some good days on the job, when he felt he was actually making a dent in this disgusting cesspool of a world, doing what good guys are supposed to do—put the bad guys away.

The Owen case had been a feather in his cap, no doubt about it. It was a landmark case, one he'd been working on for over three years. Poor old Ethel Owen, he thought, back in the parking lot again headed to his car. They'd never found her body after all these years, but he'd managed to stockpile enough evidence to get a conviction for second-degree murder just a few days before. First homicide in Ventura County to go down without a body, and he was the man who'd made it happen. That makes a guy feel proud, he said to himself, reaching the door to his unit.

He got behind the wheel and then leaned out and looked at the sky, thinking it might actually rain. He missed the seasons, got sick of the sameness, and was terrified of earthquakes.

If a plane flew overhead or a large semi passed and caused so much as a slight shake or rattle, his enormous frame was in the nearest doorway in seconds. He had seen more bodies than you could shake a fist at, stared down the barrel of a dozen or more guns, but he hated the earth moving beneath him. Everyone teased him about it, including his wife and kids. His wife, Sharon, insisted that it wasn't the earthquakes that made him dream of leaving and returning to Omaha. It was the gangs, the violence, the senselessness of it all. At night sometimes, when his wife and kids were asleep, Cunningham would sit at the dining room table for hours poring over their finances, trying to figure a way out, a way back, wishing he'd never left to begin with, asking himself if it had been worth it. Then he'd get up the next morning and have to stand over a tiny body on the street, the victim of another insane drive-by shooting, and wonder if one of these days, God forbid, he'd roll up and find one of his own kids spread out on the sidewalk, shot dead while they were merely walking to school.

He pulled out of the parking lot and headed to the morgue, his mind returning to the Owen case. He'd known Ethel Owen's slick young boyfriend had killed her from day one. They'd found physical evidence of a homicide at her home: blood and obvious signs of a struggle. The boyfriend had caught a flight out of the country as soon as he'd cleaned out old Ethel's bank accounts and sold her brand-new Cadillac, forging her name on the pink slip. When the jury had delivered a guilty verdict, Cunningham had walked out in the sunshine and could have sworn he saw Ethel's face smiling down at him. Maybe he stayed because of people like Ethel, he thought now, pulling into the parking lot of the morgue.

Once inside, he flashed his badge, asked to see the Hernandez case, and followed the skinny, effeminate lab attendant to one of the tiled autopsy rooms. The attendant checked the name and number on the man's toe, attached like a price tag in a discount department store, and then left Cunningham, prancing to a corner of the room to work on a chart.

Pulling down the white sheet, he noted that the victim fit the description of about eighty percent of the homicides in Oxnard and about fifty percent of the suspects: Hispanic, early to late twenties, five-nine, one hundred fifty pounds, criminal history. Cunningham looked over his shoulder and made certain the attendant's back was turned. He then removed a small jar of camphor from his coat pocket and dabbed a little in both nostrils. He didn't mind looking at dead people; he just hated to smell them.

The cause of death was obvious: a huge hole in the center of his chest where his heart used to be. A glimmer of stainless steel from the table made him think for a moment that something was inside there. He moved closer and bent down to look. The skinny attendant turned and chirped, "We have the missing parts in a jar if you want to see them." Cunningham just sneered. He always wondered what kind of sickness caused people to want to seek employment among the dead, particularly on county wages. The strangest part was they were always so cheerful, making him think they were going to start whistling or break out in song.

He had removed only a portion of the sheet before it snagged on the upper right portion of the body. He pulled harder, yanking it down all the way. The reason was suddenly apparent: one arm was connected only by threads of rubbery, exposed ligaments. The word *overkill* came to mind.

"You got body fluids back yet?" he asked the attendant.

"Let's see." The man flipped open the chart and glanced at it. "Not complete, but looks like blood alcohol was .07 and no drugs. Give us a break here, this guy only checked in this morning, and a lot more guests were registering than checking out."

"Cute," Cunningham replied without a chuckle. "Hell, the guy wasn't even legally drunk." After he said it, he remembered that the crime had occurred early that morning. He removed his tape recorder from his jacket and started speaking into it, describing the man's injuries. Finished, he hit the stop button and pulled the sheet back over the body. He'd seen all he needed to see. On his way out, he puckered his lips and made smacking noises at the attendant. "Stay away from the merchandise, sweetie," he said.

In his unmarked unit he radioed the station: "Six-five-four, Station One," he called.

"Station one, go ahead, 654."

They usually didn't answer right away and he was still turning pages. "Stand by." There it was: the only eyewitness, the victim's brother. "Station, call 495-3618 and have a Manny Hernandez meet me in front of his house in thirty minutes." Cunningham didn't just walk up to doors and ring doorbells like the rookies did. He wanted to live a few more years.

Pulling up at a Stop 'n' Go, he bought a few packs of cigarettes and a bag of Doritos. He placed the open bag next to him and tossed chips into his mouth as he drove. A few drops of moisture struck the windshield and then quit. Typical California rainstorm—lasted all of five minutes.

Moving the bag of Doritos, he confirmed the address. A Hispanic male resembling the deceased stood at the curb with his hands in the pockets of his baggy denims. Pretty good-looking guy, Cunningham thought. Brother hadn't been bad-looking either back when he was still in one piece. The boy was wearing a red shirt, L.A. Raiders baseball cap, and black sunglasses. The detective motioned to him from the open window.

"Get in," he said.

Hernandez shuffled over and climbed in. A woman was standing in the yard, a baby slung over her hip, chattering away in Spanish to an older woman. Probably still talking about the murder. Neighborhood entertainment, he thought, Colonia style. Driving down the street past a few houses, Cunningham pulled to the curb and parked under a large oak tree.

"Want a Dorito?" He extended the open sack to Manny.

"No, man, I don't want no fucking Dorito. They fucking blew my brother away." He was fidgeting in his seat, tapping his feet and rubbing his hands back and forth on his pants.

"You wired, Hernandez? What're you on?"

"Nothing, man. I ain't on nothing."

Cunningham threw three or four Doritos into his mouth and crunched them loudly with his teeth. A speck of Dorito hung in the thick hairs of his mustache. Tapping the back of an open pack of Marlboros, he slid one halfway out and extended it to Manny. "Want a cigarette?" A thin hand reached forward to accept. Inside the knuckles were tattooed letters. "You in a gang, Manny?"

"No, I ain't in no gang," he said but sucked so hard on the cigarette that his cheeks caved in. He looked defiantly at the detective as he spoke and blinked his dark eyes every few seconds, like lights on a Christmas tree.

Cunningham had a theory that people blinked when they lied or when they were high on drugs. Might be a little of both going on here, he thought. He brushed his hand through his mustache; the Dorito fragment disappeared. "Tell me what you saw here this morning."

"I told all I knew already. I don't know nothing else."

"Tell me again," Cunningham said gruffly. "I'm stupid. I can't read."

"I was dozing . . . heard a shot . . . then right away another . . . boom. I ran to the front door and saw my brother down . . . bleeding from a motherfucking hole in his chest." Manny's own chest started to rise and fall. He started talking faster. "Man, there was blood all over the sidewalk and his arm was blown off. But—but this guy . . . this guy was a fucking ghost." His eyes were wide in terror. "He was a spook . . . tall white guy . . . skinny. Face looked like those guys with AIDS. Bald. I dunno."

Cunningham's eyebrows arched in question. "Bald? You told the officers this morning that he was wearing a blue knit cap. You never said the man was bald."

"He was wearing a cap, man . . . but for some reason . . . I think he was bald under that cap. No fucking hair at all. I gotta go, man." He reached for the door handle, but Cunningham grabbed his shirttail. He slapped him back against the seat.

"What about the car? Did you get the make and license?"

"Spook was standing behind the car . . . red . . . box car of some kind . . . Nissan, Toyota . . . Volkswagen . . . dunno. I didn't get the plate. I dove, man . . . dove when I saw the barrel of that gun." He flicked the cigarette out the open window. "Gotta go." This time he flung open the car door and made it clear. Cunningham reached for him, but he was too fast. He slid across the seat, knocking the package of Doritos and the file to the floorboard and was almost out the passenger door when he saw Manny reach inside his pants and shoot a stream of gold urine at a tree. He then returned to the vehicle. "Told you I hadda fucking go."

Cunningham turned to him and barked, "Don't move a muscle even if you have to take a shit or I'll cuff you. *Comprende?*"

"Station one, 654," he said into the mike, his eyes glued to Manny. "Get the sketch artist to stand by. I'm coming in with a witness for a composite drawing." There was no answer, only other radio traffic. Then: "10-98, 654, just made it. He was leaving for the day. He's standing by."

Manny looked up and down the street and hunkered down as they drove away. Cunningham continued the questioning. He was beginning to like this case.

"So you're certain you don't know the shooter?"

"How many times I gotta tell ya . . . not a homeboy . . . not anyone . . . weird fucking spook."

"Your brother just got out of jail. Did he get in trouble inside? Was he into drugs, dealing, robbing?"

"He called from the jail. Told me to bring the car. We waited and then split. I left the keys with the desk. Hadda do some things. I didn't know he was out till I saw him laying there dead. He ain't into anything."

Depositing Manny with the police artist, Cunningham went

to records and filled out slips on both the victim and Manny. "I want everything you have," he told the chubby records clerk, "F.I.'s, bookings, any units responding to that address in the past, any intelligence info."

F.I.'s were small printed cards, Field Intelligence, that officers filled out when they had contact with someone in the field that looked suspicious but did not warrant arrest. There were places for several names so that the officer could identify subjects who were with other subjects at the time and place they were contacted. It was an excellent source of information and had solved many a crime.

The rows of desks in the Investigation Bureau were empty. Cunningham carried a cup of mucky coffee pilfered from the radio room and a Snickers bar from the vending machine. Tossing the Snickers into the drawer for later, he lit a cigarette and started going through his other cases. He loved working this shift, with no brass around and no phones ringing off the hook. In the quiet he could think. The brunette from records stomped into the room, always pissed over during her job, and slammed the requested information on his desk. "Did you hear the news?" she said. "The jury found *not guilty* on those officers in L.A.—the Rodney King case. They're rioting in South Central L.A. now, burning down buildings. Buildings! Can you believe it? They're going to burn the whole city down."

He hadn't heard the news, but it didn't surprise him. How any jury could completely ignore what the tape had clearly shown was beyond him. He'd seen the tape. Half the world had seen the tape. The guy could have been cuffed about five blows back, yet the officers kept on beating him until they almost killed him. Cunningham was just glad he wore plain clothes and not a uniform and worked in Oxnard right now instead of L.A.

He bent his head to the task in front of him. He had to admit that the Hernandez brothers were pretty clean. In addition to the recent attempted rape and kidnapping that had been dismissed, Bobby had a five-year-old arrest and conviction for burglary. Manny had several busts for being under the influence of cocaine, also a number of years back. Crack was of course the inexpensive drug of choice today, but there was nothing to indicate the brothers indulged. Thinking the whole mess amounted to nothing, he started to pull out the Snickers. He wouldn't go home to dinner until nine o'clock, and it was only eight now.

He began working his way through a stack of F.I.'s. After five or six, he was getting bored—nothing but a bunch of names and places. Then he picked up the sixth one and read the names off again. They had been stopped for an open-container violation about two months before, but the officer had passed on citing them. Bobby Hernandez had been driving his van, Manny was a passenger, and the other passengers were listed as Carmen Lopez, Jesus Valdez, and Richard Navarro. Cunningham sat up and felt his body surge with excitement. Carmen Lopez had been brutally murdered with her Anglo boyfriend, Peter McDonald, the previous month in Ventura. Two of the suspects in custody pending trial along with three others were Valdez and Navarro. Bingo. This had been his lucky night; he'd have to go to the Catholic church on Wednesday now and really try his luck. The first bingo tonight had been small—the tattoos that were a sign of Manny's involvement at one time in a gang. The second was a much larger prize.

He went to retrieve Manny and found that the sketch had been completed. If this was the man Manny had seen, he was right in calling him weird. His mouth was small and perfectly shaped, his jaw softly rounded, and the whole picture had a strange quality about it. According to the drawing—actually, a computerized composite—the cap had been pulled low on his forehead, riding high on the back of his head. There was no hair around his ears or his long neck at all, probably why Manny got the feeling the man was bald.

"Make copies and fax this out to every agency in California. Make sure every member of this department gets a copy," he barked at the artist. "Remember to note that he is armed and dangerous and wanted for murder."

The composite artist was tall and dark, a neatly groomed young man, a relative newcomer to the department. "Hey, I'm off duty now. I have plans with my wife tonight. Get records to do it. It's their job anyway. I just make pictures on my computer here, remember?"

"Fuck records. They'll just put it aside for the day shift. You make the copies and stand there while they fax it. Do it or I'll have your asshole for dinner instead of chicken."

Shoving Manny in front of him, he said, "Walk. You and I are going to have a real heart-to-heart. We're gonna get real friendly before this night is over."

CHAPTER 13.

After two hours of tormented sleep, twisting and thrashing amid dreams of red-robed men with knives and jagged holes in their chests, Lily drove to the rented house. She left Shana out cold from the medication with her father. Opening the front door, she was assaulted by the sickening odor of vomit, and she ran to the kitchen for Pine Sol, fighting back her own nausea. Once the bathroom was clean, she took a plain dust rag and wiped every surface the rapist might have touched. The slip of paper with his address, torn the night before from the office file, was carefully taped back together from the back. After the police had left, she would stop at the copy store and Xerox it, placing the photocopy in the file. She called for the crime-scene unit and collapsed in a heap on the kitchen floor. The screen door was open and it had clouded over. Even a few drops of rain had fallen and were glistening on the rose bushes.

The gloom seemed right for this day. She recalled how as a child it had always rained on Good Friday, the day they had crucified Christ. Her mother told her that the sky would get dark around three, the time He might have died, and as Lily recalled, it frequently did. Those were the days when she dreamed of becoming a nun and used to dress up in white sheets and roam around the house when everyone was outside. Those were the days before her grandfather and that first summer. Lily had prayed then and no one had heard her prayers. She soon stopped praying and dreamed of becoming a person who could punish other people.

The first night it had happened, even now she could not really blame him. It was she who had crawled into his bed, after he'd been into the brandy that Granny no longer allowed him to drink due to his diabetes. Granny was small, like a child, barely five feet tall, and he had mistaken her in his drunken stupor, aroused by memories of the past. Afterward, he had kneeled by the bed and prayed and washed her and begged her to keep the "secret." He'd told her that his elbow had slipped and hurt her so bad, and at only eight years old, she didn't know any better. The next day, on her birthday, he had a beautiful chestnut pony delivered to the ranch.

But the perversity would continue for five more summers. He wanted to stroke her, feel her, put his fingers inside her. Each time she allowed him to do so, he rewarded her with an extravagant gift. The pawing wasn't really so bad. Sometimes it even felt good. She would close her eyes real tight and think of what she wanted him to buy her: a new doll maybe, or a new saddle for her pony, Bay Boy, or a beautiful new dress. As the years went by, she became aware that their "secret" afforded her something most children never have: power. If she wanted to, she could make him cry, saying she was going to tell. It was like a cruel game she played with him, and she played it often. To everyone else he was a hero: rich and generous, lieutenant governor of Oklahoma, past president of the Rotary, board member of various charities. When her mother spoke of him, her eyes became alive, and her father admired him. He and her grandmother would roll into town in their big Lincoln Continental, loaded down with gifts for the family, each visit like Christmas. As Lily digressed, she pulled her knees to her chest and began rocking back and forth on the kitchen floor.

On one sweltering Dallas day, Lily had been riding her bike up and down the block all morning, playing jacks on the porch, and spraying herself with the garden hose in the backyard. School had just let out the day before for the summer vacation. The year had been one of nightmares and bed-wetting, but she had kept the terrible "secret" locked inside. She came in to change her wet clothes and found her mother in her room, the suitcase open on the bed.

"I'm not packing a lot this summer," her mother said. "You always come back with so many new things." She suddenly realized Lily was sopping wet, dripping water. "Get those wet clothes off before you get sick. Look what you're doing to the carpet." Her voice got higher. Lily didn't move. She couldn't.

"What's wrong with you? Go change . . . now. Do you hear me, young lady?"

"I'm not going," Lily screamed. "I'm not going . . . not going." She placed her hands on her hips in defiance, shaking her head from side to side, water from her wet hair spraying the walls. She marched to the bed and pushed the suitcase with both hands; it toppled to the floor. Folded underwear and socks spilled out.

"Look what you've done. You change your clothes this minute and put everything back exactly as it was. I'm going to get the belt and spank you if you don't stop. What brought this on?" She glared at the child, her chest heaving.

"I don't want to go. I don't like Granddaddy. He's creepy. He's not like Daddy. I wanna stay here."

Her mother sat on the edge of the bed, sighing deeply, pushing a long lock of auburn hair off her face. "You should be ashamed of yourself, Lillian. After all your grandfather has done for you . . . for us. He adores you. He would be heart-broken if he heard you saying these things. Haven't I always told you that you have to respect older people? When people get older, they act different, but they're not creepy, just old."

"He hurt me." There, she had said it. She couldn't keep his old "secret" no matter what he bought her. It made her feel funny inside, bad funny, like when she was sick with the flu and about to throw up.

Her mother's soft face tensed with annoyance, but she tried to speak calmly. "And just how did he hurt you? Did he spank you? He's supposed to spank you if you're bad. He's like your dad in the summer, and your dad spanks you. You bring that on yourself, Lily, with your temper tantrums."

Lily started shivering, the wet clothes pulling warmth from her body; chill bumps rose on her skin. "His elbow slipped and he hurt me bad."

Her mother stood and picked up the suitcase, placing it back on the bed, open again. "Oh, is that all? You're such a little actress. Everything is such a big production." She turned and started removing clothing from the chest of drawers and faced Lily with her arms full. "Did he say he was sorry?"

"Yes," she answered, hugging herself, thinking she was bad, seeing that reflection of herself in her mother's eyes. She wet the bed, threw temper tantrums, made her mother nervous and upset. That's why they sent her away, so her mother could rest because Lily was so bad. They said it was because it was hot and miserable in Dallas in the summer and nice and cool at the cabin, but she knew it wasn't true. This year she had tried so hard to be good, but she wasn't good. "When he touches me with his old creepy hands, I hate it."

Her mother took hold of Lily's shoulders and turned her in the direction of the bathroom, giving her a little push to get her moving, the conversation over. "He's just old, Lily. You have to feel sorry for him. He just wants to love you. You're his little angel. Besides, you don't hate him when he buys you all those pretty dresses and dolls and ponies. Go now. Get dressed."

Every year when the suitcases came out, Lily regarded them in horror. She saw herself inside those bags, like a puppet case being handed over to the old puppeteer who would stick his hands inside and make the puppet do whatever he wanted and the puppet had no choice, no voice, because no one would listen. When the old puppeteer put the puppets away and shut the lid on the case, Lily knew the poor puppets cried.

The next time she spoke disrespectfully of her grandfather, her mother spanked her with the belt until angry welts rose on her spindly legs. She never spoke badly of him again. He died of a massive heart attack the year Lily turned thirteen. At the funeral she wore her best dress, one she had earned in his hands, and she curled and combed her hair as she would for a birthday party. Walking by his open casket behind her sobbing and hysterical mother, her solemn and downcast father, Lily held her body erect and tossed her silken curls. She looked down at his waxy face, lingering with fingers locked on the edge of the coffin, a tragic and touching picture to those in the church watching, the hundreds who had come to honor the great man. "Now you're in the case," she whispered and smiled. "And I bet you're going to cry when they close the lid."

A few days later, when she was alone in the house, she removed every single item he had ever given her and carried it to the big trash can in the alley. There were so many dresses with crisp petticoats that she had to jump inside the can itself and stomp them down. Then she came back with handfuls of shoes, hair ornaments, old dolls, beads, and bracelets, tossing them in and slamming the tin lid down with a loud, satisfying clang of finality.

She could hear the metal ring of that lid now as she sat on the kitchen floor. Then she realized the doorbell was ringing: the crime-scene unit had arrived. It was four o'clock. She'd been waiting over an hour. Once they gathered their evidence and left, the urge was overwhelming to call the Oxnard police or local hospitals to see if the rapist was dead, but she dared not. In two hours she would watch the local news.

Her thoughts turned to cases she had handled in the past

and the Judicial Council rules regarding circumstances in aggravation and mitigation that were used to determine the severity of sentences. Lily thought of the rule: Did the defendant show remorse for his or her actions? Remembering days in courtrooms when she had argued fiercely for maximum terms, citing callousness and lack of remorse, pointing to the blank, emotionless faces of defendants with an angry, accusing finger, she realized that a lack of remorse was a primary emotional defense against guilt. Lily had to believe in what she had done. The knife had been at her throat, the blade against her skin. In his eyes was the ability to end both her life and Shana's. She knew the look. She'd seen it in her own eyes in the rearview mirror on the way to Oxnard.

When she called Butler's office, his secretary informed her that he was in a meeting due to end any second.

"Buzz him for me, please, it's important."

Soon Butler came on: "Lily, hold on a minute." There were male voices in the background on the open line. "That will be fine. Tomorrow at ten, then." His deep voice was consoling from the onset. "I am shocked, Lily, quite simply shocked . . . deeply sorry. Your daughter? How is she?"

"As good as can be expected." Taking a deep, raspy breath, she continued, "I'd rather speak to you in person, Paul. I can be there in forty-five minutes if you don't mind waiting."

"Take your time. I'll wait."

The shower was steaming when she stepped in; it hit the back of her carpet-burned calves and she jumped, almost losing her footing. The water cascaded over her head and ran off the tip of her nose. Her entire body ached; she felt battered. Placing both her palms against the still cool tile, she realized that she was crying, but the tears ran off with the water.

"Why? Why? Why?" she cried. With each utterance of the word, she slapped her palms against the tiles until they were stinging and red. "What have I done to deserve this?" She kept hitting the tile until the sharp pain in her wrists stopped her.

She carefully painted her face with makeup. It was her mask. She wanted to face Butler looking exactly the same as she always did. Nothing has changed, she said to herself. Nothing at all has changed.

The elevator was crowded with people leaving, and Lily smiled and exchanged a few words mechanically. The receptionist buzzed her through the security doors. "How're you feeling?" the girl asked politely. Lily's head jerked and she wondered how many people in the office knew. In the next moment, though, she realized that the girl probably just thought she had been ill. They had to tell people some reason why she hadn't been in the office all day.

"Must be a twenty-four-hour virus or something," she said, placing her hand on her stomach. Stopping at records, the clerk already gone for the day, she dropped the Hernandez file and several others in the basket. She had Xeroxed the copy of the report on the way over.

Butler's secretary was also gone, and she walked directly into his large office. The room was not lit by fluorescent lighting like all the others. Butler had real lamps, making it appear more like a well-appointed library in a stately home.

He stood and walked around the desk, extending both his hands. "My dear," he said, pulling her to him in a brief embrace. "Sit. Sit. Tell me all about it." He waved his hand at one of the high-backed leather chairs. Not returning behind his desk, he took a seat in the chair next to Lily's and turned, facing her, waiting for her to speak.

"There's not a lot to tell, Paul," she said softly, controlled. "I guess I left the back door open, and he came in and threw my robe over my face, like putting a blanket over me. He had a knife. He then got us both on the bed and forced me to orally copulate him and raped Shana." Lily inhaled deeply when she mentioned Shana's name, pressing her body back into the seat. "He was scared off by some sirens in the neighborhood."

"But where was your husband during all this?"

"We just separated a week ago. I was renting a house in Ventura, not far from here."

Butler's brows were knitted and his mouth tense. "Had you ever seen this man? Was he someone you prosecuted?"

"No, I never saw him before. Shana was waiting earlier on the porch when I came home. Maybe he saw her and decided to come back later. Who knows? He was a rapist, though. I don't think his intentions were to rob us. No, not at all."

"Your daughter? How is she handling this? How old is she, Lily?" Butler's demeanor was calm and soothing.

"She's thirteen." Lily's voice cracked. She hated the sound of compassion in his voice, as though she were a child. "She's resting now, sedated."

"You know you can take some time off," he said, but flicked a glance out the window and she sensed the lack of sincerity in that statement. It would create mammoth problems.

Unable to remain seated in the chair, she stood and started pacing. "I'm coming back to work tomorrow. I'll probably even send my daughter back to school." She had just arrived at this decision as she spoke. "The more we let this disrupt our lives, the larger it will become." She stopped and faced him. "The appointment. Richard told me. Has it been filled?"

"I'm sorry," he said, turning away, refusing to meet her gaze. "Carol Abrams was appointed and accepted a few hours ago. It was a tough situation. Attenberg had to be replaced at once. You were considered—"

"Was the deciding factor my rape? Tell me, Paul. I have to know."

"It was a factor. I won't lie and say it wasn't, but the deciding factor? They wanted a female. It was between you and Abrams, and you were both highly qualified. There'll be other situations. Although nothing like this has ever come up, I'm confident the bench can accommodate you in the future." Seeing the conversation had returned to business, Butler moved to the large chair behind his desk. Lily continued to pace.

135

"Who's going to prosecute Lopez–McDonald now?" she retorted, her disappointment almost at the verge of anger. "Shit, I'm up to my eyeballs in cases now. I have no one with the experience to handle a case as complex as this one."

"Lily, if you'll relax a little and just listen, I'll tell you how we're going to handle it. I realize you've been through a terrible ordeal. Perhaps this should wait?"

She had picked up a pen and was twirling it between her fingers. "Go ahead. I want to know where I stand."

"You and Richard Fowler are going to handle the unit and the case. I'm moving Silverstein back to cover Richard's unit temporarily. You'll split the workload right down the middle."

At the mention of working with Richard, Lily's muscles contracted and the pen flew through the air like a rubber band, barely missing Butler's head. "Shit," she said. Then quickly: "I mean, about the pen. If that's what you want . . ."

"Can you handle a case like this?" he asked.

Lily was indignant. "Of course I can. How could you even ask?"

He fixed his eyes on her, looking down his nose. "I mean emotionally, uh, after what you've been through."

Picking up her briefcase and purse, she said firmly, "I'm a prosecutor, a mad dog. You know, after the kill. Guess I'll have even more reason to win, don't you think?" *After the kill*, she thought, how appropriate. The more real and horrible her life became, the more absurdity she saw in the entire charade. Little words, little gestures, little feelings, all marching in one big line to the finish.

"Exactly my own thoughts." Butler stood. "I'll walk you to your car."

When the phone rang, Richard was at home sorting through the day's mail at his desk in the spare bedroom he had made into a study.

"Can you talk? It's me." She was at a service station only a few blocks from the house. It was drizzling again and she was standing outside. The traffic from the freeway was deafening. "Hold on. A semi just went by. I can't hear."

He yelled, "Where are you? Are you okay?"

"I'm at a service station. I just left Butler's office and he told me. I'm on my way home to see if Shana's awake. I don't know why I called, but I said I would."

"Did he tell you about the appointment?"

"Yes, and he told me about your moving back to the unit to work with me, about us prosecuting McDonald–Lopez together."

"How do you feel about that?" He was still yelling even though she could hear him fine now.

"I can hear you, don't yell. I'm numb about everything now. You know, no sleep and all." She paused, noting the rain had stopped.

"I guess it will work out. I need a friend and I'm going to need a lot of help. Better go now. I plan to come to work tomorrow. If I can't, I'll call."

"Take care of yourself, Lily. If you're worried about me pushing myself on you, don't."

Her last comment was an understatement, to say the least. "That's not one of my big concerns right now. Tomorrow, huh?"

On the way home, she stopped at a pet store and bought Shana a precious puppy. Life seemed to be going in circles. Puppies, ponies. They were all about the same.

14.

Lily was driving John's Jeep and pulled it alongside her Honda in the garage. She carried the tiny Italian greyhound puppy in her arms and grabbed some towels from the clothes drier, which she placed in an empty cardboard box, and then bent down to put the little animal inside. When she stood up, vertigo momentarily engulfed her and she thought she was going to black out. Right in front of her eyes was a blank spot in the garage where her father's shotgun had leaned for years before she moved out. If John had not forced her to take it with her along with the rest of her things when she'd moved, she would not be a murderer. The garage door was open and she looked outside, walking to the edge of the garage and searching the street for any cars she didn't recognize. The police could be watching her. Satisfied no one was there, she hurried past the Honda into the house.

John was in the kitchen, about to place a chicken in the oven to roast. He leaned back against the counter, facing Lily. His light blue cotton shirt was wrinkled, and dried rings of perspiration stained the armpits. "She's still asleep," he said.

Lily felt his gaze follow her as she headed to the den and fell onto the sofa. The local news was in progress.

"Did you hear me, Lily? Can you at least answer me?"

"I heard you. I want to watch the news."

She sat upright, her hands folded in her lap, her eyes glued to the screen. John opened the oven door and slammed it shut, took out a smaller pot and banged it on top of the range. She could hear the flick of his lighter. They were showing footage of the riot in L.A. At present they were reporting at least eleven major fires, numerous injuries, and two firemen injured, one shot. Nothing registered. Lily stared, waiting.

"Should I wake her for dinner?"

The female newscaster was speaking, returning to the regular broadcast. "Another senseless act of violence claimed the life of a twenty-eight-year-old Oxnard man early this morning in what police are calling a gang-related drive-by shooting. As the man's brother looked on in horror . . ."

"Lily."

She screamed, "Shut up, John."

". . . unknown assailant opened fire, killing the man in front of his residence in the Colonia section of Oxnard."

The newscaster turned with a plastic smile to the weatherman. "So, it looks like the rain has stopped, Stu. We could certainly use a little more with those fires burning." Lily pressed the off button on the remote control and got up, walking to the kitchen bar.

"I'm sorry, John." Their eyes met and Lily swam there, searching. An eyewitness, the man's own brother, had watched her kill him. I'm sorry, she said to the dead man's brother. I'm sorry, she said to John. I'm sorry, sorry, sorry. The words kept playing like a mantra in her head as the images washed in blood played red before her eyes. She wanted to say the words, tell him what she'd done, have him run to her and comfort her, but he could not offer comfort. His eyes bore into her, burned through her, but she couldn't speak. He was too weak, too unpredictable. In the beginning, she'd seen him as a safe haven in the storm, but he had been only a lean-to.

John pulled hard on his cigarette. The smoke swirled from his mouth; twin streams exited his nostrils. The puppy began whining in the garage and John looked toward the noise, puzzled.

"I bought Shana a puppy. It was the only thing I knew to do right now. Tomorrow I'll get a referral from Social Services for a good psychologist." Lily fetched the tiny greyhound from the garage, and as she headed to Shana's room, she stopped and looked back at John. "I'm going to wake her. That way she can sleep tonight and go to school in the morning."

A look of astonishment swept over John's face. He stabbed the cigarette out in the already overflowing ashtray. "Are you trying to tell me that you're going to insist that the child goes to school tomorrow after what she's been through? You're incredible, Lillian."

"Don't call me that. You only do it to annoy me." She inhaled, puffing her chest out. "Yes, she's going to school. If you baby her and give in and stay home from work and sit around all day with her, she'll end up afraid of her own shadow. Let her go back to her friends and her school work, things that are normal. Please listen to me on this."

"Whatever you say. Whatever you say." He turned and started taking plates from the cabinet.

Walking down the dark hall to Shana's room, Lily imagined them coming to arrest her. She saw the police cars pull up in front, the neighbors gathered watching, Shana crying as they led her away, her hands cuffed behind her back. She was holding the little dog so tightly that it whined in pain and tried to jump out of her arms.

She crept into the room and tapped Shana gently on the shoulder. With the covers pulled up around her, her soft face on the pillow, she looked so young, so fragile, so untouched. Rolling over onto her back, she opened her eyes to her mother, pushing herself up in the bed. Lily placed the puppy in her lap. "This is your new pal. What do you think?"

"Oh, how precious. What breed is it? It's so tiny." She picked up the puppy and held it to her face, nose to nose. "I love it. Oh, I love it. Is it a girl or a boy?"

Sitting on the edge of the bed, Lily answered, "It's an Italian greyhound and a girl just like you. And you must name her. But first, throw on some clothes and come in for dinner. Dad's got it all ready and it smells great."

Both Lily and Shana ate everything on their plates, taking seconds, leaving very little to John, who said he had eaten lunch and didn't mind. The puppy jumped around on the floor, squatting and making a puddle.

"I brought all your new clothes over here from my house. They're in the car," Lily said after dinner as she carried the dinner dishes from the table and John planted himself in front of the television. "You can wear one of the new things to school tomorrow if you want." When she turned to see Shana's response, she was shocked to see the child picking up the dishes off the table and walking to the sink. Shana never cleaned up of her own accord. Not without a fight.

"Okay," Shana said, looking at the puppy at her feet. "Let's call her Princess Di, no, Lady Di. You know, like *Lady and the Tramp* and Princess Di? Hey, Di. Come here, Di. Come to your mummy. Come here, little princess."

The dishes done, Lily and Shana went to her room for the remainder of the evening. After Lily helped her select an outfit for the next day, she sat behind her on the small bed and brushed her long hair. She tried to sense what her daughter was feeling. Finally, Lily dropped the brush and wrapped her arms around her. Shana's head fell back into the crook of her mother's neck. Lily lightly trailed her fingers over her brows, her eyelids, let them trace the slope of her slightly upturned nose. "When you were little," she whispered, "I used to put you to sleep this way. Do you remember?"

"Yes," she said softly.

"Do you remember the Christmas when you found all the presents in the hall closet and unwrapped them and played with them and then put them back without anyone knowing? I thought I'd die laughing when I found out. You were such a case."

"Yes."

"How about the time when we went skating together and we skated into the boys' bathroom by mistake and scared all those boys to death?"

"I remember. What about when Grandma went into the men's room at the movie theater and we were too embarrassed to get her and sent the usher in? Grandma couldn't come out because her girdle got stuck and she was too nervous to get it up. That was funny."

"Yeah," Lily said. But neither of them could laugh; the laughter was out of reach. Even the memory of its sound was distorted, like a foreign tongue they had once spoken fluently but no longer comprehended. "Can you sleep now?"

"No."

Lily left and returned a few minutes later with one of the sleeping pills they had given her at the hospital, handing it to Shana with a glass of water. "Do you want to sleep with me in our bed?"

After swallowing the pill, Shana pulled the puppy into the crook of her arm, rolled onto her side, and stared at the wall. "I'll sleep here."

"You don't have to go to school. I thought it would be a good way to get your mind off everything, but not if you can't handle it."

"I'll be fine, Mom."

Kissing her before leaving, Lily whispered to the child, "Life goes on. That might not be the greatest thing I could say to you right now, but it's a basic truth."

Lily went to the bedroom and fell across the bedspread facedown, fully clothed. She rolled over onto her back and stared at the ceiling. Her eyes shut and her body started falling into the blackness, but each time she fought it, springing back into consciousness, her eyes opening, seeking the familiar sights around her. She imagined she had a rope and she could tie it to the nightstand or the big green chair and then wrap it around her waist. Then she would not fall all the way down into the pit, then she would have a way to pull herself out again. He was dead, she was alive. Yet in the murky netherworld of dreams, he would never die. The door to Shana's bedroom was open, and she heard John telling her good night, their voices muffled.

Eyes on the ceiling, Lily heard him enter and softly close the door behind him. "Open the door," Lily said. "I want to hear if Shana needs anything."

"I'll open it in a minute. I just want to talk to you, and then I'll sleep on the sofa." He paused, leaning against the door, his hands behind him, his voice low. "What do we do now?"

Lily rolled over onto her side and looked at him. "We go on living, John. What else can we do?"

"I mean about the police, about Shana, about us."

"The police will investigate, try to find him. Until they find him, nothing much will happen."

"I don't know what to say to her, what to do."

"Do what you always do. Just be there for her and listen if she wants to talk." Lily got up and went to the bathroom, thinking she must take off her clothes. John followed her.

"Are you going to stay here? What about the house you rented?"

He was standing close and Lily backed away. His breath, his clothes, even his hair, all reeked of cigarette smoke. "I can't live in that house, John. Shana would never feel safe there again. I'll have to give it up." She stepped into the bathroom and closed the door in his face. Letting her clothes fall in a heap on the floor, she put on his robe hanging on a hook. When she opened the door, he was still standing there. "You could move out."

His features became twisted with anger. "I'm not moving out," he snarled. "This is all your fault, you know. You even left the back door unlocked. That's how he got in."

Her back stiffened and she felt the blood rush from her face. "Get out," she snapped, trying to keep her voice down. "Leave me alone."

"I'm not moving out. Don't try to use this, Lily. I'm staying here with my daughter."

"Then stay," she said, disgusted. "But you can't ask me to leave. Whether you realize it or not, she needs me. She needs both of us. And your needs don't mean shit right now, John. Nothing else matters."

He turned and started to leave the room. "Leave the door open," Lily said.

She rolled over onto her face on the bed, grabbing handfuls of white sheet in her fists, pulling them until the fitted corners lifted and the mattress was exposed. Sitting up, she yanked the sheet off, looking for the old stains, wanting to see them. In the center of her side of the bed was the reddish-brown circle where she had miscarried when Shana was only a few months old. It was all that remained of what should have been a brother or sister for Shana. If she had not miscarried, she would never have gone to law school and Shana would have never been raped. It was a spot of death, only a spot.

She threw the sheet onto the floor and slept on the mattress, placing her face over the stain, the bedside lamp still on.

Soon she was walking in deep, dark water, up to her knees. It was splashing against her as she moved, her stride more like a march than a walk. As she walked, the water got deeper and deeper, but she couldn't turn back. Far ahead, Shana stood, calling to her, her hair blowing straight out, her voice a crystal soprano.

Lily's eyes suddenly sprang open, her body bathed in sweat. She turned and saw Shana standing in the doorway. "My God, what happened. Are you all right?"

"I can't sleep, Mommy. I'm so scared." Her voice was small

and cracking, the voice of a very young child. "He's coming back. I know he's coming back."

Lily patted a place next to her on the bed, and Shana walked over. "Sleep with me, sweetheart." Once Shana was in bed, Lily turned off the lamp and they talked in the dark. "Shana, I want you to listen to me and try to believe me. I know it's hard, I know you're afraid, but he's never coming back. Do you hear me? I promise you he'll never hurt you again."

"You don't know that—you can't promise me that."

Lily stared into the darkness. There was nothing more she could say. She'd taken a life, committed the ultimate sin, and still there was nothing she could do to stop the pain.

CHAPTER 15.

Waking long before the alarm clock went off, Lily panicked seeing Shana gone from the bed. She rushed to her room and found the door open, the room empty, but she heard noises in the kitchen. As she stood inside the room, she thought Shana must have risen hours before, for her room was spotless, everything in its place, every piece of clothing hung neatly on hangers. A coldness settled over Lily: she felt she was standing before a set on a stage. The props all belonged to Shana, but were no longer infused with her presence. This was not her daughter's room, this ordered perfection.

She found Shana dressed, sitting at the kitchen table with schoolwork in front of her, her little puppy in her lap. Lily went to her and stroked her hair, placing her hands on her shoulders, peering down at the papers in front of her. "What time did you get up?"

"About four. I couldn't sleep."

"Are you sure you want to go to school today?"

"I sure don't want to stay here all day. But I don't really want to leave Di either." She paused. "I'll go."

146

Later, as Lily drove her to school, she told Shana that she would have her new bedroom set with the canopy bed moved to her room in a day or so from the rental house. The bed where the rape occurred, Lily's bed, she planned to have hauled off to the dump and burned.

Shana looked at Lily with soft, dreamy eyes. "That would be nice, Mom. I really liked it."

John had left before Lily that morning and she had been forced to drive the Honda. As she approached the government center complex, her fingers tightened on the steering wheel. Perhaps they were waiting in the office with an arrest warrant and would cuff her and march her out in front of the entire staff. "Take me," she said in defiance to the windshield. If not for Shana, she'd welcome an end to the waiting, would accept the consequences of her actions. Then she would not have to perform, continue to function as if nothing had happened, constantly fear arrest. Then the tangled, twisted knot of horror and guilt might leave her.

She rode the elevator up in silence, burst through the security doors, and hurried to her office, keeping her eyes on the floor, shutting out the chatter and ringing phones and printers spilling copy. Someone said her name, but she ignored him and walked even faster, her heart racing, beating erratically as she listened, deep inside her own body. Her office was dark and the halls around it empty. She flicked on the light and tried to reassure herself with the sameness, checking her desk to see if anyone had been going through her papers and finding it all as she had left it. Letting her body sink in the upholstered desk chair, she felt momentarily safe. This was the place she loved, the work she lived for, her refuge. Here she was a respected professional. Here she was a righteous person.

"Good morning," Clinton said, strolling in energetically and taking a seat in front of her desk. "How're you feeling? Touch of the flu, huh?"

He didn't know. Thank God, she thought. Clinton was one who could never keep knowledge under wraps. "I'm fine today.

I'm just a little weak." Say something else, her mind screamed. For a bizarre moment she saw herself standing there completely naked, her victim's blood dripping from her fingernails. "So, you're getting quite an opportunity here. Even though you may only be acting supervisor of the Muni Division, it could lead to a permanent promotion later. Are you pleased?"

"Sure, but back to the same stupid cases, when I was finally getting something to sink my teeth into here." He grimaced and then suddenly his face came alive; he sat forward excitedly in his chair. "I almost forgot because it happened yesterday when you were off, but Hernandez got bumped off. Can you believe it?"

Clinton could be baiting her, she thought. He could even be a plant, wearing a wire. "Hernandez? Which case is that?"

"The prostitute case. The one I dismissed the other day. Oxnard P.D. called me yesterday asking all about the case. They think it was a gang thing, a drive-by. Anyway, someone saved the taxpayers a hell of a lot of money."

Lily gripped the arms of her chair and tried to remain calm. They were asking questions about the Hernandez case, she thought, panicked. Clinton could have already told them that she'd taken the file home with her and had it in her hands at the time Hernandez was murdered. What should she say now? She felt her mind drifting off track and imagined them throwing a big party to celebrate all the salvaged taxpayers' dollars, throwing confetti in the air while the Hernandez body rested on a slab in the center of the room. Seeing her glasses under a file folder where she had left them, she put them on and started to shuffle papers on her desk, moving them to one side and then back to the other.

"The detectives are asking about the victim on that case. They tried to interview her and it's pretty strange. She's still missing."

As Clinton continued, Lily started tapping her pen on her desk frantically. She saw the expression on his face and stopped. "What's strange? She's a hooker and she moved on.

That's not too unusual." She knew her voice sounded annoyed, grating, taut.

"Hey, I know you have a million things to do," he said, standing to leave.

"No, I'm interested. Go on . . . finish what you were saying." She placed her hands in her lap to keep them out of sight.

"Well, seems like she left a couple of kids behind, little ones at that, and according to the detective, her sister said she was a pretty good mother. She didn't have any skills, and she started working the streets for the money, basically for the kids. So, they haven't heard word one from her. And get this, Hernandez was picked up on an arrest warrant four days after she filed charges. No one's actually seen her since he was arrested."

The night of the rape was coming back in full force, and sweat broke out on Lily's upper lip as she recalled the knife and his words: "Taste a fucking whore's blood." She pressed her hand to her cheekbone and held it there like a compress. "Does Oxnard think he might have murdered her to keep her from testifying? Did they search his house for any evidence?" The image of his house was in front of her, the sidewalk stained red with his blood. Had dogs licked her vomit from the asphalt, or had the crime-scene officers scraped it up and sent it to the lab? Maybe the prostitute's body had been cut up into pieces and they were locked inside that old refrigerator on the porch with the big padlock.

"They work pretty slow over there, you know, with an average of three or four homicides a month, but I'm sure they're on top of it. They've impounded his van and are going in all the right directions. Bruce Cunningham is handling the case. You've heard of him. Pretty sharp man."

Lily's phone started ringing. She heard it but thought it was down the hall. She looked up to find Clinton staring at her. With a jerky movement of her hand, she hit the intercom. "Hold all my calls, Jan."

"You might have been right on this one from the start, Lily. I've got to hand it to you."

"Keep me posted, Clinton. Get everything you have on this from Cunningham and let me see it." Of all the detectives that could have received this case, it had to be this one, Lily thought, feeling her fear and panic escalate. He was the best detective in Oxnard, possibly in the entire county. She knew him—knew what made him tick. They had worked together several times in the past, and the man's record was flawless. Taking a case that Cunningham had investigated to trial was an almost certain conviction. The man never erred, never rushed, never compromised his standards of excellence. He was a prosecutor's dream, a criminal's worst nightmare. And now he was her adversary.

"This whole thing could be even bigger. I mean, I don't want to get you all excited for nothing, but . . ."

Lily's hands were locked on the edge of the desk, her body straining forward. "Spit it out, Clinton," she said, unable to play out this scene any longer.

"Well, Cunningham is tight-lipped right now—merely putting out feelers. Seems Hernandez and his brother were F.I.'d a few months ago in the company of guess who? Carmen Lopez, and get this, Navarro and Valdez."

Lily practically leaped out of her chair. It might mean the first real break in the McDonald–Lopez massacre, but it carried even more weight. It could be the taste of salvation. If Hernandez had killed the prostitute and orchestrated the slaughter of two others as well, he could be a multiple killer, a deadly psychopath.

"I want Cunningham to report to me immediately on any morsel he gets on this, no matter how insignificant. I want our own investigators apprised of this at once. Call and inform Butler and of course Fowler. Don't let a word leak to the press. Got it?"

"Right, boss," Clinton replied, feeling the same rush. At the door he turned, looking back at Lily. "You know, I didn't want to work for you. I thought you were going to be too tough, like, unreasonable. I was a damn fool. I'd like to come back when manpower allows it."

She peered at him over the rim of her glasses. "Too tough, huh? Not because I was a woman, because I was too tough. That's a new one. You can come back, Clinton. Just keep using that conditioner on your hair."

He started laughing and Lily longed to catch the golden sound, steal it, and swallow it inside her. Only the corners of her lips rose and then fell.

"It's expensive. You going to pay?"

"Not hardly," she replied, trying to crack her face with a bigger smile. Once he had left, she stood and walked around her desk in a circle, unable to sit still. She felt claustrophobic in the small office, but if she left, she would have to talk to more people, make polite conversation, listen to drivel. All she could think about was Cunningham, Cunningham, Cunningham. She kept repeating his name again and again. He was really quite well known, almost famous in a way in the legal community. The Owen case had made all the papers. How the man had managed to put together enough evidence to get a conviction without an actual body Lily couldn't fathom. The woman could just walk in one day, alive. She was filled with abject fear. If he could put together a case like that, he was going to figure out that she killed Bobby Hernandez.

Hernandez's own brother had seen her. How could she have possibly thought she could shoot someone in broad daylight and get away with it? She was living on borrowed time. Her actions had been sheer insanity. Suddenly, Richard was standing in her doorway, his brows knitted with concern, watching her pace.

"I've been calling you all morning, but Jan said you weren't taking any calls and then Clinton called and told me of the developments in McDonald–Lopez. Are you okay, Lily?"

She backed up, moving behind her desk, wanting something between them. "No," she said. "I guess I'm not, but I'm working on it.'' He was a stranger from another time, another place, a part of someone else's life.

"Will you have a drink with me after work? We can go somewhere quiet.''

"I can't. I have to take my daughter to the psychologist.''

He stood and crossed the room, taking one of Lily's hands in his own. She let it lay there lifeless, cold. "When can I see you again? I want to hold you, touch you.''

Lily pulled her hand away. "I don't know,'' she said. "I just don't know.''

"You mean you don't know when you can see me or you don't know if you want to?''

"I'm living at home right now.'' She looked him in the eye. "I don't know what's going to happen. Right now I don't know anything.'' The phone rang and Lily grabbed it. Jan said she had Bruce Cunningham on the phone and asked Lily if she wanted to take the call. "I have to go, Richard. I'll get back to you.''

Once he had gone, Lily took a deep breath and pushed the flashing button. The detective started talking before Lily even answered.

"Silverstein called me at home and started barking orders at me. Who is this guy and what makes you people think you have the right to tell me how to run an investigation?''

"I'm sorry, Bruce. Accept my apology. Obviously, I know you're on top of this . . . but . . .'' She tried desperately to separate herself, not fall over her words, play the part. Like an animal, he would sense her fear. "This Lopez–McDonald case has everyone crazy over here. It's one of those cases that grabs you.''

"Yeah,'' he said, the anger diffused. "Well, I'll let you know the minute I have anything. The whole thing may be nothing.''

She could tell he was getting ready to hang up. The words were in her throat, trapped there. Finally she spoke. "What do you actually have on Hernandez?''

"I thought I had something good, but it didn't work out.

152

Neighbor got a plate. Swore she copied it down exactly right, but it came back to the wrong vehicle and a sixty-nine-year-old registered owner in Leisure World." Cunningham must have been eating something, for smacking noises came out over the line and pans rattled in the background. "We've got a composite drawing of the suspect: white male, five-ten, thin, fair-skinned. Could be a professional hit. Never know. Looks like someone just did us a favor on that one."

"Thanks, Bruce," Lily said. "Call us if anything new develops." She hung up the phone in a daze. Some favor, she thought, wondering if people realized the meaning of their offhand comments. She visualized herself sitting on the floor in a circle with the big detective standing in the center like a schoolteacher. He would look over the heads of the children, saying: "Now, which one of you did us the favor of murdering the bad Mr. Hernandez?" Lily would raise her hand proudly.

She felt like she was losing her mind.

Without the Magic Marker she would already be marching to a jail cell. They were looking for a man, a professional assassin. That's what he had said. But Cunningham was smart, cunning, and she knew very well that he could be setting her up, having her followed, waiting for confirmation from the lab. She put her head in her hands, laced her fingers through her hair, and pulled as hard as she could. She was looking for the pain of reality, but she felt the nothingness of abstraction. When she removed her hands, sizable tufts of red hair were locked in her fingers.

CHAPTER 16.

As they sat in the psychologist's outer office, Lily reviewed a case she had brought along, while Shana thumbed through a magazine. A woman about Lily's age walked out, and both Shana's and Lily's eyes glanced up at her, certain she was the doctor. Then a much younger woman appeared in the door and motioned for them to enter. She had soft brown eyes in a small, round face, and camel-colored hair to her shoulders. She was dressed in a calf-length floral skirt and green sweater, wearing loafers and socks. "I'm Marsha Lindstrom, Mrs. Forrester, and this must be Shana."

Lily stood and quickly shoved the case file into her open briefcase. "I thought you would be older," she said without thinking.

"Well, that's a nice compliment." She smiled at Shana. "Why don't I talk to your mother first and you wait out here? We won't be long."

Shana was standing and spoke up. "Why don't you talk to both of us? It happened to both of us. We were both there."

"That might be true, but sometimes people express themselves better when they are alone. Just give us a few minutes, okay?"

Instead of an office, the woman led Lily to a room with a sofa, coffee table, and two large, overstuffed chairs. Lily had already had Ventura P.D. fax the woman a copy of the police report. With a clipboard in her hands, she started quizzing Lily on her childhood, her parents, her marriage.

"I don't think any of this is relevant," Lily stated, annoyed and restless. "I want you to counsel my daughter, not me."

"So you don't believe you have suffered any personal trauma over this incident? Is that correct?"

"I didn't say that. Sure, I've suffered trauma, but I'm used to it." Lily paused, feeling trapped and stupid. Everything she said, everything she did came out wrong. Her control was slipping away. "What I mean is that—"

"Have you ever been raped before, Mrs. Forrester? Lily . . . can I call you Lily?"

The woman held her soft brown eyes on Lily's face. Lily looked down at her loafers and white socks. She looked like a graduate student. She was too young.

"What real difference does that make?" The lights were low and soft guitar music played from hidden speakers. "I'm an incest survivor. Does that qualify as being raped? I think it does. Is that what you wanted to hear?"

"Can you tell me how you feel about that . . . the incest?"

Lily had finally said the words to someone other than John, and the floodgates cranked open, releasing a torrent of emotions. It was another category, another title, she thought. District attorney, incest survivor, murderer. What else could she become: inmate, prisoner, jailbird? She saw herself with a number across her chest, staring into the camera, heard the click of the shutter. "How do you think I feel?" Lily stood and glared at the young woman. "Let me tell you how I feel. If someone ever tries to tell you that lightning doesn't strike twice, tell them to fuck off. Now, call my daughter in here and see if you can help her. It's too late for me."

Lily walked out the door and didn't look back.

She took a seat and waited. She'd acted like a complete ass when the poor woman was only trying to help. She just couldn't deal with the incest now. It set her off, made her crazy. When Shana came out an hour later, Lily jumped up and knocked all the paperwork she had in her lap on the floor. "May I speak to you again?"

"Certainly," Dr. Lindstrom stated calmly, "but my next appointment will be here soon."

When they were once again in the small room, Lily apologized for her earlier behavior. "I'm sorry I was rude. I realize you're only trying to help me, to do your job. The incest, well, it's just too painful. I can't break myself open and bleed all over your carpet now. Do you understand? Sometimes things go too far. Years ago, maybe. But now? Now I have to focus my concern and strength on my daughter and not bring up things that will disturb me."

The woman didn't reply. Silence hung heavily in the room, and Lily heard her own breath seeping in and out of her mouth. Perhaps this woman would one day be called into court to testify on her behalf, telling the jury that she had killed a man because of the incest. Maybe she would state that she was cold and heartless, recite how she had refused professional help, stomped out of her office. "How do you think my daughter is handling this?"

"Remarkably well, at least on the surface. Her greatest concern appears to be the fear that people know about the rape. Your daughter is a very strong young woman, very determined, very controlled."

"Just that," Lily said, leaning forward in her seat, "what you said about her being controlled. That's not like Shana. She's never been controlled. She's always been spontaneous, almost a little erratic sometimes. And now she's suddenly neater, quieter, more respectful. I'm afraid she's going to suppress all this and let it build inside her for years, maybe all of it surfacing when she's a woman."

"Is that what happened to you?"

"I guess it did," Lily said in a child's voice. "One of my greatest concerns is my daughter's sexuality and how this will affect her. She's a beautiful young woman and I want her to have a complete life."

"Perhaps you should share your experiences with her. Tell her just what you told me. Give her a reason to work at therapy."

"I can't," Lily said, looking at the floor, then raising her eyes tentatively. "And I believe it's the wrong thing to do. The world used to be a safe place for her and that's gone. If I tell her what happened to me, then she'll see even more danger, evil, menace. She'll see it all around her. She needs to feel this was an isolated incident that seldom occurs and will never happen again. I don't want her thinking it can happen twice in a person's lifetime."

"But it can and it did in your case. Correct?"

"Correct." Lily stared at her. "I'm not telling her."

"That's your decision."

"Lately, everything's my decision."

"That appears to be the way you want it. Life is sometimes full of choices, decisions. You know, sometimes we end up with an unwelcome role in life, but it's a role we've selected. You don't have to deal with everything alone. Even if you don't feel you can talk to me, there are groups for incest survivors. But here again, it's a choice you have to make."

As Lily walked out the door, she had a flash of herself standing over the car with the shotgun pointed at Hernandez. Was this really a choice she had made, to become an executioner? Had she waited all these years for that moment, waited for someone to step over the line and release the pent-up rage? Or was this a role created for her alone at birth, her entire life leading to that one moment? Did the universe prepare her by the earlier abuse to be a predator, to thin out the population of evil? No, she thought, she had stepped off the edge of the world and fallen into the abyss, into the dark, tormented waters of the insane.

"Mom," Shana said, standing as her mother appeared, "what's wrong?"

Lily was shivering, her arms wrapped around herself. "Nothing," she said, "nothing at all."

17 ∎

The remainder of the week passed in slow motion. Days disappeared into sleepless nights, sleepless nights turned into blurry daylight, and Lily felt she was swimming the icy waters of the English Channel, pushing her body to perform, fighting the exhaustion, desperately trying to reach shore.

She had to get her hands on the police report filed by Oxnard P.D. on the murder of Bobby Hernandez. It was the only way to know exactly what evidence they had, to know where she really stood, and she had to see the composite drawing. She had instructed Clinton to order the reports, but they had never arrived. Clinton had taken over Richard's unit, and Richard had moved into Carol Abrams's old office. Everyone was buried in work, and the Hernandez murder was insignificant in itself and only of importance if he could be linked to the McDonald–Lopez case. Nothing further had developed on the missing prostitute. Everything was in limbo. Lily wanted to scream at Clinton to get the report, call and demand it from Cunningham, but she knew she would be a fool if she did so. That could be exactly what the detective was waiting for.

Every day when she backed out of her garage, she searched the streets for unmarked surveillance vehicles, looked in her rearview mirror as she drove to work, and every night she sat in her house thinking they were out there somewhere, watching her house.

"I'm going out tonight," John said at about four-thirty Saturday afternoon. "I thought I would tell you so you could make your own plans."

He had just come back from dropping off Shana at a friend's house for a slumber party. Lily had case files spread out all over the oak dining room table. She had her hair in a ponytail, tied back with one of Shana's "scrunchies," as she called them, and was dressed in running shorts and a sweatshirt.

"What does that mean—you're going out?" she said, removing her glasses and pushing the high-backed dining room chair away from the table. With no room in the house for a study, Lily had made a habit of working there: it afforded her more space than a desk. She had a classical tape in the stereo: Tchaikovsky's Sixth Symphony. "Does that mean you have a date or something?"

"Let's just say I'm going out with a friend from the office. We both know you have friends from the office, don't we?" he said sarcastically. "As soon as you're certain Shana is stable, you're going to move out again. You know it and I know it. There isn't a life anymore for the two of us." He walked over and turned the stereo down, as if the soft strains of classical music annoyed him. "You can stay here as long as you want, but I'm going on with my life. I have a right to have a life too."

Looking deep into his soft brown eyes, she knew that he didn't love her anymore. The love had ended long ago. He needed someone who made him feel important, who was eager to listen to his stories, and who saw him as an attractive and desirable man.

"Anyway," he said, "you'll have to get your own dinner." His look was triumphant as he marched down the hall.

160

Lily remained in the dining room and attempted to regain her concentration as he showered and dressed for his "date." The situation was becoming bizarre. Half an hour later, he came into the living room all decked out in one of his better suits, drenched in Drakkar cologne, making a point that she see him, and left, a lively bounce in his step. She hadn't seen him walk that way in years.

Early date, she thought, wondering where he was going and with whom, trying to imagine what the woman looked like and asking herself if they would kiss, even have sex. All these years he had shunned her and made her feel dirty about her sexuality. Who was this woman? Some broken little girl he could comfort and protect? Why did he have a right to go on with his life when her life was destroyed? She should have stopped him, told him what she had done, sucked him into the nightmare. He should have been the one who avenged his daughter's rape.

She stood and shoved the papers onto the floor, consumed with anger and self-pity. She walked through the silent house, from room to room, peering through the blinds, through the cracks in the drapes, looking. Since she had forgotten all about lunch, her stomach was empty and turning, acid bubbling into her throat. She opened the refrigerator and found a piece of cheese, two slices of sandwich meat, and a foil-wrapped, dried-up piece of leftover chicken. Slamming the door and grabbing her purse off the kitchen counter, she discovered that she had only three dollars in change. She hadn't gone to the bank since the rape. Thinking she might find a few bills hidden inside the corner compartment of her checkbook, she pulled out the piece of paper with Richard's phone number on it. On impulse she dialed the number. After two rings the machine picked up and a woman's voice spoke on the recording. She immediately hung up, even though she was certain he had merely failed to change the recording after his wife had left.

Lily flipped on the television and stared at the screen. The inner city of Los Angeles had almost burned to the ground during the riots. Thousands of buildings and homes had been destroyed, and hundreds of people were injured or dead. It looked like a war zone. After fifteen minutes, she called Richard again, listened to his wife's voice, and was about to hang up when he picked up, speaking over the recording, his own voice blending with the recorded voice of his wife.

"Hold on," he said. "I've got to turn the machine off."

"It's me," Lily said, "your office partner. What're you doing?"

"Well, you got me at a really bad time. You see, I have these twin nineteen-year-old blondes over here, and we're about to get in the Jacuzzi."

"Sorry. I'll see you at work Monday. Have a good time." Lily believed him and felt humiliated.

"Wait. That's a joke. Actually, I'm sitting here all alone perusing the take-out menus, about to make the big decision. And what are you doing?"

"My husband has a date," she said flatly, knowing how silly it sounded, yet needing to talk with someone.

"Well, isn't that just special? I think that's about the best thing he could do, if you ask me. Now, why don't you get in your little red car and head my way? Can you find the house if I give you the address again?"

"I think I can," she said, wanting to run out the door and leave the empty house behind.

"All you have to do is get here. I'll take care of the rest. How long will it take?" He was anxious and it showed.

"Let's say an hour."

"See how easy this New Age living is. Now you have a date too. The Ozzie and Harriet days weren't really any fun, anyway, were they?"

He was so light, so breezy. "Maybe I shouldn't come, Richard. I may ruin your evening."

The lightness disappeared and his voice lowered. He uttered only one word: "Come."

The sun was going down, and dark shadows were lurking

in the corners of the empty room, marching toward her. "I'm coming. Right now."

"I'm waiting."

Lily hung up and, grabbing her parka draped over a kitchen chair, rushed from the house. She had not showered, her hair was unwashed and her face bare of makeup. As she drove, she watched the cars around her, behind her, weaving through side streets so that no one could follow her. When she arrived, after getting lost in the narrow, steep hills leading to his house and after huffing and puffing up the eighteen steps leading to his door, she started to turn and leave. You were an idiot to come here, she told herself. Standing on the doorstep, she looked back down at the steps and then back at the door. She released her hair from the ponytail and shook it free. She grabbed her compact from her purse and glanced at her face. Finally she rang the doorbell, standing there like a waif, her bare legs freezing.

As he flung open the door, his eyes registered shock at her appearance. Then he reached for her and held her in his arms. "My God, what're you wearing shorts for this late in the evening? You'll catch pneumonia. Come in. Come in." He moved his arm, directing her into the living room and made a little bow like a headwaiter.

The house was now fully furnished, with lots of black marble and shiny, uncluttered surfaces. The lights were low and the stereo playing "Unforgettable" by Nat King and Natalie Cole. Lights were twinkling in the picture window overlooking the city. The dining table was set. Two candles in silver holders were the only lights in the room.

"I bought tequila and a blender," he said. "Or, I have an excellent bottle of champagne. What will it be?"

He was dressed neatly in slacks and a sweater, and the familiar lime scent drifted to her nostrils. She felt smelly and disgusting, like she'd been living on the streets, like a homeless person. "Maybe a bath or a shower?"

"Sure. No problem. Here's the plan. You take a shower and I'll start dinner."

Lily let the hot water cascade over her head. She washed her hair with Richard's shampoo and dried herself with Richard's towel. She sprayed her underarms with Richard's deodorant. Then she saw the bottle of lime cologne and poured some onto her hands and touched her body with it. She was safe here among Richard's possessions, in his home. Here no one could touch her. Wrapping herself in his big, fluffy bathrobe, she padded barefoot into the living room.

They sat side by side on the sofa facing the floor-to-ceiling glass windows and looked at the city lights stretching out beneath them. He started a small fire in the fireplace. Lily asked to use his phone and left his number at the house where Shana was spending the night. He wanted to know how the girl was doing.

"It's funny, but she's doing fine. She saw the psychologist again yesterday, and the doctor feels she's handling everything remarkably well—on the surface, anyway."

"Kids are survivors, Lily. They're much stronger than we think."

"But she's different, Rich. She's quieter, neater, more helpful around the house. I don't know. Something so terrible can't have a positive effect. I keep thinking these are all indicators that she's more deeply disturbed than anyone thinks." As Lily took a sip of the champagne, concern etched itself in her face, causing her brows to knit.

"Sometimes when a tragedy occurs, in anyone's life, at any age, it makes them more aware of the value of life. Maybe she just matured."

Lily didn't respond but got lost in her thoughts. What if Shana thought this terrible thing had happened because she was a bad person, and by trying so hard now to be good, she was trying to protect herself, redeem herself, so to speak? Lily decided to discuss this with the psychologist next week. Then she realized Richard had just been sitting there, and she felt a flush of appreciation for his silence.

"Why don't I serve dinner while you relax by the fire? Are you hungry?"

"Starving," she said. "You didn't make it yourself, did you?" She didn't want Richard to have any domestic skills at all, not like John. That she couldn't handle.

"No, but I know how to reheat it. The restaurant even wrote it down on a little card." He smiled and left the room.

After a candlelight dinner of roast duck in orange sauce, which was excellent and prepared by Monique's, one of the better French restaurants in town, he put a Nat King Cole record on the stereo and they danced by the fire, their feet barely moving, his arms loose around her waist.

"Did I tell you that you look absolutely gorgeous tonight? I've never seen you like this," he said.

Lily was embarrassed, knowing he was lying, trying to make her feel good. Without makeup she felt naked, exposed, homely. He placed his large hands on her back, letting them slide down to her ass, pressing her tightly against him. Lily pulled back, seeing where it was heading. She took his hand and led him to the sofa.

"Tell me about yourself," Lily said. "You know, the real stuff, not the stuff I already know."

"Let's see. I grew up here in Santa Barbara, a spoiled rich kid. My parents owned a house right across from the beach, but we seldom went on it. Funny, when you live so close it becomes old hat. My father was a surgeon, and his father was a surgeon, but I didn't have the inclination or the aptitude to follow in their footsteps."

"Was it a disappointment to him?" she asked, comparing her own past to his, wondering what it would be like to have no greater trauma buried there than simply not having an aptitude for surgery.

"No doubt. But he handled it well. I was on the swim team

and made decent grades. He wasn't unhappy when I went into law. He viewed it as a respectable profession." He stopped and a glint of moisture appeared in his eyes. "He died two years ago. My mother moved to Florida. I have a brother in Pasadena, also a surgeon. That's about it."

"How's your son? Greg, right?"

"Still surfing. His hair's so long now that he looks like a girl, but we're getting along pretty good. We see each other several times a week. I might eventually get him to move in with me. Who knows? He's a good kid."

They were sitting close now, staring at the fire. He suddenly stood and took her hand. "I'd like to take you in the bedroom and hold you. I don't expect you to have sex with me, but I'd like to hold you in my arms."

In the bedroom, Lily slipped off the robe and let it fall to the floor. He removed his clothes and tossed them onto a chair. They got under the covers and held each other, pressing their naked bodies together, not saying a word. The warmth of his body, his strong arms around her, made her want to stay there forever.

After a while he began stroking her lightly with a feather touch, using the soft, padded tips of his fingers. Soon his hands were between her legs, but only so softly, barely touching her. She moved his hand away. "Don't do that, Richard," she said. He was breathing heavily and reached for her breasts. Leaping from the bed, she grabbed his robe and placed it in front of her. She backed to the wall, standing next to his chest of drawers.

"Lily," he said, sitting up. "What's wrong?"

Her chest was rising and falling rapidly, and she couldn't speak. Her skin felt cold and clammy.

He got up and came to her, wrapping her in his arms.

"Don't," she said, pushing him away from her with both hands. "I'm sorry."

His shoulders drooped and he sat on the edge of the bed,

his head in his hands. "It's all my fault," he said. "I just wanted to hold you, but I got carried away."

Lily slipped on the robe and tied it around her. She left the bedroom and headed for the living room. Richard followed, wearing only his pants. She sat on the sofa, her legs pulled underneath her, and stared at the fire. He sat down next to her and put his hands on her shoulders, gently turning her to face him.

"I was wrong. I pushed you. Please forgive me."

She looked into his eyes. "There's nothing to forgive."

"Lily, I can wait. Do you hear me? I can wait. However long it takes you, I'll wait. I want it to be like it was before."

"It may never be like it was before." As she said the words, tears began falling down her cheeks.

He took her head and placed it on his shoulder. "Yes, it will, Lily. We found each other after half a lifetime. There was something wonderful there, beyond the sex. It's just too soon. I should have known."

"You don't even know me."

"I know you enough that I want to marry you. I've watched you for years. Possibly I was even a little in love with you for years."

She broke away and stood, walking to stand in front of the fireplace, her back turned. "Do you know what it means to be sexually dysfunctional?"

"Certainly I know what that means. But you're not sexually dysfunctional. My wife might fit that description, but you're a perfectly normal woman with normal desires. You've just suffered through a rape and it's too soon. That's all."

She turned and faced him. "Maybe there was more than just the rape, Richard." Now, an inner voice screamed. Tell him now. He's not weak like John. Tell him. But the words were locked inside, the key lost.

"What are you trying to tell me? Just tell me one thing. Do you care about me?"

"Yes."

"Then that's all that matters. I'm going to marry you. And you're going to be happier than you've ever been in your life."

If she could only believe him, delude herself into thinking it could actually happen. Maybe they would never find out, and she could suppress it all like the incest. She had to get back to the place she had been before, had to find the road back. She told him, in a voice so low it was almost inaudible, "I want you."

She turned and walked back into the bedroom. No one was going to take this away from her. She untied her robe and let it fall to the floor. There was no past, no memories, no fears. There was only this moment. Tomorrow or the next day they might come and arrest her. She wanted to live first, wanted to taste his love one last time. She was a condemned prisoner sitting down to her last meal.

Under the covers again with Richard beside her, she moved against his body. He didn't reach for her or stroke her, but he became aroused. They turned on their sides, facing each other, and he entered her. Only their connected hips moved back and forth in a slow, unhurried motion, more like a dance than the hungry sex they had experienced before. Lily felt the pleasure begin somewhere in her toes and creep up to her genitals and then her breasts, hitting her brain like a shot of heroin and washing away the pain. She moaned, but he did not stop and did not speed up. Then, with his hands on her ass, he pushed into her deeply for the first time and his body trembled. He did not cry out.

His lips next to her, he whispered, "I love you, Lily."

And she knew it was the truth, for she felt the same. "I'm in love with you too, Richard," she said, the words bringing tears to her eyes and profound sadness. It was all just an illusion, a mirage.

"I'm going to love you for the rest of your life. Nothing

you can do can stop me. However long it takes, and whatever it takes, we're going to make it work."

She took the words, the smells, the feelings, and tried to enlarge them inside her mind. She saw a photo album, the pages all empty, and saw herself carefully inserting these images underneath the plastic, filling the album. Then she saw the last page. On the last page was a bloody, disfigured corpse, but it wasn't Hernandez, it was her. He rolled onto his back, and Lily sat up on the bed. Then she ran to the bathroom and closed the door, falling to her knees and vomiting into the commode.

Richard tapped at the closed door. "Let me in. Let me help you." It sounded as if he was leaning against the door, his voice only inches away.

"Please," she said. "Please don't come in." She flushed the toilet and washed her mouth in the sink. Finding her clothes on the floor, she dressed and opened the door to find him sitting on the edge of the bed, still naked. He stood and she started backing out of the room. Each step he took forward, she moved backward. "Don't love me, Richard. There's nothing to love. Nothing. Do you hear me?"

"Lily, please," he pleaded.

She turned and ran out of the front door, down the steps to her car, looking back at the house as she drove off. Heading down the steep, winding roads, she floored the Honda and drove as though the hounds of Hell were yapping at her feet. The road in front of her was a blur as tears filled her eyes and spilled onto her face. She had no right to happiness, she told herself. No right to pleasure.

After thirty minutes, she found herself on 3rd Street in Oxnard, slamming on her brakes in front of Hernandez's house. She stared at the front of it, watched as the curtains billowed out and were sucked back in by the breeze in the broken window. She saw herself walking in the door and entering the house, finding his bed and sleeping in it, waking to search his room until she found the red sweatshirt and pulling it over her head. Then she would walk out the front door and spread her arms while bullets tore her flesh and her blood pumped on the pavement.

They were locked in an eternal dance, she thought, a bride and groom. When she'd pulled the trigger that morning, the vows had been sealed, the books inscribed. His soul was free, his sins washed clean in blood. She had been left to stand forever at the altar.

With the back of her hand, she wiped her wet face and runny nose, slowly pulling the car away from the curb. Her head fell back and a great hacking noise rose from her chest and echoed off the windows and steel of the car. Laughter. She was laughing. A shotgun wedding, she thought, spewing forth another burst of the hawking. It had been a shotgun wedding.

18.

The phone rang in the darkened bedroom, and at first Lily thought it was the alarm clock. She had been in a deep sleep, the black-out drapes blocking the morning sun. It was Shana.

"Can you come and get me, Mom? I'm ready to come home," she said.

Lily sat up in bed and looked around the room for John, but he was not there and his side of the bed looked undisturbed. Somehow she had forgotten that they no longer slept together, and everything that had happened seemed like a dream. He was probably on the sofa and had not heard the phone. "What time is it?" she asked.

"It's only seven-thirty, but I'm ready to come home. Sorry I woke you. Where's Dad? Did he feed Di today?"

"I don't know . . . maybe he went out for breakfast. Give me the address and directions, and I'll be there as soon as I get dressed." Once she hung up, concern began to rise. Slumber parties almost always lasted until ten or eleven in the morning, the girls staying up late and sleeping late, waking to donuts and milk provided by the parents. In the past Shana had been the last to leave, since the girl who had hosted the party always begged her to stay over far into the day.

As Lily dug in the bottom of her closet and pulled out a pair of rumpled jeans, which she shook to make them somewhat presentable, it dawned on her that her closet was now in worse shape than her daughter's. Looking for some type of top and seeing nothing but dirty laundry, she decided to try Shana's closet.

She walked into the room wearing jeans and her bra. John was asleep in Shana's small bed, his suit, shirt, and tie from the night before flung over a chair. Shana's little puppy was curled up at the foot of her bed. So, this is how it's going to be, she thought. Even John was going forward with his life— while she was sinking deeper and deeper into a bottomless pit. She resisted the urge to kick him, pull the few strands of hair on his head, do anything to inflict pain. Picking up his shirt, she held it to her nose and sniffed it, trying to catch a whiff of perfume, thinking she could then picture the woman he'd been with. She let it fall to the floor, realizing that it didn't matter. As she grabbed a sweatshirt from a stack of freshly washed and folded clothes Shana had stacked on top of her dresser, the thought crossed her mind that she'd probably seen John sleeping more than she'd ever seen him awake during the course of their marriage. When he was awake, he wasn't much different from when he was sleeping anyway.

She saw Shana sitting on the front step of the girl's house as soon as she drove up. She hurried to the car, carrying her sleeping bag, and tossed it in the backseat before getting in the front. Her hair was uncombed and she looked tired.

"Is something wrong?" Lily asked. "Why did you want to come home so early?"

Shana reached into her purse and, taking out her brush, started brushing her hair in the visor mirror. "It's just a bunch of baby stuff. All they do is giggle and act like monkeys."

Shana then pulled out a tube of lipstick, tangerine pink, and carefully applied it to her lips. Satisfied, she pulled the visor down and looked at her mother.

"I want to change schools. I'm sick of this school and the same kids. I've known them all since the first grade."

"Shana, there's only one junior high in Camarillo and you know that. If you tough it out one more year, you'll be in high school and several junior highs feed into that school, so there'll be a lot of new faces."

Lily suddenly wondered if someone had heard about the rape, a fact she'd feared all along. "Shana, has anyone said anything to you . . . you know . . . about what happened?"

"No," her daughter said and her eyes clouded over.

They were stopped at a light and Lily faced her. "Are you telling me the truth?" she asked.

"Of course I am, Mom. No one has said anything and I haven't told anyone either." She wasn't angry that Lily had doubted her, which was out of character. "I've been thinking a lot, and I know you are going to move out again." Lily started to reassure her that she wouldn't leave, but Shana stopped her as her mouth opened. "Just listen, okay. I want to move out with you. We could get a place in Ventura, not *that place* for sure, but another place, and then I could go to Ventura High School. They start in the ninth grade and I would go to high school next year. That would be rad."

Lily took a deep breath, not believing her ears. It was all she had ever hoped for and could solve everything. "What about your dad? I thought you didn't want to leave him."

"Oh, he'll be fine. He has a girlfriend, you know." She caught herself for a moment, putting a hand over her mouth. "I shouldn't have said anything. I promised him I wouldn't."

They arrived at the house. Lily opened the garage door and saw that John's white Jeep was gone. "I knew anyway. He went on a date last night." She thought of herself and Richard, wondering how she could face him at the office after last night, knowing she had no right to criticize John's behavior. "He has every right to go out. We were separated and planning to divorce, so . . ."

Tossing her sleeping bag in a corner in the garage with a sense of finality, as if she would never go to another slumber party in her life, Shana followed her mother into the kitchen. She grabbed a banana, peeled it, and with her other hand started picking food particles out of the cracks in the brown kitchen counter tile. Then she went to her room and came back with her puppy Di in her hands and held her while they talked.

"He's had this girlfriend for a long time, Mom. I know, I've heard him talking to her a lot of nights when you worked late. Sometimes a woman would even call the house and I picked up the phone. Then he up and told me the other day." She started eating the banana, her sapphire eyes bright and wide. "Just can't imagine ol' Dad making out with some woman. If you move out and I stay, this lady will be over here all the time. It makes me sick." She set the puppy on the floor and watched as it scurried off.

Lily had put up a pot of coffee, and not wanting to wait for it to perk, she stuck her coffee cup under the drip pan and removed the pot. Coffee started leaking out onto the counter, and she mopped it up with a paper towel. Shana tossed the banana peel under the sink in the trash can and picked up a sponge and began cleaning the counter.

"But what if I want to see someone . . . you know, a man . . . go on a date? Is that going to make you sick too?" Lily said the words but didn't envision it actually occurring after the night before. All the same, the revelation that John had been seeing someone for some time made her wish that she had given him a swift kick that morning. All the guilt he'd laid on her and he had been carrying on behind her back. She promised herself that she would follow him and spy on him the next time he went out, give him a dose of his own medicine.

Shana tossed the sponge into the sink and threw up her

hands. "Dad's gonna be dating . . . you're gonna be dating . . . shit . . . guess I'll start dating too. We'll be the dating family."

Shana never used profanity. Thinking she was upset, Lily said, "We're all only human. Everyone needs someone in their life, even if it's just for friendship's sake."

"I'm not angry, Mom," she said, smiling. She even walked over and hugged Lily from behind around the waist. "You're pretty, Mom, real pretty, and you're a lot younger than Dad." Lily turned to face her and her eyebrows arched and her eyes sparkled. "All the guys are gonna want to go out with you. I just know Dad's going to bring some boring old lady over here and she's gonna try to be my mom. Besides, Dad babies me to death. He's always hanging on me, kissing me, treating me like I'm still a little kid, his baby doll or something." She grimaced. "I can't stand it. I'm not a baby anymore."

She looked Lily straight in the eye. More was said with that look between them than words could ever say. Lily knew exactly what she was feeling, knew it would be a long time before she would be comfortable with any man, even her father. Even though she was certain that John's behavior was just fatherly love and nothing inappropriate, she knew Shana couldn't tolerate it any longer. "No, you're not a baby anymore, Shana. You're a bona fide young woman." Lily felt tears about to fall. She placed one finger under each eye in an attempt to hold them back. "I'm really, really happy that you want to live with me. I'll do my very best to make you happy."

"Ventura is so cool, Mom, with the beach and all. Let's drive over there today and see where we want to live. Okay?"

Thinking of Richard and the cool breezes and towering trees in the foothills, the feeling she got when she'd been there of being far removed from the city below, Lily knew just where she wanted to look.

"Your dad will have to sell this house. I don't think he can afford it without my salary."

"So, why does he need such a big place? What's he gonna do anyway? Let his girlfriend move in here. I don't want to move back here, not ever."

Lily opened her arms and Shana walked into them. "I love you so much," she said, holding her tightly. "Just your saying that you want to live with me, well, it's all I ever hoped for. You can't possibly know how much I needed to hear this."

Shana pulled back and brushed her mother's hair off her face. "I know a lot more than you think, Mom. Everything's going to be great. Just you wait and see."

CHAPTER 19.

Sunday was visiting day at the Ventura County Jail, and Manny Hernandez was standing in a long line, waiting to sign in, have the metal detector waved over his body and be patted down by one of the jailers. Thursday they had buried his brother. Not much of a funeral, and even that cost enough that his father had to get a loan at the produce company where he worked. Their mother had split years ago, when Manny was a baby and Bobby about six years old.

Finally getting into the visiting area, Manny took a seat in one of the cubicles and picked up the phone to speak with the inmate, while they looked at each other's faces through the thick glass. The prisoner started jabbering in Spanish.

"I dunno what you're fucking saying, bro," Manny said. The man knew he didn't understand Spanish but was always forgetting. His father knew only a few words himself, having been raised in the States.

"You not 'spose to be here, man. Like they check the sign-in to see who's comin' in here to see who."

"My brother is fucking dead an' the cops are all over my

ass. Someways they found out 'bout Carmen. It's bad shit, man. Bad shit. You heard?"

"I hear." The man's face twisted with menace and rage, threatening. "I hear you fucking sleepin' with the cops, man. You gonna be dead meat. That's what I hear."

Manny got up to leave. "I don't got to take shit from no one," he yelled. The man behind the glass stood and put both his palms on the window, jerking his head for Manny to return. Manny took his time, shuffling his feet. Then he picked up the phone again.

"You ain't heard nuthin' 'bout what I say. Not saying shit, man. Not shit. You the ones inside, not me. You ask 'round. Some skinny white guy blowed Bobby away and I want his ass, you hear me? That man's dead I find him. Dead. You get the word or you'll hear plenty."

Manny threw the phone receiver in the metal bin used to pass papers and things to the inmates. The noise was loud enough to attract the attention of the jailer. He was around the corner in seconds.

"Dropped it, man," Manny said, holding his hands up as though he were under arrest and to show he wasn't concealing anything. "Just dropped it, man." With that, he left.

When Manny pulled up to his house, he saw an unmarked police unit at the curb and Cunningham motioning for him to come over. "Motherfucking detective," he yelled, squeezing his fingers on the steering wheel until the knuckles turned white. "Making my skin crawl. Everywhere I go, every time I take a piss, I see this mother."

Slamming the car door, he walked to the police unit and stuck his head in the passenger window. "What you want now? It's Sunday, man. I just got back from mass for my brother. You harassing me, comin' here all the time."

Cunningham sneered, flicking the ends of his mustache with his fingers. "And who are you going to complain to, Manny, my boy? Just who is going to be real concerned about me harassing you? The chief maybe, or the mayor?"

"So whatta you want now? Wanna smell my dick and see if I took a piss today?"

"You lied to me about Carmen Lopez, and you can't imagine what it does to me when people lie to me." Cunningham reached inside his sharkskin suit and pulled out the .38 Smith & Wesson he carried there. He held the gun in his hands and played with it, checking the chamber, taking the edge of his jacket and wiping it down. "I just fucking hate to be lied to by jack shits like you. You said you had never seen Carmen before that night and only picked her up for a cruise. Well, that wasn't true, was it?"

Manny started blinking. Sweat became visible on his brow and upper lip. He slapped the top of the patrol car with his palms. "So I was with her a few times 'fore she moved. Lotsa guys were with her. That ain't no crime."

"Word is that Bobby was hot for her—real hot for her— and maybe he got real pissed when she decided to clean up her act and started dating a high school guy." Cunningham replaced the gun in the shoulder holster.

"Fuck you," Manny said. "Bobby's dead and she's dead. They got the guys who wasted her. Why don't you fucking find the guy who killed my brother? Fuck you."

Manny turned and went into the house. He knew even Cunningham had his limits and would not follow. Things were getting heavy, real heavy, and Manny was getting scared.

CHAPTER 20 ·

The line at In-n-Out Burgers was about twelve cars deep, but Cunningham didn't care. Sunday night was diet night at his house, and he made it a habit to eat out instead of going home as he normally did. His wife, Sharon, as well as all three of their kids, had a tendency to gain weight, so diet night consisted of plain chicken breasts cooked on the grill, with salad and a baked potato without butter. Just thinking of those little dry pieces of meat made him want to gag. His mouth was watering and his stomach roaring for a double-double with cheese and an order of fresh-cooked fries.

While waiting in line, he reviewed all the information he had collected. As far as a lead on the homicide of Bobby Hernandez, he had little or nothing. When one of the little Mexican ladies on the block had called the station and advised a Spanish-speaking officer that she had copied down the license plate of the red compact car, he'd known right away that it was too good to be true. She insisted that the plate was correct, saying she'd checked it several times while the car was parked right in front of her house, a few doors down from the murder scene. Said she got up early to go to work, and her kitchen window looked onto the street. Seeing the car there, parked with the engine running, she smelled trouble and wrote down the license plate just in case. But the lead went nowhere. So far everything had been a dead end. Even the National Crime Information Center in Washington, where he had faxed the composite, and the FBI had no one who was a close enough match to follow through on.

He had a make on the weapon and two slug casings from the scene, but no prints and no weapon. He'd played with the thought of a professional hit, but there was nothing to substantiate it. A professional would have known the first shot was the kill shot and never stayed around, risking apprehension, to fire again. Also, the Hernandez brothers were just not big enough at anything, and in Oxnard, if you wanted somebody dead, it could be had for as little as five hundred bucks and you'd have your choice of shooters. They might not be pros, but they'd stand in line for the job.

The only thing that crossed his mind was the boy who had been murdered with Carmen Lopez, Peter McDonald. If the Hernandez brothers had committed that crime and the family had learned the truth without reporting it, possibly they could have hired someone to murder Hernandez, or even one of the family members themselves had sought revenge. The compact car and the fact that the killer was distinctly Anglo could support such a premise.

He finally made it through the line and got his little sack containing his double-double and fries. He parked and popped the can on his diet soda, purchased at Stop 'n' Go earlier. He liked to save pennies whenever possible. While he sank his teeth into the hot burger, he made a mental note to call the detectives handling the Lopez–McDonald murders in the morning and find out what he could on the McDonald family.

Officially it was not his case, occurring about twenty minutes away in Ventura, but no one would mind, not one little bit, if he could put something together on this baby. And

Manny Hernandez was dirty, as dirty as they come. Not only that, he thought, he was running scared, real scared. One thing Cunningham had a righteous nose for was fear, and he could smell Manny a city block away.

As far as the disappearance of Patricia Barnes, the fat hooker that Hernandez had been dismissed of trying to rape and kidnap, there were no leads whatsoever. No body had been found, even unidentified, and he had checked the entire state. The van had turned up hairs matching those on one of her brushes supplied by her sister, but they already knew she'd been in the van. There were no blood stains or any other evidence in the van or the house that could suggest a murder. Barnes more than likely would waltz in one day in a month or a year and claim her kids. She probably just took a hike. Of course, she could be buried somewhere and her body might never be found. Old Ethel Owen was still out there somewhere. Never know, he thought. That was another benefit of the job: suspense. He thrived on it.

Back at the station, he went to the records counter and seeing Melissa, he smiled, relieved that the bitch was off today. "God, Melissa," he said across the counter, "I'm stuffed like a pig." He extended his stomach and opened his jacket to prove it. "Want me to get you something to eat?"

Melissa placed her cigarette on the edge of the ashtray and sneered at Cunningham. "Thanks but no thanks," she said, bending back down over whatever she was working on and ignoring him. When she picked up the cigarette, he spotted the calluses on her right thumb from writing. She was the best damn worker in the department. The only problem was the girl weighed only about eighty-five pounds dripping wet. She was either anorexic or on speed. No one had figured out which, and everyone wondered.

Melissa's father was an ancient, decaying ex-Hell's Angel, crippled now and in a wheelchair with some rare illness stemming from years of drug abuse. For such a low-life background, the young woman made every attempt to present herself with a degree of class. She wore inexpensive but stylish clothes and wore her dark hair swept back in a sleek knot at the base of her neck. Lately she had become so emaciated that she had to sit on a pillow, no flesh whatsoever on her tailbone.

"Melissa darling," he said, "I have a little project for you and only you. You know you're the best there is in my eyes."

She didn't smile, but she did get up and walk to the counter, leaving the ever present cigarette smoldering in the ashtray. Being sweet-talked was old hat, as she did extra work for half the department. The calluses came from writing patrol officers' reports from their own scribbled notes when they were too lazy to write them.

"I have this murder case with nothing, absolutely nothing," he said. "All I have is this license number, and it's got to be an error."

She looked up at him with her big, soulful eyes and waited for him to fish the number out of his file. "So, you want me to run it with every possible combination. What are we looking for exactly?"

"We're looking for a compact car, red, and I'll take anything with a registered owner in the local area, say a radius of fifty miles or so. Then run D.M.V. for the owner and if it looks even halfway possible, let me see it. Also, check all combinations on anything stolen in the past week or so."

"See you around Christmas, Bruce. That's how long it's going to take for this little job."

She took the paper and returned to her desk, slipping it under her desk blotter. She might act annoyed, but he knew she loved these kinds of projects. Pity, he thought, navigating his big frame down the hall to the detective bureau. She would've probably made the best cop the department had ever seen, but there weren't that many that weighed only eighty-five pounds, not yet anyway. Just then a little man in uniform passed him and he shook his head. As hard as he tried, he just couldn't get used to the munchkins, as he called them. When he had entered this line of work, it had been a world of giants, jock straps, and balls. They were all big and brave then, the town heroes. Now it was midgets, in more than physical stature, men and women who had to resort to brutality and force to make themselves feel superior, to maintain control. Because of a few L.A. cops, and a population that was morally bank-rupt, half the city had been burned down in the riots, and thousands of people were homeless and out of work. Shit like this just didn't happen in Omaha. There was crime, but what was going on around here was madness, moral decay, the end of the line. People were becoming desperate. They had no heroes, no warriors, no protectors, no one left to draw the line. When the cops didn't even know who the good guys were anymore, it was a sad day to be sure.

Yep, he thought, dropping into his chair and swinging his feet on top of the desk, the job just wasn't the same anymore. Trouble was, the fucking world just wasn't the same anymore. Might be getting high time to take out the pencil and paper again and try to find the road out before it was too late, he told himself, before he too was sucked into the sewer with the rest of the rats.

CHAPTER 21 .

After spending the afternoon looking at houses in Ventura, Lily took Shana out to dinner and a movie at her insistence. In the dark theater, she sat and stared at the screen, unable to follow the film. Once they were home and Shana in her room with the door shut, she asked John to discuss something with her in the backyard.

The back door creaked on its hinges as John stepped outside. Lily was sitting in the dark, waiting. There was a full moon and she could see him clearly, her eyes tracking him until he made himself comfortable in the lounge chair.

"So what do you want to talk about?" he said, stretching and yawning.

She sprang from the chair, stood over him, and brought her hand across his face as hard as she could, listening to the loud slap. "You had the unmitigated gall to hit me and order me to move out of this house when it was you . . . you're the one who has been cheating behind my back. If it wasn't for Shana, I'd get a court order and have you physically removed. Do you hear me?"

"I hear you," he said, standing and starting to return to the house.

Lily grabbed the back of his shirt and pulled it. "Don't you dare walk away . . . don't you dare. If you hadn't forced me to move out, Shana would've never been raped and I would never be living this nightmare. You're the one responsible, not me."

Once she let go of his shirt, he faced her, moonlight reflecting off the whites of his eyes. "And you, you're going to look me in the eye and tell me that the other night was the first time you ever cheated on me. What do you take me for, a fool? You're a slut. You've always been a slut. You may be a hot-shot attorney, but you're nothing but a slut."

The back door of the neighbors' house opened, and both Lily and John turned. He moved closer to Lily and lowered his voice. "Now the whole neighborhood is going to know what's going on in this house."

Lily felt his warm breath on her face. "Just tell me one thing, John. How can I be a slut when I've only slept with a few men in my life and one of them raped me?"

"You know what I think? I think you just fabricated that whole stupid story about your grandfather to cover up the fact that you weren't a virgin. I've always thought that."

She was stunned. Letting her body drop to the lawn chair, she laced her fingers through her hair and stared at the ground. She wasn't married to this man, she told herself. There was no way she could have lived all these years with this man, slept in his bed, shared his life, given birth to his child. She listened as he entered the house and shut the door behind him. The train had finally derailed and the cars were all overturned. All that remained was the baggage.

Staying in the chair until the night air burrowed deep in her bones, she looked at the moon and the stars and tried to imagine herself floating there in the dark serenity, far away. Then she walked to the back door and turned the knob. After a few moments of fiddling with it, she realized it was locked.

She started beating on the door with her fists and kicking the wood with her feet.

"Is there anything I can do?" a familiar voice said in the dark.

Lily looked over her shoulder and saw her neighbor peering over the top of the fence. "No, Ruth," she said to the woman, "the door's just stuck. I'll go around to the front. Thanks anyway."

Waiting until the woman disappeared, she walked in the moist grass and tried the front door and found it also locked. Finally she discovered a cracked window, removed the screen, and climbed in. All the lights were turned out and the door to the bedroom bolted from the inside. There was no energy left in her body to continue the fight. She felt small and frail, invisible; she felt erased. Taking a pillow and blanket from the linen closet, she curled up on the sofa. "One one-thousand, two one-thousand, three one-thousand," she counted.

About to leave for the day, early, due to their appointments at the Ventura Police Department to look at photo lineups of possible suspects in the rape, Lily punched the hands-free button on the speaker phone for what had to be her last call. She hadn't arrived at the office until almost noon, waking late in the morning on the sofa in the empty house, and she was now trying to wade through the deep pile of cases on her desk and make one last assignment before leaving. The deep voice of Bruce Cunningham was recognizable without introduction.

"Thought I would let you know what's going on," he said hurriedly, excitedly. "I'm heading out now to Moorpark, where they're digging up a body that fits the description of Patricia Barnes. Seems they were bulldozing for a new housing tract and spotted a leg or something after the first level of dirt had been removed."

Lily slammed back so hard and fast in her chair that it slipped backward on the plastic mat. She pushed herself to the desk with the heels of her shoes and grabbed the receiver. "I'll get one of our investigators over there too," she said. "I want one of our men present when the body is exhumed." She then added quickly, "If you get there before he does, try to preserve the crime scene before they destroy it." Wanting to have him call her at the police station, she hesitated, not willing to disclose her reasons for being there. "Let me give you my home number. Call me around six-thirty or seven. I should be home by then."

She rattled off her number and disconnected, swearing she would purchase a cellular phone, her heart jumping and her mind racing. What she wanted to do was get into her car and go to Moorpark, actually be where she could feast her eyes on death brought about by Hernandez. She wanted to smell the putrid odor, lean over the grave and take the cold, lifeless hand and hold it in her own, seal in her mind the bond they had, both of them victims, sisters. Then perhaps she could exonerate herself, free herself from this nightmare of guilt. But Shana was waiting and the fact that Hernandez had murdered Patricia Barnes was still no more than speculation. The body buried in Moorpark might not even be the prostitute.

She made the necessary call to Investigations and started someone rolling. Then she called Clinton.

He was huffing and puffing when he answered the phone. "Did Cunningham call you?" she asked.

"No, I just walked in the office this second. What's up?"

"They found a body in Moorpark and it may be Patricia Barnes. He's on the way now and I have one of our guys responding."

"Fuck . . ." he said, letting the word roll off his tongue and linger. "You had the guy nailed from the beginning."

"Don't get ahead of yourself, Clinton. It might not be her. That's a virtual dumping ground for homicide victims out there from all over the state." She paused, trying to read his thoughts, knowing how she would feel in his position. "If this is her, she was already dead when you dismissed, so there was nothing you could do. Hernandez is dead anyway."

"But we had him and released him, and I wanted to plead him on a misdemeanor."

"All water under the bridge now," she said, glancing at her watch. "It was only a wild guess on my part in the first place, or woman's intuition, if there is such a thing. Listen," she said, "fill Richard in on what's going on when he gets out of court. I'm leaving now."

"No telling what other crimes he could have committed if someone hadn't killed him." Clinton was thinking out loud, persecuting himself.

Concluding with assurances that she would fill him in on whatever developed, she hung up and rushed from the office to pick up Shana. If he only knew, she thought.

CHAPTER **22** ▪

"Shana," Lily yelled the moment she walked into the house. "Come on, we're late."

John had a pile of raw hamburger in a big bowl and was mixing it with ketchup, raw egg, and onions. He was making his second favorite dish after roast chicken: meat loaf. When she came through the door, he wiped his red-smeared hands on a paper towel, and Lily thought instantly of blood and severed arms. Shana appeared in the kitchen, dressed neatly in a button-down blouse, a black skirt, and the low heels they had purchased for her to wear to the last dance at school. Her hair was pulled back with a clip at the nape, the way Lily frequently wore her own hair, and she looked more like fifteen than thirteen. Her eyes were solemn.

"Go ahead and get in the car, sweetie," she said. "You look so pretty. I just have to run to the bathroom."

"Isn't she gorgeous?" John said, walking over and grabbing her around the waist and hugging her.

Just as he started to kiss her, she pulled her face away and glared at him. "Stop it. I told you not to do that anymore. I'm too old for that stuff."

John stepped back, his mouth open, obviously hurt. Exchanging only detached eye contact with him when he looked at her for an explanation of Shana's behavior, Lily rushed to the master bathroom and closed the door behind her, removing a little bottle from the medicine cabinet. She dropped on her knees in front of the white porcelain commode, feeling nauseous, but nothing happened. Her child was living through the same pain and confusion she had suffered, not knowing why she felt the way she did, uncertain who to trust, isolating herself from other young people. Removing one of the little pink pills, Valium, and tossing it into her mouth, she leaned down to the sink and swallowed it with tap water. There was only one pill left. She would have to get it refilled tomorrow.

The Ventura Police Department was housed in a brandnew building, on a street named after a sergeant who had been killed in the line of duty: Dowell Drive. Lily recalled when the department had been housed in a couple of trailers, attached to an old run-down building. Now it was all carpet, and each desk sported a computer terminal. The detective met them in the lobby. Lily had known the woman for years.

Detective Margie Thomas was close to retirement—or beyond, for that matter, probably surpassing the twenty-year mark several years before and electing to stay on as long as she could pass the physical. There was no doubt that this was her life and adjustments following her retirement would be difficult. She was the first woman police officer in Ventura, the first to make detective, and the first to earn the respect of her male counterparts. Her hair was tinted a shade too dark to be flattering; she was heavy in the lower section of her body, making it look like she had an old-fashioned bustle underneath her shirtwaist navy blue cotton dress. With thick, painted-on eyebrows and eyes almost a shade of lavender, she made Lily think of Elizabeth Taylor during her boozy, blubbery days.

Margie took one of Shana's hands, sat down on the lobby

sofa with her, and just looked her over. "How you doing, doll?" she asked. "Boy, are you a pretty thing. You've got your mom to thank for that hair, that's for sure."

Shana didn't smile and slipped her hand from the detective's. "I'm doing fine," she answered politely. "I'd feel a lot better if you caught him, though."

Realizing she had never discussed this possibility with Shana, Lily wondered if she thought about this often, maybe at night in her room before she went to sleep, or in the early hours when she got up long before anyone else. If she could only assure her that he would never hurt anyone again.

"Okay, this is what we're going to do today," Margie said, her voice light and breezy, as if they were going to have fun or something. "I've prepared some pictures of men who resemble the man you and your mother described and have backgrounds that make them possible suspects. I'm going to let you sit at my desk, Shana, and look at half the pictures. Your mom will sit in the other room and look at the other half, and then you'll exchange. If you see someone that resembles the man who attacked you, you write down the number by his name. You may see several faces and not be certain, but that's okay. Just be sure to write down all the numbers." She paused and looked at Shana only, aware that Lily was all too familiar with the routine. "If you do see someone, then we can try to get this man in for a real lineup so that you can be absolutely certain." She stopped and stood, adding, "Any questions and I will be right across the room. Okay?"

Lily started thumbing through the photos, seeing a number of men she'd prosecuted through the years, sometimes amazed that they were back on the street and trying to recall the exact particulars of each case. One face she remembered from years back, noting how he'd aged and recalling the ten or twelve counts of indecent exposure she'd prosecuted and plea-bargained down to two counts and ninety days in jail. They called these men "weanie wavers," and statistics proved they seldom committed more serious offenses. Shouldn't even be in the lineup, Lily thought.

After about ten minutes, she was eager to pick up the phone on the desk of the small, glass-enclosed office she was occupying and call Oxnard P.D. to see if she could contact Cunningham. It was too early, anyway, she decided and continued to look at the faces, no longer actually seeing them, letting her thoughts roam.

Looking at the photos the way they were presented made her think of the proofs professional photographers give their clients to make their selections, and she realized that it had been over a year since Shana's last portrait. She would have to have one done in another month or so. She glanced through the glass and saw her daughter intently staring at each face on each page at Margie's desk. Thinking this whole process was a catharsis in many ways for Shana, she was glad that John had called the police. Considering the way things were shaping up, and with the simple fact that what she had done was done and there was no going back, Lily thought that someday she might be able to detach herself from that terrible morning in Oxnard.

If he had murdered Patricia Barnes in order to prevent her from testifying against him, merely fulfilling that first mission that Lily had suspected all along—to kill her—then he might have followed the same pattern with her and her daughter. Perhaps God had intervened and it was His hand that guided her that night. It was His voice Lily had heard in her mind and not the ghost of her dead father. Recalling the religious fervor of her early childhood, she vowed she would take Shana to the Catholic church one Sunday.

Deep in thought, she jumped when the door to the small office opened and Margie appeared with Shana. The policewoman was holding something in her hands and she took a seat next to Lily. Shana was ashen and wide-eyed, her hands by her side, an excited expression on her face. Margie opened her mouth to speak, but Shana blurted out: "I found him. I know it's him. I'm certain. Show her," she urged, reaching over and pushing Margie's shoulder. "Show her. She'll know it's him too."

Lily felt perspiration oozing from every pore in her body and knew that she would be drenched in seconds. Waiting for the heavy pressure in her chest signaling a heart attack, she felt blood rush from her face.

Margie saw her distress. "My God, you look ill," she said and turned to Shana with a degree of urgency. "Go and get your mother some cold water from the water cooler—right at the back of the room you were in. And bring some paper towels from the bathroom and soak them in cold water. Hurry, now." Shana ran from the room.

"Do you want me to call an ambulance?" she said to Lily, seeing the moisture darkening the pale green blouse she was wearing, watching as beads of sweat dropped from her forehead, over her nose, and down her chin. "Are you having chest pains?"

Lily tried to monitor her breathing and calm herself. She felt like there was a tight band around her chest and suddenly remembered the shingles. She was just having a panic attack, long overdue. Shana had seen a photo of someone who resembled Hernandez, and she would realize it was the wrong man as soon as she saw him in person. "I'm okay. Just too much pressure, I guess. I've even had a case of shingles, so . . ."

"I had those too one time," Margie said sympathetically. "Boy, do they hurt. Nerves. That's what they said caused it."

Shana returned, her mouth tight with concern, carrying the wet towels and a cup of ice water. She handed them to her mother and stood back, watching while Lily wiped her face and the back of her neck, and then left the soggy, cold paper towels resting on her neck while she sipped water from the Styrofoam cup. "I'm fine," she said, reassuring Shana. "Might even be coming down with the flu or something." She placed her hand on her forehead as if checking for a fever. "Just give me a minute and I'll look at the photo."

"Relax," Margie said. "You can even go home and come back in the morning. One more day—"

"No," Shana said, her voice louder than normal, insistent, "let her see it now. Then you can put him in jail."

The detective turned and took Shana's hand. "Just give your mom a minute, honey. This has been real hard on her too. Even if your mom agrees that this man resembles the man who attacked you, we can't just go out and arrest him. You'll have to see him in a real lineup, and we'll have to get an order from a judge to arrest him. That's the way it works."

Shana stared impatiently at Lily, impervious to whatever was wrong with her, wanting her to confirm her selection. Lily could see her chest rise and fall visibly with each breath.

"Okay," Lily said. "Let's see the photo."

Asking Shana to return to the desk she had been at previously, the detective handed Lily a stack of pages with photos just like the ones she had been looking at before they had entered.

"Go through each one slowly and don't respond just because she has told you she saw someone. I told her to remain outside, but she followed me in here. If you do select someone, it should be completely independent." Seeing that Lily appeared in control, she said, "I'm going to step outside. Come out when you're through."

As she searched each page, she now was really looking, wanting to see the man Shana had seen, certain that he resembled Hernandez but knowing that half of Oxnard resembled Hernandez. She occasionally glanced out the window of the office, looking for Shana. She was out of visual range. Margie had more than likely taken her to the vending machines for a soda or to the rest room. On about the twentieth page of photos, she saw him.

My God, a dead ringer, she thought, leaving no question

as to why Shana had become so excited. Even if he was not the right man, simply seeing his face propelled her back to the fear and humiliation, the degradation of that night. Her pain for what her daughter had suffered was agonizing. The man had an almost identical shape to his face, his eyes, his nose, his mouth. Even the way his hair was cut was similar to Hernandez's. He looked younger, however, and Lily knew he was not the rapist. He couldn't be. The rapist was dead.

She took her time and studied his face closely. She recalled how photographs were sometimes miles apart from the actual person. They were one-dimensional, and this man in the flesh, in profile, in body conformation, could look entirely different, she rationalized. Removing the paper towels from her neck, she felt the crisis had passed. Just go through the motions, she told herself, and even agree that he looks somewhat like the attacker, because it would be absurd to say anything different. So what if the guy had to be yanked in for a lineup? He'd done something at one time or another to place himself in this position. She certainly wasn't going to worry about some unknown man with a criminal history at this point. Once they saw him, the whole thing would be dropped. Lily would state that he wasn't the man and that would be it.

She picked up the package of photos and calmly left the office. Margie and Shana were walking through the doors to the detective bureau, where six desks were lined up, three to a side. It was six-thirty and only one detective was still working, files open, phone in his ear, his feet on the desk. Shana held a Coke in her hand and appeared subdued but anxious. Lily had her finger on the page containing the photo of the man she was certain Shana had picked.

The three of them met in the center of the room. "I admit, I have one that's real close, but I'm pretty sure it's not the man," Lily said without enthusiasm. Seeing the taut look of frustration in Shana's eyes, she quickly added, "But it's real close and worthy of additional investigation."

Setting the photos down on Margie's desk, she turned to

the correct page and placed a finger on his face. "Number thirty-six is the one I picked." Her look was questioning, but she didn't have to wait long for a response.

"That's him," Shana said, turning to the detective eagerly. "Told you. That's him. Number thirty-six."

"Shana, I don't feel as positive as you. I want you to know that from the start, and remember, I got a better look at him when he was leaving. You were terribly distraught."

The visual image of him standing in the light from the bathroom appeared in Lily's mind: the red sweatshirt, the profile—she even recalled the top of his head as he bent down to snap his pants. She glanced back down at the photo, but also noticed the other men on the page. Out of six, two were wearing a red T-shirt or sweatshirt. Red was a gang color. She knew that—every other Hispanic in Oxnard wore red and those silly baseball caps. She then started thumbing back through the pages and saw more red shirts. One man was wearing a gold chain with a crucifix. She turned the page and saw another one, only smaller. If she let her imagination go now, she might end up in a mental institution. The man she had shot was the man. It must end there and end now.

"*Mom*, you didn't even have your glasses on that night, and you don't have them on now," Shana snapped. "He raped me, remember, and I can see perfectly." She turned to Margie and said sarcastically, "She's supposed to wear them when she drives too, but she never does."

"I only really need them to read—just a little farsighted," Lily informed the detective. "Anyway, arguing over it right now is counterproductive. Can you pull him in for a lineup?"

"I'll get right on it and call you as soon as it can be arranged. Why don't you two go home now and get some rest and try to put this out of your mind?" As Shana walked past her mother, heading for the door, Margie gave Lily a look with those Liz Taylor eyes and shrugged her shoulders. "Life's a bitch, isn't it?" she said.

"You got that right," Lily replied and started walking out, trying to catch Shana.

Margie's voice projected and echoed in the large room. "Oh, I'm sure I don't have to mention this, but it might not be a bad idea for you to wear those glasses when I can get this guy in here for the real thing." She returned to her desk, sat down, shifting from side to side until her flesh-and-blood bustle was comfortable, and then turned her back on Lily.

By the time Lily made it out of the building, Shana was waiting by the passenger door of the Honda. As she started the car, Lily told her, "They'll get the lineup together and we'll go from there, okay?"

The girl was staring straight ahead. They rode in silence for quite some time. "Why don't you turn on the radio?" Lily suggested.

"He's still out there. I know it now. I thought he'd run away. He didn't. He's still out there. You told me he'd go far away and never come back so he wouldn't get caught."

Lily hesitated, torn now, not knowing exactly what to say and thinking she must call the psychologist and get Shana in to see her tomorrow. She felt that assuaging her rising fear was the right thing to do, even if she became angry. "I really feel he's long gone, honey, and like I said back there, I don't think it's him. I can see things far away better than I can close up: that's what farsightedness means. When he was close, it was very dark, but when he was leaving, he was farther away and in the light." She reached for her hand, holding it tightly. "I don't think the man you saw was him. He's gone. You're a smart girl. You know a lot of people look alike. Even you and I look alike, but of course, I'm a lot older. If we were the same age, people could mistake us even. See?"

Shana reached out and turned on the radio, a rock station. She then said over the noise, "It was him, Mom. When you see him with your glasses, then you'll know."

CHAPTER 23.

En route to Moorpark, Cunningham pushed the speedometer up to eighty on the two-year-old Chrysler sedan and felt the chassis shake beneath him, but the large engine had the capacity to break a hundred with no problem. He sometimes missed the days behind the wheel of a screaming black-and-white, the radio turned full tilt to hear the dispatcher over the siren, the streets coming up in seconds, knowing each time he raced through an intersection he could collide in a mammoth marriage of metal, his life over, or arrive at the scene of whatever hot call he was rolling to and meet some nut with a shotgun ready to blow him to kingdom come. Those were the brawn and balls days, far behind him. These were the days when he went home with a headache instead of a black eye or a bruised kidney. These days he had to use what was between his ears.

It was hard for him to imagine any other job, no matter how much he tried and how much he complained. He quite simply loved it. With a dozen stories with open endings going on at the same time, he always had something to occupy his mind. Trying to put together the missing pieces in a homicide was to Cunningham like completing the *New York Times* cross-word puzzle in ink: always having the little puzzle in his back pocket to play with, yet aware that he had to find just the right word and make sure it fit perfectly before he filled in the blank spaces with his pen. He was not a man who made mistakes. Mistakes lead to guilty men walking free on the streets, thumbing their noses at law officers who were hasty and sloppy.

Thinking of the case at hand, and the issue of jurisdiction if the body was in fact Patricia Barnes, he was certain the sheriff's department would be more than pleased to kick the case to his side of the fence. The victim had been seen last in Oxnard, reported missing in that city, and the primary suspect was now the victim of an Oxnard homicide investigation. There were far too many Oxnards in this little puzzle and not enough Moorparks. Knowing this information already, even though a positive identification hadn't been made, the sheriff's department was probably handling it like anything else that was on the burner: to be handed off like a hot potato. And that meant mistakes.

He took his foot off the gas once he left the main road. It didn't take him long to determine that he was in the right place. Three county black-and-whites were parked along an unpaved but graded dirt road where a new housing tract was going in: a white van belonging to the medical examiner, an unmarked police unit, and a black-and-white crime-scene unit. Other than two bulldozers and a few other pieces of construction equipment, no other civilians appeared to be present and, thank God, he thought, no reporters or television remote vans as yet. The professionals themselves frequently trampled and destroyed valuable evidence. Reporters and onlookers were a homicide investigator's worst nightmare.

He flung the door to his unit open and removed his shield from his back pocket, flipped it, and hung it on his belt a few inches from the buckle. "Shit," he said, stepping out into the soft dirt and sinking. The day before, he had finally taken a few minutes to have his worn-out black shoes polished and shined while he had a haircut. Now they were filthy again and would look even worse than they had before. Waste of money, he thought as he started marching in the direction of the uniforms, knowing it wasn't really messing up his shoes that annoyed him. What he never got used to was finding the rotting remains of people, thrown away like useless garbage.

Charlie Daniels, the medical examiner, was leaning over the edge of the shallow grave, holding up a dirt-covered arm with a plastic gloved hand. He dropped it when he saw Cunningham. "Your case, my man?" he asked. "Go on. Take a look. Couple more pictures and we're gonna take her out."

"Who's crime scene here?" Cunningham yelled at the group, and a man dressed in a white sheriff's office shirt and black pants stepped forward.

The two men backed away from the others and, looking at the ground as they spoke, the crime-scene officer filled Cunningham in on what had transpired prior to his arrival. "My partner is reloading the camera in the unit," he said. "As soon as we got here, we made a pretty extensive search of the area before we allowed anyone else to disturb it. Even the construction worker was pretty cool. Once he saw what he thought was the body, he went and called and didn't go back. We picked up a lot of junk, and it's bagged and in the van." The name on the man's shirt read TOM STAFFORD.

"Okay, Stafford," Cunningham said. A bulldozer had run right over the whole thing, eliminating such vital evidence as tire marks or indications of how far and from where the body had been dragged to its grave. They would expand the search for evidence in a wider circle as the investigation progressed, and although they might have picked up various items, there was no way to know if they were related to the homicide until forensics got to them. "I guess you would have told me if you found a weapon or something, right?"

"No such luck. Not unless you think she was killed with a couple of beer cans, a candy wrapper, or the carcass of what looks like a cat."

Stepping to the edge of the grave now that he was satisfied that the crime scene had been secured and as much evidence collected as possible, Cunningham looked down at the corpse. He had little doubt it was Patricia Barnes. It sure wasn't Ethel Owen. Ethel was a tiny woman, and this woman was far from small.

"We dusted her off enough for you to see her face," the medical examiner offered. "She's a big one, huh?"

Almost every orifice of her body was filled with dirt, and her mouth was a large, open circle, probably the last scream of terror before death. Her eyes were also open, but small animals had feasted on a good portion of them and little was left. As Cunningham reached into his pocket and pulled out three photos of the woman given him by her sister, Daniels leaned over again and scraped more dirt off her open mouth. Scooping it out with a gloved finger, he exposed a dried-up, purplish tongue extending onto her bottom lip. Around her neck were distinct discolorations, but there appeared to be no other wounds.

"Strangulation?" Cunningham asked, expressing his opinion on the cause of death. The protruding tongue and marks on her throat were classic.

"Well now, we haven't turned her over. Just might have a knife sticking out of her back, but from this viewpoint I would agree." With that the medical examiner stood and stretched his back—he then took a white handkerchief out of his pocket and wiped the sweat off his forehead. "You give the word, and we take her out and have a look."

Before Cunningham answered, the M.E.'s assistant and one of the crime-scene men started toward the body. "Go," he said.

It was his girl. The black short skirt and bright pink sweater she had been reported wearing when missing locked it up. He watched as they removed her: three good-sized men, still straining under the dead weight. Although she was fat and out of shape, in the pictures he had seen a pretty face and a pleasant smile. Some men liked big women, he speculated, wondering just how much she got for turning a trick but certain it wasn't much. She sure wasn't pretty now.

They placed her on a plastic sheet and rolled her onto her stomach, the M.E. brushing off dirt with his hand and then lifting her sweater and checking her back. "*Nada*, my man. No reason to remove her skirt here. Nothing there that I can see. We'll cut it off later and bag it." She was still wearing what looked like panty hose. The M.E. stuck his hand up the back of her skirt, like a ventriloquist, and after feeling around, he withdrew it. "No signs of sexual assault right now, as the crotch is still in place—unless he raped her somewhere else and then had her dress, come here, and then strangled her," he said, standing. "Believe me, no one but this lady herself could get that panty hose over that ass in one piece. They feel like they're steel-belted anyway." He laughed and the laughter spread through the crowd of men. They welcomed it. Even in the open air, the smell of decomposing flesh was overpowering, and many turned away. The M.E. was waving his hands over his head, swatting at a fly.

Cunningham looked down at the large lump of flesh that had once been a living, breathing human being: a mother, a daughter, a sister to others who cared. The only thought that came to mind was that the poor creature would never suffer ridicule again over her weight, never have to suck some guy's dick to feed her two kids, and would never have to worry about retirement. Her troubles were over. Maybe this sad life had earned her another as a rich, skinny Beverly Hills beauty. Sure, he thought, like reincarnation. As far as he was concerned, that was the one good thing about death: no one really knew who the winners and losers were on the other side. It was a hell of a lot better not knowing.

While more photographs were taken of both the body and the empty grave, and Officer Stafford started looking for evidence in the grave itself, the investigator from the district attorney's office arrived, eyes squinting from the sunlight without shades, complaining that he'd taken a wrong turn and ended up in the middle of nowhere. Cunningham filled him in, but related that he would call Lily Forrester himself as soon as he could spring free.

The press arrived, complete with a film crew, just as they were placing Patricia Barnes in a body bag. The place was rapidly becoming a zoo. Cunningham removed his shield and placed it in his pocket, finding the first uniform that responded.

"Once the body is removed, you clear and write up your report and fax it to my office, with my name on it."

"It's not much," the young officer stated, "just the statement from the construction worker and who I notified, you know. My sergeant said he spoke with you, and it's your case if you claim it. With the riots and all, a lot of our men have been working in L.A., and we're hardly able to handle what we have already."

Before he could make a formal statement along these lines, he would have to get her sister to meet him at the morgue for a positive ID and clear it with the captain. "As far as the press are concerned—and anyone else, for that matter—she's an unidentified homicide victim as of this moment. Got it?" he instructed the officer. "You better write it like it's yours right now and tell your sergeant I said so. I'll call him later this evening."

He tapped Daniels on the shoulder as he walked to his unit, while they loaded the body. "I'll get the victim's sister in tonight, if I can find her. You gonna be around, Charlie?"

"Not tonight, my man. Day's over for me. Call or come by around three tomorrow afternoon," he yelled over the roar of a passing plane.

Two hours later, Cunningham exited the morgue with Anita Ramirez, the identification made. The woman was crying and blubbering, rattling on about the kids, telling Cunningham that she had three of her own and didn't know how she could raise another two. Thank God she had arrived with several other family members and collapsed in their arms, freeing him to leave. He went to a pay phone and called his captain.

After he got the okay to handle the case, he started to hang up and call Forrester when the captain stopped him. "Bruce, I have some bad news about the Owen homicide."

He froze. The case was down. The defendant sentenced to prison. He waited, holding his breath, thinking Ethel Owen had suddenly walked into the police station after an extended vacation in Europe and made them all look like a bunch of idiots.

"They called while you were out today. Franco Andrade was released on bail today pending appeal of the conviction."

"What the fuck . . . ?"

"Look, Bruce, the evidence was completely circumstantial. It was a minor miracle the jury even delivered a guilty verdict to begin with. You knew he appealed. Well, the judge felt the case was weak enough to merit his release on bail. What can I tell you, guy? Win some, lose some."

He hung up and kicked the brick wall by the phone, almost breaking his toe and putting a jagged hole in the end of his shoe. Another killer released on the street. All that work for nothing. The appeal could take years, and that slimy bastard would just find another old woman to prey on or fucking kill. He was livid. All they were doing was chasing their own tails around and around in little circles like a bunch of mongrel dogs.

"Win some, lose some," he said between clenched teeth, repeating his captain's words as he picked up the phone to call Lily Forrester. "Fucking lose some and then some is what I'd call it. Fucking disgrace is what. Judge's own mother should meet up with Franco and see how he likes it." Before he tossed in the coin, he looked up at the sky. The sun was setting and it was getting dark. The air was still thick with ashes from the fires in L.A., and his white shirt was sprinkled with it. "We tried, Ethel," he said. "That's about all we can do. We can try."

CHAPTER 24 ∎

L ily was sitting in the bedroom by the phone when Cunningham called. She had been waiting. His deep, strong
voice had somehow become her link to sanity. The knowledge
that he was her adversary disappeared whenever she heard his
voice. Even the recollection of his face vanished, and all that
remained was the disembodied sound that traveled through the
telephone lines.

"No stab wounds or mutilations whatsoever?" Lily quizzed
him, thinking of the crusty knife and also the McDonald–Lopez
case, which had involved a small-caliber handgun. "What do
we really have to link this to Bobby Hernandez other than the
fact that she disappeared just prior to his arrest?" She was
certain he was the rapist, certain he had murdered the prostitute, but everything was still a hazy gray and what she needed
was black and white.

"Not a thing. For all we know, anyone could have strangled
her in her line of work. We'll go back over the van again, but
even if he did her and transported her in that van, there
wouldn't be much evidence, not with strangulation."

He was silent. Only the soft sounds of their breathing came over the phone line. It was as if they were both in the same room, only a few feet away, both deep in thought.

"The case is certainly not closed," he said, putting an end to the strange silence.

"What about Hernandez? Any leads whatsoever?" Lily asked matter-of-factly. She then added, "You know my primary concern is Manny, his brother, and whether we can put them into the McDonald–Lopez homicides."

"No leads on Bobby and as yet nothing to write home about on that one either, other than the known associations. We could put a surveillance team on Manny if you put the pressure on. I think we can substantiate it."

"You got it," she said. "I'll make the calls first thing in the morning." Before hanging up, she added. "Bruce, we need a break on McDonald–Lopez and we need it bad. We may have a couple of innocent young men on trial for murder one."

"I hear you, babe," he said. "You know what, you're my kind of woman. I bet there's not a D.A. down at your place who gives a shit who they try as long as they get a conviction." The line went dead. Cunningham had hung up.

John came into the bedroom. "So tell me," he said, "do you think this is the guy? That animal . . . I should blow his head off."

Lily was sitting on the corner of the bed, near the nightstand and phone, the bedside lamp shooting rays of light through her bright red hair. She turned to John and her eyes narrowed and blazed an almost catlike green. "I already did that," she said.

"Did what?"

"You heard me."

"No, I didn't hear you. What did you do?"

"I killed him."

"You killed him?"

"No, I didn't kill him."

John reached into his pocket and took out a cigarette. He

rolled it around in his fingers with a baffled look on his face. "Shana said you got sick at the police station. Said they almost had to call an ambulance. Now you're talking like a nut case. What in the hell are you trying to say?"

Lily's body was still facing the wall, her head turned to John. "I meant to say I wish I could kill him."

"Yeah, well, I wish I could kill him too. But why did you tell Shana that he wasn't the right man?"

"Because he isn't the right man. Leave me alone, John." Lily was still staring, her voice a low monotone.

John started to walk toward the bedroom chair, his eyes still on Lily, a look of concern on his face.

"Don't sit down, John. I said to leave me alone and I meant it."

Her eyes stopped him; the words were hardly needed. He stood in the center of the room, his hands by his side, afraid to move.

"You know what's wrong with this world, John? People don't listen. That's what's wrong. People just don't listen."

He turned and left. Lily walked to the bathroom, looked in the mirror, and poured out the last Valium. Then she found the sleeping pills the doctor had prescribed for Shana and removed one of those as well. She put her face under the tap and let the water run into her open mouth. She stared at her face until the awareness that it was her own reflection began to fade and she searched the image. She could see her eyelashes fluttering, her nostrils slowly opening and closing, tiny beads of tap water on her open mouth. She wanted to move her flesh-and-blood body behind that image, allow the cold glass of the mirror to separate her from the outside world, where she could still see and be seen but where there was protection.

That night she didn't even bother to take off her clothes. All she could think about was the face she'd seen that day, the man so uncannily like Hernandez that he could be his brother. Then she recalled the men in the photo lineup, every one wearing a red shirt and a crucifix around their neck. "No," she kept saying, trying to force her racing thoughts to stop, waiting for the pills to hit her bloodstream. It was nothing more than a coincidence, a fluke. It had to be. Finally she entered a drugged, dreamless void in the green blouse now stained from her perspiration, still wearing her skirt and panty hose, her bra tight around her chest.

CHAPTER 25.

Lily showered and dressed for work, grabbing the first thing she saw in her closet, feeling listless from the drugs. She then saw her reflection in the bedroom mirror and realized that she had worn the same suit only two days before. She stripped and suddenly found herself holding both the top and bottom of her favorite black-and-white outfit with the buttons up the side. The top had been cleaned and returned to her closet. All of her laundry had also been washed and folded and was stacked neatly in plastic bins in the closet.

Buttoning up the side buttons of the skirt and adjusting the top, she felt the loose fabric and stepped on the bathroom scales. She'd lost eight pounds since she had last weighed herself. With her hair pulled back, her cheeks looked sunken and her face drawn. She removed the clip from her hair and brushed it out, deciding to get it cut the following day. Something neat and soft around her face maybe—something more stylish. What she really wanted was to look in the mirror and see someone else.

When she got to the kitchen, Shana was dressed and eating

a bowl of cereal at the breakfast table. Di was eating her breakfast too, right at Shana's feet. She jumped up and poured her mother a cup of coffee, handing it to her.

"You did all my laundry, didn't you?" Lily asked quietly. "That was really nice, Shana. I appreciate it a lot."

Shana was placing her cereal bowl in the dishwasher and picked up the sponge and washed off the sink. "It was nothing, Mom." She turned and faced Lily. "You work hard and you've been so tired lately. I'm worried about you."

"Come here," Lily said, holding her arms out. Shana walked into them and hugged her around the waist. "What about you, baby? Are you okay?"

Shana pulled away, mustering up a smile. "I'm fine. You know"—she looked at Lily as if she would know exactly what she meant—"some days are okay and some are terrible. Like if you let it get to you and think about it all the time. But I'm trying not to do that." She took her little puppy to her room, covered the floor with papers, and shut the door.

Lily drove her to school and watched her walk into a crowd of young people. Once she was a few feet away, her shoulders slumped and Lily had to look away. She'd never really understood her own daughter's magical personality. Shana hadn't just been born with it; she had worked to acquire and maintain it, just like a great athlete or concert pianist. But the rape had taken away the laughter and the optimism, and Lily wondered if she would ever be the same.

Richard was in the hall leading to her office, waiting when she arrived, a tentative smile on his face, a steaming cup of hot coffee in his hand, and reeking in familiar lime. "And a good morning to you," he said, his mouth dropping somewhat at her solemn expression. "You look good. Great dress, but do I sense a rotten mood this morning?"

Lily had a pink slip in her hand, handed to her by one of the secretaries on the way in, stating that Detective Margie Thomas had called. Richard followed her into her office and took a seat. Lily looked at the stack of cases in her incoming bin, and an even deeper furrow developed in her brow. "Sorry," she said, "guess it's that time of the month or something. PMS." Her smile barely lifted the corners of her mouth and then collapsed again.

Richard moved his chair closer to her desk, reached across, and picked up the entire stack of files in the bin, placing them on the floor next to him. "Now, does that make you feel any better? I got here at six-thirty and have already cleared my desk. Tell me how it went yesterday with Shana."

"First of all, Richard, I don't want you to make it a habit of covering for me and absorbing the entire work load of this unit." Lily's voice was a lot harsher than she had intended.

"Don't you think that you're defeating the purpose of me sharing the responsibilities if I can't cut you some slack when the going gets rough? You should have really taken some time off, you know. And Butler knows that too."

Her emotionalism the other night with him had diminished her in his eyes. She could see it clearly. Insisting that he put the cases back would be useless. "Thanks, Rich. The body they found in Moorpark was Patricia Barnes. Cunningham called me last night after her sister identified her."

"And . . ." he said.

"She was strangled and not much evidence links it to Hernandez, but they're working on it. Cunningham wants us to make some calls and see if we can get a surveillance team on his brother, Manny, hoping we can get something, anything, to determine if they were involved in the McDonald–Lopez slayings."

"What happened with the lineup?" he asked again, concern in his eyes.

"There's a suspect. She's positive; I feel exactly the opposite. He looks like the guy but isn't." Lily saw her glasses on the desk where she left them every day and seized them, slipping them on. "Because I don't wear my damn glasses, Shana thinks I couldn't really see him, but I'm only a little farsighted, and I guarantee you that I saw the bastard."

"But maybe she's right and you're wrong. Ever think of that? What's his status? Are they picking him up?" Richard spoke between clenched teeth, sitting up straight in the chair.

Lily bristled. "Don't get involved in this, Richard." She again regretted her harshness and hurried to close the door to her office, not wanting anyone to hear. She returned to her desk and bent over, speaking in a whisper. "I'm sorry I reacted like that . . . I know you care about me and it's natural for you to want to know what's going on, but if I let this—this . . . you know, you and I talking about it in the office every day . . . well, I just can't handle it."

"Say no more," he said, touching her hand quickly and then removing it. "I understand. Tell me what you want me to know. I won't mention it again. And let's have dinner tonight."

Lily sighed deeply, started to say no, and then recalled that Shana had softball practice tonight and she would be alone in the empty house. If she could get her in to see the psychologist after practice and John could take her . . . ? "I'll let you know a little later. It's possible," she said. "I'm sorry about the other night." Instead of looking at him, she focused on the glass partition, watched as one of the secretaries passed with an armful of papers.

"The other night was my fault, Lily. I'm the one who was insensitive. After you left, I felt like a jackass."

She tried to bring forth memories of their first night together and the next day in the interrogation room. Had that person really been her? It seemed like another lifetime. "I'll call you later," she said softly.

As he bent down and picked up the stack of cases, she pushed Butler's extension on the phone and started her pitch for a surveillance team on Manny Hernandez. Richard reached over and touched the back of her neck before leaving, causing a shiver to race up and down her spine.

After getting Butler to agree to call Oxnard P.D. and put the necessary pressure on, she tried to reach Margie Thomas. They informed her that the detective was in the field. The psychologist, however, was in and agreed to see Shana at eight o'clock. Shana and her father could pick up a bite to eat after the softball practice, leaving her free to have dinner with Richard.

"And are you going to come in?" the psychologist asked Lily.

"I came in with Shana last week," she said.

"I mean for a session. I really feel you need to work through this ordeal as well as your daughter."

Lily knew she could never sit down and spill her guts to this woman. There was far too much she could never discuss with anyone. Thinking of the woman's loafers and white socks, she felt like she would be telling her life story, with all its dark secrets, to one of Shana's school friends. "I'm really more concerned here with my daughter, and I don't have the time." The psychologist cleared her throat, sort of a humph, as if she heard this line every day. Lily continued: "I want you to talk to her about why she has suddenly decided that she wants to transfer out of the school system and move in with me. It would solve a lot of problems for me." Lily realized that sounded self-centered and corrected herself. "What I mean is that my husband and I are planning to divorce, and you're aware that I moved back in because of the rape. So, I want to be near Shana and I want to move out. But I don't want to encourage her to do something that will be harmful to her."

"It's a two-sided coin," the woman said. "Remaining in a home with two people who are obviously living together for her benefit, and specifically because of the assault, coupled with the tension that has to be present among all three of you, is not healthy. On the other hand, a radical change of environment such as changing schools and leaving all her friends behind is not advisable right now."

"Well," Lily said, expecting this type of comment—didn't all shrinks talk out of both sides of their mouth?—"could you at least find out why she wants to change schools? And try to explore if she really wants to live with me."

"Certainly," the woman said. She then replied firmly, "Mrs. Forrester, I realize you're a district attorney and used to having any information you desire, but the conversations between your daughter and me are confidential. I appreciate you informing me of any problem areas, but I can't repeat what your daughter says."

Lily felt the muscles in her face twitch and knew her composure was dissolving. "This is my daughter we're talking about and this is a serious matter. Either you're going to help me or we'll seek another therapist."

Just then her secretary, Jan, walked in and Lily flicked her hand with annoyance, causing the poor girl to retreat hastily. Lily turned her chair toward the wall.

"There's no reason for you to become excited," Dr. Lindstrom said in her placating tone. "I didn't say I wouldn't discuss it with her. I will. I just can't funnel information to you." She paused. "All you have to do is discuss it with her. She seems very close to you right now. In fact, she's exceedingly concerned about you. The greatest gift you could give her is to seek therapy for yourself. It might be premature, but I feel she's going to handle this all very well in time."

"Another reason I called is that Shana picked a man from the photo lineup that she believes is the rapist. I don't. I think when she sees him in the flesh, she'll know he isn't the right man, but I think you should discuss this possibility with her."

"Certainly," she replied and then added, "Before you go, I'd like to give you a phone number for that group I told you about—the incest survivors' group. Here it is."

Lily was doodling circles inside triangles, her head close to her desk, and without thinking, she copied down the phone number and printed the word *incest* beside it in script so small it was almost illegible.

"Maybe I'll see you there. We meet every Thursday evening."

With a voice as small as the letters, Lily responded, "So, you run the group?"

"No, Lily, I don't. I'm part of the group. I'm also an incest survivor. I guess I should have told you this the other day in the office. You're not alone."

Once she had disconnected, Margie Thomas called back and informed her that the lineup was scheduled for the next day at five-thirty. When Lily started quizzing her about the possible suspect, she refused to divulge any information. Lily suddenly felt she was on the outside looking in—she felt like a victim. In her mind she saw herself walking in a long line of women, all connected by a heavy steel chain, like prisoners of war, all of them shuffling their feet in the soft dirt, their backs bent under the weight of the past.

The phone rang and Lily jumped, crossing both hands over her chest, still deep in the cobwebs of her mind. She started wildly pushing buttons but didn't pick up the receiver, and soon the ringing stopped.

The case files sat untouched while Lily bent once again close to the surface of her desk and doodled with her pen. She crossed out the word *incest* and scribbled the word *murderer* over and over until the page was full. Then she crushed the paper tightly in her fist and tossed it into the trash can. A few minutes later, she reached in, pulled it out, and tore it into tiny pieces.

CHAPTER **26** ■

Cunningham had been running on adrenaline and sugar all day. The night before, he had fallen into bed with his sleeping wife after midnight, passing on the leftover supper waiting on a dish in the microwave. Today he had consumed three chocolate donuts for breakfast, a Snickers for lunch, and was now munching on a bag of Doritos, washing it down with a Diet Coke, as he asked to speak to the medical examiner, Charlie Daniels.

"It's not three yet, Cunningham. Didn't I tell you to call at three?"

"Yeah, yeah, but I'm in a hurry." He laughed. "And it's two. That's pretty close."

"You're in a hurry," Daniels said. "My, my, where have I heard that before?" He then yelled at the top of his lungs into the phone: "Like no one else in the fucking world's in a hurry. Everyone's in a fucking race to infinity, you asshole."

Cunningham tossed a few Doritos into his mouth and held the receiver away from his ear. Charlie always yelled like this for about five minutes and then coughed up the goods. He liked people to beg.

"Now, Charlie, please," Cunningham said sensuously, "I'll do anything for ya, baby."

He heard the click and knew he was on hold. That was a good sign.

Papers were rustling as Charlie came back on the line. "Death by strangulation . . . looks like about two weeks . . . no semen or signs of forced penetration. I'll tell you, though, there's been a lot of traffic in that little tunnel, so I wouldn't expect anything there anyway like rips or tears."

"Come on, Charlie," Cunningham pleaded, "cut to the good stuff."

"We've got tissue under her fingernails and some hair particles, not hers. That's about it for now. I was opening up her chest cavity when you called."

Cunningham took his feet off the desk and sat up, knocking the bag of Doritos onto the floor, and the guys at the two desks next to him started shouting, "You're a pig, Cunningham."

He ignored them and asked Daniels, "On the Bobby Hernandez case, do we have hair and tissue to match against what you've found? He's the suspect."

Daniels started yelling again: "You're in a hurry and the suspect's a fucking corpse."

"Charlie, listen to me. It may be an even bigger case. Do we have samples?"

"We have tissue, I'm sure, but hair . . . I don't know. Was he cremated?"

"Buried," Cunningham replied.

"Well, what we don't have, we can get. I'll get back to you later."

He crossed his fingers that they did have the sample, or he'd have to get a court order to have the body exhumed and that meant time.

The radio room called and relayed information from the helicopter he had arranged to fly over the surrounding area in

Moorpark, with an officer riding copilot, searching the ground with binoculars. They'd seen something and had dispatched a patrol unit from the sheriff's department. The officer was en route to the station with Patricia Barnes's plastic purse in a bag. It contained her identification and, in the officer's opinion, was a perfect surface for prints.

Things were shaping up, he thought. Knowing the man who killed Ethel Owen was back on the streets had made him want to load the wife and kids in the car last night and drive straight out of this godforsaken town and back to Omaha. But this case had him hooked big-time. Two young kids were dead. They'd been butchered like two sides of beef. And chunky Patricia Barnes with the warm smile and the two little kids was getting dissected right now at the morgue, old Charlie poking through the contents of her stomach while he sat here munching down Doritos and Snickers. "Not on your diet, kid," he said to her. "Beverly Hills, remember? Next life you're gonna be as skinny as little Melissa."

He called the lab and made certain they had entered Hernandez's prints on their fancy computer, informing them that he would drive the purse over himself and wait for the fingerprint analysis.

Hanging up the phone, he took out the snapshots given to him by Barnes's sister and lined them up on his desk, wanting to commit her face to memory. "We're rolling, kid. And if the man who killed you is the man I think he is, we won't have to worry about some judge kicking him out on the streets. Looks like he already met his just reward. See, there is *some* justice left out there, Patty. There just ain't too damn much."

CHAPTER 27 ∎

Shana rode the school bus home and got off two blocks from her house, her arms full of books. After walking a short distance, she felt exhausted and sat down on the curb. Every morning she woke up at four or five o'clock, and as hard as she tried, she couldn't go back to sleep. She slept during study hall, her head in her arms on the desk, and many times she nodded off in class and didn't wake until the bell rang.

The sun was bright and warm, and she lifted her face and let it wash over her. A car passed and she inhaled exhaust fumes while several ten-year-old boys passed, laughing and punching one another.

"You want to see a picture of my mom's tits?" one boy said.

"You don't have a picture of your mom's tits. You're lying."

"Yeah, I do," the boy said. "See, she had them made bigger and the doctor took pictures of them before and after, and I found them in her room. Wanta see?"

Shana turned around to glare at the boys, and they started running down the street. They were toads, she thought, disgusting little toads. The entire school she went to was full of skinny, stupid-looking little boys and dumb girls. She was sick of them all. She stood and dusted off the seat of her pants and picked up her books. Suddenly she focused on the yard in front of her and saw an entire flower bed planted in tulips. Breaking one off, she held it to her nose and then tossed it into the gutter. The only thing she hated worse than her school was her house. She hated her room facing the street, where anyone could simply climb through her window, hated the disgusting yard, hated the ugly brown tile in the kitchen, and she hated the fighting between her parents. But what she hated the most was what she saw in her mother's face.

She'd been so stupid before the rape, so immature, she told herself, so selfish and spoiled. That was probably why it had happened—to punish her. She should have told her mother about her father's girlfriend from the beginning, should have told her she would live with her. But she was going to make it right now, whatever it took.

Seeing her house, she found her key and went inside, going straight to her room for little Di. Although light was streaming in from the windows, she went from room to room and flipped on every light switch in house, the puppy following. Then she turned on the television in the den and her stereo in her room. She checked the dead bolt on the front door and all the other doors to make certain they were locked. Every day she went through the same routine. It's not like I'm scared or anything, she thought, because I'm not. She'd never been scared of anything in her whole life. She was just being safe, that's all.

The phone rang and it was Sally. "You coming to practice?" she asked in her high-pitched voice.

"Yeah," Shana replied, kicking off her shoes. "I always come to practice. My dad's the coach, remember?"

"Did you hear what happened to Heather Stanfield? David

Smith asked her out and then broke up with her an hour later, right after she told everyone. Isn't that pathetic? You should have seen her, she was crying and . . ."

Shana placed the receiver on its side on the bed and started taking off her clothes. David Smith was probably one of those boys who had pictures of his mother's tits or maybe his sister's. If she strained really hard, she could hear little sounds coming out of the phone. She imagined that Sally was inside there, shrunk. It was as though all the kids she knew had gone through a shrinking machine and she was this clumsy giant. Seizing the receiver, she listened.

". . . and then she bought me that outfit we saw in the mall and a new pair of shoes, but they pinch my toes . . ."

"Oh, really," Shana said and then tossed the phone back on the bed. She went to the bathroom and turned on the faucets in the tub. Picking the phone off the bed, she said, "Have to go. Bye." Then she reached over and pulled the plug out.

In the tub, she submerged herself until only her nose protruded from the hot water. She listened to the rushing of her breath and the sound of her heart. If she could get her mother out of the house, just the two of them, then she could make her smile again, laugh again. It would be as her mother had said, like a dorm or something. The house would be clean and neat, and all they would eat would be health food. There would be no ashtrays overflowing with her father's disgusting cigarettes and no more stupid, silly girls like Sally, thinking a new dress or a new pair of shoes was the most important thing in the world.

The room suddenly went black and Shana sprang from the tub, sloshing water onto the floor, trying to brace herself by grabbing the shower curtain. Only a sliver of light shone through the blinds in the small bathroom window. Her heart was beating like an enormous drum. He was here, in the house. Just like in the movies, he had turned off the electricity. There was a deathly silence and she lunged at the bathroom door, her fingers checking the lock. This time he wouldn't take her without a fight, she thought, desperately flinging open the cabinets and reaching in the dark for something, anything that could be' used as a weapon. She heard a clunk and a whine and music. Her image appeared through the steam in the mirror as the lights came back on. She was standing there holding a plunger. It had just been a power failure, a stupid power failure. She stabbed the plunger against the mirror, growling at her reflection; it stuck there. The fear dissolved into hysterical laughter. Sitting on the toilet seat, she bent over and held her stomach as she laughed. Tears started rolling down her cheeks, and she couldn't stop laughing. Everyone was so serious—looked at her with such funny eyes—her dad, her mom, the shrink, all her friends. They were the ones making her crazy. They were all just waiting for her to do something weird, as though they thought her head was going to explode or something.

The spasms of laughter subsided, and she started rubbing her temples as she recalled the man's face from the photo lineup. Something inside her head seemed to expand and contract. She knew it was him; she could never forget. Her mother just couldn't see without her glasses. The detective had told her that they'd find him, bring him in for a real lineup, and then her mother would know too. She stood and pulled the plunger off the mirror, and imagined him in front of her naked with his stupid thing standing straight out between his legs. Her mother and Margie would hold him while she stabbed the plunger there, and when she pulled it off, his thing would be stuck there. Tossing the plunger against the wall, where it bounced and rolled to the tile floor, she unlocked the bathroom door and opened it, peering down the hall. She ran to her room and got her softball uniform and locked herself back in the bathroom.

Shana wasn't ready when her father got home. She was still locked in the bathroom, blow-drying her hair, and John had to knock three times to get her out. "We're going to be late," he said when she opened the door. "Shake a leg. You know I like to get there on time."

At practice, she was sullen and distracted. When the girls crowded around her, she merely walked away, leaving them all standing there with puzzled looks on their faces.

John told her to line up to bat. "I don't want to practice batting today," she insisted. Her entire body ached from exhaustion, and she felt like curling up in a ball on the ground and sleeping. "I just want to work on my pitching."

Noticing several girls standing nearby, John took her arm and led her a few feet away. "This is a team sport, Shana. I can't let you and only you pitch. The other girls need practice too. You know how we do it."

She jerked away and took her place in line. Ever since the rape, he had treated her differently, had avoided her like the she had a disease and he would catch it. Watching him out of the corner of her eye, she saw him pat one of the other girls on the back and smile at her. Just because she didn't want him pawing her and kissing her all the time like she was still a baby didn't mean she didn't want his love. Her eyes narrowed, thinking that he smiled at his girlfriend like that, smiled at everyone but her. Before, he always had let her have her way, no matter what. But now that she really needed him, when she could barely get through school, he was paying attention to everyone but her.

When she came up to bat the first time, she hit the ball into center field and ran to first. The next rotation, she slammed the ball with tremendous power and it went flying outside the diamond. With the same amount of force she threw the bat, and it struck one of the girls warming up in the leg with a loud crack. John started running toward the girl, while Shana stood and watched.

Screaming in pain and holding her leg, the girl fell to the ground. The bottom of her jeans were so tight that John had to run to the Jeep and get his pocket knife, kept in the glove compartment, and cut her jeans to look at the damage. All the girls gathered around. She yelled at Shana: "You did this on purpose. I know you did. Call my mom, my leg is broken. I know it."

There was a large knot and a darkening bruise. "Thank God it's not broken," John said. He sent one of the girls to the pay phone to call the child's mother, then turned to Shana in anger. "You never throw the bat. You know that. Never," he screamed.

Shana slammed her batting helmet on the ground, stood right over the girl, looking at the injury, her face twisted in disgust. "You're just a spoiled little crybaby. What do you know about anything? What would you do if someone really hurt you, *die* or something?" She stomped off the field, turning and yelling over her back. "I quit. Take your stupid team and shove it."

Shana waited in the car. Once the injured girl's mother arrived, John told the other girls to practice throwing to one another until their parents arrived. Charlotte walked up to him as he was leaving. "You want me to take the equipment home?"

"Sure, thanks, honey," he said.

"What's wrong with Shana? Is she really going to quit?" the girl asked, shaking her head. "She doesn't even eat lunch with us anymore."

John turned and glanced at the Jeep and then back at Charlotte. "Who does she eat lunch with, then?"

"I don't know. I don't think she even eats lunch anymore."

John tried to talk to his daughter as he drove to a local restaurant. "Shana, what got into you out there? Those girls are your friends. How could you scream at that girl when she was hurt?"

"She just had a little bump on her leg, and she accused me of doing it on purpose, like I really planned it or something. What a stupid crybaby. That's what they all are. Just a bunch of babies."

"But they've been friends of yours for years. They all love you."

Shana glared at her father. "What do you know? Everyone hates me now. I'm not *Miss Perfect* anymore. All they do is hound me all the time and drive me crazy. Everyone comes up to me and keeps asking me the same lame questions. 'What's wrong? What's wrong? You're mad at me.' I just can't take it anymore. Why can't they just leave me alone?"

"They don't understand because they don't know what happened. You can't blame them for that."

"Well, nothing happened to them, did it? And nothing happened to you either. It happened to me and Mom. That's what. And let me tell you something, Mom isn't all right."

John pulled into the parking lot of the cafeteria and started to get out. "Your mom is a strong woman. She's going to be fine."

"You bet she is. She's gonna be fine because I'm not going to let her be anything else. I want to change schools and move in with Mom."

He shut the door to the car, leaned back in the seat, and turned to face his daughter. "Shana, I just can't allow that. Look what happened when you just went to visit. Besides, your mother is too busy with her career to care for you."

She leaned over in his face and opened her eyes wide. "And you're not *all tied up with your girlfriend*, right?" She slapped back in the seat, and her face got redder and redder with anger. "All you've ever told me is that Mom is too busy and doesn't care about me. She just has an important job, Dad. I'm busy with my schoolwork too. Does that make me a lousy kid? I love you, but I don't want to hear any more shit about Mom." With that, Shana got out of the car and slammed the door.

CHAPTER 28 .

Richard had asked Lily to meet him at Amechi's restaurant at six, and as she pulled into the parking lot, she saw his white BMW. When she walked in, he stood and kissed her lightly on both cheeks. "Like the restaurant?" he asked.

She looked at him with piercing blue eyes, her face more ethereal now than ever, her cheekbones high and pronounced. "I like you, Richard," she said.

The waiter placed a caesar salad in front of her and poured her a glass of wine. The little restaurant was more authentic than elegant, with red-and-white-checked tablecloths, voices chanting in Italian from the kitchen, the odorous scent of garlic filling the air and stimulating the appetite, while the tenor voice of Luciano Pavarotti serenaded them from the sound system. It was early and they were the only customers; at one table a few waiters were eating their dinner before the rush.

He held up his wineglass, and Lily held up hers, tapping her glass lightly against his with a ting. "To us," he said.

"I'm only going to tell you this one thing, and then we're not going to talk shop for the rest of the evening," she said, leaning over the table, her eyes wide with excitement. "They lifted a print off the purse and matched it to Bobby Hernandez. Cunningham called me from the lab right after you left." This was one of the reasons Lily felt she could finally eat. Right after the detective had told her, she had wanted to stand up and scream at the top of her lungs. She had killed a murderer, not just a rapist but a murderer. Now there was no doubt whatsoever.

"Bravo," Richard answered. "We're rolling now."

"Nothing yet on Manny. They have a surveillance team on him as of today, but I don't think we have enough for an arrest warrant." In between mouthfuls of salad, which she was shoveling down unladylike, ravenous, she added, "Cunningham also found out that Manny visited Navarro in jail recently, after his brother died."

"Is Cunningham going to use this to put more heat on him, maybe let him think we have something linking him to the Barnes murder?"

"I don't know," Lily said, signaling the waiter to refill her empty wineglass. "What we want Manny to do is lead us to the gun they used to shoot Carmen Lopez. That gun's around somewhere, hidden, stashed. His kind would never put it out of reach forever, like in the ocean or something, not a perfectly good gun they could use again. Waste not, want not. That would be like flushing a pound of heroin."

She sat back in the chair with the menu open in front of her. Seeing the words were blurry, she recalled that she had brought her glasses, but still refused to put them on. "You order for me, okay? No more office talk. Let's eat."

Richard ordered for both himself and Lily veal cooked in white wine and capers, and linguini in a superb marinara sauce with clams and mussels. She leaned close to the plate and inhaled the rich aroma, let each mouthful move over her taste buds before swallowing. It seemed like years since she had smelled anything, tasted anything. By now the restaurant was filled almost to capacity. Dishes were rattling, voices of other diners filled the air, and the sounds surrounded her. Everything was brighter, louder, larger. She felt she had traveled down a dark tunnel to a room blazing in light and warmth. Lily ate everything on her plate, along with several pieces of bread. She placed her hand on her stomach and felt a round bulge and thought she must look like a bloated Ethiopian child.

When they left the restaurant, he took her hand to lead her to his car in the parking lot. "I can't, Richard. Please don't tempt me. I want to be there when Shana gets home."

"But it's only seven-thirty and you said her appointment at the psychologist wasn't until eight." He continued pulling on her hand like a spoiled child and forced her to move a few steps closer to his car. "I even picked this place because it's only a few miles to my house."

He turned and took her other hand, pulling her into his arms right in the middle of the parking lot. "Claire agreed to the property settlement. That means in less than six months, I'll be free. Tonight is a celebration," he said, pushing her hair away from her face tenderly. "I need you."

Through the thin fabric of her dress, she felt his large hands on her back, warm, strong, pressing her into him. She caught a hint of his lime scent, and while he kissed her, she tasted the garlic and wine inside his mouth.

A couple passed them heading into the restaurant, the woman talking fast and with a distinct cadence to her voice. Lily opened her eyes wide and stiffened in Richard's arms.

"Don't look up," he said. "They didn't see us anyway, but . . . that was Judge Abrams that just walked by."

They quickly jumped into his car and left, Lily exclaiming loudly, "Carol, shit. Do you have any idea how many seconds before everyone—"

Richard cut her off. "They're going to know one day soon anyway. What's the big deal? You should hear the rumors circulating about her."

Lily ignored him and continued. "Butler might not want us working together if he found out." It was useless to argue with him about keeping their relationship under wraps. On this issue, they didn't agree. Since he was almost divorced and she had been separated, he thought they had every right to see each other and had told her it was silly to be so uptight. "What about Carol?"

"First, never call her Carol; she only wants to be addressed as Judge Abrams. I bet she has her husband call her that in bed. The funniest thing is that she can't sit still for long—must be genuinely hyperactive—so she keeps calling recesses and it's clogging up her calendar."

Should have been me, Lily thought, but instead said, "She's a smart woman and a hard worker. She'll work it out. Anyway, she can keep the black robe. All I want is the parking space."

They were a block from the restaurant, stopped at the light. She turned to Richard. "Take me back to get my car and I'll follow you to your house: I don't want to come back here and run into someone else from the office."

When they both pulled up in front of Richard's house, only a few minutes away, Lily got out and he swept her up in his arms and carried her through the front door and straight to the bedroom. He dropped his clothes on the floor and crawled under the covers, motioning for Lily to join him. On clean, crisp sheets, with soft classical music and candlelight, she let him hold her and stroke her gently, but she refused to take off her clothes and he didn't push. First they snuggled in the bed on their sides, Lily's back against his front. The wine had warmed her and she felt locked in a tight cocoon, safe and protected.

"This is called spooning, you know," he whispered in her ear. "We fit together just like spoons. Ever heard that one?"

"Somewhere," Lily answered. His breath in her ear tickled and she began laughing. His arms tightened around her waist, pulling her even closer. Then he placed a hand on her shoulder and rolled her over onto her back. He moved on top of her, pressing his erection against her stomach, then her pubic region, rubbing against her genitals through her dress and hose. Suddenly, Lily felt trapped, unable to move. The lights were low and she could barely see his face. All she saw was this dark figure looming over her, pinning her to the bed. "Get off, Richard," she said. He leaned down and kissed her neck with moist lips, ignoring her. "Let me up," she said in a voice fringing on panic. "Let me up."

Richard rolled off her onto his back. "Shit," he said, staring at the ceiling, refusing to look at her, his erection subsiding. "Shit," he said again in frustration, and the words flew through the air and hit her, no different than a slap across her face. Lily sat up, straightening her clothes, her sense of well-being evaporating.

"I told you it would never be the same. When you get on top of me like that, it reminds me of the rape. He held me down, held us both down."

Richard was silent. He didn't reach for her or try to comfort her. The atmosphere inside the room was heavy with disappointment. Lily could feel it.

"I think you should start dating other women, Richard. Go on with your life."

"Lily . . ." he said, finally turning to face her.

"No, please listen to me. You're not being realistic about this. Do you really want a relationship with someone with all these problems? I keep trying to tell you."

Rolling over onto his side, Richard touched her hand and then pulled away. "Do you really think I'm that shallow, Lily? Every human being has problems. I don't exactly see life through the head of my dick."

Her eyes cut to him and quickly looked away. She had tried to end the evening at the restaurant, when everything had been right. He had been the one who had insisted. If sex was so unimportant to him, why did he keep pushing himself on her every time they were together?

"Haven't we already had this conversation? You're blowing this all out of proportion now." Annoyance was beginning to show in his voice as he swung his legs to the side of the bed.

Even though she tried to stop it, she felt her anger rising.

"Blowing it out of proportion. Jesus," she said, jumping from the bed and standing there. "You don't understand shit about what happened to me. You're a fucking man, that's why. No one's ever held you down and forced you to have sex with them. Just forget it. That's what you all say. What's the big deal anyway? Right? Just wash it out and go on to the next one." She was pacing back and forth in front of the bed now, waving her arms in the air.

Slowly standing and walking to her, he took her hands and pulled her to him. "You took it all wrong. What I meant was you're blowing the sexual thing between us out of proportion, not the rape. Do you think for a minute that I don't know what this has done to you? My God, I've been prosecuting rape cases for years. Rape is a devastating crime of violence, a loss of will. I might be a man, but believe me, I understand more than most men. I love you." He put his arms around her and engulfed her. "When you love someone, you take the bad with the good. You hear me?" He lifted her chin to his face. "And, Lily, it's going to be good. Have faith. Listen to me. It's going to be great. Come on, let's go sit by the fire in the living room. You just seemed so happy tonight, so much like your old self. I thought . . . I don't know what I thought . . . that you wanted it as much as I did."

"Obviously, I don't know what I want right now," she said, following him down the hall. It was the truth.

Classical music still filled the air, and Richard left Lily sitting by the fire while he went to the kitchen, returning with a big crystal bowl filled with strawberries. The fire was warming her back, crackling and popping. Sitting Indian-style in front of her, Richard started feeding her strawberries, but her taste buds were dead again and they were nothing more than mush in her mouth. Impulsively she pushed him over onto his back, the bowl of strawberries spilling out on the carpet. Then she pinned his arms down with her own and looked down in his face. "How do you like it?" she said, pushing down hard on his arms, feeling in control again.

He looked her right in the eye and smiled. "I like it any way you like it."

Still holding his arms down, Lily bent down and kissed him tenderly on the mouth. She then let go and collapsed on top of his body. "I really do love you," she whispered. "I never knew a man could be like you. I never thought I could feel so close to another person."

He put his hands in her long hair and she sat up. "It's almost nine," she said. "I have to go."

While Richard picked up the strawberries, Lily got her purse and opened her compact to put on some lipstick. "Sorry about the mess," she said, leaning over to help him. When they finished, she began to brush the tangles out of her hair. Richard took the brush from her hand and started slowly pulling it through her hair, causing her scalp to tingle. "Do it like this," she said, turning her head upside down while he continued. Then she tossed her head back and grabbed him, pressing her body against his.

"You'll have to beg," he said, smiling. "That's my new philosophy. If you want me from now on, you'll have to beg." They walked arm in arm to the door.

"Beg, huh?" Lily said, arching her eyebrows. "And what happens if I don't?"

The smile fell from his face and he leaned against the door frame, remained there as she walked down the steps. When she reached the bottom, she looked back up to wave at him, but the door was closed and he was gone. She stood there staring at the door, hugging herself against the chill. The shrill sound of a siren rang out in the distance, and she could see flashing red lights streaking down the street far below. If things didn't change, she told herself, and soon, real soon, Richard's door would be closed forever. She saw herself beating on it until her fists were bloody, pleading with him to let her in, while inside he was moving his body up and down on top of a faceless woman.

CHAPTER 29 ∎

"Bruce," the voice called from somewhere faraway, and he saw his mother's rosy cheeks and smelled her Ivory soap-scrubbed skin as she leaned down to tie his shoelaces. He was in the kitchen, warming his hands over the open furnace before heading out into the cold for school. "I'll make you some scrambled eggs and bacon, even if it is lunchtime, if you get up right now." The voice belonged to his wife, Sharon, calling from the doorway of the small bedroom. He tried to shut it out, to return to the dream, wanted to go back until his mother had given him that big sloppy kiss she gave him every morning, but it was gone.

He rolled over onto his back and opened his eyes to the ceiling. Somehow he had managed to sleep through the daily door slamming, toilet flushing, water running, and arguing that woke him every morning as his three kids prepared for school. Normally he would have gotten up and headed for the bathroom, trying to keep his eyes half closed, urinate, and then return to catch a few more hours of sleep once the front door shut and the house was quiet. Still in his white boxer shorts,

234

he trudged toward the kitchen, down the narrow hall, toward the sound of bacon crackling in the skillet. The aroma made his mouth water. Sharon knew he'd go for the breakfast; there were few surprises after twenty years.

She was wearing an aqua sweat suit, one of four identical sweat suits she kept in a little bin in the closet, allowing her to dress in there with the door shut and not wake him each morning. He had not worked the day shift for at least a year, and although he seldom saw the kids, except when he stopped by the house for dinner and on his days off, his wife didn't object. From the old school, long married to a cop, she didn't look to him for much in the way of parenting other than acting as a disciplinarian. On those occasions, mere threats of their father's wrath was sufficient to do the job.

The bacon was out of the pan now, the eggs in, and she placed a steaming mug of black coffee in front of him before returning to the stove. The sweat suits were so unflattering, he thought, worse now that she'd gained weight again. Her backside was as broad as it had been when their last son was born. But as she set the plate of eggs and bacon in front of him, with two pieces of wheat toast buttered just right, he looked at her soft brown eyes and lovely face without regret. Given the chance, he'd marry her again, broad ass and all.

She took a seat in the cane-backed chair across the breakfast table from him. "Tommy needs money for the yearbook by tomorrow. I told him he could buy it because it's his senior year. The insurance on the car is due, probably overdue, and yesterday the orthodontist said they couldn't continue treating Kelly if we don't make the last three payments. I have three hundred and seven dollars in the checkbook and it's eight days till payday."

Cunningham spoke with a mouthful of eggs. "You got any good news?"

"I'm pregnant," she said, looking him square in the eye.

"No, you're not," he said, almost choking on a piece of bacon.

"Yes, I am," she said, and not a muscle twitched in her full face.

Cunningham dropped his fork on the table and tried to recall the last time they had had sex. He didn't remember. He knew it had been a long time because the need was getting real bad. He'd been tempted to wake her the other night at two o'clock when he'd finally got off work. He smiled and shoved the empty plate away, downing what was left of his coffee.

Placing his fingers inside his boxer shorts, he sucked in his stomach and tried to make the muscles that were left in his biceps bulge. "Follow me," he said, shaking his butt from side to side like a girl. "I have something to show you in the bedroom."

Her aqua sweat suit on the floor, his shorts under the covers at the foot of the bed, he pulled her to him and felt her warm, soft breasts against his chest. He nuzzled his nose deep into her neck and said in her ear, "You're not really pregnant, are you?"

"Nah," she said, "but it worked, didn't it?"

"I'll show you what really works," he said, taking her hand and putting it between his legs. "Works every time." At least that was one thing about his body that functioned as well as it had twenty years ago, he thought. This was one of the reasons she liked the night shifts.

Before he left, he told her, "Be sure and have the kids watch the local news tonight. Might see a face they recognize."

Cunningham strode past the records department en route to the investigation bureau, knowing he must stop at the captain's office briefly to go over everything again before he met the Channel 4 News team due at the station in an hour. He saw Melissa head down at the desk, the ever present cigarette smoldering in the ashtray. "I'm going for chicken-fried steak with cream gravy in a few minutes," he lied. "Want to go?"

She looked up, took a pull on the cigarette, and blew the

smoke out with the words: "You're such an asshole, Cunningham." She then bent back down to her work.

Her hair was slicked back, her face carefully made up, and from this range she looked dramatic and pretty, almost like a ballerina. He stopped and slapped his hands on the countertop. "Got anything for me, gorgeous?"

"I've got herpes. Want some?" she said without smiling, still head down.

After a few moments she removed a stack of computer printouts and walked to the counter. She was wearing a mid-calf black rayon dress, belted around her tiny waist with a wide patent-leather belt. Through the sheer fabric her hipbones protruded on either side of her concave and nonexistent stomach. Cunningham thought of his wife's abundant sponge-rubber flesh, how good she'd felt beneath him that morning, and wondered if Melissa was even able to engage in sex. Her body looked as though it would snap like a dry twig.

She fixed him with her soulful eyes, lined in black eyeliner. "I've narrowed it down to about fifty red compact cars. I'm waiting for D.M.V. and records checks on the owners." She took a sheet off the top of the printouts, with the license plate given by the neighbor printed at the top in her cramped handwriting, and lines and lines of number and letter combinations listed below with slashes drawn through them. Turning the paper so he could see it, she said, "See, what I'm doing now is trying look-alikes. Some people have learning disabilities or they just can't see as well as they think." She showed him an example by drawing a number three on a piece of paper and then making it into an eight. "Also, the letter *B* can be mistaken for an eight."

"Melissa, doll," he said, "how many times do I have to tell you that you're the best? If you would just gain some weight, I bet you could pass the next exam. You'd make a damn fine officer."

Her eyes drifted down and she suddenly started coughing, a deep, hacking cough that shook her frail body and caused her eyes to tear. Once the spasm had passed, she said, "I'll let you know when I have something interesting."

As he passed the end of the counter, he saw her back at her desk, lighting a fresh cigarette with her lighter held between her callused fingers, sitting on her cushion, spreading her elbows out and leaning close to the work in front of her.

He called the officer tailing Manny Hernandez on his cellular phone, but Manny had been in all day, showing his face only once to get into his car and drive to the local market at about one in the afternoon, returning with what looked like groceries. Manny's prints hadn't been found on the purse, or he would already be in custody instead of lounging around his house, probably high on drugs. He wasn't even aware that his brother had been made on the homicide, but by tonight he would know, and the heat inside that house should rise about fifty degrees, Cunningham thought. Hot enough to make him want to get out, to make him possibly do something rash.

After clearing his press release with the captain, Cunningham leaned back in his chair, feet on his desk, with the composite drawing made from statements made by Manny in his lap, waiting for reception to call him when the news team arrived. He glanced down at the drawing, leaned back, and looked at the water spots on the ceiling, then glanced back at the drawing again. These drawings never looked that realistic, but this one took the prize. It reminded him of those sketches made from people who said they were abducted by space aliens, like something from a dream that was distorted.

Hell, he thought, sitting up and slamming his feet on the floor, the little fucker could have made the whole thing up. Maybe he knew the shooter and planned retaliation on his own after things blew over. He tossed the paper on his desk and hurried to the men's room to check his hair and tie before the news team came. He was wearing a brown jacket that he reserved only for court appearances and turned his head, trying to see which side looked better today. Thank God, he thought, they only filmed from the waist up, and his shoes would be out of camera range. He hadn't even been able to wear the brown ones. Sharon had thrown them away last week.

Back at his desk, he removed the best picture of the three given to him by the victim's sister, one taken at least four years ago with one of her little girls. This was the one that made her look pretty, with her cheek pressed to her daughter's and both of them smiling. She must have been fifty pounds lighter then, he thought. He had promised her sister that her record of prostitution would not be released to the press; it was the least they could do for her, for the kids.

The filming with the press went well. Cunningham didn't stumble over his words and felt he came off looking good for the department. Once they filled in the spot, they could bring up the fact that the murder would not have happened if Bobby Hernandez had been arrested immediately following the offense, which didn't make the department look so great but was just how the wheels of justice turned any way you wanted to look at it. At least the wheels turned, Cunningham thought, thinking bitterly of Ethel Owen. There was also that little ironic twist to the story that the reporter liked a lot, that the murderer had himself been murdered. Cunningham kind of liked that part himself. Made it all neat and tidy, at least on the Barnes case. The only problem was that it was still his job to find the person responsible for Hernandez's death, and he was swimming upstream on that one. Back at his desk, he opened the gray metal filing cabinet and counted the open homicides, some so cold that he would soon have to place them in inactive status. There were twelve. Just then the phone rang and he grabbed it. It was Sharon.

"Guess what I'm doing?" she asked, her voice slurred.

"Don't know, darling. Tell me." He was opening files and looking inside, trying to figure out which ones he was going to put in inactive and which ones he thought he still had a slim chance of solving.

"I'm getting stoned." She giggled.

Cunningham grabbed the phone and took it off the speaker.

"What the fuck are you talking about? My God, woman, this is a police station. Don't even tease about something like that."

"Well, there was a day when I wasn't married to a cop, remember? When I was in college, I was a tiny bit wild. Kinda know what I mean?"

"Sharon," he barked, "what in the hell is wrong with you?"

"Just found this little cigarette in your oldest son's drawer and thought I'd smoke it and see what it was. It's pot, all right, and pretty good too."

"You're fucking joking. This isn't funny, Sharon. You found *marijuana* in Tommy's drawer?" The last part of the sentence he whispered, looking around the room to see if anyone was listening. Only one detective was at his desk, and he was on the phone and out of earshot.

"Sure looks that way. One puff and I'm totally stoned. Maybe you better come home and we'll finish what we started this morning."

Suddenly he was angry. He loosened his tie. "That's it," he said, "we're moving back to Omaha. I knew this was going to happen. This whole city is nothing but a fucking garbage can."

"Calm down, Daddy. It's not that terrible. I mean, just because he smoked a little pot doesn't mean he's going to be sticking needles in his arm next week. He's a senior this year, and he's simply feeling his oats."

"When he gets home today, don't let him leave the house. Soon as I get there, I'll handle this. And Sharon . . ."

She was still silly and giggling. "Yes?"

"Go drink some coffee or something. This isn't funny. It's definitely not funny." He slammed the receiver down.

So, he thought, this is what it was going to be. His own children couldn't survive in this stinking hellhole without resorting to drugs. The next thing he knew they'd be smoking crack and stealing. He started shoving all the files on his desk into a big stack and instead of putting them back in the file, he was so disgusted that he just dropped them on the floor by his desk. Then he stepped over them and headed for the door.

"Cunningham, you asshole," the other detective said. "Look at the fucking mess you made, man. What's wrong with you? You losing your fucking mind?"

"Lost it, Snyder. You got it. I've completely lost it. Anyone wants to know where I am, tell them to go fuck themselves, okay?" He punched his way through the double doors and marched to his car to go home and deal with his son. No kid of his was going to use drugs. Not as long as he was around to stop it. And he'd damn sure stop it, he thought, gunning the engine on the Chrysler and roaring out of the parking lot.

30 ▪

On the way to her office, Lily stopped at records and asked the clerk to give her the file on Bobby Hernandez. All the current data regarding his commission of the homicide of Patricia Barnes would have to be compiled and a hearing held before the case could be closed. In the attempted rape and kidnapping, they had dismissed the charges due to the victim's failure to appear, and certified copies of both their respective death certificates had to be obtained and placed on file. She held her briefcase in one hand and the file in the other, unsure if the autopsy photos of Hernandez had been forwarded from the medical examiner yet and horrified of actually having to look at them. Even more horrifying was the thought that she would soon be looking at the composite drawing.

That night she and Shana were going to the Ventura Police Department for the lineup. She had to look at the mug shot of Hernandez one more time. If Shana identified the same suspect, or another suspect, she wanted the strength of conviction to carry her through what was surely going to be a scene. Coming from records, she headed to her office down the back corridor at a brisk pace until she saw something that stopped her cold. Richard was talking to one of the new A.D.A.'s, a young, good-looking blonde. His back was turned, his arm against the wall over the woman's head, and the woman was laughing. Lily's skin felt like it was on fire. She turned and headed back the way she had come. She was ducking into another hall when she collided with Marshall Duffy. Her file and all its contents spilled onto the floor.

"We've got to quit meeting like this," he said, chuckling as he bent down to help her pick up the scattered papers.

"I'll pick them up," she said, "it was my fault. I wasn't looking." Her fingers were trembling as she reached for the papers, trying to scoop them all up in one sweep. Marshall had a stack in his hands, and Lily saw her own likeness on the front sheet. He was holding the composite drawing!

"So, what's been happening, lady? I never see your face around here anymore. They must have you buried back there."

Lily watched as he dropped the hand holding the papers to his side. She wanted to reach out and grab it, but she stood quietly, in a daze.

When she didn't answer, Marshall moved closer, scanning her face. "Are you feeling okay?" he asked.

"Yes . . . no . . . I mean, I have a lot on my mind." Her eyes were still fixed on the composite, and finally she couldn't hold back any longer. She snatched the papers from his hand and stuffed them back into the file. "Sorry," she said. "Thanks." She took off, feeling everyone's eyes on her, the incriminating file burning in her hand.

As she passed her secretary's desk, the girl held out a stack of pink slips, messages, but Lily ignored her, left her sitting there with her mouth open, about to speak. Out of the corner of her eye, she saw Richard back in his office pinning up crime-scene photos on a large bulletin board. She hit the door to the ladies' room with her shoulder like a quarterback and slipped into a stall, pulling the latch. Setting her briefcase on the floor, she sat down on the commode and opened the file. "Oh, my

God," she said, one hand over her chest. She was looking at her eyes, her mouth, her nose, her long neck. "No," she whispered, shaking her head, trying to swallow and finding her mouth too dry. All the same, no one would ever see her likeness on this piece of paper. The eyes were too menacing, the mouth too compressed, the face too rigid.

Several mug shots were clipped together, and she saw a small triangle of Hernandez's face sticking out the side of the file. She reached for it but couldn't force herself to do more than shove the composite inside and open the door to the stall. Standing in the mirror was a person she didn't know, a stranger, the face in the drawing. She had traveled a thousand miles through Hell to come face to face with her worst nightmare— her own image.

After swallowing two Valiums, Lily tore the clip from her hair and brushed it down around her face. She put on fresh lipstick, blush, and eyeshadow and again looked at the reflection. Of course, the composite drawing resembled her, but no one would attach her name to it. If she was actually a suspect, she'd have been arrested by now. Cunningham wouldn't talk to her all the time, work with her, and then just waltz in one day and place her under arrest. In her mind, he was a shadowy hero, an old-fashioned cowboy. He didn't know, she reassured her mirror image before leaving. No one knew.

Pouring herself a cup of coffee from the pot they kept on a little table in the unit, near the secretarial pool, she stuffed the file under her arm, picked up her messages, and hurried to deposit it on her desk before checking in with Richard. When the file left her hands, she noticed her hands were still shaking. Valium and coffee, she thought, breakfast of champions. She took two sips and left the styrofoam cup on her desk.

Richard's office was cluttered with a bulletin board and a blackboard, and he was busy pinning up crime-scene photos from the McDonald–Lopez case with little punch pins, using the medical examiner's report as a guideline to place them in the order the injuries were possibly inflicted. Her eyes found the eight-by-ten glossies of the mutilated body of seventeen-year-old Carmen Lopez; the thought that Shana's little body might have ended up on a board made chills run up her spine.

"God, what time did you get here this morning?" she asked, looking at all the work he had already done.

He turned and smiled. "Have the words good morning ever come to your mind? It's a nice way to start the day." He waited until she walked over close to the board he was working on and then added in a lower voice, "Especially after last night . . ."

"Good morning," she said, trying to sound cheerful, seeing the blond D.A. in his arms, in his bed. She had left him frustrated, failed to perform. It was just a matter of time.

"I've been thinking of the issue of the gun," he said, "and the fact that they were stopped only a few miles from the crime scene without it. The area has been combed and combed, as our first thoughts were that they tossed it right after the murder. If the Hernandez brothers were involved in this, it could explain the absence of that weapon." He picked up his coffee cup from the desk and took a swallow. Having discarded his jacket and loosened his tie, he was prepared to get to work while Lily was just sitting there with a blank look on her face.

Flashbacks of that early morning and her father's shotgun tumbling down the hill behind the church were playing in her mind. Had someone found it? Had they kept it or turned it in to the authorities? Hernandez had used a knife on her and Shana. If he still had the gun, he surely . . . Seeing Richard looking at her, waiting for her to say something, she said, "I'm thinking. Give me a minute. Remember, I'm not used to working with a partner, so this may be a little awkward."

"We'll get the hang of it," he said cheerfully, returning to the board and pinning up more photos.

Hernandez had strangled Patricia Barnes, which blew her

belief that it was her blood on the knife that had been forced into her mouth, along with the statement he had made about it being the "blood of a whore."

"Rich, are we absolutely certain that none of the wounds on either victim were inflicted by a knife?" she asked. "The tree limb forced into her vagina caused tremendous lacerations, I know, but possibly some of those were caused by a knife prior."

He walked to the desk and picked up the fifteen-page autopsy report, handing it to Lily. "You're welcome to read it again or even call them if you think there could be another weapon. I only recall that the lacerations were listed as tears —jagged—not consistent with a knife."

"If Manny Hernandez kept the gun while his brother was in custody, which is feasible, particularly since arrests had already been made in the case, it wasn't in the house or in Bobby's van," she said. "But did they search Manny's car?"

He turned from the board excitedly, swiping his dark hair off his forehead. "Good question, Lily. Damn good question. My bet is they didn't, since Manny was in no way a suspect in the homicide of his brother."

"Guess we should call Cunningham and ask," she said, picking up the phone and dialing the number from memory. The receptionist advised her that the detective's shift began at three o'clock and it was only nine o'clock. "Go ahead and ring the homicide bureau, then." One of the other investigators put her on hold and came back on the line with the file, retrieved from Cunningham's desk.

"Hold on . . . I'm reading."

"Take your time," Lily said, hitting the hands-free button. Returning to her chair, she removed a yellow pad and a pen from her briefcase.

The man finally responded. "Just the van. We impounded the van and searched the house. Nothing more."

"Thanks," Lily said, turning to Richard. "Want me to start

preparing a search warrant for that car? I can have someone walk it through. We should have it by this afternoon."

"Go," he said. "Once Manny hears the news about his brother going down for Patricia Barnes's death, you can bet that weapon is going to disappear."

"They're tailing him, though, and if we catch him actually disposing of it, it makes a far better case than just finding it in his car. He could merely claim his brother placed it there without his knowledge. All we have on him is that one association with Carmen and his visit to Navarro in jail."

They decided that Lily would prepare the request for a search warrant, and once it was in their hands, they could decide when to execute it.

The request for warrant dictated, Lily kept picking up the Hernandez file and then setting it aside to work on other cases stacked in her bin. Richard had not taken her cases this morning, and she talked herself out of opening the file until her other work was completed.

She skipped lunch and worked straight through, against Richard's protests. One of the new cases they had was a multiple-count child molestation in which the victims involved were now all adults, all sisters. The reports stated that they had been talking one night, and one confessed that their father, now divorced from their mother, had molested her. This led to the other sisters admitting that they too had been victims and deciding to report the crimes, all three insisting that they wanted to prosecute their father. The man had been a school bus driver for over fifteen years, and Lily knew there were probably other victims out there who had never come forward. Cases like this one were unusual, yet cropped up here and there now that the statute of limitations had been extended to ten years on some crimes involving the sexual abuse of a child, and indefinitely in regards to specific offenses. This might be an important case, since the long-term psychological damage caused by such crimes would not be mere future projections and speculations, but could be documented and testified to in trial.

She had told Shana she would pick her up at school at three-thirty, and it was now almost three o'clock. After John informed her of what her friend had said about the child not eating, and the scene at the softball practice, Lily had decided to take her to lunch before they went to the lineup. She reached with tentative hands for the file that had haunted her all day, no longer able to avoid it.

There were no autopsy photos, only the original mug shots, and there were duplicate copies in the file. Lily removed one and touched her glasses with one finger, pushing them tightly on her nose. She stared at the picture and instantly brought forth the image in her mind of him looking down on her only inches from her face. Then she tried to visualize him standing there in the light from the bathroom those few panicky seconds before he fled. Swallowing and trying to remain calm, she removed her glasses and stared again at his face. There was a definite difference as she looked at the less distinct features. There was no way she could lie to herself.

Before she left, she placed the extra mug shot in her purse, removed the bottle of Valium, and swallowed two of the pills with a mouthful of cold coffee. When she walked out of the office, she was wearing her glasses, her stomach in knots.

Shana was standing on the curb in front of the school, arms full of books, glancing up and down the row of cars, searching for Lily. Other kids were hurrying down the steps, passing her and dispersing in all different directions; some were congregating in small groups, talking and laughing. Everywhere around her were the sights and sounds of pent-up youthful energy being released into the sunny California afternoon. Shana stood ramrod straight like a cardboard figure.

The scene reminded Lily of a double exposure in which the shadowy and distorted image from one photograph appears in another, out of place, like a ghost. Would the magic ever come back? she wondered, recalling Shana's melodious laugh and how making her laugh had been like winning a prize on a game show. Shana was wearing the new jeans purchased only last month, but now they were baggy in the seat, and she had used a belt to hold them on her waist. She spotted Lily and walked over to the car, ignoring several kids who passed her and started to say something to her.

"Boy, I'm starving," Lily said. "I skipped lunch today. So, let's you and I go somewhere and have something nice. What sounds good?"

"Not much," Shana said, sighing deeply.

"Did you eat lunch?"

She didn't answer and tossed her books in the backseat, where they tumbled and rolled to the floorboard. "I got an *F* on my math test today."

"You can make it up. Naturally, with all that's been going on . . . well, you just can't expect . . ." Lily paused, thinking, trying to find the right words. "To tell you the truth, I haven't been doing so great at work either. What about a tutor? Maybe we should get you a tutor for the remainder of the year."

"I want to change schools," she said, her voice strained. "I told you that already."

"But, Shana, it's going to be extremely hard on you to come into a brand-new school so late in the year. You wouldn't have any friends, and I don't know if it's in your best interest to do something like that right now. Why is it so important?"

The girl brushed her hair back behind her ears and turned to her mother. "Because I think everyone is talking about me behind my back all the time. That they know. Everyone hates me anyway."

Lily pulled into the parking lot of a Sizzler restaurant and turned off the ignition. "I'm sure they don't know, but I appreciate how you feel. I felt the same way at first at my office, but I forced myself to stop thinking that way."

"You know what you sound like, Mom? You sound just like that psychologist, and I can't stand her."

"Let's eat, okay? I won't pick on you and you don't pick on me. Deal?"

Finally a hint of a smile appeared on Shana's face. "Is that like me pulling your hair?"

As they walked into the restaurant, Lily put her arm around her and took a handful of her hair in her hand but didn't do anything more than hold it. "You're one up on me on that. I just might collect one of these days."

"You're something, Mom, you know," she said, turning her bright blue eyes to Lily's face. "You're about the best friend I have right now."

"Then you're going to eat, right?"

"Yeah, sure, I'll eat. We'll see who can eat the most. You're pretty skinny yourself." Shana was smiling as she reached for Lily's skirt and put her fingers inside the waistband, feeling the loose fabric.

At the police station, Margie Thomas took Shana in to view the men in the lineup first and Lily sat outside, nervously crossing and recrossing her legs, unable to sit still. Recognizing one of the detectives handling the McDonald–Lopez case walking by, she snagged him and asked if there were any recent developments. Arnold Cross was young, no more than his late twenties, and had probably just made detective. He had that fresh-scrubbed, blond, starched, wet-behind-the-ears look.

"I had a long talk with Carmen's brother the other day, and he did admit that she was in with a very bad crowd before she transferred to Ventura High, but he couldn't give us any names. Hell, the kid's only twelve." Cross looked at her and started to say something but stopped.

Lily realized that he must be aware that her own thirteen-year-old daughter had been raped, the very reason she was at the precinct house. Excusing herself, Lily went to the water fountain at the back of the room and reached in her purse for another Valium. She felt the man's eyes on her back and hoped he couldn't see her tossing the pill down her throat. When she returned, Shana and Margie were walking toward her. The younger detective had taken the cue and left.

"We're all done. Now it's your turn," Margie said, then turned to Shana. "Get yourself a cold drink or something if you want. It won't take long."

"Mom, give me the keys to the car. I'll wait there. I can start working on some of my homework."

Lily desperately wanted to know what had transpired inside that room, yet she knew she was forbidden to ask until it was over. She tried to read Shana's eyes, searching for something, but she appeared remarkably composed, calmer now than before. If she had just seen the man who actually raped her, would she be this composed? It must have been exactly as she'd thought from the start—that once she saw him in person, she'd know it wasn't him. She started to follow Margie, who was already headed toward the room with the two-way glass where they conducted the lineups.

"Give me the keys, Mom," Shana asked again.

"Here," Lily said, handing over her purse. "They're in the bottom somewhere."

Looking at the men assembled, it took only seconds before she saw him. Then she could look at no one else. The lights were low in the viewing room, and Margie sat without speaking. "Tell them to turn sideways," Lily told the detective, and listened as she spoke to the men from a microphone. She walked to the glass and placed her palms on it, staring at his profile. He looked older than in the mug shot. "Was the photo of number three that we saw the other day recent?"

"I thought it was because he was just in jail on a parole violation, but it wasn't. It was five years old, from an old booking. Someone forgot to put the new one in the file."

"Tell them to bend down like they're tying their shoes or something," Lily asked, and the woman detective complied.

Finally she left the window and collapsed in the seat, her head in her hands. In the past, every time she'd recalled the rape, the face of Bobby Hernandez had appeared instantly.

Her mind was reeling like a boat about to capsize. The man in the room below was more than a face in a mug shot; he was a presence and that presence reached through the glass and seized her with fear. Could it be possible that she murdered the wrong man? She raised her eyes again and looked at him. She could taste the crusty knife in her mouth. It was him! Shana had been correct. Then the boat tipped again and she saw Hernandez. Like a form of denial, she was battling her own will. There was still a thread of doubt. If she could only see Hernandez again, in person, then she might know. Bile rose in her throat and she swallowed it. Hernandez would never be seen in person again. She'd made sure of that.

Removing her glasses, she reached down for her purse to look at the mug shot she'd brought from the office. Her fingers brushed against the carpet, then her palm. Shana had her purse. Her purse had the mug shot of Hernandez in it. Leaping from the seat, she rushed to the door, Margie right on her heels.

"Come back," the detective yelled, thinking she was having another panic attack. "We have to finish this and then you can leave."

Lily was out the door and actually running through the squad room, passing the records bureau, where every head turned, as she slammed through the double doors to the lobby. Her breath coming hard and fast, she bent down and held her stomach just as Margie caught up with her before she was out of the building.

"Please," the detective said, also gasping from chasing Lily, "I have to know if you've seen enough." Her dark eyes were full of annoyance. "My God, you're a D.A. Get a grip." Once she had said it, her eyes filled with regret. "I'm sorry, okay? That was a low-down thing to say, but I'm only trying to do my job." Her Elizabeth Taylor lavender eyes looked worn and tired, garish; there were beads of perspiration on her forehead beneath her jet black bangs.

"It's number three," Lily snapped at her, refusing her apology, knowing she was making her feel like shit. "I'm going to get Shana, and we'll come back and give you a statement." The woman had her hand on Lily's arm, and Lily jerked it away. "I'm only doing my job too. It's my daughter." With that, Lily turned and walked out of the station.

She went directly to the passenger side of the Honda and tried to open the door. It was locked. Shana saw her and rolled down the window. In her hands was the small picture of Hernandez.

"Who is this?" she demanded, no longer composed, her eyes wild with confusion.

"It's just an old defendant in a case at the office. Someone gave it to me, thinking he looked like the man I described. It's nothing." Lily reached inside the car and tried to take the photo from Shana's hands. The girl held it away where Lily couldn't reach it.

"No! It looks just like him. I want him brought in for a lineup. I thought it was the guy in there—number three—I was so sure. But now . . ."

"Shana, please give me the picture. You were right. I picked number three too. This other guy isn't the guy." Lily tried to still her racing heart by taking several slow, deep breaths, hoping the Valium was kicking in, willing herself not to think of all the ramifications of what was happening. She had to stop it now. "He's dead. It was a mistake. I just found out."

"What do you mean, he's dead? Does Margie know about him?"

"The man who gave me the photo didn't know that he'd been killed. He was killed in a gang shooting or something a long time ago, months before the rape. He means nothing to Margie or to anyone now. I told her we'd come right in and make a statement. She's waiting."

"Everyone looks alike. Maybe that guy isn't the one either." Tears started falling from her eyes.

Lily pulled the latch on the door and opened it, reaching

in to Shana, leaning down beside the car. "Honey, we're not the judge and jury. All we're doing is telling the truth—that the man in there appears to be the man who attacked us— nothing more. Once I learned this man in the picture was dead, I just forgot to put the picture back." Shana let her remove it from her hands. His name was printed at the bottom of the photo.

"Get my purse and we'll go in, and then we can go home and try to put this out of our minds. Okay?"

Once the photo was back in her purse and she and Shana were walking back to the building, she said, "Don't mention this to Margie. We'll all be confused and it will be a waste of time. I wasn't supposed to take this photo from the office and I'll get in trouble."

Shana looked at her mother only a moment, but her expression was one of disbelief. "I won't tell Margie," she said quietly. "It doesn't even look that much like him anyway. His face was thinner and he was uglier, meaner-looking. He had pimples like the man I saw in there. That's the man."

As they entered the lobby and Lily started to ask the girl at the front desk to page Detective Thomas, Shana made one last statement: "I wish this guy was dead too."

CHAPTER 31

It was five o'clock and Cunningham wanted to leave in a few minutes and get home before the local news came on. He always enjoyed seeing himself on television, knowing how it impressed Sharon and the kids. He didn't earn enough money to give them all the things they wanted, but he knew they were proud of him, and times like this when they saw him on television were the best times of all. After the row the other day with Tommy over the marijuana cigarette Sharon had found in his room, he'd also made himself a promise to spend more time at home.

Nothing new had turned up on the surveillance of Manny Hernandez. Fowler had called and informed him of the search warrant, having it delivered to the station, ready to be executed. His captain also called him and indicated that he simply did not have the manpower to continue the surveillance for more than twenty-four hours, particularly since the original matter was outside their jurisdiction. Cunningham crossed his fingers that once Manny heard the news of his brother's involvement in the Barnes homicide, he would dump the gun if he actually had it, and they could arrest him on the spot, evidence in hand. If this went down, he would buy himself a new pair of shoes for sure. He'd be a righteous star in everyone's eyes and maybe even get another interview on television.

On his way out, he passed Melissa, headed in his direction, her hands full of computer printouts. "You got something for me, babe, or are you going to finally take me up on that chicken-fried steak?"

His comment was ignored. "I have something, but who knows what it is? Thought I'd run it by you anyway."

"Shoot," he said.

A uniformed officer passed them in the hall. He stopped and patted Cunningham on the back. "Good work on that case, buddy," he said. He then squeezed by them and kept walking.

Melissa had the stack of papers held against her chest. He wasn't allowed to enter the records section where she worked, so she stated: "Do you have time to go back to your office? I need to spread this out to show you where we stand."

It sounded interesting. Enough that he thought he could always catch himself on the ten o'clock news if he missed the six. "Follow me . . . my dear. I always have time for you."

The squad room was empty and he landed in his chair hard, causing it to squeak and slide under his weight. Melissa sat in the chair next to him and leaned over, placing the papers on his desk. He reached out to pick up the printouts, and she knocked his hand away as with a child reaching into a cookie jar. "Stop that," she said, "you'll mess everything up."

"Wow," he said, "aren't you a bossy little thing?"

"Okay, this is the plate the witness copied: EBO822. Playing around, I ran all these plates and came back with red compact cars and registered owners in the area."

"Keep going," Cunningham said, "you got my full attention."

"Well, I've narrowed it down to about ten, as you can see. I thought I'd let you look at the names and addresses first, and see which ones you want to exclude. Then I'll run the owners for wants and warrants and criminal history." She got up to leave.

"Come on, Melissa," he said, "just run them all."

Her face was tense and she coughed. "I'm leaving now for the day. They just took my father to the hospital and it doesn't look good."

He felt for her. For years she had been saddled with the burden of caring for her father's needs, and every day she got more emaciated. Possibly this time he would die and she could finally go on with her life. "I'm sorry, doll. Thanks. I'll look everything over and let you know."

He watched her make her way out of the office, and then began studying the papers in front of him. As he began reading, he didn't recognize any of the names, so that left out the possibility of the killer being a known offender in the area. Then he came to the eighth name on the list and froze, staring at it. The plate was close, FPO322. It could have easily been misread for the real plate, EBO822. But it was registered to John and Lillian Forrester. "Shit," he said, laughing. Of all the names to pop up, it would be hers. The plate was restricted. Because Lily was a district attorney, the Department of Motor Vehicles didn't list her address on the registration in order to prevent some nut she'd prosecuted from walking into their office and filling out a form and getting her address. Just for the fun of it, he called the computer room and had them run her driver's license, curious as to where she lived. They said they'd call him back in a few minutes, and he sat there thinking about her, her face appearing in his mind.

He'd worked with Forrester numerous times in the past and thought highly of her, a lot more so than he did for her associates. He considered most of the attorneys in the D.A.'s office to be pompous legal eagles more concerned with their conviction records than what actually happened to the people involved in the cases they prosecuted. But Lily was tenacious, hardworking, and genuinely concerned with the outcome of every single case that came across her desk. In many ways they were alike. Once she sank her teeth into a case, she was like a dog with a bone. There was no way it was going to get away from her if she could help it. The phone rang; it was the computer room.

"You ready," the girl said.

"Shoot."

"The address is 1640 Overland, Camarillo. I ran her through records and we have her listed only as a victim in a rape that occurred in Ventura on April 29th of this year. I can have them fax you the report if you like."

He was speechless. This was a recent crime and she'd never mentioned a word, never missed a stride. He hadn't even asked the girl to run records on her. He'd just been playing around, using his authority to feed his curiosity. A lot of the officers did that, calling and getting the address of some good-looking babe they saw driving down the street. They weren't supposed to do it, but they still did.

"Hey," the girl said, "do you want the reports or not? I've got another officer on hold."

"Send them," he said, "mark them homicide and put my name on them." He replaced the receiver back on the hook and reached for the Hernandez file.

He knew what he'd find; he just had to confirm it. There it was: Bobby Hernandez had been murdered the morning of April 30, the day after Lily had been raped. Lily drove a red compact car with a similar license plate, one close enough to be mistaken. The next item he removed with considerable trepidation: the composite drawing. Before even looking at it, he glanced around to make certain the other detectives had left. "Nah," he said, looking at the face, "you're out of your fucking mind, Cunningham." Lily, as he remembered her, was actually fairly attractive. He sure wouldn't throw her out of bed, he thought, and this guy in the picture was certainly not someone he'd want to wake up to in the morning.

Just then the buzzer went off on the fax in the corner, and

he went to retrieve the reports. He started reading them as they came out of the machine. "Good lord, her daughter was raped, her thirteen-year-old daughter." He yanked the last sheet out and carried them all to his desk and started going through each page, committing every detail to memory. It all fit. Even the description they'd given of the rapist matched Hernandez perfectly. Mentally he was ready to reach for his pen and fill in the blanks in his little crossword puzzle, but he stopped himself, hoping it was simply a coincidence. That itself went against the grain, for he'd never been a big believer in coincidence or half his cases would have never been put to bed. According to most of the people he arrested, it was always just a big coincidence.

For the next hour, he sat at his desk, poring over the reports. Why on God's green earth, he kept asking himself, would a district attorney not report a crime like this for over six hours? Her husband had additionally called the police and reported her missing after the rape. She had not returned to the house until an hour after Hernandez had been blown apart on his sidewalk. What car did her husband have the police looking for—none other than the red Honda. That evidently was her car and not her husband's, which could have put the entire matter away and eased the throbbing pain Cunningham felt building in his temples. If her husband had been at home with the daughter with the red Honda in the garage, then . . . ? No, he thought, that still would not erase all suspicion. The husband might have left while the child slept and shot Hernandez.

He went back to the report again and found the time John Forrester had originally called the police in concern about his wife's whereabouts, and the time the police had arrived at their home in Camarillo. Forrester might have called the report in on his missing wife from a pay phone, shot Hernandez, and then made it back to Camarillo in the eighteen-minute time span before the police actually arrived. It was possible, but he would be one stupid son of a bitch if it really went down that way, giving the police the description of the very car he was driving. Lily Forrester had driven up in that Honda, so he was getting way out in left field . . . or had she . . . had the officers really seen the car . . . any car? Had the two of them, John and Lily, conspired together after deciding to execute Hernandez?

Linking the Forresters to Hernandez was a done deal. The Patricia Barnes matter had been handled under Lily's supervision and the matter dismissed the day of the rape. Removing the composite drawing again, Cunningham let it sit on his desk, and with both hands he shoved the other papers aside so that only the drawing met his line of vision. He took a piece of paper and covered the upper section of the face, leaving only the nose, mouth, and chin. Then he turned it over on his desk and left.

At records, he yelled at the dark-haired, chubby girl he despised, "You got any colored pencils?"

"No, I don't have any colored pencils," she said sarcastically.

"You got one of those little pencils that you use on your mouth? You know what I mean. My wife has one and you make a mouth first and then fill it in with lipstick."

She reached for her big black purse and removed a smaller plastic bag, holding up a reddish pencil in the air like a prize. "Is this what you mean?" she asked.

"Give it to me."

"Why should I give it to you?" she said, her nose in the air. "You've never done shit for me. Not only that but this little pencil cost me about three dollars. You got three bucks and you can have it," she said, smiling now, thinking it was a game, like a scavenger hunt.

He reached into his pocket and pulled out a fiver, slapping it on the counter. "Keep the change. Buy yourself some diet pills or something. Just give me the fucking thing, okay?"

Back in his office, he outlined the lips on the composite drawing, making them a little larger. The squad room had been empty, but now one of the detectives walked by on the way to his desk, a day-shifter working overtime. "You coloring now, Cunningham? That's what you do all night down here, huh? What is it, a little porno coloring book you got there?"

When he got no rise out of the detective, the other man went to his desk and started writing. Once the outline was drawn, Cunningham filled in the lips with the red pencil and stood up, looking at his handiwork. "That's it," he said, pacing up and down in front of his desk, stopping to look at the drawing and then too agitated to return to his chair. "That's it."

Grabbing all the files, he told the other detective, "I'm outta here. Do me a favor and tell dispatch that if anything comes in for homicide, they'll have to call me at home. I'm on sick leave."

On the way home, he pulled into a Stop 'n' Go and just parked, sitting in his car, watching people wander in and come out. His head was splitting, the pain like a vise now. Intending to go home and take some aspirin, maybe eat something, he was instead contemplating buying a six-pack of beer and driving somewhere to guzzle it down alone. It was still early, only eight-thirty, and the kids would drive him crazy if he went home. Seeing himself on the ten o'clock news meant nothing now. If his suspicions were accurate, this Hernandez story was big enough to go national, even a full fifteen-minute segment on one of those crime shows like *Hard Copy*. He opted for the six-pack and headed for the beach.

He parked the car on a remote area of the beach, near the sewage-treatment plant. It was an area where bodies frequently washed up on the shore: dead surfers, boaters, victims of homicides dumped into the ocean. The currents from miles away carried their lifeless bodies and placed them on the sand right next to the treatment plant, the sea regurgitating something noxious that was not its own and placing it where human waste was recycled.

By the time he popped the can on the third beer, his headache was receding. He had left Omaha for more reasons than the cold, and memories were flooding his mind.

While still assigned to patrol, Cunningham and his partner had been dispatched to a burglary in progress in a local grocery store and pharmacy. They had called for backup, seeing one of the rear windows broken and thinking they heard noises inside the building. His partner had taken up a position at the rear of the building, while Cunningham covered the front. Before the backup unit arrived, he heard glass shattering, gunfire, and then his partner's voice screaming on the portable radio for an ambulance as he ran for the back of the building. On the ground, bleeding from an enormous head wound, was a young boy.

His partner was bent over him. "It's a sock . . . a sock," he said, his voice and eyes indicating that he was on the verge of hysteria.

Cunningham pushed him aside and started C.P.R. on the boy. Pressing up and down on his chest, he looked at the concrete next to him and saw the spongy tissue in the pool of blood and knew that he was looking at the boy's brain, blown out the side of his head. Attempting further resuscitation was a waste of time. He stopped and wiped his bloody hands on his uniform pants.

"I thought it was a gun . . . do you hear me . . . ?" The man grabbed Cunningham's shirt with both hands. Sirens were wailing in the distance, getting closer by the second. "He came through the window . . . I saw something white in his hand . . . I thought it was a pearl-handled revolver. I fired. I didn't know he was a kid . . . I didn't know."

Cunningham looked at the kid's right hand and saw that he'd wrapped a white sports sock around his fist to prevent cutting himself when he smashed out the window.

His partner reached into his boot and pulled out a .22 pistol wrapped in plastic—what they called a throwaway—an unregistered, clean weapon. Many officers carried them for situations just like this one—in case they mistakenly shot an unarmed suspect. Cunningham stood speechless as the man leaned down and removed the sock from the boy's right hand. Holding the blood-spattered sock, he placed the gun into the lifeless hand and then let it fall to the ground.

"I've got to know you're with me," the officer pleaded, the ambulance and other units converging on the scene. "I've got five kids, for chrissake. I'm supposed to make sergeant next month."

It turned out the boy was a fourteen-year-old runaway, a victim of child abuse living on the streets. He had entered the grocery and pharmacy not for drugs or money, but for food. His partner made sergeant the following month; Cunningham made detective. When the same man worked his way up to deputy chief, Cunningham left the department.

He popped the can on the last of the six-pack and looked out over the darkened beach, illuminated only by the lights from the treatment plant and what little moonlight managed to break through the foggy night. He searched the stretch of sand, thinking idly that he might find a body there. What would he do if someone raped his daughter and he not only knew who had committed the crime, but had access to their address? Would he let the process of law deal out punishment, whatever it might amount to, or would he allow the beast of outrage and fury lead him to take matters into his own hands? Lily Forrester was a good woman, a dedicated and hardworking prosecutor. She was a mother. His partner all those years ago had been a good man too, and a father. But Cunningham had hated him for placing that gun in the dead boy's hand—and hated himself for collaborating on his story—a lie that was forever attached to the poor boy's memory.

Bobby Hernandez had been one of God's defects, he told himself. He'd been a killer and a rapist—a violent and deadly being who stalked his prey like an animal. He thought with repulsion of the unspeakable acts committed against Carmen Lopez, a girl who had managed to rise above the crime-infested neighborhood she had grown up in, who had been in line for

a scholarship and a decent life. Her boyfriend, Peter Mc-
Donald, had never received so much as a citation in his short
life. Although he couldn't yet prove that Hernandez had been
involved in that crime, his gut instinct told him that he had.

He hadn't seen Lillian Forrester in person for maybe six
weeks, but her image was clear in his mind. She wasn't one of
those attorneys who pranced around the courtroom, in love
with the sound of her own voice, eager for convictions because
they were wins, feathers in her cap. He remembered her har-
ried face during the last homicide he had worked and she had
prosecuted, her somewhat wrinkled suit, her red hair escaping
and falling across her forehead. She lived for the job; it consumed her. They were alike, a kinship born of conviction.

Killing the last beer, he drove home.

CHAPTER **32** ∎

Lily and Shana were on their way home from the Ventura Police Department after both signing statements to the effect that Marco Curazon, an American-born Cuban, was to the best of their knowledge the man who had perpetrated the crimes of which they were both victims. He had a prior offense for burglary, an extensive juvenile record, and had been sentenced to prison five years before for rape. By failing to maintain employment, he had violated the terms of his parole and had served five days in county jail in April.

He had been released the evening of the rape.

Margie Thomas had informed Lily that evidence obtained from the medical–legal exam conducted at Pleasant Valley Hospital on Shana had contained several hair follicles recovered from her pubic area, and these would be examined against hairs which they would eventually obtain from Curazon. Prior to signing the statement, Lily had asked that he be returned to the lineup and asked to read the words "taste the blood of a whore" from a piece of paper while she listened from the viewing room. Shana remained outside.

There would be a bail hearing the following day, but even if the court did set bail, the man's parole agent had indicated that he would place a hold on Curazon preventing his release. With his prior conviction, which could be pled as an enhancement, extra time for violation of parole, and the current offenses, his prison term if convicted could add up to almost twenty years. Lily didn't feel the need to advise Shana that he would only serve ten of these years. She wanted the child to be free from fear.

Her emotions numbed by the Valium, Lily was floating in a sea of disbelief and shock. The only solace she could find was in the knowledge that Hernandez had murdered the prostitute. She needed more. She needed to know that he was involved in the McDonald–Lopez massacre. Then the death penalty she had wrongfully imposed would be less barbaric. And she still wasn't fully convinced that Curazon was the rapist, but this time she was going to let law enforcement and the courts determine his guilt. This time there was no rage—the only emotion he had generated as she had stood and watched him through the one-way glass was disgust.

Coming up from her thoughts, she noticed they were passing the government center. "Want to stop at my office and see the new building?" she asked Shana. "I won't be more than a few minutes. I left early today and I should check on a few things."

"I don't mind, but I have to do my history."

"Take your history book and notebook, and you can work at one of the desks outside my office while I make a few calls. I'll call your father and tell him we'll be late."

"I already called him from the station and told him the guy's in jail," Shana said, a look of relief on her face. "I just wanted him to know." She turned and looked at Lily.

Almost eight o'clock, the parking lot was deserted except for a few cars scattered throughout the huge space. Right in front of the doors to the Hall of Justice, where Lily was headed, was a white BMW exactly like Richard's. As she got closer, she recognized the plate and knew it was his. She started to turn around and leave; she was seconds late. He had seen her and was waving as he exited the glass doors.

"Who's that?" Shana said.

"That's a man who works with me in my department. He was the chief before I got the post, and they kept him on to help me." Richard was walking toward the car as Lily and Shana opened the doors. He had a big smile on his face and didn't bat an eye when he saw Lily wasn't alone.

"You have to be Shana?" he said, extending his hand as he would to an adult. "I've heard so much about you from your mother, and of course, I see your picture on her desk every day."

Lily introduced him. "Shana, this is Richard Fowler." She then turned and seeing a young man behind the wheel of the BMW, she realized that it must be Richard's son. Even though the windows of the car were rolled up, the car seemed to be vibrating from the deafening stereo inside. Lily felt self-conscious and tried to push her hair off her face and pull her shoulders back. When she had first seen the BMW, she had visualized him walking out of the building with the young blond D.A.

Richard spoke directly to Shana. "Stay there a minute, but put your hands over your ears before I open the door or you'll be sorry. I want you both to meet my son." He then turned to Lily. "I left my wallet in the office and we're out foraging for food. Can't get too far on five dollars. Wait . . . I'll get Greg."

An enormous blast of what sounded like rap music struck their ears and then was silenced. A handsome young man started walking toward them. He had his father's dark eyes, but his hair was blond and hung down his back like a rock star's—silky and sun-streaked, as well cared for as a girl's. The way he moved, the long, fluid strides, was definitely a trait inherited from his father, as were the rakish grin and confidence.

"Greg, this is Lily Forrester, the D.A. who took my position, and this lovely girl is her daughter, Shana."

Tossing her full head of hair to one side of her face, Shana peeked up at him in such a way that her eyelashes looked like they were going to stick to her lids. A slight tinge of pink spread across her face, but she managed to produce a smile unlike any her mother had ever seen. Lily knew she was nervous; she also knew she was taken with Greg.

Richard started to take a few steps toward his car, and Lily toward the doors to the building. "See you tomorrow," he said. They both then stopped and stared at their children and then back at each other. Greg and Shana were in their own little world.

"Where do you go to school?" Greg asked, leaning over the top of Lily's Honda.

"Next year I'm going to Ventura High. Right now I'm still in Camarillo. I hate it." Shana pushed one hip out and also leaned against the car.

"Radical. I'll be a senior there next year. Ever go to the beach around here?" he asked, flipping his hair with both hands.

Richard's expression darkened, but Lily was pleased. What she was seeing was a hint of the magic, the old Shana. She didn't want it to stop. Now was the perfect time for the child to resume her life.

"Rich, I have a case I have to check on. I could use your advice." She turned to the two young people. "Do you guys want to talk for a few minutes while we run upstairs? It won't take more than ten minutes max."

"No problem," Greg said eagerly. "I just ate some burgers a few hours ago."

Richard looked at Lily, puzzled, but followed her into the complex. In the elevator, he questioned her. "What case are you talking about? McDonald–Lopez? Nothing new." His brows were furrowed with concern. "You know, I haven't told you much about Greg. He's quite the man with the girls."

"I noticed," Lily said. "Like father, like son."

"To be frank, I would rather they got to know each other once our relationship is out in the open. I don't want Greg putting the make on her." He grimaced. "Christ, he will. She's a beautiful girl. Looks just like you. I mean just like you."

At the floor, they needed a key to get in. "Got your key?" Lily said, replaying his last statement about their "relationship." She had him jumping in and out of bed with every available woman at the office, and he was still talking about their relationship. "I think I'm going to get one of those key chains that fastens to your belt."

Richard fished out his key, but kept glancing back at the elevator. "I'm going back down. Do you mind?" He was nervous, rubbing his finger back and forth over his chin.

"Please, you're being silly. Shana needs this desperately. This is the first time since everything has happened that I've seen her come alive. So what if they flirt a little?"

"What did you come here for anyway that couldn't wait until tomorrow?"

Her intention had been to call the jail and find out exactly what time Hernandez had been released on the night of the rape, something she should have done long ago. Now that Richard was there, she hesitated, unable to find a valid excuse for her actions. "Let's go," she said. "Shana has homework."

In the elevator, he tried to corner her, but she slipped away, ducking under his arm. "The kids could be standing there when the door opens," she said.

"That's just the point. I want them to know we love each other. I want us all to be a family someday. That's what I dream about all the time. You'd never believe all the dreams I have. I've even thought about us opening our own law firm." The elevator doors closed.

Lily felt warmth course through her veins, wondering if she

was reacting to Richard's words or the Valium. Opening her purse to reach for her car keys, she saw the mug shot of Hernandez and quickly closed the purse. It was the Valium. Dreams were for people who had not stepped over the line, who had not made a grave error.

Richard was holding the elevator doors open; they kept trying to close and were emitting a horrendous noise that echoed in Lily's ears. She was leaning against the back of the elevator, unable to move.

"Are you okay?" he asked. He then slapped his forehead with his hand. "You went for the lineup tonight, didn't you? God, how could I forget? I was so preoccupied today and then Greg came over . . . What happened?"

She ignored him and walked from the elevator, looking through the glass to the parking lot. The kids were no longer standing there, and Lily began to panic. "Where are they? My God, where did they go? I shouldn't have let her stay down here."

Richard walked behind her and smiled. "They're in the car, Mom. Probably listening to tapes. I thought you were the one that thought this was such a good idea."

They both hit the double doors at the same time. "Remember, I did warn you about Greg. I wouldn't trust that boy five minutes with my thirteen-year-old daughter," he said.

"She'll be fourteen in two months, but I get the picture. Send her to the car and I'll see you in the morning." She then added, "We both picked the same man. He's in custody. I'll fill you in later."

Shana jumped into the car and waved to Greg out the window as they drove off. "He's so rad, Mom," she said, pulling the visor down and trying to see how she looked even though it was dark. "He's gorgeous . . . totally gorgeous. He's a surfer. He wants to take me to the beach someday. I can't believe it . . . a senior. Wait till I tell Charlotte and Sally. He looks just like one of the Nelson twins. Jeez." The words were spilling out in youthful enthusiasm. "I've gotta get a tan."

Lily didn't want to dampen her excitement, but she couldn't let her think she was going to start dating a boy as old as Greg. The whole thing had been a mistake. Everything she did seemed to be a mistake. "He's too old for you, Shana. And from what his dad says, he's a little wild. But there are other boys your own age."

Shana sat upright in her seat, angry. "Don't treat me like a baby. A lot of girls my age date older guys. He probably won't call anyway."

"We're going to have to have a boy talk soon," Lily said. "We've really never talked about things like that." They used to talk about the boys in Shana's classes, but that was quite a while back, and Greg was far out of that league.

Shana shot Lily a look like she was the dumbest person alive and turned on the radio. She then spoke loudly over the music. "Really, Mom, don't you think I'm a little bit more mature than other girls my age? Why don't you just accept it? I have."

Lily's heart started to race. Kids were survivors, Richard had said. She didn't want her daughter to be a survivor. Rats were survivors. What she wanted to believe was that nothing had changed, at least not with Shana. But that was far from the truth.

"No, I don't think you know everything. And I don't want anyone to take advantage of you."

"You're being ridiculous, Mom. I mean, it's not like someone I know is going to hurt me."

Lily turned onto a side street and parked, turning off the ignition and letting her hands fall into her lap. "I'm going to tell you something awful . . . something that happened to me when I was a girl, something that has been with me all my life like an ugly scar. I never thought I could tell you, but . . ." Lily's voice was soft, her mouth dry. "I don't want you to think that people you know are harmless and only criminals pose a threat. When I was eight years old, my grandfather raped me."

Shana's mouth fell open and Lily could hear her sucking in air. "Your grandfather?"

"Yes. It's called incest. It continued from the time I was eight until I was your age, thirteen."

"But why didn't you tell someone . . . your mom?"

"I tried to tell her, but she didn't listen. She didn't listen because I was a little girl and because people didn't talk about things like that back then. Not only is incest common, there are other situations that develop with teachers, neighbors, people you see everyday. And don't ever think that just because a boy looks nice that he might not try to force himself on you. That happens a lot too."

"I can't believe this happened to you. I can't believe you're telling me this," Shana said, shocked.

Lily sighed deeply and looked straight ahead. They were parked in front of someone's house in a residential neighborhood, and a man was getting into his car, looking at them. "Well, it did happen to me, Shana. And I did the worst thing I could possibly do. I tried to pretend it never did; I suppressed it, buried it deep inside." She turned and looked at her daughter. "Now, after all these years, I think that's the reason I never let anyone get really close to me, because this horrible secret was there. It feels so strange to talk about it . . . and to you, my own daughter."

"You can talk to me about anything you want, Mom. Everyone's always talked to me about their problems. I don't know why, but they have. What happened to him—your grandfather? Did you hate him?"

"He died. I thought it was all over. I was happy he died. But you know what? Now I wish he'd lived and that I'd been able to confront him, tell him what he did to my life, tell everyone." Lily started up the car, the radio started blasting, but Shana reached over and turned it off.

"You know, Mom, I've thought about all kinds of things since the rape: God, dying, why things like this happen. In school once I read this book and it said that God never gives you more than you can handle. Maybe these bad things happened to us because we can handle them and some other person couldn't. I mean, you became a district attorney and you put people like that in prison, so . . ." She reached over and placed her hand on Lily's. "And me, well, I'm gonna do something important someday, just like you. I'm going to be happy too and I won't let myself be afraid of every little thing . . . every person . . . every sound."

"You're a remarkable young woman, baby," Lily said, squeezing her hand. "I'm so proud of you . . . so proud you're my daughter."

"Hey," Shana said, "there's a Baskin-Robbins." She smiled. "How about a great big hot fudge sundae with nuts and whipped cream? Yum. Doesn't that make your mouth water? Let's get one."

When they got home, John was asleep on the sofa. Lily went to the linen closet for the blanket and gently tossed it over him, looking down on him as with a child. She then tiptoed around him, turned out the lights, and locked the doors.

In Shana's room, she told her to forgo the homework for the night and finish it in the morning. Shana grabbed her around the neck and kissed her on both cheeks.

"You know that guy—Greg's dad—is he your boyfriend?"

Lily started to blush and didn't know what to say. "He's someone I work with and I like him a lot."

"You can tell me. Dad told me about his girlfriend and he said he thought you were seeing someone too."

Shana went and flopped down on her bed on her stomach, bracing her head in her hands. "I liked him. He seemed like a nice man." Di peeked out from the covers.

Looking back at her from the door, Lily smiled and said, "You just liked his son. Don't tell me you're going to want to pick the men I date and they all have to have good-looking sons."

"Why not?" Shana said, her eyes sparkling. "We're gonna be roommates, remember?"

In the big bed alone, Lily turned off the light. For years she had been two people without even realizing it. She had gone about her affairs during the day exuding strength and purpose, a woman in control, just as she had gone out and played as a child the morning after her grandfather fulfilled his disgusting desires. But inside there was another Lily, a terrified woman possessed by hatred and rage. This was the night person, the dark one. Her grandfather's face kept appearing in front of her, and she could smell the sickening odor of Old Spice aftershave. "You," she said out loud. "I hope you're rotting in your grave. You stole my life. You drove me insane. I've done something worse than even you now. I've killed someone. You made me hate so much I killed someone."

She stared open-eyed into the darkness. With the blackout drapes, it was like a grave. Only a glimmer of light from the alarm clock made a small circle on the wall. What did it feel like to die? she thought. Was it blackness? Was there a rebirth of some kind? Was there a purgatory like the Catholic church had taught her to believe?

The ticking of the clock seemed unbearably loud, and she could hear her own heartbeat. In a court of law there were defenses and mitigating circumstances. Was there a final court, a final judgment? If she had killed the wrong man, then it was not God's hand that had guided her. That was delusional, insanity. God had not appointed her as His executioner. She rolled over onto her side in the darkness, pulling her knees to her chest in the fetal position. But was there forgiveness, redemption? What was required to clear her mortal soul?

Suddenly the bedside phone rang, jarring Lily back to reality. She grabbed it and whispered, "Hello."

"It's me," a deep, familiar voice said, but she couldn't quite place it. "You know, Bruce Cunningham."

"Cunningham?" she said, bolting straight up in bed. It was

almost eleven o'clock. What in God's name was he calling about? "Did something go down on Manny?"

"Nah. I've just been thinking. Thought I'd call you up."

Lily couldn't believe it. His words were slurred; he'd obviously been drinking. She didn't know what to say. Her heart was racing. Had something happened? Maybe another witness had come forward, pointing the finger at her. Or the shell casing, she thought, panic rising. Ballistics had found her prints on the shell casings. She raised a finger to her mouth and started chewing on the skin there.

"That Hernandez was an animal. He butchered that poor girl. Just fucking butchered her like a side of beef."

Lily took her finger out of her mouth. She wanted to turn the light on, but she couldn't move. "He strangled her," she said softly. "It's sad, but she was a hooker and that's a dangerous line of work."

"I'm not talking 'bout the hooker," he said loudly. "I'm talking 'bout Carmen Lopez. They did her. They shoved that tree limb in her vagina and shot her breasts like a fucking game. We got to get them. Manny, I mean, and the rest. You got a daughter?"

"Yes, I do."

"Me too. It makes you think, huh? Makes you think it could happen to your own kid."

Lily pulled the covers up to her neck and started twisting one of the corners with her hand. What was he getting at? He hadn't simply called her up at home this late at night to talk off a drunk. He wasn't that type of cop. It was hard to even imagine Bruce Cunningham intoxicated. Holding her breath, she listened for sounds that the call was recorded.

"I believe in the law, you know," he continued, his words less slurred, in almost an intentional effort. "No one else does much anymore. Not in the ranks. Everything's become a big fucking joke. Cops just do whatever they want." He was silent and then he said: "People too."

That was it. The conversation had gone too far. What was she going to do? Sit here and discuss vigilantism with the man who could march her to prison? "Good night, Bruce. Let me know if anything develops with Manny." She quickly replaced the phone and tried to tell herself the phone call meant nothing. He had her number, he'd had a few drinks, so he just decided to call her. They were working together on a major series of brutal crimes, she told herself. They'd known each other for years, working on cases together, drinking coffee together. It wasn't really so unusual. Even a seasoned cop like Cunningham might feel the weight of it all now and then. But it was too close. Too close. Every possible negative thought in her mind surfaced and played again and again. She'd killed the wrong man. Cunningham was on to her. Over and over the thoughts turned. Then she tried to rationalize them away, like a trial inside her tortured mind. She was both prosecutor and defense. She had lost her ability to be a judge even in her own fantasies.

The clock ticked and she watched the hands move until the dial read four o'clock. She crawled out of bed and fell to her knees in prayer. "Father, forgive me, for I have sinned, and it's been . . ." She didn't remember when she'd made her last confession. She didn't remember anything except Bruce Cunningham's last statement: "Cops do whatever they want . . . people too."

"Please, God," she continued, "I don't have the right to ask you to save me from what I've done. Please just give me the strength to handle it and protect my precious child."

She remained on the floor, on her knees, leaning over the bed, staring into the darkness. Finally her exhausted body gave up and she slid to the floor in sleep.

Outside, the sun was rising.

CHAPTER **33** .

Officer Chris Brown was parked a block down on 3rd Street, in a black '65 Caddy borrowed from vice to use as a surveillance vehicle. He could see the front of the Hernandez house from his position, but had to use the pair of binoculars on the seat next to him to make out facial features of anyone coming or leaving the house. It was eleven o'clock and Brown had just relieved the previous officer. Shucking his uniform in the locker room only a few minutes before, he was pulling a double shift. He needed the money.

He poured a cup of black coffee, only lukewarm, from the thermos on the floorboard and sipped it, hoping it would do the job and keep him awake. It was going to be a long night. Finishing the coffee, he slid down in the comfortable velvet seat, rolled down the window, and stretched out his long legs. He started to doze, with his arm out the driver's window, when suddenly he felt a wet, sickening touch on his hand and almost went for his revolver. A large mixed-breed dog had been licking the remnants of his fried chicken dinner off his hand. "Shit," he said, sitting up in the vehicle, his heart still jumping. In this neighborhood he was lucky that wet feeling hadn't been his own blood after some dude sliced his arm off to steal his wrist watch. He turned on the ignition and rolled up the automatic windows, flicked the door locks, and looked down the street at the house.

He stiffened as he spotted a male shuffling to the car in the driveway, already down the front steps of the residence. Grabbing the binoculars off the seat, he saw it was his man and watched as he entered a black '75 Plymouth and backed out into the street. Waiting until the taillights were almost out of sight, he cranked up the Caddy, speeding until the vehicle was once again in sight, catching him just as he turned the corner, and then dropped back at least three car lengths behind.

Starting to reach for the radio, Brown recalled that he had been instructed to follow the suspect and make contact only if he appeared to be disposing of a firearm. Then he was not to approach unless he had backup. He could relay information to the station via the portable cellular phone; the radio was off limits due to the possibility that the suspect had a police scanner.

There was still traffic on the streets, and on several occasions he almost lost the black Plymouth. He was darting in and out of the side streets, but it was almost like he was merely cruising, his speed well within the posted limits. Looking at the street signs, knowing the area well from patrol, Brown thought he was headed to the beach area of Porte Hueneme. It could be that he was going to score drugs. Should he only watch and disregard it? He assumed they weren't interested in busting him on possession.

The Plymouth pulled up to a deserted area of beach and parked. Brown watched as he exited the vehicle on foot, both hands in his jacket pocket. There were no other cars in sight, and he was walking rapidly in the direction of the water. If Brown didn't follow him on foot, he would lose him. He picked up the cellular phone and held it in his hand. If he requested backup and the guy was merely going to take a piss, the surveillance would be blown and Brown knew he'd never make it out of patrol. He shoved the portable phone into the back pocket of his pants, following on foot, hoping he hadn't already lost him.

Pulling the nylon parka up around his neck, Brown strolled nonchalantly toward the beach, looking for anything that could provide cover. There were a few light standards near the sidewalk, but the light didn't reach to the sand. Ducking behind a large garbage can, he saw Manny just as he removed his hand from his pocket. From this distance it was impossible to see the object in his hand, but there was something, and Brown knew he had to move fast. The suspect was now standing at the water's edge. If the object was the .22 pistol, it would be gone in seconds, tossed into the ocean, any prints obliterated.

No time to call for backup. He pulled his service revolver from his shoulder holster, crept closer in the dark, and was only steps away from shoving it into the back of Manny's head when he turned, saw Brown, and fired. The bullet smashed into his shoulder and he hit the sand, frantically grabbing for the portable to call for help. A second shot rang out and this one struck his leg. He tried to reach the phone with his left hand; his right shoulder had been hit and his own weapon had fallen to the sand. Manny was running now. Brown dragged himself up and, grabbing his gun with his left hand, started after him.

Stumbling in the deep sand, his leg throbbing and warm blood saturating his pants, he went down on his stomach and clasped his gun between both hands, forcing his injured arm to move. Manny was a good distance away, but the sand was slowing him down and he had not yet reached the sidewalk. Brown sighted and fired. The explosion caused the gun to pop out of his weakened hand and fall to the sand several feet away.

He had missed. Manny was turning with the gun again, about to fire at him, this time at close range.

He scrambled to retrieve his weapon, his shoulder wound shooting white heat down his arm. He had the gun. Terror of his impending death brought strength and stillness. He fired. Manny went down.

"I'm shot. Jesus fucking Christ," Manny screamed in terror. "I'm bleeding to death. Help me, man. I'm gonna die."

Wildly stabbing the tiny button on the cellular that dialed the station, finally hearing the familiar voice of the dispatcher and the beeping of the recorded line, he yelled, "Officer down. I've been shot and suspect shot. He's still armed. Need ambulance and backup." He tried to recall the cross street nearest the beach. "Anchors Way," he screamed. "I'm at the beach at the end of Anchors Way . . . Porte Hueneme."

"Stay on the line," the dispatcher said. "Keep talking until we get there. Where's the suspect in relation to your location?"

"Near the sidewalk. I'm on the sand behind him."

Manny struggled to get up and fell down again. Brown tried to fire once more, but his right hand was now useless and his left hand shaking and weak. He had to brace it with the injured arm. When he saw Manny make it almost to his feet, he squeezed off another round. This time the man hit the ground face first, sand rising in the night air like a dust storm around him. He didn't move. He didn't get up. There was dead silence, but in the distance Brown could hear the emergency vehicles en route.

By the time help arrived, Manny was in cardiac arrest with two .38 slugs in his back. One must have raced through tissue and muscle and lodged in his heart. The paramedics started C.P.R. and loaded him into an ambulance before they loaded Brown into a second one that pulled up, siren blaring.

Although Brown was losing blood fast, the .22 had done no major damage, and his condition stabilized once they applied pressure and tourniquets to stop the flow of blood.

More than sixteen black-and-whites converged on the

scene, but Brown had been alert enough to warn them of the importance of protecting any prints that might be on the weapon. It was bagged immediately and the area sealed off for the crime-scene units.

CHAPTER **34** ·

Cunningham was in a deep, beer-induced sleep when the call came through. His wife answered the phone, punching him and handing it to him.

"The officer," he asked, "you certain he's going to pull through?"

"No doubt at all. I hear he's awake and they're removing the slugs. He's lucky it was only a .22. Plus, the second shot was from a good distance, so that wound is pretty minor," the patrol sergeant advised. "But your guy was pronounced dead in the E.R."

"The weapon . . . sounds like what we've been looking for . . . hot damn," Cunningham said. "We may have just put together that Ventura homicide." He then added. "Impound the Plymouth. No telling what else we'll find."

As he hung up the phone, Sharon rolled over and rested her head in the crook of his arm. "You smell like a brewery. Are you going in?"

"Nah," he said, "nothing on my end till tomorrow. Go back to sleep."

"Have you ever thought of getting another job, Bruce?" She was drifting off as she spoke. He didn't reply; she knew the answer.

He went to work at ten the following morning. The weapon was still in the lab and the fingerprint analysis was not complete, but the department was buzzing with rumors about the connection to the double homicides, and everyone came up to Cunningham, asking questions. The officer, Chris Brown, was in excellent condition and was due to be released the following day. Cunningham went to the hospital to see him.

"You did good, buddy," he said, taking a seat in the small chair next to the bed and pulling it closer. "How're you feeling?"

The young officer looked pale. He'd lost a lot of blood. "I'm going home tomorrow. Maybe if I'd called for backup right when it started going down, no one would've got shot."

"You did what you were instructed to do. He might have been taking a stroll on the beach and you would have blown it. You kept him from disposing of the weapon. That was the game." Cunningham brushed his fingers through his mustache and looked at the white tile floor. He pulled out his pack of Marlboros and then realized he couldn't smoke in the hospital. "This guy had a big red target on his back. Someone else would've taken him out if it hadn't been you. There's no telling what all he and his brother were into, but you can bet it was all bad, real bad. In a few hours we'll know if the weapon was the one used in the double homicide in Ventura." The detective watched as the young officer gazed at the ceiling. He knew the look. "Never shot anyone before, huh?"

The officer tried to pull himself up on the pillows. He was too weak and fell back. "No one has ever shot me, or shot at me. I've never even fired my gun outside of the pistol range. I always knew it might happen, but then it really happens and it's not at all what you thought it would be." He looked over at the detective. "Seconds, that's what it is. It's all over and you're still trying to figure out what went down in those seconds. Everything they teach you doesn't mean shit."

"Yeah," Cunningham said, standing to leave. "You've got that right, my man. You rest now. I'll see you later."

Heading back to the station, Cunningham pulled through Taco Bell and ordered two burritos and a diet soda. He didn't feel like stopping at Stop 'n' Go to save the few cents on the drink. His head was throbbing from the beer he'd consumed the night before. He hadn't stopped with the six-pack on the beach. He'd come home and downed three or four more. This was a sure sign of age, this hangover, he told himself, recalling the nights he had drunk three times as much and leaped out of bed the next morning ready to tackle the world. But the other thing was troubling him, the reason he had downed the beer to begin with, the fact that he still had an open homicide and the suspect was a district attorney. He belched loudly. Now his stomach was churning and bubbling. Getting close to a Maalox moment, he thought. Getting close to a damn ulcer, that's what.

Back at the station, he found Forrester's home phone number and sat in his chair, hesitant to speak with her. Conclusive reports on the fingerprints removed from the weapon wouldn't be available until Monday. Did he really have a reason to call her at home again on a weekend? Then again, she would hear of Manny's death, he told himself, and she would want to know if a weapon had been recovered. He picked up the phone and then gently replaced it on the cradle.

Why had he called her last night? He really didn't know. If the weapon did prove to be the one used in the McDonald–Lopez slayings, this would amount to the finest police work of his career. He had followed the lead on the missing prostitute and hit pay dirt. It was his eagle eye that had spotted the F.I. card noting Carmen Lopez's association with the Hernandez brothers, tying them to the mutilation murder. He had pushed for the surveillance on Manny even if Lily had been the one who suggested the weapon might be hidden in Manny's Plymouth. That one he had to give to her. No doubt about it. That one he'd missed. But the rest was old yours truly, he thought with pride. He'd put the whole thing together from day one.

He could see the front-page headlines. Oh, not just the ones that would go out today, but the ones that would come when the case was completely broken open like a ripe watermelon. And it would be. That, he could feel in his gut. He'd already taken his imaginary pen and filled in the blanks of his puzzle.

Why had he called her? He still didn't know. The case was sensational as it stood, but if Lillian Forrester, District Attorney, had murdered Bobby Hernandez . . . ? "Now, we're talking national coverage," he said. "Now we're talking big." As his excitement rose, his stomach turned.

That's why he'd called her. Was it time to go formal with this: the investigation of Forrester for the death of Bobby Hernandez? On this case the bomb was ticking and the detonator was in his sticky palm. He dialed her number.

She answered the phone. "Heard the news?" he said. "Oh, this is Bruce Cunningham."

Lily had just scrubbed out the master bath and was getting ready to vacuum the carpet. "No, I didn't hear anything. What's going on?"

"We shot Manny Hernandez last night. He's dead. He fired first at our surveillance officer, but the guy's okay. We have the gun: a .22 caliber."

"My God," Lily exclaimed, sitting on the edge of the bed, a sponge still in her hand. "The prints?"

"Won't know anything until around noon Monday. It's looking good, though, isn't it? Looking real good. You may get that break you've been waiting for real soon."

"You've done a great job on this, Bruce," she said and then paused, thinking. "Can't you come up with something on the other two suspects we have in jail? If this is the weapon and Bobby and Manny were involved, it makes their stories seem feasible."

"Why don't I come to your office Monday, and we'll sit down and put everything together? My suggestion is to go for Nieves. If his prints aren't on it, he could be the lightweight in the whole picture."

"You mean offer him a deal?"

"You can think on it. I know you guys don't want anyone to walk, but if he pled on the rape and possibly an accessory to murder charge and he spilled his guts, you'd have the case in hand. But what do I know . . . ?"

"I'll discuss it with Richard Fowler and, of course, Butler. Come in around eleven. You might be able to interview Nieves and get him to talk without a deal."

"Not without a pair of brass knuckles," he said, laughing, "but I'm not proud. I'll give it a shot. Clear it with his attorney."

"It won't be a problem; it's Kensington, the public defender. He tends to lean in our direction."

After Cunningham hung up, he took out the composite drawing of the so-called man Manny Hernandez had seen. On impulse he folded over the paper that he'd drawn the red lips on and began tearing it into tiny pieces. Lily's soft voice, with the barely distinguishable Texas accent, played over and over inside his head. There was something about her that reached him in a place he couldn't describe. When they talked, some unknown presence hung heavy in the air, so thick that he felt he could reach out and touch it. It was fear, and it wasn't just her fear, it was his. He looked down at the shredded papers in his hand. He was holding her life there, her future, her child's and husband's future. Moving his hand over the trash can, he let the papers fall like confetti.

He then replaced the drawing with a duplicate minus his artistic enhancements. The only eyewitness in Lily's case was Manny and he was dead. The woman who'd come forth with the license plate hadn't seen the driver's face. Once again he looked at the composite and tried to see what Manny had seen. It all seemed so wild. They may have shot a suspect in one case, but they'd shot a witness in the other. Speculation was a funny thing, he thought. Maybe there was some pale, effeminate killer out there, running around shooting people while Cunningham was sitting here trying to pin it on one of his own kind.

No, what he saw, no matter what he tried to tell himself, was the face of Lily Forrester, her hair shoved under that blue knit ski cap, blasting away at the man who had raped her daughter.

It was going to take something a lot stronger than a six-pack of beer to make him forget. It might take something stronger than his stomach and his conscience could handle.

35.

He called Friday morning before she left for school.

"This is Greg," he said. "You know, I met you the other night with my dad."

"Hi," she said, stretching the phone cord as she walked over and closed her bedroom door, her puppy right on her heels. "I was just leaving to go to school."

"Wanna go surfing with me tomorrow?"

"I want to go, but I can't surf."

"Wanna learn?"

"Sure," she said. As she recalled her mother's admonitions about him, a plan of getting around any objections was already formulating in her mind. "Tell me what time you want to pick me up. I'll be at a friend's house."

In the background Shana heard the garage door open and knew her father was parked in the driveway, waiting to drive her to school. Greg had his driver's license. What a trip. Gorgeous and he could drive.

"'Bout five-thirty. Give me the directions. Wait, gotta get a pen . . . Go," he said.

Spending the night with Charlotte would be no problem, but sneaking out at five-thirty, when her father got home from work, that might be a real problem. "I don't know," she said. "Can't we do it another time?"

She heard one quick tap of the horn outside; her father never honked. It must mean she was going to be late for school.

"Don't want to get up that early, huh? That's the best time."

"You mean five-thirty Saturday morning?" Once she had said it, she realized it made her sound dumb. Everyone knew people surfed early. "Sure . . . that's fine."

That night at Charlotte's, where she was staying overnight, Shana spent most the evening going through the girl's closet and drawers, pulling out things and trying them on and then tossing them on the floor. "Don't you have anything at all new?" she asked. "I'm going on a date with a senior." She smiled, raising her shoulders and hugging herself with apprehension. Both girls giggled.

"He's not a senior till next year. That's what you said." Charlotte was spread out on her stomach on the bed, her face supported by her hands. "You're only going surfing. What do you think you're supposed to wear anyway? Here," she said, leaping off the bed. "Wear these and this."

The girl held up a pair of cutoff jeans and a U.C.L.A. sweatshirt. Shana grabbed them and pulled them on, letting them drift down on her hips. Charlotte's clothes used to fit her perfectly, but now they were too big. As she looked at herself in the mirror, pulling her nightshirt up and exposing her navel, she liked the look of the oversize shorts. With her bikini top, she would look like the girls she saw at the mall with guys who looked like Greg.

Instructing him merely to pull in front of the house and park, Shana was awake at five o'clock and perched by the window in Charlotte's bedroom, overlooking the street. After what seemed like hours, a green Volkswagen van with a surf rack on top pulled to the curb and parked. She nudged Charlotte, but put her finger to her lips so she wouldn't wake the rest of the household. Charlotte had agreed to tell her parents that Shana's mother picked her up early to go see her grandmother. "He's here," she said, "but don't let him see you looking out the window."

As they were driving off, Charlotte's face was as noticeable in the window as a pumpkin on Halloween. Greg saw her and waved like a celebrity. Shana slid down in the seat in embarrassment.

From Camarillo they headed toward Los Angeles and then dropped into Topanga Canyon to Malibu. The van rattled and shook as they drove the winding canyon roads in the dark. The back was full of McDonald's and Burger King sacks, towels that reeked of mildew, and wet suits. She had pictured him picking her up in his father's white BMW.

"Like my van?" he asked. "Got it at an auction for seven hundred. I love it."

"It's great," she lied.

Soon he pulled alongside Pacific Coast Highway, on a cliff above the beach, and parked. "Hurry," he said, tossing her a wet suit from the backseat. "Put this on and I'll get my board. I won't look. Don't worry."

Shana scrambled into the backseat and peeled down to her bathing suit, thankful for the wet suit, not ready to be seen yet with so little clothing.

They paddled out together on his board. He practically was on top of her as she lay on her stomach. He didn't go all the way out, where a dozen or more surfers were congregated, just sitting there on their boards waiting for a wave. He stopped close to the beach, where the water was shallow.

"This is what we're gonna do," he said. "When I say so, I want you to stand on the board. I'll help you. Then bend your knees and pretend they're rubber. Don't worry. We'll catch a real small one."

Each time a wave came, he grabbed Shana around the waist and pulled her up, but her feet slid out from under her and she fell under. Soon her eyes burned from the salt water; her hands and feet were like ice. On about the sixth try, she willed herself to stand and rode the wave, his arm around her waist. She wasn't sure if she loved the thrill of riding on the water or the thrill of his arm around her waist. Finally, he turned and looked far out at the other surfers.

Reaching into the little zipper pocket on his wet suit, he handed her the keys to the van. "'Nuff for today. Why don't you go to the van and sleep or whatever? I'm gonna go out." He tossed his wet hair in the direction of the other surfers. "There's a blanket in there if you want to sleep on the beach."

Feeling abandoned, she waded to shore and climbed the steep hill to the van, shivering, wrapping her arms around herself to stay warm. She crouched down again in the back of the van, looking first to see if anyone was around, and took off the wet suit, pulling Charlotte's sweatshirt over her head. Then she carried the smelly blanket down to the sand and tried to spot him. All she could see were a bunch of bobbing heads far out in the ocean.

She allowed her eyes to close, and soon sleep overtook her.

A short time later, she woke with a scream trapped in her throat, her body drenched with sweat, her legs locked together like steel, her arms folded over her breasts, just as she did almost every night. She removed the heavy sweatshirt, now drenched, and pulled the blanket over her head, rolling onto her side. She tasted the fear and swallowed it. "No," she said inside the smelly tent of the blanket.

Just then he tapped her on the shoulder. The sun was beating down and real people, not surfers, were spreading beach towels out and sticking umbrellas in the sand and smearing their bodies with suntan lotion.

"Hey," he said, "want to share that blanket with me?"

She was rolled up like a mummy. Spreading out the blanket, he flopped down on it on his back. He was wearing a bathing suit and his body was muscular but slender, his skin golden and dusted with sand. "My father told me I couldn't go out with you . . . said you were only thirteen. That's not true, is it?"

Shana tried to swallow before she answered, to clear her throat, to stall for time. "I'll be fifteen in two months," she lied.

"Awesome," he said. "You look older. I thought we were the same age. Doesn't matter." He then looked at her curiously. "Do you think your mom and my dad are getting it on?"

"What makes you think that?" she asked.

"I know my old man has something going on because some nights he calls me at my mother's and talks real stupid. Asks me what I'm doing and then tells me he's going to bed early and not to come by and wake him. The next day, I sneak in his room and there are always two glasses in there—one on each nightstand by the bed. One always has lipstick on it. Parents are so stupid. They always lie about dumb things."

His hair was beginning to dry in the sun; it was almost colorless in some places, completely bleached out, and in others it was golden blond. He was leaning back with his arms bracing his body and his hair grazed the blanket. "So what do you think?" he said.

"Maybe. I even asked Mom the same thing. She said they were just friends."

"Yeah, well, don't believe anything. My mom . . ." His eyes clouded over, but he looked at Shana and smiled. Then he looked out at the ocean. "I love it here. I love the ocean. What I'd really like to do is study oceanography at the institute in San Diego, but . . ."

"Then why don't you?" she asked, uncertain exactly what oceanography was, or what he would actually do.

"My dad has never once asked me what I really want. All he does is tell me what a loser I am and how I won't be able to get into any college but a stupid junior college. It's like he thinks if I can't be a lawyer, then I'll be a garbage man or something."

Shana laughed. "My mom said once that I would have to

be a waitress because I didn't study hard enough, but it was just to scare me. She didn't mean it. That's just the kind of thing parents say—you know, like they're supposed to say things like that. Why don't you talk to him and tell him how you feel?" Shana reached over and touched his arm. "He seemed so nice."

"You're nice. My dad's an asshole. But he's okay. Everyone's okay with me. I don't care what they do." Greg reached over and tousled her hair with his hand. "You're only thirteen, aren't you?" he said.

Shana looked down at the blanket as she spoke. "I'm sorry I lied. I don't feel that young, and it seems like all my friends are babies."

"Tell you what," he said, standing and wiping sand off his body, stretching, "you're gonna be a knockout."

Shana glanced down at her breasts, barely visible in the small bikini top, only little lumps under the fabric. She was embarrassed and wished she'd never come. Her skin was white next to his, her legs long and skinny. "Want to take me home?" she said softly.

He picked up the blanket and Shana grabbed her clothes, her feet sinking in the deep sand as she followed him. When they reached the van, now surrounded by cars parked up and down the coast highway, he turned and picked her up in a bear hug, and then put her back down. "Wanna get some donuts? I'm starving."

"Me too," she said. She grabbed her purse from the back of the van and began brushing her hair as they drove.

"I asked you to come today because my dad said you'd been having problems."

Shana felt her breath catch in her throat. Everyone did know about the rape, just as she had thought all the time. It was sickening. How could her mother tell everyone?

"He said your parents were getting a divorce and still living together. Boy, is that tough. I know what you're going through because my mom and dad just split up and I'm living with my mom and some amazon tennis player. It's not even our house, it's hers.''

The muscles in her back started to relax. Then she thought he still might know. Searching his soft brown eyes, she saw sympathy yet it was impossible to know if he merely felt sorry for her over her parents' divorce or if he knew. Every time she started to feel comfortable with someone, the same thoughts entered her mind and she couldn't even remember what they said because she was too busy trying to figure out if they knew. She pressed her fingers to her temples and held them there, thinking her head was about to explode. Suddenly she turned to him and blurted out, "I was raped.''

He turned off the engine; they were in front of a donut store. "Does your mother know?'' he said. "Was it an older guy? Someone you went out with?''

"My mother was there . . . she was raped too . . . he broke into our house . . . he had a knife. He's in jail now. We picked him from a lineup that day I met you.'' When she stopped, it felt as though a hard knot in her stomach had dissolved. This was one person she didn't have to wonder about anymore. Her mother had said that keeping things inside was the worst, and having admitted what had happened, she believed her. It was great to talk about it openly. Suddenly she felt a wonderful emptiness in her stomach, for the first time since the rape. She allowed her head to fall back on the headrest. "You're the first person I've told. I haven't even told my best friends.''

"Well, my mom is a lesbian. If you want to talk about heavy stuff, you picked the right guy. I haven't been discussing *that* with my friends either. Come on,'' he said, taking her hand, "let's go get some donuts.''

Shana ate two chocolate-covered donuts and Greg ate three. They had to drink ice water instead of milk because between them, they only had $4.50. It was hot in the van and Shana sat there eating her donuts, letting the crumbs fall onto her bare stomach. She then started talking and couldn't stop.

"My mom . . . you know, she was so brave. Before this,

we didn't get along. She was always working late and Dad made it seem like she didn't care that much about me. But that night . . . she was great. She tried to get the knife from him and he almost stabbed her. It was terrible." She watched as Greg tossed the empty donut sack in the backseat. "I mean . . . maybe you can talk to your dad about things. I don't think of Mom in the same way anymore. She's like my very best friend."

"Do you know what a lesbian is?" he asked, reaching for Shana's brush and running it through his own long hair.

"Sure I know. I'm thirteen, not in the third grade. Did your mother tell you? What did she say?"

"That's the point: she didn't tell me shit. And Dad didn't tell me shit." His voice was abrupt and filled with anger. "Three years ago, I came home one day and my mom and this woman were in the bedroom, coming out of the shower together, both of them wrapped in towels. She didn't know I saw them. Then I saw them kissing a few days later and it totally blew my fucking mind." He looked at Shana, sorry that he'd used the word *fuck,* but she was undisturbed and leaning toward him in the seat, locked on every word. "It was so sick . . . you know, to see your own mother kissing some woman right on the lips like a man. I knew this thing and Dad didn't know, and I didn't know what it all meant. Anyway . . ."

"Well," Shana spoke up, "being a lesbian is not so awful. It's not like a crime or something, and it's not like sick. It's just different, that's all. I mean, if your mom loves this woman, then that's her business and not yours. How would you like it if she told you who you could love?"

She felt so grown-up, so mature. She'd never had a real conversation with a boy before. She looked up and found him studying her.

"I have a girlfriend, you know."

"Oh," she said, her heart sinking to the bottom of her stomach. "That's nice." She turned and stared out the passenger window, watching people in the parking lot.

"Hey, the things you said to me made a lot of sense. I mean, about my mom and all."

Shana didn't answer. She refused to look at him.

"I'm really sorry about what happened to you. I know it took a lot for you to tell me."

"Yeah," she said, feeling tears dampen her cheeks.

"I like you. I want us to be friends. I might have a girlfriend, but I don't have a friend like you, someone I can really talk to. You know?"

"I know."

The smile fell from his face and was replaced by a look of concern. He reached over and touched her hand. "Anyone gives you a problem, you call me. Call me even if they don't. Next time, I'll take you farther out. We'll ride some real waves."

CHAPTER **36 ■**

After speaking with Cunningham and learning of Manny Hernandez's death and the recovery of what could be the murder weapon in the McDonald–Lopez homicides, Lily finished cleaning the bedroom and was ready to attack the kitchen. John had gone out the night before, and with Shana at her friend's, she had spent the entire night alone in the house. Richard had tried to talk her into coming over, or even going to a club to listen to jazz, but she'd refused. After an agonizing, sleepless night, she knew she had to tell him. The man was planning a life for the two of them, living for the day when they would be together. Even if her actions were never uncovered, she could not go on without telling him. She had to give him the option of walking away. She loved him.

She had her little bucket of cleaning products sitting by the door in the bedroom, but her eyes kept returning to the bedside phone. Compulsive cleaning was her way of avoiding the last unanswered question, and it wasn't working. She dialed the records department at the jail.

"This is Lily Forrester with the district attorney's office, and I need booking and release times on a case. Let's see," she said, pretending she was trying to locate the information, "the suspect's name is Bobby Hernandez. Looks like the booking was near the end of April."

The clerk put her on hold and then returned. "He was booked on April 18th and released on April 29th. Do you need the charges?" she asked.

"I need the time he was released on the 29th," Lily replied. Her hands were perspiring and she changed the phone to the other hand. She could hear the taps of the computer terminal while she waited.

"Here we go," the clerk said. "It looks like he was released about eight o'clock."

She had been holding her breath and now let it out and her body relaxed. There was still hope that Curazon was not the rapist. Starting to thank the girl and disconnect, she heard her add, "But wait, we didn't release him then; that's the time we got the paperwork processed. Here it is: he was released at eleven-fifteen that night."

"Are you certain?" Lily asked.

"It's right here on the computer. They had about fifty releases to process that night—you should see them. That guy was lucky he got out. Some of them weren't released until the following day."

She had shot the wrong man.

"Do you need any additional information?" the girl asked.

Her voice to Lily was faraway, bodiless, surreal. "No. Thanks," she said, letting the phone fall from her hand to the carpeted floor. There was no doubt about it now. When she had gone into the kitchen that night, the bedroom clock had read eleven o'clock. Bobby Hernandez had still been in the Ventura County Jail.

Lily closed the drapes in the bedroom and opened her purse and swallowed two Valiums. She threw herself on the bed and waited for the pills to work, hoping that she would fall asleep and not have to think. Holding the bottle in her hands, she dumped out the pills on the bedspread and counted them, moving each one aside with her fingers, finding them sticking to her skin, damp with perspiration. It would be so easy, she thought, so incredibly easy. One by one, the pills could go from her sticky fingers to her tongue and then roll down her throat. The blackness called to her with a seductive whisper. Through a slim slit in the black-out drapes, a razor beam of light fell across the row of pink pills like an omen. She pressed down on a pill and placed it on her tongue, leaning her head back and swallowing it like a delicious piece of fruit or candy. There were only twelve remaining. It was not enough.

And there was her daughter and Richard and even John to consider. She had too many obligations to commit suicide; it would only cause more pain.

Possibly if she confessed and threw herself on the mercy of the court, she could purge herself. By submitting to punishment, even imprisonment, the guilt might subside. But that would be suicide in another way, for she could never practice law, never be the person she was today, and it would inflict tremendous psychological damage on Shana. There were really no alternatives. She saw herself as a jigsaw puzzle that someone had thrown on the ground, a million tiny pieces. The one missing piece was locked in the lifeless hand of Bobby Hernandez, and he would never release it. In killing him, she had killed a part of herself.

CHAPTER 37 ∎

Shana had Greg drop her off a block from her house and she walked home. Her father was in the garage, trying to fit together pieces of pipe from what she guessed was the sprinkler system. "Where's Mom?" she asked.

"Her car's here, so she must be inside somewhere. I haven't seen her. I just got home."

"Did you leave her here alone last night?" she said accusingly. "What'd you do, spend the night with your girlfriend?"

Her father dropped the pipe and stood, wiping his hands on a rag. "I won't allow you to talk to me like that. Do you hear me? I haven't done anything to be ashamed of. Your mother and I are separated. She moved out, remember?"

Shana didn't answer and hurried into the house, slamming the door behind her. "Mom," she yelled, but there was no answer.

She walked into the darkened bedroom and saw her mother on the bed curled up in a ball. "Mom," she said, her concern rising with each second, "are you okay? What are you doing in bed in the middle of the day?" Lily remained motionless on the bed. Shana ran over and started shaking her. "Wake up. Mom, can you hear me? What's wrong?"

Lily rolled over and moaned. She then apparently went back to sleep. Shana saw her open purse on the floor and pulled out the bottle of pills. "That's it," she yelled, this time getting her mother's attention. "I'm flushing these stupid pills down the toilet."

Sitting up in the bed, Lily pleaded, "Don't, Shana, please. I need those pills to sleep. You're being absurd."

It was too late. The toilet flushed.

Shana came back into the room and pulled the drapes, letting the afternoon sun flood the room. "Get up," she said. "Go take a shower and put on some makeup. You and I are getting out of here." She faced her mother and put her hands on her hips. "And if I see you take any more pills, I'll just throw them away too. And if you keep using them, I'll start using drugs. I'll buy them at school. It's easy." Her arms fell to her side, but her chest rose and fell with emotion.

Dragging herself from the bed, Lily looked at her daughter and couldn't believe that the child was chastizing her as if their roles were reversed. "Where are we going?" she asked.

"We'll go out to dinner somewhere and go to a movie. I'll look for one in the paper and you get dressed."

Shana found the newspaper rolled up in a cylinder with the rubber band still on it on the kitchen counter. She pulled off the band and glanced at the front page before looking at the bottom for the entertainment guide. Then she saw the photo layout.

There were three pictures, one of Manny Hernandez, Bobby Hernandez, and the police officer involved in the shooting. She read through the text quickly, until she got to the paragraph that stated that Bobby Hernandez had been shot by an unknown assailant on April 30—the morning after the rape, Shana thought. It then stated that the suspect was described as a white male, five-ten, wearing a blue knit ski cap and driving a red compact car. Shana dropped the paper on the counter as though it were on fire, her mind spinning.

Her mother had lied about the date this man had been killed. Her mother drove a red compact car. Other details were forcing their way to the surface. Shana remembered that she'd been gone all night and had returned only the next morning. The picture of her mother crouching down behind the Honda when she had come into the garage and the strange odor, like paint or paint thinner, was as clear as the day it occurred. What had she been doing?

She heard footsteps on the wood flooring and quickly rolled the paper back up and placed it in the trash. Now was not the time for questions. All she knew was that something was wrong: her mother was in trouble. Looking at her as she entered the room, she could see the strain in her face and the dark circles under her eyes.

"You look great," she lied. "Let's go. I couldn't find the paper, so we'll just drive over and see what's on at the mall."

"The paper was right on the counter," Lily said, looking around, her eyes glassy and swollen. "Maybe your dad took it. I don't know."

"Come on, it doesn't matter. We have to eat anyway. I'm starving."

They stopped and ordered hamburgers at Carl's Junior on the corner. Lily drank a cup of black coffee and took only two bites from her sandwich before she set it aside.

"Eat it all," Shana insisted. "You told me I had to eat or I'd get sick. Well, you haven't been eating. What is it? Is it okay for you and not for me?"

Lily put her hands over her ears and smiled in spite of herself. "God, is this what a mother sounds like? I'll eat it. You're pretty tough, you know."

"Yeah," she said. "I guess I got it from you." She then leaned over the small table and looked her mother square in the eye. "At least you used to be tough . . . before you started taking pills all the time."

Looking around the restaurant to make certain no one heard them, Lily said, "Don't get carried away with this pill stuff. I'm not an addict or anything. A lot of adults take tranquilizers, particularly people in very stressful jobs. You know I've never taken anything before—"

"I know you've been taking a lot of them lately. I've seen you and I've seen them in your purse." Shana remembered the day she'd first seen the pills, the same day she had discovered the photograph of the man in the newspaper today, the man who looked almost like a brother to the man in the lineup. She wanted to ask her about him, but she held back, refusing to let her imagination run wild.

They left the restaurant and walked to the parking lot. The sky was clear, the sun shining, and the temperature was at least seventy-five degrees. This was the type of day to spend outside in the sunshine, Shana thought. It was the kind of day that should make you happy to be alive.

In the car, Shana tuned in a rock station and rolled down the window, letting the fresh air caress her face and blow her hair. "I know," she said. "Why don't we go look for houses again? It's too pretty to go to a movie. We can always go later when it gets dark."

For the first time that day Lily's face lit up. "I have some houses for us to see. I'll have to call the real estate agent to meet us there, though. They may be out, but we can try."

"You know, Mom, you need to move out of the house. What's driving you crazy is living with Dad when you guys aren't really married anymore. I mean, I know you're married, but you know . . ."

"But I still don't think it's such a good idea for you to change schools right now. Maybe if you waited until school was out. It's only another month. I doubt if we can even get a house until then anyway."

"Here's the deal," Shana announced. "We move as soon as possible, like yesterday, okay? But I'll stay in my school for the remainder of the year. You can drive me a few days and I'll stay with Dad a few nights, so . . ."

"That just might work," Lily replied, breaking her tight grip on the steering wheel and fanning her fingers before closing them again. "We'll see."

They stopped at a pay phone and were able to make arrangements to see two homes, both in the foothills of Ventura. As they had an hour to kill, Lily stopped and purchased a portable cellular phone.

"This is so cool," Shana said, grabbing the phone from her mother. "Can I call someone?"

"Later," Lily said. "But at least you can reach me now no matter where I am. You really want to live with me?"

"Yes, yes. How many times do I have to tell you?" She leaned across the seat and kissed Lily on the cheek. "It's gonna be perfect, Mom. That creep who raped us is going to prison and we're gonna be happy. See, I made up my mind about that this morning. I'm going to be happy. No matter what happened. We're alive—he didn't kill us. And you're going to be happy again too."

The first house was overgrown with weeds and smelled like mildew. The paint was peeling and the kitchen was a disaster. As they walked to their car, they both put their fingers on their noses. "What was that smell?" Shana asked. "It smelled like someone forgot to flush the toilet or something." They laughed and Shana draped her arm over Lily's shoulder.

The second house was perfect. It was small but adequate, and there was even a tiny study off the living room. An older adobe, with brown tile floors and two bedrooms located at opposite ends of the house, each with their own baths, it had a wooden hot tub in the backyard and a lovely patio, lush with plants. On the wall by the front door was a panel for an alarm system. As Lily spoke with the realtor, Shana ran her fingers over the black box with the blinking red dots. Here they would be safe, she thought. There weren't going to be any more tears or fighting or nightmares.

"I love it," Shana said enthusiastically, looking at her mother. "Let's take it. Just think, Mom, the whole yard is grass, not half dirt. And the hot tub is great."

"We can't make a decision today," Lily informed the realtor. "I'll call you tomorrow after I check a few things out."

Outside, Shana pushed her to go back in and tell the woman that they would take it. She wanted to move in today, start her new life today, this very minute. That was one of the problems with adults. They always made everything so complex when everything was so easy.

"That just wouldn't be right, Shana. We have to talk it all over with your dad. There are plenty of houses around to rent."

"I've talked to Dad about it."

"Well, why don't you let me talk to him tonight?"

"He can't say no," she said, her mood deflating. "I'm almost fourteen, and when Sally's parents got divorced, the judge let her pick who she wanted to live with."

"We don't want that . . . to go to court. Just let me handle it. I want us all to stay close—for your sake."

"No," Shana said flatly, "don't say for my sake, Mom. This is for our sake, yours and mine." A cloud passed over her face. She could hear the arguing and fighting, her father's protests. Thoughts of the newspaper article she had seen and the morning after the rape flooded her mind. Had her mother done something terrible to this man, thinking he was the one who had raped them? Was this what she saw in her face, heard in her voice? She sat up stiffly and faced her mother. "From now on, everything we do, we do for us. Got it? We're a team. We went through this together and we're going to get over this together. I love Dad and I'm going to spend time with him, but he's not going to come between us anymore." Lily was looking straight ahead at the road. "Look at me, Mom. Promise me you won't let him talk you out of this."

"I'll do the best I can," Lily replied.

"No," she said, shaking her head, "that's not good enough. Promise me you're not going to take any more pills and you're not going to treat me like a baby. I'm gonna help you and you're gonna help me. I'm gonna tell you everything and you're gonna tell me everything. That's the way it's going to be."

"I promise."

"Good. Then everything's going to be perfect." Shana leaned back in the seat and closed her eyes, allowing her thoughts to wander. They would pack all of their things and move to the new house. All the bad things they would leave behind. If her mother had done something wrong and anything happened because of it, they'd have to punish her too. Whatever her mother had done, she had done for her, and no one was going to ever hurt her mother again.

38.

When they got home, John was watching television on the sofa, his cigarette smoke swirling to the ceiling. Shana glanced at him and then scurried off in the direction of her room, her little dog right behind her, jumping and touching its pink nose to the tips of her fingers. Walking past Lily, she leaned close, whispering in her ear, "Do it now. Don't wait."

The second she left the room, Lily's shoulders fell and she stared at John through the opening from the bar to the den, pressing her body against the kitchen counter. She swallowed, feeling a strange sensation in her mouth similar to hunger but not hunger, and when she reached for a glass, her fingers shook and the trembling spread throughout her body. She needed a Valium. Her body was screaming to be fed the chemicals she had poured into it, and there was nothing she could do to satisfy its demand. Flinging open cabinets, she searched for anything, knocking over bottles of cough syrup and cold pills and vitamins that she never took.

"What's going on?" John said, glancing at Lily and then back at the television.

She stood in the middle of the kitchen, in the stark overhead light. Half the cabinet doors still stood open. "Give me a cigarette."

He stood, hiking up his polyester pants, and padded into the kitchen, shoving a pack of cigarettes across the brown tile. On his feet were large, furry bedroom slippers, and when Lily saw them, she started laughing. He looked like a dwarf. They were supposed to be some type of animal—an elephant or something. She bent over and placed her hand on her stomach, her body still heaving, tears rolling down her cheeks. "Where did you get those?" she said, pointing at his feet and once again doubling over with laughter. John glared at her. "Did your girlfriend give you . . . did she give you . . . those . . . ?"

His eyes narrowed with annoyance and he turned to walk away. "No," Lily said, sticking the cigarette in her mouth, stifling her laughter. "Give me a light."

"When did you start smoking?" he said, watching her draw on the cigarette, the smoke coming out in one big cloud that she fanned with her hands.

"When you started wearing elephants, that's when," Lily said, about to explode again but quickly checking herself. Her head was spinning from the cigarette. She tried to put it out in the ashtray, but it broke in half and continued burning. "Shana wants to move in with me. She said she discussed it with you." He started to say something, but Lily raised her hand to protest. "Before you get all excited, let me tell you what I've been thinking. We can rent this house for about what it costs us each month. That way we'll still have the tax write-off, and neither of us will be saddled with the payment. Shana can complete this year at school, and I'll drive her or you'll drive her when she stays with you, and then start her new school next year."

His face was stern and he snapped, "I forbid it. You work late and she'll be alone. I forbid it. You've always been a shitty mother anyway."

Lily felt her temper rising but forced herself to take a few deep breaths and try to let the last comment roll off her. It wasn't as if he hadn't said the same thing to her a dozen times. If she had to kiss his ass, she was prepared to do it. Besides, she thought, looking at his feet, he was too absurd to be a threat. Why had she never seen it? Why had she ever let him upset her, make her angry? He was a joke, a cartoon. She could gobble him up in one bite.

"I appreciate how you feel and I know how close you are to Shana. You have my assurance that I will be home on time every night. I have only one case to try and then it's strictly supervision. What I can't do at the office, I'll do at home." She leaned back against the counter and searched his face. His brows were still drawn and his mouth a thin slit.

"You're trying to use the rape and the fact that Shana identifies with you now to steal her away from me."

"You're so wrong, John. Not only that, but you're being unfair to your own daughter. You're not going to lose her. She loves you. She'll probably spend as much time with you as she does with me."

Lily paused, staring at him, waiting.

He ran his hands through his hair and met Lily's gaze. "I guess if this is what Shana wants and it will help her to put things behind her, then . . ."

"Oh, John," Lily said, moving closer to him, reaching out to touch him and then placing her hand over her mouth. Relief flooded her body, a wave of tenderness touched her, and for just that moment she wanted to hold him and thank him, wished that they could love each other again. "I want you to be happy too. I don't want to close the door on our relationship as friends or parents." She saw tears forming in his eyes and fought back her own tears. "If we stay in this house together, the way things are now, then we're going to end up really hating each other. I don't want that."

He reached out and put a finger on her lips, like a kiss. Then he got up and left the house without saying another word.

Lily couldn't sleep. At three in the morning, she went to

the kitchen and searched for a bottle of wine, anything to put her to sleep. There in the dark, on the sofa, John was awake and smoking.

"I don't mind if you sleep in the bed," she told him impulsively. "I can't sleep."

"Well, I guess you're going to have to learn to deal with it. Right?" he said softly. "And I'm going to have to learn to deal with it too."

Back in the bedroom, Lily closed the door behind her and leaned against it, bringing the bottle of wine to her lips and, afterward, wiping her mouth with the back of her hand. She surveyed the room, searching the dark corners and shadows. The only eyewitness was dead. Now both the brothers were dead. Tomorrow she would meet Cunningham face to face. Tomorrow, she thought with a degree of relief, would be either the beginning or the end. Either way, she knew she was ready. She'd been in the tunnel too long.

CHAPTER **39** ■

Cunningham was standing naked on the bathroom scale, watching the needle quiver around the 225-pound mark. He tried moving his feet around and the needle dropped slightly. Sharon opened the door to the bathroom and snatched the bath towel from his neck as she dropped her pants and seated herself on the commode. "I'm an old pro at this stuff, remember," she said.

Without the towel, and with more foot shuffling, the needle fell to just under 223 pounds and Cunningham sighed with relief. If he passed the 225-pound mark, even at six-four, he would be in trouble at the next department physical.

"What are you doing up this time of the day anyway?" she asked, standing and flushing the toilet.

He threw his large arms around her and lifted her a few inches off the ground, then sat her down with a thud. "You're taking a big chance right now, lady. I'm feeling pretty good this morning. I might drag you to bed and have my way with you."

"Yeah," she said, undaunted. "Put your money where your mouth is."

"You're nothing but a brazen hussy, you know that?" He turned around and smeared shaving cream on his face as Sharon left to drive the kids to school. He wondered if Lily Forrester drove her daughter to school, wondered if she was driving her in her red Honda right this minute.

He took out his best brown jacket and sniffed the armpits. He hadn't had it cleaned in a long time and it had a slight odor. He went to the bathroom and got the bottle of cologne the kids had given him for Father's Day. The name on the bottle read Hero. Not exactly a designer cologne, he thought, spraying it on the fabric of the jacket, but the name was a real winner. It was a set. He had Hero deodorant, Hero shampoo, and Hero after-shave.

Driving to the crime lab, Cunningham had all the windows in the car rolled down, and the air was fresh and clean, morning fresh. The exhaust fumes and smog hadn't settled in yet, and it reminded him of a spring morning in Omaha. Feeling a tingle of excitement in his stomach as he exited the car and took the steps to the crime lab two at a time, he knew he was still addicted to the job. It was the thrill of the chase, the constant surprises, the satisfied feeling he got when he closed a case and put it to bed.

Inside the lab, he ranted and raved, his booming voice bouncing off the walls and echoing in the tiled room. At ten-thirty, he finally had the report on the seat next to him and was weaving through traffic to the government center complex. He was standing in the lobby of the district attorney's office at ten-forty, twenty minutes early, just as he'd planned. He flipped his shield and flashed it at the receptionist.

"Who are you waiting to see?" the girl asked him. "I'll check if they're available."

"Why don't you just hit that little buzzer with your finger, honey, and leave the rest to me?" He stuck his head through the small opening. "Now," he said. The girl jumped and hit the buzzer.

He ambled down the long hall past the row of clerks and

secretaries until he was standing outside Lily's door. He remained outside the glass watching her. Her head was down and she was writing. He couldn't see her face. Finally he moved in the doorway and cleared his throat. She jerked and looked up, dropping her pen on the desk, looking quickly at her watch. There was no doubt that she'd been waiting for him. This was what he had planned: to surprise her, confront her, to watch her squirm.

"Bruce," she said, swallowing, trying to control her nervousness at confronting the big detective. "You're early. I didn't recognize you at first. I think I'm losing my eyesight with all this damn paperwork."

He stepped inside the office and patted his gut. His jacket was open because it was too small and when buttoned, it pulled. "Put on a few pounds probably," he said and strolled to her desk, slapping a stapled stack of papers down. "Here's your report."

She looked up excitedly. "On the weapon?" she asked. "I thought you said noon."

"I went by and put the squeeze on them," he said but didn't break the news. Lily started thumbing through the pages of the report and then tossed it on the desk.

"Look, I don't have a lot of time." She couldn't get her eyes to focus or her mind to remain still enough to read. All she could think about was the fact that he was standing here only a few feet away and staring at her face. "What's the verdict? Is it the gun or isn't it?"

"Read it. You'll see." He leaned against the wall by her desk and smiled at her.

She picked it up again and started flipping through the pages. Without the Valium she was tense and impatient. Just his presence was enough to make her feel like she was coming apart at the seams, and now he was playing silly games with her. She slapped the report down on the desk and glared at him. "Is it the fucking gun or not?"

He pushed himself off the wall, annoyed. "It's the gun."

"And . . . ?" The suppressed fear was rapidly turning into anger. She couldn't contain it. She felt cornered—trapped inside this small room with the very person who could destroy her.

"Can I smoke in here?" he said, reaching into his pocket and pulling out his cigarettes.

"No, it's against the rules," she said, her heart pounding. He was too close. Her eyes tracked his every movement.

"Oh, I see," he said, replacing the pack and continuing to stare back at her, flicking his mustache with his fingers. He walked over to her desk and leaned over her shoulder, practically breathing down her neck.

She could smell him, feel his warm breath on her neck. Her hands began trembling and she placed them in her lap, hoping he wouldn't see. Any second, she thought, and I'm going to explode, tell him everything, put an end to this insanity. "Cunningham, will you sit down and tell me what I want to know? We don't have all day here, you know."

He moved around to the front of her desk, but he continued to stand. "Well, it looks like we've got a positive match on the prints belonging to both Bobby and Manny Hernandez as well as Richard Navarro. The weapon was additionally found to be the same weapon used on Carmen Lopez. So, I guess the answer to your question is it's definitely the right fucking gun." He smiled.

She placed a hand on her chest and then looked up. "They were both involved. Jesus. And we have Navarro made as well."

"You still want me to talk to Nieves?" he asked, lighting a cigarette anyway and looking around for something to dump the ashes in. Seeing an old styrofoam cup with remnants of coffee in it, he walked over and flicked his ashes in it right in front of Lily. She was nervous, afraid. He could sense it. If he pushed a little harder, he thought, just a little harder . . .

"Butler wants you to try to scare him. Get him to talk without promises. The only thing you can offer him is protective custody now and the chance to serve his time in a federal facility if he does talk.''

As she spoke, her voice started to crack. Her face was pale and gaunt. Dark circles were visible under her eyes. He couldn't keep his mind on the conversation. No matter how tough she talked or tried to appear, she looked fragile, delicate, vulnerable. She looked like a woman on the edge. There was a small sprinkling of freckles across her nose and cheeks. "My little sister has freckles just like yours," he said without thinking.

"Oh," Lily replied, pausing, not raising her eyes. For that instant they were somewhere else, no more than two human beings. Then she cut her eyes to him. "Do you mind if we discuss your interview with Nieves instead of my freckles?"

"Well, without anything to offer him, I think I'm wasting my time."

Lily suddenly lost her composure completely, standing up and smashing her fist on her desk, causing the coffee cup filled with his ashes to spill all over the carpet. "Wasting your time?" she yelled. "You're wasting my fucking time right now. I want you to interview Nieves and that's the end of it. I don't give a shit what you offer him. He's a damn murderer. There's no free rides here."

Cunningham covered the few feet to her desk in seconds and put both his palms down on her desk, sticking his face right in front of her, so close that he could smell her breath. "No free rides, huh?" He paused and let his words hang in the air, thinking she should think before she mouthed off, particularly under the circumstances. He watched the color drain from her face when he repeated what she'd just said. She reacted. He saw it. An inch or two more and she'd crack.

"Well," he said finally, "he'll be risking his life if he talks, federal facility or not. Someone can always get to him. I wouldn't spill my guts and risk getting my throat slit one night in the john just to spend time in a nicer prison facility." He had been pacing and now he spun around and faced her.

"Would you?" he asked. She just looked at him. He continued, "You're asking him to give you a pound of cocaine in exchange for a lid of marijuana."

Her eyes were blinking, perspiration was breaking out on her forehead. She backed away from him and dropped into her chair, speaking to him in a low voice, looking down. "Butler said he'd consider a plea . . . try it straight first . . . doesn't want us to play our ace until our hand is forced."

The words came out in little spurts and then dropped to such a level that he had to strain to hear her. Inside his jacket, Cunningham felt warm and sticky. He reached up and loosened his tie. This wasn't turning out at all the way he had planned it. All he wanted to do right at that moment was walk out the door before he did or said something he'd later regret. The case was too weak to arrest her without a warrant. The eyewitness was dead and he simply wasn't one hundred percent certain. If and when he decided it was time to put a district attorney behind bars, he'd damn sure better know what he was doing.

His face solemn, he said, "I'll go talk to Nieves now." He headed for the door. The windowless room was filled with cigarette smoke, and several people walked by and looked as if they wanted to chastise him, but he glared at them and they scurried off without a word. Then he leaned in the doorway, facing the hall, his back to Lily. He looked down at the butt of his cigarette and walked back to pick the cup off the floor and toss the butt into it. For a moment he studied her face and wondered what she would look like with her hair pushed up inside a knit ski cap, without makeup.

He knew what she'd look like and it was scary. She'd look exactly like the composite drawing.

"This your daughter?" he said, picking the silver frame off her desk. "She's a beauty. Guess no one ever told you she looks just like you."

For a moment the tension left her face and she smiled, taking the frame from his outstretched hand. "She's the greatest kid in the world." Her face turned red with embarrassment. "I'm sure every parent feels that way."

"Not every parent," he replied, studying her face intently. "I sure wouldn't want to claim the Hernandez brothers if they'd been my sons. Something went haywire there for sure."

He watched as a cloud passed over her face and she reached for her glasses, her hand trembling visibly. Yep, he thought, reckoning he knew what she was thinking. They had parents too. "By the way, for what it's worth, we found a crack pipe in Manny's Plymouth and some vials with residue. They were probably loaded when they did Lopez and McDonald."

"Crack," she said, slamming a file down on her desk.

Cunningham left, leaving behind a wake of cigarette smoke mixed with the sweet odor of Hero cologne, the face of Shana Forrester entrenched in his mind. It wouldn't really be so bad, he thought, being a chief of police in a small, quiet town. Right now he could use a little boredom, a little peace of mind. If someone offered him a job right this minute, he might just take it.

He stuck his head into the receptionist's cubicle by the security doors. "It's the big, bad wolf again, sweetie," he said in a menacing voice. "I know you want to let me out."

The buzzer rang instantly, and Cunningham hit the double doors with his fists and headed to the jail. Things were getting bad, really bad. Seemed like both the good guys and the bad guys were wearing black hats these days. Before long, everyone would be carrying 9mm revolvers or submachine guns every time they left home. The days of the white hats were over, and the time to move on was drawing near. "Black is black and white is white," he said out loud as he walked across the court-yard, but no matter what he said, all he saw in this situation was gray.

Because he was a police officer, Cunningham was allowed to interview Benny Nieves in a small room, containing a table and two chairs, like the type found in a grade school. The detective took a seat in one of the chairs and Nieves the other. The boy was so small that Cunningham thought of a seesaw on a playground and knew that it would take two or three kids the size of this one to balance the board. He couldn't weigh more than 115 pounds dripping wet. His hair was neatly cut, probably at the insistence of the public defender. His small dark eyes were ravaged with fear.

Cunningham looked at him and breathed a sigh of relief after the way the meeting with Lily had just gone. Benny Nieves he could handle any day of the week. But Forrester, well, he thought, that was something altogether different.

"Okay, Benny. I'm Detective Cunningham with the Oxnard Police Department and I'm here to save your soul. You going to church services here?"

"Yeah," he said meekly, completely thrown by what this had to do with the case.

"You believe in God?"

"Yeah, man, I believe."

"Do you think God forgives those who sin? Do you think there's a Hell for those who don't repent of their sins?" The last time he'd used this approach, it had worked. When people sat in a cell, day after day, they frequently turned to religion. Even Kenneth Bianchi, the Hillside Strangler, now claimed that he was a minister.

"Bible says you repent, God has to forgive you," the boy answered, dead serious.

Cunningham had been right. Benny had found Jesus in the Ventura County Jail. "And what does it mean to repent of your sins?"

"Say you sorry, man. And that you won't do it again."

"Well, Benny, my man, you're close, but not close enough. See, I'm not even a detective assigned to your case. God just talked to me this morning and said, 'There's a boy who needs help down at the jail and his name is Benny Nieves.' Cunningham watched as the boy's eyes got as round as saucers and his mouth fell open. "You could even say that I'm a little like a guardian angel." Cunningham leaned far over the table, only inches from Benny's face. "Because you're going to get the death penalty, Benny, and God thinks you can be saved."

"Shit, man, you crazy," Benny said. "You shitting me, man. You just a fucking cop. You ain't no guardian angel." Even though his words were tough, his eyes were still glued to Cunningham's. He was trying to find hope in a pool of fear.

"Now, Benny. You listen to what I've got to say, 'cause I'm offering you a chance to repent and that chance may not happen again. See, we have the gun that was used in the murder, and you probably know that both Manny and Bobby are dead. There's also fingerprints on that gun, but none of them are yours. I think that those two boys in jail now who say they just hitched a ride with you guys are telling the truth. And I don't think God would think too highly of you if you let them pay for something they didn't do."

Benny jumped up from the chair, walked the two feet to the back wall, and leaned back against it. "They didn't do nuthin'. They just boys on the street. Guys we know. Just caught a ride."

"Fine, Benny, but that's not going to clear them. What's going to clear them and save you from the death penalty is to tell me exactly what happened that night. We don't think you did any shooting, and we don't think you smashed that boy's head in with that rock. Those were the worst things, know what I mean?"

The metal doors outside closed with an electrical whine and clang, and Benny turned as if he could see through the door, as if someone was outside listening. He didn't answer.

"If you talk, we'll move you to protective custody, and any time you serve will be at a federal prison facility. You've heard of those, Benny. They're like country clubs compared to the state joints. They have swimming pools and golf courses and decent food. That's where the big fat cats go who just steal people's money."

"I don't care 'bout no fucking golf." He looked at Cun-

ningham and his face started to twitch. "I don't wanna die."
He returned to the chair and leaned forward, whispering,
"They'll kill me, man."

"If you get the death penalty, you'll die for sure. And the
worst thing is that you'll die without forgiveness. You want to
go where the streets are paved with gold, or you want to go
to the fires of Hell?"

Cunningham stood and signaled for the guard. "You let
me know. You think it over. Here's my card." He tossed it
on the table just as the guard arrived to unlock the door.

Standing in front of the electronic doors to the lobby, Cunningham looked up at the television monitor and belched. He
reached into his pocket and found a roll of Rolaids he had
bought the day before and tossed one into his mouth. "Hey,
open the damn door," he yelled at the monitor. "I'm beginning
to feel like a fucking prisoner." He waited. No one came. He
gave thought to returning to Lily's office and confronting her
again, but the ball was in his court now and it was burning its
way through his stomach like a red-hot poker.

"What the hell is going on here?" he yelled again, his
frustration level rising. He couldn't possibly imagine what it
would be like to be locked inside this place, behind bars, no
privacy, no sunshine or fresh air, no way out. He only knew
one thing, reaching up and hitting the monitor with his fists—
he'd just as soon die. The world outside might be a garbage
dump, but this here was a cesspool. This was the end of the
line.

"Sorry, you had to wait. I was in the bathroom," the unseen
voice of the deputy rang out over the speaker. "It's raining
like hell outside."

"My favorite subject," Cunningham said.

"Rain?" the voice asked.

"No, Hell, my man. Hell."

CHAPTER 40

Before Shana left for school, she called Greg. "Aren't you going to school?" she said. "It's after eight already."

"Sure," he mumbled, "I'm going. I just overslept. Who is this anyway?"

"It's me. You know, Shana. If you don't go to school, you might end up a garbage man like your dad said." He didn't answer right away and she thought her statement might have been cruel, but then, he could have just rolled over and gone back to sleep. "If you're awake, I wanted to ask you to pick me up at school today. I want to talk to you about this thing with my mother. Are you listening?"

"Yeah. I'm putting on my clothes. I'm not really into garbage. I'll pick you up. What time?"

"We get out at three-thirty, but I'll wait if you're late."

"I won't be late," he said.

After her father had gone to the car, Shana retrieved the newspaper article from the trash can and put it inside her notebook before rushing out the door for school.

* * *

Shana strolled out the front doors of Camarillo Junior High with at least six girls surrounding her. She kept trying to get away, but it was impossible. Then she saw him, and the girls with her saw him. He was leaning against his Volkswagen van, posing, his blond hair sparkling in the sunshine, wearing a white T-shirt, jeans, and Ray-Ban sunglasses. Shana took off at a jog, leaving the girls standing there gaping and crowding together to speculate. He must love the attention, she thought, because he tossed his hair and flashed the girls a rakish smile.

"I'm moving to Ventura next week," she said, struggling to get the rickety van door to stay shut. "Where do you live?"

"My dad lives in the foothills," he replied.

"I can't remember the name of the street our new house is on, but it's in the foothills. Isn't that totally cool? We'll be neighbors."

Greg looked at her and smiled, but without enthusiasm. "You know, Shana," he said, "I meant what I said about having a girlfriend." He pulled down his Ray-Bans and peered at her over the lenses, like he wanted her to understand what he was trying to say.

"That's cool," she said and then pushed out her lower lip. "You don't think I asked you to come today just to show you off to my friends? I mean, I don't expect you to take me to the prom or anything."

"All right," he said with relief. "Now that we got that established, lil sis, what's this stuff about your mother?"

"Go to the park up the street and I'll tell you. I don't have anyone else to talk to and it's driving me crazy."

Once they got there, he pulled the smelly blanket from the back of the van and they sat on the grass. When a bunch of small children erupted screaming on the playgrounds, they got up and moved the blanket away from the racket. Shana started at the beginning, telling him how her mother had stayed out all night after the rape, and then how she'd found her in the garage behind her car that morning with something on a rag that smelled like paint thinner. She told him about the photo of Hernandez that was in her mother's purse. He was spread out on his stomach, listening.

"Now see," she said, removing the newspaper article, "this is the man right here." She pointed at the picture. "He looks just like the man that raped us, but he's not."

"So, what's the big deal? I don't get it."

"Mom told me this guy was killed by someone a long time before the rape and that wasn't true. The paper says he was killed that very morning. You know, the morning after it happened. So, she lied to me about that."

"I told you they all lie."

She continued, "In the article they say the person who shot this man was driving a red compact car. My mom drives a red Honda."

Greg was reading as she spoke. "Wow, this is deadly. You mean you think your mom shot and killed this guy, thinking he was the dude who raped you? But they're looking for a man. Says it right here."

"Maybe they thought my mom was a man," she said, looking at Greg to see his reaction. "She's tall and she might have been disguised or something."

"I bet it's nothing," he said, handing her the newspaper. "Your mom didn't kill somebody. I mean, maybe your dad might have done it if he'd known where the guy was, but your mom? That's radical. My mom can't even kill a little spider."

"Yeah, but your mom isn't my mom."

"You really, really think that she's tough enough to kill someone," he said, completely awed by the whole conversation, looking around the park as though he didn't know what he'd got himself into.

"She did it for me," Shana said, choking up. "She did it so he wouldn't come back."

"Okay, calm down. Don't get upset."

"What should I do?"

"Nothing, man. What do you think you should do? Even if by some wilder than wild thing your mom did kill this guy,

I don't think I'd go around telling everyone. Think about it."

"But what about my mom? Should I tell her about what I think? Maybe she can explain it to me. At least I should tell her I'll stand by her no matter what. What if she gets caught and they take her away? I'd just die."

"Listen to me. You asked my advice and I'm giving it to you. You want me to act like a brother, so pay attention. Your mom figured out who the rapist was and where he lived. She went there all done up like a man and she blew him away." Greg put his hands together and clapped. "A little round of applause for the old mom there." Shana smiled weakly. "She came home, did something weird in the garage. We won't talk about that. It might be gory or something." He made a face, raising his eyebrows. "Maybe she shot him and then she ran over him and part of his body was stuck on the car. Gross."

"You're making fun of me," she cautioned, shaking her finger. "This isn't funny."

"Sorry. So, she killed him. He's dead. See, I bought it all. But," he said, raising his hand in the air, "your mom now lets another guy go to jail. No way. It all falls down, the whole nightmare on whatever street."

"She didn't know he wasn't the one. She didn't wear her glasses. At first she said the man in the lineup wasn't the right one."

Greg took both his hands and made a *T* with them, like time-out. "That's it. No more. When the big brother speaks, that's it. The peon under sister shuts up. Got it?"

Shana was silent. "Forget it, huh?"

"One last try and then I'm going to leave you here to walk home alone by yourself if you don't listen. Put yourself in your mother's place. Say all this did happen. Would she want you to know, anyone to know? Would she want to have little talks with you about the time she shot a rapist?"

Impulsively she reached over and pecked him on his bronze forehead. "I wish you were my brother."

He stood and yanked the blanket, causing Shana to fall onto her side. "After all this, I *am* your brother."

In the van on the way to her house, Shana was silent. Greg turned up the stereo so loud that she wanted to scream, but she didn't. He was nice. He'd picked her up at school and listened, but nothing had really changed. She was just as confused as ever. Playing over and over in her mind the events of that night and morning, she knew something terrible had happened, maybe something more awful than even the rape. And no matter what Greg said, it was her mother they were talking about and she was afraid.

41 ▪

Cunningham pulled in the driveway and lumbered to the front door. His stomach was in knots, but he'd promised Sharon he'd come home for dinner. "Diet night," he said, kicking a skateboard off the walk. Inside, it was quiet and the kids were nowhere to be found. He yelled, "That stupid kid left his skateboard on the sidewalk again, and I almost broke my fucking neck."

Sharon stuck her head out of the kitchen door and smiled. "Don't do a thing," she said. "Go straight to the dining room."

He yanked his tie off and tossed it on the sofa. "Where are the kids?" he said.

She came out all decked out in a tight pair of jeans and a long sweater that concealed her large hips but plunged at the neckline, carrying a platter with a large roast and potatoes. "Surprise," she said. "Thought we could use a nice dinner, just the two of us, so I sent the kids to my mother's."

He stared at her and belched, holding his stomach. "I feel like hell. I've had it with this fucking shit."

"You're sick, aren't you? Look at you. I hope you're not

having a gall bladder attack or something. You know your dad had gallstones and that belching is a symptom. I'll get some Maalox."

"Would you stop it, just stop it for chrissake. I don't have gallstones. I don't have an ulcer. I'm fed up. Can't you understand anything? Right to here, see?" He made a gesture with his hand under his neck.

She grimaced and set the platter down on the table, looking at it with disappointment. After all the trouble she'd gone to, he was in one of his black moods. "Want to talk about it?"

"Sharon . . ."

She stood there while he went to the sofa and collapsed. "I mean, maybe if you eat something," she said, glancing at the table and the food.

"Sharon . . ."

"Want a beer? We've got a whole six-pack in the refrigerator. I'll get you a beer, okay? You relax awhile and then I'll warm everything up again and we'll eat later."

"Sharon, I don't want a beer. I don't want Maalox and I don't have gallstones. I want to go home. For the last time, I want to go back to Omaha."

She dropped into one of the dining room chairs and turned it to face him. "Bruce, we talked this all over the other night. Tommy's been accepted to U.C.L.A. He's worked years for this. It means the world to him. If we go back to Nebraska, he'll have to pay out-of-state tuition, and we simply can't afford it. What we've saved for his college education will never cut it. We're surviving on a shoestring as it is now."

His chin had dropped so low, it was almost resting on his chest. His legs were flung out in front of him, and he had slouched down low on the sofa, still holding a hand over his stomach. He peered up at her, his eyes black and penetrating. "What you're saying is that I don't make enough money on this miserable job to even send my son to college."

"Bruce, please. You work hard. You do a job that needs to be done, a job you've always loved. Think of Tommy. You'll destroy him if you take this away from him and make us move now.''

He stood and started pacing around the small room. "Do you really want your son to go to college here? Do you know what's been happening in L.A.? This is a city in ruins, kid. This is a city beyond salvation, let me tell you."

"The riots are over. You're just finding excuses. Is it a case, Bruce? Usually when you're like this, it's a case. Is it over that Owen thing, that old lady?"

He ran his hands through his hair. "It's a lady, all right, but not Ethel Owen. This lady . . ."

Sharon turned white. "Are you having an affair? Is this what this is all about?"

He ignored her, almost as if he was talking to himself, continuing to pace. "We can sell the house. Real estate is much lower in Omaha. I'll get my old job back and they'll probably promote me in six months. I could even make captain there or deputy chief with my experience. They don't have the problems there that we have here: the drugs, the gangs, the crime, the blasted corruption, the smog."

The phone rang in the kitchen and she left him there, pacing. She came back and said softly, "It's for you. It's the jail."

"Cunningham," he barked, seizing the phone in the kitchen.

"This is Deputy Clark at the Ventura County Jail. I really feel bad about disturbing you at home, but Benny Nieves has gone completely psycho on us, and he's screaming that he has to talk to you and that you'll have us all fired if we don't call you. I'm probably going to get him transferred to the medical facility and let them shoot him up with something. Either that or put him in lockup."

Sharon was standing right next to him in the kitchen, staring up into his face. He turned his back on her. "Don't do anything," he ordered the deputy. "Separate him from the other prisoners and keep him on ice until I get there, or I *will* have your fucking job. Got it?"

"You're going in, aren't you? You're not even going to stay to eat the wonderful dinner I fixed for us." Her eyes were moist and she sniffed. "I worked on it all day. I thought just this once we could have a romantic dinner."

"Look, I have just a few loose ends, Sharon, and then we're leaving. There's a few cases I have to put to bed, and then I'm putting in my notice."

The sniffing stopped and she stared at him. "You never answered me before. Are you having an affair? Is this over some woman? Tell me. I have to know."

He headed to the door, Sharon following him, insistent. He turned and faced her. "I am *not* having an affair, okay? And yes, this is over some woman, but you don't even want to know about it. Trust me." He opened the door and let the screen bang on the way out. Then he kicked the skateboard again, sending it flying into the neighbors' yard.

By the time Cunningham got to the jail, it was six o'clock. He had stopped and picked up a cup of black coffee at Stop 'n' Go on the way and a couple of backup batteries for his tape recorder. He hoped like hell he was going to need it.

They were back in the same interview room, in the little chairs, staring each other down from across the table. Benny's eyes were wild and his olive face ashen. Cunningham sipped his coffee and waited.

"I had this dream, man. There was fire 'round me and people standing over me with faces like monsters. I was in Hell, man. I was burning in Hell. My skin"—he grimaced with fear—"my fucking skin was burning right off my body."

"Benny, I told you God sent me to help you. Are you ready to talk now?"

"Yeah, I'm ready."

His eyes were glued on Cunningham as he removed the small tape recorder from his briefcase and pushed the play button, setting the machine on the table between them. "This is Detective Bruce Cunningham, and I'm speaking with Benny

Nieves." He then proceeded to advise him of his rights and asked him each time if he understood. He nodded, but the detective insisted that he speak out loud for the tape recorder. After he'd read every item from the little card he carried, he asked Benny: "Are you making these statements of your own free will without any promises or harassment?" Benny stated that he was and the interview began.

"Start at the very beginning," he instructed Nieves. "Before the crime and everything leading up to the crime."

Benny coughed, looked around the small room nervously, and then began. "Manny was seeing Carmen last year, but his brother wanted her bad, so he just hands her off to him, you know?"

"Benny, you have to say everyone's name clearly. You're talking about Bobby Hernandez? Is that correct?"

"Yeah, man, who else? So Carmen sees him a few times, but she don't like him much and she's all mad 'cause Manny hands her off, see? Manny did whatever Bobby wanted. They was like that. Bobby wants her—has a fucking hard-on for her and he's smoking crack and talking 'bout her all the time. She moves to Ventura and shuts him out. Bobby. Won't even talk to him. We go out cruising and he cruises to Ventura all the time, driving by her house, saying he's gonna fucking kill her. See, Bobby's always got the women, you know? They always go for him. He was always bragging 'bout killing people too. Wanted us to think he was bad."

Should have believed him, Cunningham thought, but kept his mouth shut. He sure wasn't bad like Michael Jackson, more like good ol' Charlie Manson. "Did he ever tell you that he'd killed someone?" he asked.

"No way, man. Just talk. So, word comes out on the street that Carmen takes this fancy test and does good and that's she's going steady with this white boy and bragging that she's gonna go to college and all. Bobby stops talking 'bout her and no one thinks shit, man, until that night."

"And what happened that night?" Cunningham asked,

quickly checking the tape recorder heads to make certain they were revolving.

"My throat's dry," Benny said. "When they gonna know I talked?"

"No one's going to know anything until the preliminary hearing next week, and you'll be in protective custody by then." Cunningham shoved what coffee was remaining in his cup across the table.

Benny took a sip and complained: "Cold, man." He looked at the recorder and the red light on top, and then he looked at Cunningham. He put his head down on the little table for a few minutes, and then continued. "That night, man . . . that night I wish I'd been in church. That was one terrible night. Okay, Manny calls me up and says he's got some good stuff —crack, regular coke, smoke. Talking like he's got a fucking drugstore. Says for me to get Navarro and Valdez and meet them at this street in Ventura to cruise. Guess they were already there. Dunno.

"We get there and all get in Bobby's van, and he gives us what we want. They got a pipe and Manny, Bobby, Navarro, and Valdez pass it around and get high, man, like crazy high."

"And you, Benny?" Cunningham said. "What did you take from the goody bag?"

"Smoke. Fucking smoke is all. I do some white, but they ain't got white. They lie 'bout the white. They have only the crack pipe and I don't smoke that shit. It's addictive, man." He leaned over and placed his hands on the table, like he was about to tell Cunningham a big secret. "Seen guys who'd kill their own mother just for that shit."

Cunningham rubbed his eyes and glanced at his watch. He still had to go back to the station after this, and it had been a long, mean day. He banged on the door and when the jailer came, he asked for two cups of coffee. "What do you think this is, a twenty-four-hour diner?" the man said, pissed. While they were waiting, Cunningham changed the batteries on the tape recorder, just to play it safe.

When both of them had fresh cups of coffee, Benny continued:

"We drive by this high school, and Manny and Bobby stop and tell us to get out. I see Manny shoving a pocket shooter in his jacket, but it don' mean nothing 'cause he carries all the time. But they know what they up to, see, 'cause they lead us right to the spot where they're fucking."

"Who's fucking?" Cunningham asked.

"You know, man. Carmen and her white boy. They musta followed them and seen them go behind the bleachers. Bobby and Manny grab the white guy and punch him out cold. Then Bobby tells Navarro to fuck her and he watches. She not screaming or nuthin'. Too scared. She just lays there and spreads them. Even take her own pants down when Bobby says. Navarro does her and then Bobby tells me to do her. He says she loves it, calls her a fucking cunt. He's got his dick out and playing with it—watching, man. So I do her. It's like she kinda likes it 'cause she doesn't fight."

Benny stopped and sipped the coffee, relief spreading across his face. He slid down in the chair and stretched his short legs out under the table. Cunningham urged him to go on with the story.

"After I did her, I go back under the bleachers to take a piss. Only gone a minute, but I hear them even when I'm pissing. I see the boy and his head is bashed in, and Bobby is bloody and he's got a big rock and he's beating his head. Carmen's screaming and everyone's crazy wild. Bobby says she's the one who caused it all and takes this tree limb that's there under the fucking bleachers and he shoves . . . God . . ."

Benny stopped, his eyes focused above Cunningham's head, as though he were watching the entire thing playing on a big-screen television, too mesmerized and horrified to continue.

"Benny, tell me what happened next," the detective urged, trying to keep his voice low, fearing Benny was slipping under.

"Blood gushes out of her and her eyes go wild—open but not seeing. I think she's dead now. Not moving, eyes open, blood fucking everywhere. Manny starts shooting at her like she's scary-looking and he's jumping and shooting. Then Bobby grabs the gun and shoots and laughs and says her tits, shoot her tits, and grabs Navarro and shoves him up to her and makes him shoot her tits and then Valdez. I start running. They running behind me 'cause they know the gun's gonna bring cops."

"This must be when you passed the schoolteacher in the parking lot," Cunningham said.

"Yeah. I pass someone—dunno who—running fast, you know, but they hardly turned to look till the others came. They run to the car and get in, and then we go to our car and they leave in their car."

"Why did Navarro stop and pick up the other boys?"

" 'Cause they nobody, man. Just little pussy boys and he says they'll say we was with them if the cops ask and they're like an alibi and no one will know. Would have never been stopped if Navarro had registered his fucking car, man."

"Life's a bitch, isn't it?" Cunningham said after he had pushed the off button on the tape recorder. He stood and stretched. "You did it, Benny. You're on your way to redemption, my man."

"What'll they give me?"

"I told you before that there are no promises. The judge and jury will be impressed that you came forward, and that will count a great deal. But the best part, Benny, is that you don't have to dream of Hell anymore. I'm not God, but I truly think you've earned a ticket out. Maybe not from the joint, but from Hell, which is everlasting."

Cunningham returned to the station, the tapes secure inside his briefcase. The watermelon had burst. The McDonald–Lopez case was down. Now there was the other matter to contend with, he thought, his stomach on fire, his nerves still frazzled. There was Lily Forrester. He reached into his jacket for the

Rolaids and popped one into his mouth. "One will never do," he said, picking up the file on the homicide of Bobby Hernandez and slapping it down on top of his desk. Breaking open the package, he dumped all the Rolaids out on his desk. Then he tossed them one by one into his mouth like peanuts while he stared at the composite drawing before him.

42.

ily was sitting alone in Richard's office, her chair facing the bulletin board. She was staring at the crime-scene photos, specifically the mutilated body of Carmen Lopez. Richard was in conference with Butler on another matter.

This was the man she had killed, she told herself repeatedly. This carnage was his handiwork—the man who had tortured and ravaged this poor girl, the same man she had executed. He wasn't innocent, or merely a disturbed sex offender. What she was looking at was evil incarnate. Over and over she sequentially eyed each photo, faster and faster until the scene came alive in her mind like animation. She could hear the screams, see the blood, taste the horror. Her fingers tightened on the arms of the chair.

She stood. She was free. There was no remorse. There was no guilt. When she brought forth the image of Hernandez on the sidewalk in front of his house, his lifeblood pouring out, she felt nothing but satisfaction. Carmen Lopez and Peter McDonald had been avenged. Patricia Barnes had been avenged. Case closed, she said. An eye for an eye. All she had done was don the executioner's mask. The judgment had been rendered by a greater power, and she had been no more than a pawn, a drafted soldier, a means to an end.

She walked out of the office and closed the door. The meeting with Cunningham had unnerved her. She'd gone in this morning prepared for the worst, expecting him to arrest her, contemplating confessing and putting an end to the waiting and fear. But now she was calm. She wasn't hiding from him. He knew where to find her. In a twisted way, she wanted to tell him straight to his face that she was in fact the person who had killed this animal. Then she would march him to Richard's office and make him stare at the crime-scene photos while she challenged him to arrest her, punish her, expose her. This morning she had trembled before him, felt his eyes bore into her soul. Now she felt her body fill with strength. If she was apprehended, she would fight conviction, claim insanity, put her entire life on the table and let it stand against the life she had taken. And she would win. She had already defeated her worst adversary—her conscience.

On her way back to her office, she picked up her messages. Cunningham had called and left word a few hours before that he had spoken to Nieves without result. She had already informed Butler about the morning's developments, and he had reiterated his position: no deals at this time.

She sat at her desk and methodically examined each case, her mind clear and focused. It was time to clean house, settle up, get on with the process of living.

Several hours later, Margie Thomas phoned. "Thought you'd like to know that we searched Marco Curazon's vehicle and found a big, old hunting knife under the seat, just like the one you described."

"Have you sent it to the lab yet?" Lily asked. "Was there blood on it like I thought?"

"No blood, just a lot of dirt. He kept it under the front seat of the old Chevy he drove. But your prints are on it, so

I think Mr. Curazon and his public defender will soon be receptive to just about anything you want to offer them."

If they plea-bargained the rape, possibly dismissing the oral copulation in the deal, there would be no trial and Shana would never have to testify. But she couldn't proceed with a plea or any reduction in sentence with the belief that he had used that knife on another woman. "I just can't believe there was no blood on that knife. You're certain they did a thorough test on it? He told me it was blood."

"Jesus Christ, he was a rapist, woman. Did you really expect everything the man said to be the truth?"

Margie's deep, throaty laugh rang in her ear. "But it tasted so vile, so repulsive. I'll never believe that was dirt on that knife. Never."

"I wasn't going to tell you this, but since you're so determined to know and it's in the report anyway, we found old dried semen on that knife. That's what you tasted. He's a sicko from the word go. Guess he liked to jerk off on his knife. It's a new one on me, and trust me, I've heard it all."

After Lily hung up, she had a compelling urge to brush her teeth. Instead she headed for the vending machines and bought a pack of gum. Comparing what she knew about Bobby Hernandez to what she now knew about the rapist, she decided that she might have shot the wrong man, but in the long run, she had shot the one who deserved to die.

"You were talking about when we could get together," Lily said to Richard on the phone. "How does tonight sound?"

"Now, that's about the best thing I've heard from you all day. You got it."

Only a few minutes before, Shana had called her mother and informed her that she was going to continue playing softball. Her father would drive her to the psychologist afterward.

"Why don't we pick up some Chinese food and go by my new house?" Lily suggested, waiting for Richard's reaction.

"New house. What new house? Are you telling me that you've finally decided to move out?"

"I rented a house yesterday only a few blocks from yours. I have the key."

"Hot damn," he said. "I can't believe it. When are you moving?"

"I have to get the utilities turned on and everything packed, but we're shooting for this weekend. Shana's moving in with me." She picked the photo of Shana off her desk and held it in her hands as she talked.

"Not only do you finally get around to asking me out for a change, you actually made a plan. This is sounding better all the time. This is sounding like a genuine relationship between two people about to be single adults. I'll meet you in the parking lot in ten minutes."

When they reached the front door of the house, Richard placed the sacks of Chinese food on the doorstep and waited for Lily to turn the key in the lock. Then he swept her up in his arms and carried her over the threshold. Setting her down, he put his arms around her. "This is the first house for us. My house will always have Claire's presence lurking in all the corners. But in this house there are no ghosts of Christmases past." He pressed his lips against hers in a tender kiss. "Now, let's eat."

They sat on the floor in the little kitchen, eating with plastic forks out of cardboard containers. "It's a nice house," Richard said, looking around while they ate, "but it's really small."

Lily dropped a sweet and sour shrimp in her lap and jumped up to wash off the stain. "Look, there's water," she said. "And it's even hot." She went to the switch and turned on the overhead light even though it wasn't dark outside. "I guess they still have the utilities on." Her eyes lit up and she said, "The hot tub. Can you figure out how to turn it on and heat it up?"

"I'm very handy, you know. Everywhere except the kitchen." He wiped his hands and went outside, returning a few minutes later. "Your wish is my command," he said, throwing his hands out to his sides and taking a deep bow. "Your hot tub will be ready in about forty-five minutes."

"But we don't have any towels," Lily stated.

"I think I have a few beach towels in the trunk of my car," he said. "I'll go get them in a few minutes."

He walked up and took her in his arms, burying his head in her neck, pressing her body to his. "I love you," he said.

She responded, "I love you too." With one hand he started to pull her blouse out of the waistband of her skirt, but she pushed his hand away. "We have to talk. It's important," she said. Whereas things had been standing still in the days before, they were now moving at lightning speed. She had to tell Richard. She had already decided in the car on the way to the house. Either she told him or she ended it. If she didn't tell him, she was going to tell someone else.

The heavy-lidded look of lust in his eyes was replaced with concern. He removed his tie and tossed it with his jacket in the corner. Lily went and sat down on the floor in the living room with her legs crossed in front of her. He spread out on his side and waited for her to speak, staring intently at her face.

"What I'm going to say is going to shock you. I only hope you understand why I didn't tell you before and why I have to tell you now." She paused and bit the corner of her lip. "I'm actually putting you in a very bad position just by telling you."

Concern was deepening in his face and he sat up, facing her now, his long legs stretched awkwardly beside her body, trying to brace himself with his hands. He was uncomfortable now, fearful of what she was about to say. She was stalling, trying to find the words and the courage. The silence hung ominously in the room; the sounds of dogs barking and television sets playing and cars traversing the street seemed far away.

"I killed Bobby Hernandez," she said. "I thought he was the man who broke into our house and raped us, and I drove to Oxnard and shot him with my father's shotgun."

For a moment Richard's eyes were blank, the words not registering. Then he pulled himself upright, his eyes wide and incredulous. "Repeat what you just said."

"I killed Bobby Hernandez," she repeated slowly, her bottom lip trembling. "I had his file in my briefcase that night— Clinton had told me he had dismissed the charges—and he looked exactly like the rapist. The rapist even had on a red sweatshirt. I thought he followed me home from the jail, that they gave him back his same clothes when released. I had his address." She stopped, sucking in air, knowing there were no words to describe the way she had felt that night and the insanity that had driven her.

He tried to measure his words. "But why didn't you just have him arrested if you knew who he was? My God . . ."

The expression of disapproval on his face and the tone of his voice caused tears to well up in her eyes. "I wanted him to die, okay? I watched him rape my daughter; he put a knife in my mouth and told me it had another woman's blood on it. I thought he would get out and come back and kill us both." Unable to control herself, she started sobbing, and Richard moved to take her in his arms. He placed her head on his shoulder and patted her on the back.

"Don't cry," he said. "I can't bear to see you cry." Once she had stopped sobbing, he gently pushed her shoulders back and asked her, "Then who is the man in jail right now for the rape?"

"The rapist," she said, fixing him with red-rimmed eyes, her makeup streaked with tears. "He's a dead ringer for Hernandez, but he's the one. It wasn't Hernandez. They even found the knife he used with my prints on it. I shot the wrong man."

"Jesus fucking Christ, Lily," he said, springing to his feet and throwing his hands in the air. Leaning over, he screamed

in her face, "You even shot the wrong man. You killed someone. You blew someone away and you never found the time
to so much as tell me about it. Great relationship we've got
here," he said, turning and stomping into the kitchen. Grabbing the bottle of wine, he sloshed it into a plastic cup and
drank the whole glass in almost one swallow. Then he leaned
against the counter in the kitchen and glared at her, the muscles
in his face twitching as she watched from the floor in the living
room. Finally he seized the whole bottle and started back in,
handing his glass to Lily and filling it up to the brim. Then he
turned the bottle upside down and drank from it as he paced
in front of her.

"Who knows about this?"

"No one knows," she said. "I haven't even told John. I
didn't tell anyone."

He'd read the report on the Hernandez homicide, but
couldn't remember the details now; his mind was going in a
million different directions, his eyes darting wildly around the
room. "Do they have anything on you? Any evidence? Any
witnesses?"

"Manny was the only eyewitness and he thought it was a
man." She stopped and took a sip of the wine. "A neighbor
copied down my license plate, but I had altered it with Magic
Marker, so it came back to another vehicle."

His eyes turned to her in shock and disbelief. "Magic
Marker? You changed the plate? My God, that's premedita-
tion. What possessed you to do such a thing? . . . To kill
someone. God." He looked like he was about to grab her and
shake her. She didn't answer. He continued to pace, shaking
his free hand, stopping to take another slug of wine. "Okay,
okay . . . let's think this through. Let's not panic."

Lily wanted to stop him, tell him the time for panic and
planning was over, but she merely looked at the floor.

He flopped down next to her, his body a dead weight. "So
you're clear? If Manny is dead and they have nothing more
than a bad plate, they really have nothing."

"Cunningham is handling it. Don't you think we would know if he had anything on me? Christ, I met with him today. I talk to him all the time. Even if he suspected me, he apparently has no proof and no witnesses."

Richard reached for her again, knocking over her cup of wine. A pink stain appeared on the carpet. "You've been keeping this inside all this time. You should have told me before."

She didn't answer; he stroked her hair like a child.

His mind was spinning. The woman in his arms was not the person he had fallen in love with—he'd never known her, he thought now. She had committed an act of premeditated murder. Sure, she and her poor child had been raped and it was horrible and disgusting, but to kill someone in cold blood—it was beyond comprehension, beyond acceptance. Even if someone stabbed Greg right in front of him, he didn't know if he could kill them, take another life. It went against everything he believed in, the very nature of his job as a prosecutor. But it was done. There was no way to take it back. And now he was a part of it. He would have to swallow it like a bitter pill. It was stuck in his throat, and he had to find a way to force it down.

"Hernandez was an animal, okay. A killer. There's no doubt he would have gone down for the death penalty. I guess you saved the state a fortune in warehousing him on Death Row. Look at it that way."

"Believe me, Richard, I've looked at it every possible way. I still killed someone. I committed a murder." Lily put her face in her hands, unable to meet his eyes. "I just couldn't take it. Don't you see? He raped my little girl right in front of me. All the violence . . . everyday . . . all around us."

"Listen to me," Richard said, trying to keep his voice under control. "If you hadn't killed Hernandez, we would have never known about his involvement in the Lopez–McDonald murders. Not only that, while we were sitting there preparing to prosecute what's probably two innocent boys, Hernandez might have killed again. The first homicide whetted his appetite. Isn't that what we've been saying? Then he picked up Patricia Barnes with every intention of killing her for no reason other than the sheer thrill of it. When he failed, he went back and finished the job later. What we're talking about here is the birth stage of a serial killer."

"Can you live with what I've done?" she asked. He didn't reply and their eyes locked. For all his words, she saw in his eyes uncertainty and doubt. He was looking at her as if she were someone he didn't know, a stranger, a curiosity, a freak. "I shouldn't have told you. It was a mistake."

"I love you," he said softly. "I just can't say any more than that. No matter what happens between us, I have loved you. Please believe that."

She sipped more of her wine and Richard refilled her glass, finishing what wine was left in the bottle. Then he rose and went to the car. Lily stood at the window, peering through the mini blinds, certain that he was going to get in and drive off. She watched as he unlocked the trunk and removed two beach towels.

As Lily continued to stare out the window, her hands on the mini blinds caused them to bend and crack until there was a large hole she could look through. Richard slammed the trunk of the BMW, the beach towels in his arms, and glanced at the house. His shoulders had fallen forward as if under the weight of an enormous burden. His face was tight and drawn, and he walked with an old man's gait down the steps to the front of the house. Halfway down, he turned his head from side to side to see if anyone was watching him and then continued his descent with his head dropped, his arms limp at his side, the beach towels unfurling and dragging on the ground without him noticing.

Lily was possessed with a wrenching, twisting agony and she screamed: "What have I done? What have I done?"

She had told Richard not because he had to know, but to relieve herself of her unbearable burden, to enlist his support.

"I'm despicable," she thought, "a blight on the face of the earth." Her self-loathing became so intolerable that she ran to the front door and quickly locked it just as the handle started to turn, pressing her face and then her entire body against it like a barricade. "Go away, Richard," she said through the door. "Go home."

"Open the door," he said, his voice still low, still in control. "Please, Lily, don't be silly. Open the door."

They were really only inches away, and she placed her palms on the wood just as he started to beat on the door with his fists, first like a knock and then stronger. "I've completely compromised his ethics, his entire life," she told herself. He was now withholding evidence, an accessory after the fact, a criminal. While Richard's pounding became more forceful, she ran to the kitchen and retrieved her purse. Pulling out the cellular phone, she dialed.

"Oxnard Police Department," the voice answered. "Is your call an emergency?"

"Yes," Lily yelled, looking through the front window and seeing a flash of white, Richard's shirt. He was walking toward the back of the house. "Detective Cunningham. Get me Detective Cunningham."

Richard was in the backyard approaching the glass windows.

"Detective Bureau, Cunningham," he answered.

"This is Lily Forrester. I killed Bobby Hernandez." As Lily spoke, her eyes were glued on Richard, now beating on the back door. He leaned against the glass and peered through his hands, trying to see inside.

"Lily!" he yelled. "Lily!"

The line was silent except for her labored breathing. Her nose started running and she wiped it with the sleeve of her blouse. Richard started trying the door, then went to the kitchen window.

Cunningham's deep voice seized her through the phone,

and she looked away, turning her back to the windows. "Where are you?" he asked.

"I'm in Ventura."

"Where, Lily? The address. Give me the address."

"On Seaview . . ." Suddenly her mind was blank, and she carried the phone as she went back to her purse and dumped everything on the counter. Finally she saw the rental receipt and read the number. "It's 11782 Seaview."

"Are you alone?"

"Yes."

"Stay right where you are. Don't leave. Don't move. I'll be there in fifteen minutes."

Lily didn't respond. Richard was no longer in the backyard. She heard noises in the rear of the house, where the bedrooms were located.

"Did you hear me?" Cunningham said. "I'm leaving now."

The phone went dead. Lily let it fall from her hands. Richard appeared in the hallway.

"What in God's name . . . ? I had to crawl through the bedroom window. You scared me to death." He started moving toward her, but she backed away. The relief on his face turned to anger. "Stop this right now. Why in the hell did you lock me out like that? I thought you'd hurt yourself."

"You have to leave this minute. Cunningham is on the way now. I confessed. I told him. It's over."

Richard's eyes expanded with shock. "This is insanity. I can't believe this. My God, this is a nightmare." He started turning from side to side, moving toward the door and then back toward Lily.

With one last furtive glance at Lily, he turned and left, leaving the door wide open as he ran up the steps to the car, got in, and drove off.

"Good," Lily said. She fell back against the wall and slid to the floor. "Good." Her body felt weightless, boneless, empty of all interior parts. She looked at her feet stretched in front of her. Her big toe had popped through her nylons, and she reached over and touched it. Her blouse was outside the waistband of her skirt, and a few drops of wine had stained it. She let her head drop to her chest and closed her eyes. The house was dark. Lily was traveling backward in time, unable to stop herself, lost in the dark regions of her mind, reliving the memories.

She was ten years old and walking up the path from the fish ponds at the ranch in Colorado. When she got to the top of the hill, her grandfather was waiting. His stomach seemed enormous and only his head appeared over the bulging flesh. In his mouth was a cigar, which he moved from side to side between his clenched teeth. "There you are," he said. "There's my little dolly. Come to me."

"Where's Granny?" she asked.

"She went to town, darlin'. I sent her to get some of that peanut brittle you love so much. Wasn't that sweet of me to think of you? Don't I always think of my doll? Is there anything in the world I wouldn't buy for my dolly?"

Lily turned and started climbing down the hill. She fell, landing on her seat, and with her hands she pushed herself in the dirt. "You promised," she said, great sobs shaking her body. "Not now. Not in the daytime. You promised."

"You get up here now or you'll be sorry. You're being disobedient. You can't talk like this to your grandfather. What would your mother say? What would your father say?"

Finally on level ground, Lily pushed herself to her feet and started running. She ran around the mushy perimeters of the pond, ran through the bushes and into the trees. She stumbled, fell, picked herself up, and kept running. Branches scraped her and she swung her arms wildly over her head. When she was so deep in the woods that she no longer recognized her surroundings, she stopped and fell face first onto the ground. Then she climbed to the top of the embankment, to the clearing, and sat there waiting until she saw her grandmother's Cadillac turn onto the gravel road leading to the house. It was dark. She was not allowed out after dark. She dusted herself off and headed to the house.

Her grandmother was standing in the kitchen in her town clothes, her eyes an ashen gray. Behind her stood her grandfather, a smile on his face. With his hand he moved her grandmother aside and picked Lily up, holding her like a rag doll or a sack of flour against the side of his body. "No use to cry to Granny now. You know you're not allowed out after dark. But since you're so brave, so fast, so disrespectful . . ." He walked to the door and turned to her grandmother. "Start dinner. I'll be back with this little roughneck in a few minutes."

The ranch was located about three miles from the Colorado State Reformatory for Boys. Lily was in the front seat of his Lincoln Continental, her hand held tightly by her grandfather's. She saw the tall brown brick buildings getting closer and closer, and her eyes filled with terror. She tried to extract her hand. She pushed her body forward in the seat and bowed it, her head back, her pelvis thrust upward, her feet kicking furiously. "No, Granddaddy. No, Granddaddy." With her free hand she pulled down her pants and exposed her genitals. "Don't leave me there. I'll be good. I'll be good." She tried to pull his hand holding hers to her nakedness, to the place he liked between her legs, but he yanked it away. She could see the bars on the windows and the shadows of the men inside. They were approaching the front gate.

"It's too late now, isn't it? Too late. They're waiting for you now. They love little girls." Then he turned and snarled at her. "They love to eat them. Remember, Lily, my little dolly, my bad little dolly. They don't feed them. They're hungry. It's dinnertime." He drove through the gate, simply waving at the guards, his body blocking Lily's. It was a minimum-security institution and he was a frequent caller, a friend of the warden.

Right under the looming buildings, he stopped and reached over her to open the door. Then he shoved her out, and she tumbled head over heels onto the asphalt, her feet tangled in her corduroy pants, one shoe off, one toe protruding from a hole in her socks. Rocks flew in her face as he drove off, the exhaust fumes choking her and causing her to cough amid her tears. She grabbed her knees and held them tightly, shut her eyes and refused to open them. She listened for the sounds of them coming, coming to eat her like a big chicken. They would sink their rotten teeth into her and tear her limbs off and pass them around. "Good," she said. "Good. Eat me all up. Until I'm gone, gone, gone." She waited.

The gravel crunched and the ground began moving, roaring. Then it stopped. "You ready to come home with Grandpa now? You ready to be a sweet little girl? Or do you want me to just leave you here?" The car door opened and Lily silently stood, pulled up her pants, and climbed in. "Now dry your eyes and when you get home, you go straight to the bathroom and wash the dirt off your face. Then I want you to put on that beautiful white dress I bought you and come in for dinner."

"Yes, Granddaddy," she said.

"That's my little darlin'. Give me a kiss. Just a little kiss on my cheek."

Lily leaned over and let her lips touch his coarse skin and then fell back onto her seat, her hands folded neatly in her lap, her eyes trained straight ahead. The last time when Granny had been out of town, he'd left her there to walk the three miles back to the ranch alone in the dark.

43 .

Cunningham sprang from his desk and reached for his jacket, shifting his shoulder holster to the right position. The new detective in the homicide bureau was busy putting his personal items in his new desk. He was one of the men Cunningham had investigated for shooting a drug dealer and pocketing the cash, and he'd just been reassigned to homicide from narcotics. No one had told Cunningham he would be working only a few feet away, sharing the same space, breathing the same air.

"Got something hot?" the man said, looking up.

"Fuck yourself," Cunningham growled, moving rapidly to the door. "Or better yet, stick one of those extra shooters you have in your ear and pull the trigger."

The man stood and started to come around the desk. Cunningham opened his jacket and put his hand on his weapon. "Two more steps and I'll do it for you."

"You're gonna hear about this, shithead. I'll go straight to the chief, and you'll end up out on the fucking street, begging someone to hire you."

Ignoring the man's last comment, Cunningham burst

through the double doors leading from the detective bureau and was in the driver's seat of his unit roaring toward Ventura in what seemed like seconds. The traffic on the police radio was heavy. He started to pick up the mike and advise the dispatcher that he was leaving the city perimeters, a department policy, but instead replaced the mike in its holder.

"Station one, 2-Boy," the voice of the dispatcher rang out. "Robbery just occurred at White's Market, Alameda and 4th Street. Suspects are two males armed with nine-millimeters, last seen EB on 3rd in a brown Nova, unknown license. Clerk has been shot, and ambulance and rescue en route. Code three."

Cunningham was only a few blocks from the scene the patrol unit had been dispatched to, and his eyes scanned the vehicles as he flew past them, but all he could see was the face of Lily Forrester. He reached over and turned the radio off. Why had she called him and told him she had shot Bobby Hernandez? Why hadn't she left well enough alone? He had no evidence now that Manny was dead; she was almost in the clear. It was such a stupid thing to do, he thought. It was exactly the type of thing a woman would do: confess after they had practically gotten off without a hitch. She had committed the perfect crime, executed it brilliantly, and then she had dissolved into a sniveling fucking female answering some inner need to do the moral, ethical thing. Anger rose inside him; acid bubbled like a witch's caldron inside his stomach.

"There are no ethics anymore," he said. "Presidents commit crimes and lie, preachers steal and fornicate, fathers murder their own children—children murder their parents." That very morning he'd read an article in the newspaper about a fire captain charged with twelve counts of arson. On the next page was a piece on an L.A.P.D. detective who had conspired to commit a murder for hire. Sitting at a desk right next to him, carrying a gun, wearing a badge, was a man he was certain was a cold-blooded murderer. Where would it all stop? How much lower could society sink? His eyes searched the streets in front of him, took in the houses and faceless individuals milling about. "Get back in your houses, assholes," he yelled at them, "or someone will come along and shoot you just for the thrill of it. Bolt the doors. Hide under your beds. Can't you see this is a war zone? Don't you know half the people walking around have more firepower in their pockets than the cops?"

He passed under the freeway and sped down Victoria Boulevard, where the government center was housed. "Cops. Police officers. Lawmen," he uttered with complete disgust, slowing down and searching the street signs and then making a quick right, the car fishtailing as he turned. In one of the driveways, a teenage girl was getting inside a car. "Call a cop and he just might rape you, little girl. Or maybe he'll club your boyfriend to death because he's had a rotten day. See, no one sane wants to be a cop anymore, and there's no such animal as a lawman."

Now he was climbing into the foothills, searching for the address Lily had given him. It was dark as pitch. He couldn't read the numbers. Suddenly he saw a red Honda parked at the curb and slammed on the brakes. The house was dark. Cutting the ignition, he sat perfectly still and listened. It was too dark, too quiet. His nose twitched and he thought he could smell death. "No," he yelled, slapping both hands on the steering wheel, imagining what he was going to find inside that house: strands of red hair stuck to the walls and ceilings, sweet little freckles scattered like dust in the air, her mouth sucking on the same shotgun she'd used to blow Hernandez away. Then he would have to make the notifications, tell her precious little girl, already ravaged and violated.

He held his breath as he approached the front door. It was standing open. All he could hear was his own heart tapping out a staccato beat. Then he saw her in the shadows. She was on the floor, against the wall, motionless. He thought the worst. His breath stopped, his eyes searching for blood, a shotgun. But when he reached out with an icy finger to touch the pulse point on her neck, his finger rose and fell with life. She was alive.

"Lily," he said, shaking her gently, falling to his knees. For reasons he could not explain, he engulfed her in his arms and crushed her to his chest.

"Daddy," she whispered, her words muffled, her voice that of a child's.

"It's going to be okay. I'm here. It's going to be okay." He held her and rocked her, repeating the words again and again. She had lost contact with reality, was in the midst of a psychotic break. She had fallen through the crack, but he had been there to catch her. He recalled his childhood love—the circus—the trapeze artist, how he had looked up in awe as a beautiful young woman in a shiny costume had fallen into the air and an upside-down man with muscular arms caught her and held her until they both reached the perch and dismounted, their arms in the air in triumph. He grabbed Lily's shoulders and pushed her from his body, shaking her more forcefully now.

"It's Bruce. Bruce Cunningham. Lily, do you hear me? It's Bruce. Say my name. Say it. Say Bruce."

"Bruce," she said, repeating the sound like a parrot.

He let go of her and she fell back against the wall, her eyes still closed, her body rigid. Running his hand along the wall, he found the light switch and flooded the room with light. Then he bent down again and slapped her across the face. Her eyes sprang open. "Fight," he ordered her, "fight for your life. It's Bruce Cunningham. Detective Bruce Cunningham. Look at me."

There it was. He saw it: recognition, realization, reality. She was back. He had caught her in his strong hands, and he was swinging her through the air to the perch.

"I killed Bobby Hernandez," she said. "I thought he raped my daughter. I was certain he raped my daughter. I shot him in cold blood."

"Where are you, Lily?"

"I'm in Ventura. At my new house."

"Who's the president of the United States?"

"George Bush," she said flatly, her eyes focused. "Why are you asking me this stuff?"

She didn't even remember where she'd been or where she'd been heading: to the ground without a net. He picked a towel off the floor and went to the kitchen and soaked it with water from the tap. Then he stood over her and dropped it into her lap. "Wash your face. You'll feel better," he said tenderly, a father to a child. She buried her face in the towel and after a few moments looked up at him with those big blue eyes, the freckles intact, still dotting her nose and pale cheeks.

"You slapped me."

"Yeah. Let's get out of here."

"Are you going to cuff me?"

Pushing herself up with her hands, she faced him, and a wave of emotion washed over him, causing his body to shake. One arm moved underneath her knees as he collected her in his arms. Still holding her, he carried her to the car and placed her in the front seat. He touched his lips to her forehead and tried to speak, but words had left him. Her head fell back against the seat.

Leaving the car door open, he ran down the steps and into the house. He grabbed her jacket, her purse, turned the lights off, closed the door, and ran back up the steps. He noted no shortness of breath. His body moved like that of a conditioned athlete.

Entering the car on the driver's side, he reached over her, brushing her chest, and pulled the door closed. "Put on your jacket," he told her. Once she had done what he said, he reached over again and fastened her seat belt. "Hold on."

In seconds they were on the flats and the speedometer was inching its way to seventy, then eighty, then ninety. The windows were down and the cold night air beat against their faces;

the roar of the big engine was deafening. He reached for the mike, flicked the radio on and yelled into it. "Station One, Unit 654."

"Six-five-four, go ahead."

"Where's the victim of the 211? The robbery at White's Market?"

"Community Presbyterian, but it looks like a D.O.A."

"I'm en route." He glanced at Lily and then back at the road. The steering wheel was vibrating in his hands. He dropped the mike on the seat between them.

They didn't speak for the remainder of the drive. Lily's eyes were wide and her hands were braced against the dash. The car skidded to a stop in the parking lot of the hospital, and even though she had her seat belt on, Cunningham put his arm across her to keep her from falling forward.

"Come with me," he said, throwing the car door open and then leaning in toward her. "Don't say anything. Don't do anything. Just stay beside me."

He crossed the parking lot in great, long strides. Lily was almost running in her high heels to keep up with him. The automatic doors to the E.R. opened, and bright, glaring lights struck their eyes. Cunningham flashed his badge and kept walking, the nurse pointing to one of the examining rooms. Lily's heels tapped on the linoleum behind him, her eyes on the floor.

On the table was the body of a young dark man, an Indian from the looks of him, uncovered, still. His shirt was ripped open but his chest was unmarked except for red circular spots where they had possibly placed the paddles used to shock his heart in what had been a futile effort to save him. One side of his head and face were completely gone, unrecognizable as anything but bloody tissue, hamburger meat. The room was empty except for the three of them. Lily reached for his cold hand, with tapering fingers, so dark around the white nails, and touched the thin gold band around his finger. Tears welled up in her eyes, and she looked with an unspoken plea at Cunningham. He jerked his head toward the door, and she followed him out and down the hall. He kept walking through corridors, turning down one hall to another, and then he stopped and faced her. They were alone, apparently in a section of the hospital under construction or renovation.

"What you saw back there was a product of a Bobby Hernandez. Do you understand me?"

There was a black intensity in his eyes, and she had to look away. Another person spoke with her voice, mouthed the words from her lips. "Yes," she answered finally. "I understand you."

"The world doesn't need him, the Bobby Hernandezes. You stepped on a cockroach. There are thousands more. They're in all the cabinets, under all the sinks, crawling under every stinking toilet."

He stopped and his body fell, his years reappeared, the lines sank in his face, his stomach bulged over his pants. His face was flushed; perspiration dampened his forehead. His large chest expanded and contracted.

"What happened between us back there didn't happen. What you said to me on the phone you didn't say." He stuffed his hand in his pocket and pulled out a twenty-dollar bill. Prying her fingers open, he pressed it there, then closed them with his fleshy hand. "You're going to get in a cab and go back to your life. You're going to forget this night ever happened. If you see me tomorrow or the next day, all you're going to say is 'Hi, Bruce. How you doing, Bruce,' and you're going to fight the fight and build a new life for you and your daughter."

"But you can't do this," Lily exclaimed, her voice high and shrill, her body shaking. "You can't just listen to me confess to a homicide and then walk away. What about the law?" She started waving her hands around excitedly, her eyes wild again with hysteria. He jerked his head behind him. There was no one around. They were still alone.

Cunningham moved to her and grabbed both of her hands with his own and pinned them against the wall. His face inches from hers, his breath was as hot and heavy as a blast furnace.

"I am the law. Do you hear me? I'm the one who lives and breathes it. Not the judges on their high benches too far from it to even smell it. I'm the one who gets shot at. The one who has to inhale the rotting flesh of the society we live in. I'm the one who comes when people call, when they're robbed or beaten or raped. I have every right to make this decision. Every right."

Beads of sweat fell from his forehead like salty rain onto Lily's upturned face. "Justice," he said, spitting out the words. "How can the interest of justice be served by trying you for avenging your child, by locking you up, by leaving your daughter so badly damaged that she'll never recover?" He suddenly dropped his hold on Lily and stepped back. Her arms fell to her side, her mouth trembling. "There is a God, lady, and He lives down here in the gutter with the likes of me."

With that, the big man turned his back and started walking down the hall, his scuffed and worn black shoes clanking across the linoleum, the cheap fabric of his suit jacket pulling tightly across his back and broad shoulders. Lily's eyes followed him until he turned the corner and disappeared.

EPILOGUE

L ily walked out of the government center office in Los Angeles that housed the United States District Court of Ap-
peals and headed to her car in the parking lot across the street.
It was late, after six. She made it a routine to stay late every
night, waiting for the traffic to pass before making the long,
grueling drive to Ventura, almost two hours away. Even though
she hated to miss precious hours with Shana, the child had
surrounded herself with enough activities that she seldom arrived home before her mother. She was a cheerleader now at
Ventura High School, had joined the debate team, and was
presently campaigning for president of her class. Thinking of
her as she started her car and pulled out into the traffic, Lily
knew that Shana's love and support, her constant optimism,
and her enthusiasm for life had been her lifeline.

It had been eight months since her encounter with Cunningham in the corridors of Presbyterian Community Hospital.
She thought of the big detective and smiled. He was gone now.
Shortly after that night, he'd given notice on his job and moved
his family back to Nebraska. She thought of him often, some-

times wanting to pick up the phone and call him, but what they had shared was not pretty, and she knew it must remain forever where they had left it. He had gone on with his life, and she had done just what he'd told her to do—returned to the battle, fighting the only fight she knew how to fight. Her conscience and Richard Fowler had led her to resign her position as a district attorney. She couldn't jeopardize his career or his life. She had resigned the next day. But she had located a new job a short time later, reviewing and analyzing cases up on appeal. There were no courtroom dramas, no cases to win or lose, but she made a difference in her own way, tirelessly poring over law books and transcripts in the small corner office she had on the thirty-fourth floor. She would never be a judge. It didn't seem to matter anymore.

The traffic was thinning and she was making good time now. She picked up the car phone and called Shana at the house. "It's me, baby. You doing your homework or talking on the phone?" Some things didn't change. Teenagers were teenagers.

"Homework's all done, and Dad and I are going to a movie. He's on the way to pick me up now."

"A movie on a weeknight? Hey, kid, since when did the rules include a movie on a school night? Your dad knows that."

"Mom," she said, "this is a special occasion. All my homework is done and we'll be home by ten o'clock. Besides, an old friend of yours is coming over for dinner."

The traffic suddenly slowed and Lily hit the brakes. "Who? My God, Shana, I won't even be home for another hour. I didn't invite anyone to dinner. I don't even have anything in the house to cook."

"It's a surprise, okay? Don't worry about anything. Karen next door gave me a ride to the store. I've got some pasta and sauce, a salad, some bread and a cake. Sounds pretty good, huh?"

Lily had no idea what she was talking about. "Shana, I'm not up for surprises, particularly after I've worked all day and driven for hours in the traffic. Tell me who this person is this minute."

"You're breaking, Mom. Must have a bad connection. See you later." The line went dead.

Lily held the phone in her hand, staring at the road ahead of her, baffled. It was a perfectly good connection. She could hear Shana fine. She was up to something, and with all the subterfuge, it could only involve one person: Richard. Shana had done something. She'd called him and told him Lily wanted to see him. Lily felt tension gripping her neck and rolled her head around. Snatching the car phone, she dialed Shana back. "Listen," she said when the girl picked up the phone, "if you don't tell me what you're up to this minute, I'm going to ground you."

"Can't hear you, Mom. Connection's still bad." Click.

Lily was both annoyed and amused at the same time. It was obvious what Shana was trying to accomplish. This was nothing new. She'd been pushing Lily to date, get out of the house, join clubs, do anything to put herself back in the mainstream of life. She'd become Lily's personal social director. She had to admit, Shana had chosen a tough job for herself. Lily hadn't felt too sociable in the past eight months. The only thing she attended without fail was the incest survivors group that met on Thursday evenings at a local elementary school.

She passed Camarillo as she did every day heading home, and every single day her foot let up on the gas as she passed the church with the avocado trees where she'd tossed her father's gun down the hill that awful morning. In her bed, in the dark, the horror still haunted her. She had slowly learned to live with it like a person learns to live with a serious illness, an amputated limb, a disfiguring scar. Even if she was free to go on with her life, she knew all too well what she had done. She would always know. In that, there was no escape and no one could free her. That knowledge she would carry to her grave.

She saw the white BMW the moment she turned onto

her street. Her heart started pounding and her face flushed. They'd seen each other on several occasions at the super-market—random meetings, usually with Shana present—and he'd called, but Lily had refused to speak with him any longer than it took to tell him what was going on in her life and inquire about his own. Now he was here. Shana had somehow manip-ulated this reunion into reality. Lily had told her the truth about her relationship with Richard. She had told her just about everything in the long hours they'd spent together talking in front of the fireplace or outside in the hot tub—everything except what happened the night and morning of the rape. Shana had finally asked. Lily had lied and sworn that nothing had happened. It had to be that way.

Richard was getting out of his car when she pulled into the driveway and hit the garage door opener. "Hi, stranger," he said, walking into the garage as she got out of her car, a ten-tative smile playing at the corners of his mouth. "I thought you'd never call. Pleasant surprise."

Lily didn't know what to say. Just his presence made her feel flustered and clumsy. They started walking toward the house and she almost tripped on the step and fell. "Shana called you, right?"

"No," he said, puzzled. "Your secretary called my office and said you wanted me to come for dinner tonight." He looked at her face and could see there was something wrong. "Is this the wrong night or something? Did I get the time wrong?"

Lily smiled. He was so handsome, more so than ever. When they had worked together, he had had a few strands of gray in his thick, dark hair, but now he had them sprinkled through-out his whole head and he was tan and distinguished-looking. "No," she finally said, "everything's fine. Anyway, let's go in-side."

Lily went into the kitchen and found the items Shana had purchased, and tossed the pasta in a pan to cook. Then she found the salads already made in the refrigerator and brought them to the table. "Do you want something to drink? I don't keep a lot of alcohol, but . . ."

"Got any tequila?" he said, moving closer to Lily in the small kitchen, a sly smile on his face.

"Oh, Richard," she said, feeling warmth course through her veins with the memory of that first night. "Those were the days, as they say. Guess there just weren't enough of them, you know?" She had to turn away. He was standing far too close. "I have a beer. That's all I have. Beer or iced tea. Take your pick."

"Beer. And, Lily . . ."

"Yes?" she said, still with her back to him. "Just give me a minute and we'll sit down at the table and talk. I want to put the sauce on."

He was behind her, his arms around her, his warm breath on her neck. "I think about you all the time. I can't get you out of my mind. I date, you know, but . . ."

Lily pushed her elbows out, breaking his grip. She turned and faced him. "I don't date, Richard. It hasn't been easy. What I did . . ."

The color drained from his face. He leaned against the kitchen counter and sighed. "Let's not talk about it, okay? It's over. It's far in the past. I want to see you again."

"I can't, Richard. I just can't. My God, you're up for a judgeship. You don't want to get involved with me again. Think about what you're even saying."

He stared at her. "You mean you're never going to see me again?"

"I didn't say that."

"Then what did you say?"

Lily brushed the bangs of her new short haircut off her face. Richard hadn't even noticed. "Like my hair?"

"Your hair looks great. I liked it better long, though." He paused, his eyes probing hers. "Are you going to see me again?"

The atmosphere was heavy with words she couldn't say. She longed for him to hold her, take his arms and wrap them around her, but she couldn't. "I'm seeing you now. I'm glad to see you. I've missed you."

The pot was boiling, and Lily rushed to the stove and turned down the heat. She grabbed a beer from the refrigerator and handed it to him, their fingers touching briefly. His shoulders dropped and he walked away, heading to the dining room.

The meal was a tense affair.

"How's Greg?" she asked.

"He's fine. He likes his school in San Diego. He comes home on weekends. He sees Shana, you know."

"I know. They're friends. At first it concerned me, but it seems to be platonic, so . . ."

"How is she?"

"She's Shana . . . good—you know, better than I ever expected."

"And you?"

Lily dropped her fork on her plate and sucked in air. "Me, well, I'm getting by. The work is challenging. I hate the drive, but I like the job."

After the salad and pasta, Lily cleared the table, without mentioning the cake. Richard stood to leave and Lily walked him to the door.

"Can I call you, talk to you? Can we at least be friends? Somewhere down the line, in years to come, we could—"

Lily couldn't contain herself any longer. She only had to think it and look into his eyes and he was there, in her arms. They held each other and then she gently pushed herself away. "Call me," she whispered, closing the door. She stood there long after he'd left, leaning back against the door, dreaming of how it could have been between them.

It was a beginning.